Praise for Lisa Scottoline

"Lisa Scottoline is one of the very best writers at work today."
—Michael Connelly

"In novel after novel Lisa Scottoline has proven herself a master."
—*The Washington Post*

"Lisa Scottoline has been added to my shortlist of must-read authors."
—Janet Evanovich

"Scottoline knows how to keep readers in her grip."
—*The New York Times Book Review*

"Scottoline is a powerhouse."
—David Baldacci

"Scottoline writes riveting thrillers that keep me up all night, with plots that twist and turn."
—Harlan Coben

"Scottoline is a star."
—*Time*

Praise for *Someone Knows*

"[A] heartfelt tale that touches on family, marriage, justice, and how emotional wounds drive the choices people make. Scottoline's fans will be well satisfied."
—*Publishers Weekly*

"This fast-paced tale is sure to astonish readers with a huge twist at the end. . . . A gripping page-turner full of gritty suspense."
—*Library Journal*

"Lisa Scottoline shows once again why she's the queen of suspense, delivering a relentless gut punch of a thriller that's sure to stand among the year's best."
—The Real Book Spy

P9-EJU-358

"*Someone Knows* has all the requisite turmoil, surprises, action and introspection of an enjoyable page-turner."
—*Book Reporter*

Praise for *After Anna*

"A deliciously distracting thriller . . . Scottoline illuminates the landing strip of revelations and truths in a deliciously slow and intense way."   —*The Washington Post*

"Scottoline, a master at crafting intense family dramas, expertly twists Maggie's reality with a page-turning mix of guilt, self-delusion, and manipulation."   —*Booklist*

"A nail-biting thriller."   —*Kirkus Reviews*

"Filled with plenty of twists and complex characters, this entertaining story builds to a satisfying conclusion."
—*Publishers Weekly*

"Once again, Scottoline has written a gripping stand-alone psychological thriller; fans of domestic suspense will snap this one up." —*Library Journal* (starred review)

Praise for *One Perfect Lie*

"This twisty thriller about high school secrets and deadly consequences is impossible to put down."   —*People*

"Scottoline is the master of inventive plots and relatable characters."   —*The Huffington Post*

"One thrilling ride on the roller coaster." —*Kirkus Reviews*

"Scottoline has become the master of understated terror and leaves no stone unturned in crafting a potboiler of rare depth and emotion."   —*Providence Journal*

"Bestselling Scottoline's latest promises plot twists that will keep readers flipping pages."   —*Booklist*

Praise for *Most Wanted*

"In novel after novel, Lisa Scottoline has proven herself a master of stories that combine familial love—especially that of mothers for their children—with nail-biting stories of spirited everywomen bent on finding the truth. Her new novel, *Most Wanted*, demonstrates again her skill with this kind of domestic suspense tale."
—*The Washington Post*

"This is a potboiler of a book, crammed full of agonizing choices confronting appealing, relatable characters. Scottoline has penned more hard-boiled tales, but never one as heartfelt and emotionally raw, raising her craft to the level of Judith Guest and Alice Hoffman. *Most Wanted* is a great thriller and a gut-wrenching foray into visceral angst that is not to be missed."   —*Providence Journal*

"A suburban crime tale told with Scottoline's penchant for humor and soul-baring characterization."   —*Booklist*

"A page-turner that will satisfy."   —*Library Journal*

"A Connecticut teacher's long-sought and hard-fought pregnancy turns into a nightmare when Scottoline unleashes one of her irresistible hooks on her."
—*Kirkus Reviews*

Praise for *Every Fifteen Minutes*

"A sock-'em stand-alone . . . The red herrings come fast and furious; part of the fun is how skillfully Scottoline leads us astray."   —*People* magazine Pick of the Week

"Scottoline's breezy, irreverent style prevails and her gift for intimacy—for drawing the reader close to sociopath and victim—makes *Every Fifteen Minutes* as teasingly irresistible as any of this versatile author's creations."
—*The Washington Post*

"The queen of justice, Lisa Scottoline, has yet again written a tale that will hold readers' attention while leading them to an ultimate 'shock' at the end. . . . Scottoline rocks it yet again!" —*Suspense Magazine*

"Scottoline builds tremendous suspense."
—*Connecticut Post*

"Bestseller Scottoline casts an unflinching eye on the damaged world of sociopaths in this exciting thriller."
—*Publishers Weekly* (starred review)

Praise for *Keep Quiet*

"This book shows she is at the top of her form. It's a roller-coaster ride of plot twists and cliff-hangers. . . . A fast, fun read . . . Scottoline leaves the reader sated, satisfied, and ready for the author's next thrilling ride."
—*Fort Worth Star-Telegram*

"Lisa Scottoline is an author who knows her way around a suspenseful plot. She has done it in the past and she does it again with her latest novel, *Keep Quiet*."
—*The Huffington Post*

"Scottoline keeps the tension high while portraying a family in turmoil. A heck of a twist ending wraps everything . . . A satisfying, suspenseful read." —*Booklist*

"Scottoline brings tension to a boil in her latest novel. Her characters are believable, and her protagonist is sympathetic despite making a truly horrific choice at the start of the novel. . . . This is an intriguing exploration of human frailties, justice, and family relationships."

—*RT Book Reviews*

Praise for *Don't Go*

"Lisa Scottoline is one of the very best writers at work today. *Don't Go* proves it once again. This is a story that is heavily muscled, emotional, and relevant. They don't come any better."

—Michael Connelly

"This stand-alone from Scottoline effectively tugs at the emotions."

—*Publishers Weekly*

"Scottoline spins a compelling drama that reads like the literary love-child of Jodi Picoult and Nicholas Sparks. Readers will fall in love with this war vet father who fights seemingly insurmountable odds, and his powerfully addictive story will haunt them long after the final page."

—*Library Journal*

Praise for *Come Home*

"The suspense and dread build like a series of tornadoes flattening all in their path. . . . The pace is relentless, the twists are jaw-dropping, and then Scottoline piles ending on top of ending until you turn the last page."

—David Baldacci

"*Come Home* held me spellbound."   —Janet Evanovich

"A gripping and compelling novel . . . Scottoline gets all the details right, and gives all the characters flesh and blood, breath and life. This is a novel that is as full of thrills as it is full of heart."   —Kristin Hannah

Praise for *Save Me*

"Each staccato chapter adds new and unexpected turns, so many you could get whiplash just turning a page. Scottoline knows how to keep readers in her grip."
—*The New York Times Book Review*

"The Scottoline we love as a virtuoso of suspense, fast action, and intricate plot is back in top form in *Save Me*."
—*The Washington Post Book World*

"A white-hot crossover novel about the perils of mother love."
—*Kirkus Reviews*

"Are you a good mother if you save your child from disaster? What if it means sacrificing another's child? In *Save Me*, Lisa Scottoline walks readers into this charged moral dilemma and then takes them on an intense, breathless ride where accidents might not be accidents at all. You won't be able to put this one down."
—Jodi Picoult

Praise for *Look Again*

"[A] barn-burning crossover novel about every adoptive mother's worst nightmare . . . Her best book yet."
—*Kirkus Reviews* (starred review)

"Bestseller Scottoline . . . scores another bull's-eye with this terrifying thriller about an adoptive parent's worst fear. . . . Scottoline expertly ratchets up the tension."
—*Publishers Weekly* (starred review)

"*Look Again*, if I may be so bold, is probably Lisa Scottoline's best novel. It's honest and hugely emotional, with very real characters who you care about, and will remember long after you finish this terrific book."
—James Patterson

—ALSO BY LISA SCOTTOLINE—

FICTION

After Anna

One Perfect Lie

Most Wanted

Every Fifteen Minutes

Keep Quiet

Don't Go

Come Home

Save Me

Look Again

Daddy's Girl

Dirty Blonde

Devil's Corner

Running from the Law

Final Appeal

ROSATO & DINUNZIO SERIES

Feared

Exposed

Damaged

Corrupted

Betrayed

Accused

ROSATO & ASSOCIATES SERIES

Think Twice

Lady Killer

Killer Smile

Dead Ringer

Courting Trouble

The Vendetta Defense

Moment of Truth

Mistaken Identity

Rough Justice

Legal Tender

Everywhere That Mary Went

NONFICTION (with Francesca Serritella)

I See Life Through Rosé-Colored Glasses

I Need a Lifeguard Everywhere but the Pool

I've Got Sand in All the Wrong Places

Does This Beach Make Me Look Fat?

Have a Nice Guilt Trip

Meet Me at Emotional Baggage Claim

Best Friends, Occasional Enemies

My Nest Isn't Empty, It Just Has More Closet Space

Why My Third Husband Will Be a Dog

Someone Knows

.

Lisa Scottoline

G. P. Putnam's Sons
New York

PUTNAM
—EST. 1838—

G. P. PUTNAM'S SONS
Publishers Since 1838
An imprint of Penguin Random House LLC
penguinrandomhouse.com

Copyright © 2019 by Smart Blonde, LLC

Penguin supports copyright. Copyright fuels creativity, encourages diverse voices, promotes free speech, and creates a vibrant culture. Thank you for buying an authorized edition of this book and for complying with copyright laws by not reproducing, scanning, or distributing any part of it in any form without permission. You are supporting writers and allowing Penguin to continue to publish books for every reader.

Grateful acknowledgment is made to reprint from the following:

This Is Water: Some Thoughts, Delivered on a Significant Occasion, about Living a Compassionate Life by David Foster Wallace. Copyright © 2009 by David Foster Wallace Literary Trust. Used by permission of Little, Brown and Company.

"A German Requiem" copyright © James Fenton. Reprinted by permission of SLL/Sterling Lord Literistic, Inc.

The Library of Congress has catalogued the G. P. Putnam's Sons
hardcover edition as follows:

Names: Scottoline, Lisa, author.
Title: Someone knows / Lisa Scottoline.
Description: New York: G. P. Putnam's Sons, 2019.
Identifiers: LCCN 2019001336| ISBN 9780525539643 (hardcover) |
ISBN 9780525539650 (epub)
Classification: LCC PS3569.C725 S66 2018 | DDC 813/.54—dc23
LC record available at https://lccn.loc.gov/2019001336

First G. P. Putnam's Sons hardcover edition / April 2019
First G. P. Putnam's Sons international edition / April 2019
First G. P. Putnam's Sons trade paperback edition / July 2019
First G. P. Putnam's Sons premium edition / November 2019
G. P. Putnam's Sons premium edition ISBN: 9780525539667

Printed in the United States of America
1 3 5 7 9 10 8 6 4 2

Book design by Elyse J. Strongin, Neuwirth & Associates

This is a work of fiction. Names, characters, places, and incidents either are the product of the author's imagination or are used fictitiously, and any resemblance to actual persons, living or dead, businesses, companies, events, or locales is entirely coincidental.

If you purchased this book without a cover, you should be aware that this book is stolen property. It was reported as "unsold and destroyed" to the publisher, and neither the author nor the publisher has received any payment for this "stripped book."

To my amazing daughter, Francesca, with love

It is not your memories which haunt you.
It is not what you have written down.
It is what you have forgotten, what you must forget.
What you must go on forgetting all your life.

—JAMES FENTON, "A German Requiem"

PROLOGUE

■

Nobody tells you that you'll do things when you're young that are so stupid, so unbelievably stupid, so *horrifically* stupid that years later you won't be able to believe it. You'll be on your laptop, or reading a book, or pumping gas, and you'll find yourself shaking your head because you'll be thinking *no, no, no, I did not do that, I was not a part of that, that could not have happened.*

You'll tell yourself that you were young, that you were drinking, that good teenagers make bad decisions all the time. But you know that's not it. You know that when teenagers get together, something dark can take over. Call it peer pressure, call it a collective idiocy, call it something more primal and monstrous, like whatever makes frat boys haze their so-called brothers to death. Writ large, it makes Nazis murder millions and soldiers torch Vietnamese villages. But whatever you call it, it will make you do the worst thing you ever did in your life.

And in your darkest moments, you will wonder if it *made* you do it, or simply *allowed* you to.

You know this now but you didn't then, and you'll shake your head, thinking *I can't believe I did that, I can't believe I was a part of that*, but you were, and not in Nazi Germany, My Lai, or a frat house, but in the safest place you can imagine—in the suburban housing development where you grew up, specifically in a patch of woods mandated by township zoning, confined by fences, and bordered by the Pennsylvania Turnpike. In other words, in a completely civilized location where even Nature herself is domesticated and nothing ever happens.

Except this one night.

You and your friends decide to play Russian Roulette, a game so obviously lethal that you can't even imagine what you were thinking. Days later, years later, a *decade* later, it's still so unspeakable you can't say a word to anyone, and all the books you read that you should've learned something from—*Lord of the Flies*, *A Separate Peace*, and *Crime and Punishment*—teach you absolutely nothing. You read like a fiend, you always have, but you don't let the books teach you anything. You never apply them to your life because they're fiction, or even if they seem real, they're someone else's life, not your life, except that you and your friends decided to play a prank and someone blew their brains out in front of you.

You won't be able to remember exactly what happened because of the booze and the horror, the *absolute horror*, and yet you won't be able to forget it, though you'll spend night after night trying. People say something was *a night to remember*, but this was *a night to forget* and yet you can't forget, and then you'll hear some random playlist and Rihanna singing *don't act like you forgot* and you'll realize you've been *acting like you forgot* your entire adult life, and you'll feel accused by a song, nailed by a phrase, and *don't act like you forgot* is everything, *don't act like you forgot* is all, and you'll pick up the bottle and say to yourself, *I'm acting like I forgot but I didn't, I didn't forget*, and you'll need to be put out of your own misery, so you'll drink and drink, trying to drink yourself to death.

But that takes too long. Years too long. Time doesn't move fast enough. You learned that the hard way.

One night, you'll lose patience.

CHAPTER 1

■

Allie Garvey

Allie gripped the wheel, heading to the cemetery. The death was awful enough in someone so young, agonizing because it was a suicide. The family would be anguished, wracking their brains, asking *why*. But Allie knew *why*, and she wasn't the only one. There used to be four of them, and now there were three. They had kept it a secret for twenty years. She didn't know if she could keep it secret another minute.

Allie drove ahead, her thoughts going back to the summer of '99. She could hear the gunshot ringing in her ears. She could see the blood. It had happened right in front of her. Her gut twisted. She felt wrung by guilt. She had nightmares and flashbacks. She'd been fifteen years old, and it had been a night of firsts. First time hanging with the cool kids. First time getting drunk. First time being kissed. First time falling in love. And then the gunshot.

Allie clenched the wheel, holding on for dear life, to what she didn't know. To the present. To reality. To sanity. She had to stay strong. She had to be brave. She had to do what needed to be done. She should have done it twenty years ago. She'd kept the secret all this time. She'd been living a contents-under-pressure life. Now she wanted to explode.

Allie approached the cemetery entrance. She knew the others would be there. A reunion of co-conspirators. She hadn't spoken to them after what had happened. They'd had no contact since. They'd run away from each other and what they'd done. They'd thought getting caught was the worst that could happen. Allie had learned otherwise. *Not* getting caught was worse.

They'd grown up in Brandywine Hunt, a development in a corner of Chester County, Pennsylvania, where the horse farms had been razed, the trees cleared, and the grassy hills leveled. Concrete pads had been paved for Mc-Mansions, and asphalt rolled for driveways. Thoroughbred Road had been the outermost of the development's concentric streets, and at its center were the clubhouse, pool, tennis and basketball courts, like the prize for the successful completion of a suburban labyrinth.

Allie always thought of her childhood that way, a series of passages that led her to bump into walls. Her therapist theorized it was because of her older sister, Jill, who'd had an illness that Allie had been too young to understand, at first. It had sounded like *sis-something*, which had made sense to Allie—her sister had *sis*. Until one nightmarish race to the hospital, with her father driving like a madman and her mother hysterical in the backseat holding Jill, who was frantically gasping for breath, her face turning blue. Allie had watched, terrified at the realization that *sis* could kill her sister. And when her sister turned seventeen, it did.

Allie bit her lip, catching sight of the wrought-iron fence. Her sister was buried at the same cemetery, the grave marked by a monument sunk into the manicured grass. Its marble was rosy pink, a color Jill had picked out herself, calling it *Dead Barbie Pink*. Allie remembered that at Jill's funeral she had cried so hard she laughed, or laughed so hard she cried, she didn't know which.

Allie braked, waiting for traffic to pass so she could turn. GARDENS OF PEACE, read the tasteful sign, and it was one of a chain of local cemeteries, fitting for a region of housing developments, as if life could be planned from birth to death.

Her gut tightened again, and she focused on her breathing exercises, *in and out, in and out.* Yoga and meditation were no match for a guilty conscience. She hadn't fired the gun, but she was responsible. She replayed the memory at night, tortured with shame. She'd never told anyone, not even her husband. No wonder her marriage was circling the drain.

Allie steered through the cemetery entrance. Pebbled gravel popped beneath the tires of her gray Audi, and she drove toward the black hearse, limos, and parked cars. Mourners were walking to the burial site, and she spotted the other two instantly.

They were walking together, talking, heads down.

Gorgeous, privileged, rich. The cool kids, grown up. They didn't look up or see her. They wouldn't expect her, since she hadn't been one of them, not really. They hadn't followed her life the way she'd followed theirs. She was the one looking at them, never vice versa. That's how it always is for outsiders.

Allie told herself once more to stay strong. The cool kids believed their secret was going to stay safe forever, but they were wrong.

It was time for forever to end.

Part One

—TWENTY YEARS EARLIER—

This is where we began
Being what we can.

> —Stephen Sondheim, "Our Time,"
> *Merrily We Roll Along*

CHAPTER 2

Allie Garvey

Allie ran up the hill in the woods, her breath ragged and her thighs aching. Her house was just around the corner, and she wished she could sneak home, but she didn't want to be there, either. Her sister, Jill, had died last summer, and since then the house had felt hollow, empty, silent.

Allie had to keep going, pumping her arms. When Allie had turned nine, her mother had finally explained Jill's illness, which wasn't *sis* but cystic fibrosis. Allie hadn't known that the disease was fatal back then, or any of the statistics on life expectancy, but when Jill was well enough to travel, the Garveys took trips to Disney World and Hawaii, like a do-it-yourself Make-A-Wish. Her mother said *we're making memories*, but Allie didn't know how to live in the present and the future at the same time. The Garveys smiled hard when they were happy because they were also sad, taking the bitter with the sweet, the good with the bad, every single minute.

Her sister's coughing was the background noise of her childhood, though Jill muffled the sound at night, not to keep the house awake. Every morning, Jill took antibiotics in pill form, and Pulmozyme and albuterol through a nebulizer. Every time she ate a meal or a snack, she took pancreatic enzymes, and she endured percussive therapy twice a day. Jill never complained, and everyone said she was a *trouper*, an *angel*, even a *saint*, but Allie knew the real Jill, who was funny, goofy, and naughty. The real Jill loved thick books with maps in the front and joked that she was going to smoke when she grew up. The real Jill wasn't a saint, but something much better. A big sister.

If Jill was dying on the outside, Allie was dying on the inside. When Jill was hurting, Allie couldn't stop her tears, crying in her pillow for them both. The worst was when she helped with Jill's percussive therapy. She'd beat her sister's rib cage to loosen up the mucus, which left them both drenched with effort, just to win a few puffs of something as insubstantial as air. *Air*. You couldn't see it, but you couldn't live without it. It didn't weigh *anything*, but it had all the weight in the world. It was like a bad riddle. It was even *free*. All you had to do was *breathe*. *Take a deep breath*, people said, but Jill had never had one of those in her life, which ended after seventeen years, at home.

Allie had been there when Jill died, hugging her in hysterics, clinging to her like a kitten hooking its flimsy nails into a sweater. Allie had been heartbroken, devastated, reeling at the prospect of a life that no longer included Jill. Allie didn't know who she was without Jill. She was not-Jill in a world that was Jill's, in a family that revolved around Jill's illness, specialty meds, and therapies.

Allie didn't know how her family would fill the hole that Jill left because it was everything. It wasn't a hole, it was the *whole*. So it could never be filled. Now Jill was gone and so were the hospital bed, commode, nebulizers, oxygen tanks, and pill bottles. But somehow Jill was everywhere, in the very air. Her absence was her presence, and the girl who could never get air had *become* it. The Garvey family breathed Jill every moment.

The thought made Allie's stomach knot, and sweat broke out on her forehead. Tryouts for the cross-country team were coming up, and she needed an extracurricular to get into a good college. She couldn't sing well enough to make choir, didn't play an instrument, and was too shy to be onstage. Her guidance counselor told her she should write about Jill for her personal essay, but Allie wasn't about to write *My Sister Died So Let Me into Penn*.

Allie kept running, panting hard, her legs hurting. She'd gained fifteen pounds and was falling so far behind the others she didn't know how she would catch up. It was how she felt all the time lately. *Behind*. After Jill's funeral, Allie was supposed to go to school like nothing ever happened, but that was impossible. The other girls had best friends, but Allie's best friend was Jill. She didn't fit in any of the cliques, like the pretty princesses, the field-hockey jocks, the fast girls who smoked, the goths, druggies, mathletes, or Ecology Club hippies. The boys called her Allie Gravy, and she was behind everyone, a permanent little sister to the world.

Suddenly a silhouette appeared at the top of the hill. It was Sasha Barrow, captain of the development's running team and one of the most popular girls in school. Sasha was tall, lean, and totally beautiful, with big blue eyes, a tiny nose, and not a single zit. She had on a cool blue Nike tank and silky dolphin shorts, like a professional runner compared with Allie's thick Phillies T-shirt and old gray gym shorts. Sasha ran for the development team as a way to stay in shape for the cross-country team at school.

"Hurry up!" Sasha shouted, her hands on her slim hips.

Allie sped up, but her ankle turned and she tumbled to the ground, landing on her butt. Her face went red and hot. She tried to get up, but her ankle hurt and she eased back down. Her knee was skinned, a grid of droplets.

"What are you doing down there?"

"I fell!"

"I can see that!"

Then why did you ask? Jill would have said. But Allie didn't.

"Come on!"

"Just go! I'm fine!"

"What's your name again?" Sasha came down the incline, her sleek ponytail swinging back and forth. She had on a wide black headband that Allie could never wear because they popped off her head.

"Allie Garvey."

"Are you in my class?" Sasha reached Allie and stood over her.

"Yes, in the other section. I live in Brandywine Hunt, too, on Percheron." Allie realized she was answering questions she hadn't been asked. She didn't know how to act around Sasha Barrow, who was wearing blue mascara. Allie hadn't even known that mascara came in colors.

"I'm on Pinto."

"I know," Allie said, then regretted it, wiping her brow. Sasha wasn't sweating and smelled like vanilla. Allie sweated like a pig and smelled like cellulite.

"Okay, so get up, Allie."

"Please, go back with the others. I'll be fine."

"Try!" Sasha's pursed lips glistened with pink gloss.

"I'm not going to make the team."

"Duh."

Allie's mouth went dry. She felt nervous around Sasha Barrow. She tried to think of what Jill would have said. Jill had attitude.

"Allie. You really can't get up?"

And then, Allie did it. For one moment, she summoned Jill's spirit and said exactly what Jill would have said. "If I could, would I be sitting where worms could crawl in my *vagina*?"

Sasha burst into laughter, and Allie could see why Sasha was popular, and it wasn't only that she was pretty. There was a wild spark about her, a natural confidence.

"I'll try to get up." Allie shifted.

Suddenly Sasha pointed down the hill. "Look," she whispered. "What are they up to?"

Allie turned to see that two boys in tennis whites were digging under the base of a tree with a sharp bend in its trunk, at the bottom of the hill. Leafy branches covered the boys from view, but Allie recognized David Hybrinski right away. He was dreamy, with a great smile even though he never had braces. His hair was thick and wavy, a reddish-brown color, and he was tall, with a muscular body that made him look older. Allie always saw him hitting against the backboard at the tennis courts while Jill was swimming the laps that were supposed to increase her lung capacity. When David hit the ball over the fence, he'd call to the kids, *little help, please*, and they'd fetch the ball for him like puppy dogs.

"Who's the boy with David?" Allie whispered.

"Julian Browne. He lives across the street from me, but he goes to Lutheran now." Sasha's eyes glittered. "Let's bust them."

"What?" Allie asked, but Sasha was already cupping her hands around her mouth.

"Hey, down there! Freeze, this is the police! You're under arrest!"

The boys looked up, startled, then burst into relieved laughter, which echoed in the quiet woods. Sasha pulled Allie to her feet, looping an arm around her shoulders, and started down the hill with her, while Allie smoothed her hair back, trying to look good, though this wouldn't have been the day she'd pick to meet David Hybrinski. She'd sweated off her flesh-toned Clearasil, and her long brown curls frizzed. At least her braces were finally off and her eyes were a nice blue, but boys weren't into eyes.

She pulled her damp T-shirt away from her body, so David couldn't see the blubber that made her belly button into a big O, like a mouth shouting, *LOOK AT MY FAT!*

They got closer, and Sasha called out, "What are you doing?"

"Nothing!" Julian was shorter than David and handsome in a preppy way, with hazel eyes, a refined nose, and a small mouth with thin lips. His hair was straight, brown, and shiny, and he looked lean in a white T-shirt that said CRT SPORTS CAMP. He covered whatever they were digging, then stood up as the girls reached the bottom of the hill.

"What's going on?" Sasha let go of Allie as the boys stood side by side. Their bicycles and backpacks lay on the ground nearby.

"I told you, nothing," Julian repeated, his smile sly.

"Buried treasure," David added. "Gold doubloons."

"Come on, what is it?" Sasha took a step toward them. "Tell me."

David noticed Allie and flashed her a smile. "I know you. You're in the other section."

"Yeah, and I live in the development, too." Allie couldn't believe David Hybrinski knew who she was. She felt so *seen*, and he had such a nice way about him, like a gentleman. Up close, his eyes were as brown as a Hershey bar.

Sasha gestured at the other boy. "Julian, where are your manners? Introduce yourself to Allie Garvey."

"Julian Browne," the other boy said, flashing a big grin, and Allie started to wonder if the cool kids were just big smiles hanging in the air, like the Cheshire cat in

Alice in Wonderland. Jill used to read it to Allie when she was little, and Allie had thought the title was *Allison Wonderland.*

Julian kept smiling. "I don't know if you can keep a secret, Sasha."

"Of course." Sasha snorted. "And if you don't tell me what it is, I'll come back and dig it up myself."

David turned to Allie. "Can *you* keep a secret?"

"Yes." Allie hid her excitement that he was talking to her.

"Okay, then. Come look." Julian moved the backpack, crouched, and started digging with his hands. "I had this project for Environmental Bio. Indigenous wildflower identification. I was looking for bluets."

"What's that?" Sasha asked.

"It's a blue flower." Julian kept digging as he spoke. "It's like a cornflower or a forget-me-not."

"And you have to do this over the summer? Is this a *private school* thing?" Sasha made a face, but Allie didn't think anything bad about private school. Her parents had talked about private school for Jill, but they ended up with tutors, which was how Allie learned some French. She and Jill used to say *tant pis* because it sounded like *tant pee*, then Jill started saying *tant penis*, which cracked them up.

Julian kept digging. "My mother told me that bluets don't bloom late in the summer, so I should look now, in the woods. Of course it's not a real woods. We have to leave a certain percentage of the woods or the township won't let us build."

Sasha said to Allie, "Julian's father built the development."

"His company did," Julian corrected her. "He does business as Browne Land Management."

"Oh," Allie said, impressed. Her father was an orthodontist in Exton, and he didn't do business as anything but Dr. Garvey. It bugged him that he hadn't gone to medical school, only dental, and one time, at their hotel in Orlando, one of the guests got sick and the manager called her father. He had to admit he wasn't a medical doctor.

"I saw a patch of bluets under this tree. I started taking pictures, then I noticed this paper sticking out of the dirt." Julian finished digging, and both boys moved away from the hole, revealing a wrinkled piece of newspaper wrapped around something. They unwrapped it like a gift, but it was a gun.

Allie gasped, her hand flying to her mouth.

"Whoa!" Sasha hooted. "Let me have it!"

CHAPTER 3

■

Sasha Barrow

Let me have it!" Sasha felt a bolt of excitement when she saw the gun, which had a short shiny barrel and a dark wooden handle. She leaned over to pick it up, but Julian caught her hand.

"No, don't."

"I want to hold it."

"Why?"

"Why not?" Sasha couldn't believe that Julian was asking her such a stupid question. She couldn't believe that he was saying *no* to her, either. He'd been in love with her forever. "Have *you* ever held a gun?"

"Not before this one."

"David, have you?" Sasha turned to him.

"Sure. My uncle hunts. He has rifles and a handgun just like this."

"What kind of gun is it?"

"A .38 special. A revolver. It's old."

"How old?"

"I don't know. This newspaper is from June 2, 1995." David held up a crumpled sports page. "Doesn't mean it was buried that day, but whatever."

Sasha returned her attention to Julian. "Julian, it's not yours just because you found it."

Julian smiled. "Ever hear of finders keepers?"

"How old are you? Twelve?"

Julian's smile evaporated, and Sasha reminded herself to be nicer. Her father always said *you can catch more flies with honey than with vinegar* and that her mother *should try it sometime*. Sasha knew her parents were going to get divorced someday, because her mother was human vinegar.

Sasha forced a smile. "Can I please just hold it?"

"Guys?" Allie raised her hand. "If you found a gun, I think you should take it to the police. I mean, you guys heard about Columbine. You can't have a gun. It's zero-tolerance. Just turn it in."

"Who asked you?" Sasha glared at Allie, who wasn't even a friend of theirs.

"But it could be a murder weapon." Allie shuddered. "Why would somebody bury a gun? Is it loaded?"

"No," Julian answered.

Sasha snorted. "Julian, let's load it!"

"We don't have any bullets."

"Then buy some! Don't you want to shoot it? Let's do it!"

Julian shook his head. "We can't. People will hear. The houses are too close."

"So let's go somewhere *else*!" Sasha threw up her hands. "Duh!"

"No, don't." Allie clucked. "You probably need a permit, and it's dangerous."

Sasha turned to her, angry. "Allie, don't be stupid. It's a gun, not a bomb. No police are going to know we have it. We could put it in a backpack."

David shook his head. "I agree with Allie. I don't think we should move it. Even though it's old, the owner could come back for it. We don't want to let on we found it."

"Oh, enough!" Sasha dove between the boys, grabbed the gun, and scooted a few steps away.

Julian advanced on Sasha. "Give it back, please. It's not a toy."

"Oh my God, this is amazing!" Sasha loved holding the gun. It felt heavy in her hand and packed so much power. Even without bullets, it excited her.

Julian held out his hand. "Sasha, please?"

"No, I just want to see it!" Sasha held him off with an arm. The metal was silver, and she ran a fingertip along the side, where it had been damaged. "This is scratched."

Julian nodded. "They destroyed the serial numbers so the gun couldn't be traced."

"How do you know that?"

"I researched it. The round part is the cylinder, where the bullets go. The holes that hold the bullets are called 'chambers.' There are five, so it holds five bullets. Or 'rounds.'"

"And the cylinder revolves." Sasha pressed a little lever, which freed the cylinder to spin. "*That's* why they call it a revolver."

"Exactly." Julian smiled.

"It feels really *good*." Sasha aimed the gun, double-fisted. She was pretty sure she could hit anything she wanted. It was a thrill.

David frowned. "Sasha, you're being freaky."

Allie added, "Sasha, we have to get going. They'll notice we're missing."

"Almost done." Sasha flopped the gun over in her palm and pressed the lever again. The cylinder popped open, revealing five perfectly round chambers, then she closed it again.

"Give it back." Julian held out his hand. "And you have to agree to not tell anybody about it. Agree?"

"Bang!" Sasha shouted, pretending to shoot him, and they all laughed.

Except Allie.

CHAPTER 4

■

David Hybrinski

David worried that the gun wasn't a secret anymore. He hid his annoyance as Sasha gave it back to Julian, who rewrapped it in the newspaper. Sasha had a million friends, and she wouldn't keep it to herself for long. She was used to having her own way. Pretty girls got away with murder.

"Here we go." Julian started to put the gun in the hole, but Sasha stopped him, frowning.

"I think Allie should have to touch the gun, so all of our fingerprints are on it. Like, we're in *possession*, and we could get caught, so she should be in possession, too."

Julian hesitated, but David knew that Julian would do whatever Sasha wanted. He always did. David, Julian, and Sasha had gone to elementary and middle school together, but Julian had gone to Lutheran Academy for high school. David had thought Julian was going to jump off a bridge because it wasn't Sasha's school, but his parents had made him go. They didn't think he was *challenged* enough in the public school. When David told his mother that, she laughed. Because she was a teacher in a public school.

Allie made a face. "I don't want to touch the gun."

"You have to," Sasha shot back. "Why don't you want your fingerprints on the gun?"

"It's not that, it's just that I don't, well, I don't really want to touch it."

Julian unwrapped the gun. "Allie, you should touch it. We all keep the secret. We're all in the pact."

"What pact?" Allie frowned, leaning back on her hurt ankle.

"Just do it." Sasha raised her voice, and David knew Allie was no match for Sasha, who was definitely going to win this argument. Allie was too nice, and he remembered that her big sister died. He couldn't even think how he would feel if his big brother died. The school planted a tree for Allie's sister, but David doubted that was any consolation.

Sasha met Julian's eye directly. "Give it to Allie, so she can touch it."

Julian held out the gun. "Allie, it's not that big a deal."

David felt bad for her. "Allie, do it to make them happy."

Sasha shot David a dirty look, but didn't say anything.

"Oh, fine." Allie patted the gun quickly, then handed it back to Julian. "Here."

David liked Allie for standing up to Sasha. Sasha was

too mean to other girls. He remembered how, a few years ago, some girl skater tried to break Nancy Kerrigan's leg, and he'd thought, *That's something Sasha would do*.

There was a shout, and they looked up to see one of the other runners standing at the top of the hill. "Sasha, Allie!" she called out, her shout scattering the birds from the trees. "What are you doing?"

"Allie turned her ankle!" Sasha called back coolly. "We'll be right up!"

David edged his backpack over the open hole. Sasha stepped next to him, blocking the girl's view.

The girl called down, "Is Allie okay?"

"Yes, go back and tell them we're coming!"

The girl turned around and ran off.

David exhaled slowly, with relief.

"Let's bury this thing." Julian squatted, moved the backpack, and put the gun in the hole.

"Pack it deep." David knelt next to him, shoving mounds of dirt over the gun. His father would kill him if he got in trouble. He had to get good grades and do well. He played varsity tennis and was already a nationally ranked junior player. *The next Pete Sampras*, his father always said. Meanwhile, Sasha and Allie were starting up the hill.

"See you guys," Sasha called over her shoulder.

"Catch you later," Julian said, pressing down on the dirt.

"Remember, no telling, Sasha." David pushed dirt into the hole, relieved to see that it covered the gun completely.

Sasha didn't reply. "Allie, you have to go fast or she'll come back."

"I'm going as fast as I can."

"Fine," Sasha said in a way that meant it wasn't fine.

David packed down the dirt, recognizing Sasha's tone of voice because his mother used the same one when his father worked late. He wondered when Sasha had turned into his mom, but whatever. She was Julian's crush, not his.

Julian brushed dirt off his hands. "We need leaves for on top. It can't look freshly buried."

"Good idea." David felt the tension ease in his chest. Julian was smart, even if he was a little weird. They'd been best friends since they both took tennis lessons on the courts at the development. They grew up bonding over forehands and video games like *Doom* and *Donkey Kong* and became a doubles team in middle school, winning local tournaments. David was the better player because Julian ran around his backhand. David had taught him not to. *Turn your body. Get your racket back. You can do it.* That was how David knew Julian didn't have as much confidence as he acted.

"Here we go." Julian hurried over with dried leaves and twigs, letting them fall to the ground. "What do you think?"

"Good job." David could hear the girls arguing as they climbed the hill, then suddenly Allie yelped. He looked over to see Allie sitting on the ground, holding her ankle. Sasha was standing over her, her hands on her hips, another thing that David's mother did.

Sasha yelled down the hill. "Julian, come here!"

"We're coming!" Julian stood up, grabbing his back-pack, with his tennis racket zippered into the top. "David, we can get the bikes later."

"Sasha's in a mood, isn't she?" David rose and picked up his backpack, too.

"Allie's such a baby." Julian started up the hill.

"She's hurt. She fell on her ankle."

"It's not like she broke it."

"A sprain can hurt worse than a break."

Julian snorted. "If you're fat."

"Shh." David didn't want Allie to hear, but he got the feeling that Julian didn't care. They reached the girls, and David stepped in and took Allie by the arm. "Allie, I'll help you. All you have to do is stand up. One, two—"

"Not too fast!" Allie said, nervous.

"I'll go slow, don't worry. One, two, *three*." David eased Allie to a stand and looped her arm around his neck. "There you go."

"Thanks." Allie smiled shakily.

"We'll go ahead." Sasha started back up the hill, and Julian hurried to fall into step with her. They headed off, laughing and talking in low tones.

David knew they were making fun of Allie, and Allie knew it, too. He wished he could tell her not to care. They climbed the hill slowly, with Allie huffing and puffing, holding on to his neck. He didn't have a hard time talking to girls, but he felt tongue-tied with Allie, maybe because her sister died. He didn't know whether to bring up the sister or not, then he thought that if his brother died, he wouldn't want to talk about it, so he didn't say anything. Her body felt warm against his side, and their hips kept bumping together. She smelled like flowers, but not perfume. Nice, like soap.

Allie hopped along. "I'm sorry I'm so . . . heavy."

"No, you're not."

"Yes, I am."

"Whatever, I like heavy things." David looked over, and Allie burst into startled laughter, so he realized that was the wrong thing to say. "No, I mean, like, my favorite book is a thousand pages. I'm not kidding. It's heavy but it's a great book."

Allie nodded. "I love thick books, too. With maps in the front."

"Really?" David liked her, or maybe he felt sorry for her, but either way it came out the same.

"What's your favorite book?"

David told her, and then he couldn't *stop* talking.

CHAPTER 5

■

Julian Browne

Julian stowed his bike in the garage, buzzing. He felt so good after being with Sasha. God, she was so hot. He loved to watch her talk, walk, whatever, *anything* she did he would watch. He saw everything about her, all the details, the way the sunshine brought out the gold in her hair, so blond it *matched* the sun, and her eyes were a crazy-great blue. Her fingers were long and thin, and she gestured a lot when she talked, moving them in a ripply wave like something he had seen snorkeling in the Caymans. She liked to wear rings on every finger, thin with pretty colored stones, and he knew exactly how she took them off and put them on a little glass holder in her room. He knew because he'd watched her.

Julian walked around his mother's car and let himself into the mudroom. He kept moving because he had to get upstairs before it was too late. The central air chilled his skin, and he dropped his backpack on the floor, called, "Hey, Mom," and patted Peety, their ginger tabby who came running to greet him—but none of it interrupted his thoughts about Sasha. He barely broke stride when his mother called to him from the kitchen, "Hey, honey, dinner's in an hour," and he called back, "Great," and he kept walking to the stairwell, not stopping when she asked, "How was your day?" and he answered, "Fine, gotta shower," staying in his own Sasha thoughts, which were too good to leave just yet, like a dream he was having while he was still awake.

"I'm making chicken," his mother called after him, and Julian called back, "Okay," as he climbed the carpeted stairs two by two, thinking about the moment when Sasha had said the gun was the *coolest thing ever*. Julian felt a tingling because if he *had* the coolest thing ever, then he *was* the coolest thing ever.

Julian hurried up the stairs, on fire. It had been so hard to get her attention ever since he went to Lutheran. She and David were always talking about their teachers, their homework, their schedules. Julian had become the odd man out, but he was back in business with the gun. It was lucky that the girls had come by.

Julian reached the top of the stairs and rushed into his room, then closed the door and locked it behind him, quietly. He checked his watch, 4:25. Perfect timing. He hustled into his bathroom, turned on the shower, and let the water run so his mother would hear while he stripped off his shirt, shorts, and his underwear, and raced back to the window in the front of the house.

He crouched on his knees, opened the bottom drawer

in his desk, and pulled out his binoculars, raising them so he could see out the window. Sasha lived across the street, not directly but catty-corner, and her room was on the right side of her house, so he had a great view through the front window and the two side windows of her bedroom. The only curtains she closed were on the side windows. His house was fifty feet from the curb, like all of them in the development, but his house was higher, so Julian could see down into her room, like Sasha was his own private TV show.

Her bathroom was at the back side of her house, and both houses were the same top-of-the-line model, the Unionville, except his bathroom was on the front side. Julian could watch her walking around when she was on the phone, doing her homework on her bed, especially at night with the lights on inside. She sat at her desk a lot, too, drawing on a big white pad, and once she'd told him she was sketching dress designs. Julian loved to watch her. It was harder to see inside during the day, but he'd gotten good at it, and in the summer, Sasha usually took a shower before dinner.

He pressed the binoculars to his eyes, aiming down into her room. He didn't mess with the focus because it was perfect, too, and he waited for his eyes to adjust, trying to see the moving shadows in her room as she walked back and forth. He couldn't see much because she hadn't turned on a light, but he didn't need to see. He'd seen her undress so many times, he knew every curve of her body. It excited him to think that she was undressing right now. He told himself that she was undressing for him. Only for him.

He watched her as she took off her shirt, and she was walking around as she undressed, and he realized she was talking on the phone, so he caught only fleeting glimpses of her breasts. He got stiff just thinking about it but didn't jerk off. He was saving it for later, when she went to bed. She slept naked in summertime.

He held his breath as she turned to the side, and he caught the swell of her breasts, trying to see the nipples, which he knew stuck out like pencil erasers. It turned him on so much he almost couldn't stand it. He was getting harder, and his right hand went automatically downward, squeezing himself. He was as hard as a rock, like it said in one of his father's *Penthouse* magazines.

Sasha slipped out of sight into the bathroom, and Julian knew she was taking a shower. It thrilled him they were naked at the same time, mirror images of the same bedroom, their upgraded showers running. His bedroom was filling with steam, just like hers, and Julian heard himself breathing harder, from trying to make himself wait until bedtime. His gaze shifted to behind her house, which was in the general direction of Connemara Road and the area kept wooded because of township zoning.

He'd lied to them, even David, about how he'd found the gun. Of course he couldn't have told the truth, which was that he had been watching Sasha in her bedroom one night and been distracted by a light behind her house. He had realized the light was a flashlight and watched its jittery dot for an hour, knowing that someone was in the woods, doing something they wanted to hide. Later Julian had tried to put it out of his mind, but he hadn't been able to stop wondering. It showed him he wasn't the only person in Brandywine Hunt with a secret.

Later he'd ridden his bike to the woods, searched around, and found ground that looked like it had been disturbed under the bent tree. He had started digging and discovered the buried gun in the newspaper. He had no idea who had buried it, but it was most likely somebody in the development. He'd thought about moving it, but he left it where it was, and every night when he watched Sasha undress, he checked to see if the flashlight had returned. So far it hadn't.

He'd been showing the gun to David today when the girls caught them, and that was how Sasha knew, which brought her close to him again. He was so in love with her, he wanted her so much, nothing could ever change that, not a different school, nothing. He knew that she would want him, too, someday. And then they would go into her bedroom, lie down on the pink flowery bedspread, and her golden hair would spread out on the pillowcase with the pink edges, and he would kiss her and touch her breasts, and she would get so wet for him and then he'd be inside her, rock-hard and losing himself, deeper and deeper into her, until they became *one*.

Julian's attention returned to Sasha's room because she'd reappeared. He squeezed himself again, harder, bringing a rush of pleasure and pain and anger and love and a feeling so deep it didn't have a name yet, but it drove him crazy, and he couldn't stop himself or wait another minute.

There was no saying no to that feeling.

Julian stopped trying.

CHAPTER 6

■

Kyle Gallagher

Kyle entered their townhouse, wondering if it would ever feel like home. They had moved to Brandywine Hunt two months ago, and he could still smell the paint in the entrance hall, which was Revere Pewter, the same color as in New Albany. It was the only familiar thing in the house, which had been the sample so it came already furnished with black leather sofas and glass tables. His mother had told the realtor she *preferred French country*, but Kyle knew they were in no position to *prefer* anything. They'd had to move, and the sample was the only rental available. They didn't have the money to buy. It had gone to the lawyers.

Kyle carried the last of the grocery bags into the kitchen, a small rectangle in the back of the house, ringed with white cabinets and a white built-in nook next to the window. His mother loved the granite countertops and

Mexican tile floor, but always said she *missed her island*. Kyle would kid her, *Mom, we* are *the island*.

"Oh, thanks, honey," his mother said, flashing him a smile. She was still pretty even though she was in her forties, with her brown hair in a ponytail that made her look younger. The guys on the basketball team used to call her a *total MILF*, but he never told her that. She had on her work clothes, a blue dress with a skinny belt, and she had found a job as a paralegal in Philly, only an hour commute. *Landed on my feet!* she liked to say.

Kyle set the bag down in front of the refrigerator, where his mother was unpacking the other bags. Buddy, their chubby yellow Labrador, walked from one bag to the next, sniffing the groceries, his toenails clicking on the floor and his thick tail wagging.

"Kyle, can you believe how *big* that store was?" His mother's eyes shone with excitement, on a retail high after their shopping trip. She had talked about it all the way home, trying to put a happy face on everything ever since their move.

"It was big." Kyle petted Buddy to distract him from the grocery bags. The dog was a carb monster and always managed to find the bag with the bread.

"We're so lucky it opened right down the street." His mother stowed the apples in the plastic drawer, where they rolled around noisily when she pushed it closed. "I'm excited about my rewards card. What a great idea."

"Great idea." Kyle scratched Buddy.

"We can get our prescriptions filled there, too. No more running around like at home."

"Mom, it's a grocery store," Kyle said lightly. She was always talking about how *awesome* it was here and *so much better* than home. She was trying to convince him, and herself. He knew why.

"I've never seen anything like it, have you? I mean, *that's* what took us so long. It's practically *eight o'clock*. Look!" His mother gestured at the wall clock, which didn't have any numbers but 12. That annoyed Kyle, but he kept it to himself. Actually, he kept *everything* to himself. He'd lost his friends, the guys on the team, and his high school. Nobody would ever speak to him again. Even if they wanted to, their parents wouldn't let them.

"Honey, is the ice cream in one of those bags? I don't want it to melt."

"Yes." Kyle plucked the tubs of Ben & Jerry's ice cream from the bag, her favorite, Cherry Garcia, and his favorite, Chubby Hubby.

Mom, can we still get Chubby Hubby? he had joked with her in the store, the two of them standing in the frost billowing from the massive freezer.

Ha! His mother had fake-laughed, but Kyle wished she would just be real. Like, say *that's not funny*, because it wasn't. Or maybe say *too soon, dude*. Or maybe it would never be funny. Nothing was going to be the same, ever again, and Kyle doubted it would ever be *awesome*.

He opened up the freezer side of the refrigerator with a tug, since the door practically vacuum-sealed closed. *It's a Sub-Zero*, his mother had said with pride, like it was an achievement, not an appliance. She loved their new townhouse, which had *everything top-of-the-line,* the dishwasher a *Bosch* and the washer-dryer a *Maytag*. Like, they had great appliances, so they hadn't lost anything. Except their entire life, and his father.

"I love that the store's only ten minutes from the house. You could ride your bike there, couldn't you?"

"Sure." Kyle picked up a heavy bag of canned goods, since he always put away the pantry items and she always put away the refrigerator items, one of the few things they kept the same. What had happened was one of the things they couldn't talk about, though it was always between them. Back home, he and his mother had gone to family therapy, and the therapist called it *ignoring the elephant in the room*, but it didn't feel that way to Kyle. Elephants were nice, and what he and his mother were ignoring wasn't nice.

"Won't that be perfect if I have to work late again? You can ride down and get dinner." His mother put away the romaine lettuce in the drawer. "They have that prepared foods section, and the Chinese food was good, wasn't it? I really loved my spring rolls. Not too oily. You liked yours, right?"

"Yeah." Kyle had already told her he liked his egg rolls. He brought a bag to the pantry, and Buddy wandered in after him, hoping for a treat. They kept the Milk-Bones and dog food in the pantry, too.

"It's even a family-owned business, and isn't it great that there are still stores like that?"

"God bless America."

"Wise guy." His mother forced a laugh. Her head dipped into the refrigerator, and Kyle put the cans away.

The pantry was smaller than their old one, like their backyard, which sucked. It sloped down to the thick woods around the development, and his mother didn't like it because it had big green drains, which the rental agent said were for *storm-water management* and *runoff*. Kyle didn't like it because it didn't have a fence, so he had to walk the dog instead of just letting him out.

Kyle finished with the cans, folded the brown bag, and put it in the cabinet with the others. His mother said they had moved here to *start over* and *push reset*, and the therapist had said, *one door closes and a window opens*, whatever that meant. To Kyle, they were running away, so he didn't know why they just didn't say so. His mother was legally changing their names to her maiden name, Gallagher, and now he was Kyle Gallagher, which he kept forgetting. His backpack had his old initials, KAH for Kyle Allen Hammond. Now his initials were KAG.

Awesome!

Kyle knew she couldn't help it. They couldn't stay in Ohio after what happened, but he hated his new life. He was going to be a sophomore at Bakerton High, and he dreaded the thought. He didn't know what to do, or—really—even who he was, since he wasn't Kyle Hammond anymore.

He'd played basketball back home, already on varsity because he was so tall, six foot five, but he doubted he'd try out for the team at Bakerton. His mother would be relieved, since she'd been worried it would bust them. He thought she was paranoid, but whatever. There were courts at Brandywine Hunt, but he never went to shoot or play pickup. He didn't want to meet anybody or answer questions. So he wasn't a basketball player anymore, either.

Kyle spent all day in his room with Buddy, playing *Doom* and eating Snyder's pretzels. His mother was worried about him, though he wished she wouldn't worry.

Kyle was worried enough for the both of them.

But he kept that to himself, too.

CHAPTER 7

Allie Garvey

M om?" Allie said softly, bending over the bed. Her mother was lying on her right side, facing the door, in such a deep sleep that she didn't react at all. Her face was so slack that her features seemed to be sliding off, and it hurt Allie to see, because her mother was such a pretty woman, or had been. Linda Garvey had fiery red hair, thick as a bristle brush, bright blue eyes, a pert nose, and lips like a Cupid's bow. Allie's grandmother always called her "a spitfire," but that was before Jill had been born and then died, which Allie's grandmother hadn't lived to see.

"Mom, want some dinner?" Allie touched her mother's shoulder, which was lost somewhere in the thick chenille bathrobe. Her mother wore her bathrobe 24/7, sometimes with a blue fleece hat that had been Jill's. Her mother's short hair stuck out in all directions, and Allie could see her black roots getting longer, shot through now with silvery gray strands. Before, Allie's mother would never have let her roots go and she'd be at the salon for a *touch-up* as soon as she saw what she called the *headband*, but that had gone by the wayside.

"Mom, I made dinner. Aren't you hungry?" Allie jostled her mother slightly, but it still didn't wake her. Allie leaned closer to make sure her mother was breathing, and she was, her breath smelled slightly sour. She didn't know when her mother had eaten last, when she'd lost the fifteen pounds that Allie had gained. Her father kept saying that the pills Allie's mother had been given would work in time, but Allie thought they were only making her worse.

Allie gave up. The bedroom was dark because the curtains were always drawn, and the air smelled of the dirty laundry overflowing the hamper. Allie made a mental note to run off some clothes. Her mother had spiraled down since Jill's death, corkscrewing herself into the earth, as if she wanted to be buried, too. Allie didn't blame her, because she always knew Jill was the favorite. Jill was Allie's favorite, too.

"Mom, you rest, it's in the fridge if you want it." Allie kissed her mother's cheek, left the room, and went down the hallway, passing the closed door to Jill's bedroom with its sign, NO BOYZ ALLOWED. Jill had made it after watching a VHS marathon of *Little Rascals*, one of their mother's favorite shows. Allie hadn't gone in there since Jill died.

She hustled into the kitchen, crossed to the stove, and picked up the fork just in time to turn the hotdogs over. She made them the way her father liked, fried, cut down the middle, and flattened, which he called *filet de frank-furter*. The water was boiling, so she dumped in the bag of corn. *Al dente*, her father would say, and he was due home any minute, at seven-fifteen.

Allie found herself thinking about finding the gun in the woods, her head filling with questions. *Should we turn it in? What if it's a murder weapon? Should I tell?* She heard her father's car pulling into the driveway and the garage door rattling in its tracks. The sound always reassured Allie, because oddly, she worried that one day he wouldn't come home, that he'd leave the depressed wife, the overweight daughter, and the closed bedroom.

The steam from the corn warmed Allie's face, and she remembered how she and Jill used to stand over boiling water with a towel over their heads, after Jill read that steam prevented blackheads. The steam also loosened up the mucus in her lungs, and she used to say, *Oxygen or blackheads, which matters more?*

"Hey, honey!" her father called from the entrance hall, and Allie turned off the boiling water and dumped the corn into the colander in the sink.

"Hey, Dad!" she called back, and her father entered the kitchen with a brown Staples bag. He looked older than he was, which was fifty-one, and he had lost most of his brown hair after Jill died. He was short and skinny, with alert brown eyes behind his glasses and their fine black wire rims. His lips were thin and always set in an almost-smile, which her mother used to call *benign*. Allie always liked the way her mother talked about her father, and they had a good marriage. Until recently.

"What a day!" Her father set the Staples bag on the kitchen island.

"What happened?" Allie forked his dogs onto his plate, mounded some corn beside it, and brought his food to the table, which was crowded with open cardboard boxes of envelopes stuffed with flyers about the upcoming 5K, Jog For Jill. Her father had organized it to benefit cystic fibrosis, and it was going to be held on the anniversary of Jill's death.

"What *didn't* happen?" Her father loosened his tie, then tucked it inside his shirt, easing into the chair. "We ran out of everything, but not all at once."

"What do you mean?" Allie brought her hotdogs and corn to the table, then sat down opposite him, with the boxes around them like cardboard walls. More boxes and papers covered the kitchen counter, blanketing the surfaces where Jill's medicine bottles and nebulizers used to go.

"We ran out of flyers, then envelopes, then the printer jammed and we had to call the guy." Her father cut his hotdog into skinny slices the way he always did.

"You mean the printer at work?"

"Yes, I should've had them run it off at Staples, but I knew Ellie was free and I let her handle it. I was trying to save money. What a mess." Her father squirted mustard onto his hotdog, ignoring the burping noise produced by the plastic bottle, which would have elicited gales of laughter from Jill.

"But it got done?" Allie chewed her hotdog, which was buttery and delicious, probably going to the exact spot on her waist where David had held her.

"Yes, but we have to stuff them so they can be in everybody's mailbox over the weekend."

"We'll get it done, Dad." Allie ate at a fast clip, the way they did these days.

"It will take tonight and tomorrow night to get it done."

"Dad, it won't take that long," Allie said, but her father liked nothing better than a plan. He kept a running Things to Do list and divided the tasks into Short-Term and Long-Term, which her mother used to tease him about.

"No, we couldn't possibly do it ourselves, just the two of us." Her father stabbed his hotdog, barely looking up. "There are about four hundred families in the development, and each house has to get an envelope. There are three sheets that have to go in each envelope—All About Jill Garvey, the entry form, and the waiver and release form. We lost time over the printer snafu, so we didn't get to collate. So we have to collate, then stuff."

"So we'll start now." Allie wished she could cheer him up. "We'll make it fun. We can put on a movie. If we go to the video store after dinner, it will be early enough to get a new release. We can stay up as late as we want. It's not like I have school tomorrow."

"No, it's all set up. The committee is coming over. More hands make less work. They'll be here in an hour." Her father shook his head, wiping his mouth with a napkin, which he neatly refolded and returned to his lap. "I'm herding the cats."

"Oh, okay." Allie felt her chest tighten. They were about to be invaded by a slew of women, including her mother's best friend, Fran, who'd been in Pittsburgh for some time, taking care of her own mother. Allie called her Aunt Fran and knew Aunt Fran didn't realize how bad things were with Allie's mother. "Dad, Mom was really sleepy today. I couldn't wake her up for dinner."

"She'll be fine." Her father sipped his water without meeting Allie's eye.

"I wonder if whatever meds she's on, they need to change the dosages again."

"They know what they're doing."

"But I don't even think she ate. When I came home, there were no dishes in the sink. When she eats, she leaves the dishes."

"She'll eat when she's hungry. We've discussed this. They said she's having 'complicated grief.' You can't rush it." Her father rose with his plate, gathered his silverware, and went to the sink, turning away.

"Aunt Fran's going to go upstairs."

"Fran knows she's under a doctor's care." Her father rinsed his dish, his back turned. "Besides, she might not come. Jim might have torn his rotator cuff."

"But what if she goes upstairs? They only talk on the phone. Since she's been away, Aunt Fran hasn't seen—"

"I'll tell Fran your mom has the flu. She won't go up."

Allie blinked, surprised. She had never known her father to lie, and Fran wasn't stupid. "Mom doesn't have the flu, Dad."

"It's no one's business what she has. No one's business but ours." Her father turned from the sink. "Understood?"

"Yes," Allie answered, realizing she now had a second secret.

■

CHAPTER 8

Sasha Barrow

H old on, Melanie." Sasha set the phone down and put on the flowy white dress in front of the floor-length mirror. It slid down her body, then clung to her hips. Sasha was pretty and tall enough to be a model, but she had higher hopes. She was going to be a world-famous fashion designer like Diane von Fursten-berg, Donna Karan, or Coco Chanel. She liked every-thing about designing clothes except sewing, which was boring.

Sasha spun around in the mirror, dreamy. She *loved* clothes, noticing every detail about the cut, stitching, and fabric. She practically *studied* chiffon, silk, and the tweed in her mother's Chanel suits. It was called *boucle*, Sasha had taught herself. She read *Vogue*, *Harper's Bazaar*, and *WWD* and sketched all the time, trying out ideas. She wanted, someday, to run a fashion empire like the Fendis and the Missonis, with *ateliers* in all the European capitals and seamstresses to sew for her. She'd personally oversee every *piece* in her collection before the *girls* went down the runway. The designer always walked last, and Sasha would make her runway appearance to thunderous applause. She could almost hear it now.

"Sasha, you there?" Melanie asked on the other end of the line.

Sasha came out of her reverie and picked the phone off the bed. "Chillax."

"I'm sorry, I was just saying that there's nothing to do down here."

"Where are you again?" Sasha turned this way and that, then spun around to make the hem flare out.

"Down the shore, in Long Beach Island. Come down. It'll be fun. One of your parents could take you. Are they around?"

"No," Sasha answered, distracted. Her strapless bra was making tiny bumps in the dress, and she would have to get a new one. Also strappy sandals. She had seen a pair of Manolos in Neiman Marcus.

"Where are they?"

"I don't know." Sasha's parents traveled for work, but she didn't mind. She had Bonnie and her husband, Clark, whom Sasha called Clyde, and they lived in the au pair suite and took care of her and the house. Sasha liked the freedom she had over her friends, who had to get permission to breathe. Bonnie and Clyde knew to let her do what she wanted, if they wanted to keep their jobs.

"What about Clyde? Can he take you?"

"No," Sasha answered, eyeing her reflection.

"I bet I can get somebody to pick you up. My brother might do me a favor."

"I can't, I'm busy. Hold on." Sasha wiggled out of the dress. She had three more to try on, then she wanted to message Julian about the gun.

"But this morning you said you were bored. You weren't busy at all."

"Yeah, well, I got busy." Sasha was thinking about the gun, which she couldn't get out of her mind. She crossed to the shopping bags at the foot of her bed.

"Sash? You there?"

"Hold on a minute!" Sasha rummaged in the bag, took out a box, and opened the lid.

"What are you doing?"

"Trying on dresses for my cousin's wedding." Sasha took out another dress. There were small pink flowers along the hem, which were a little young.

"Sasha, are you there?"

"Give me one more minute." Sasha put the dress over her head and smoothed it into place. Her belly was super flat, and she bet she could bounce a penny off it.

"A dress? What's it look like?"

"White with pink flowers."

"You're not supposed to wear white to a wedding if you're not the bride."

"Why? I look good in white, and I'm going to be tan by then. Hold on." Sasha unzipped the side of the dress, and got it over her head. She heard a ripping sound, but Bonnie would return it for her tomorrow anyway.

"Sash? You sure you don't want to come down?"

"Totally. Ask Courtney. She's free."

"I can't stand her."

"Nobody can. That's why she's free. Bye." Sasha hung up and tossed the phone onto the bed. She crossed to her desk, sat down in front of her computer, and dialed up the Internet. She didn't have to wait for anybody to get off the phone so she could get on, like her friends. The modem sounded, and she logged into AOL. She could see from her Buddy List that Julian was online. As soon as she appeared, he IMed her:

Heir2Throne987: do u like the new toy?

SashaliciousOne: toy? r u trying not to put it in writing?

Heir2Throne987: put WHAT in writing???? LOL

SashaliciousOne: i think we should move it

Heir2Throne987: why

SashaliciousOne: fat people yap

Heir2Throne987: she won't

SashaliciousOne: david is on her side

Heir2Throne987: he wouldn't

SashaliciousOne: i could move it

Heir2Throne987: please dont

SashaliciousOne: i know where it is & I could dig it up & then it would be MINE ALL MINE bahahahahahahahaa

Heir2Throne987: i dont want u 2

Sasha was only kidding, but the more she thought about it, the more she wanted to move the gun. She could find the bent tree on her own. She ran through the woods all the time and knew the trails better than Julian or David.

Heir2Throne987: i dont want the owner to know we found it

SashaliciousOne: how could he

Heir2Throne987: what if he watches the spot @ night

SashaliciousOne: that would be weird

Heir2Throne987: he could have binoculars & if he knows then he would move it

Sasha thought that over. Julian was right. He liked her, but she could do better and she was keeping her options open. Plus there was something about him that was a little, well, off.

Heir2Throne987: never underestimate the downside risk

SashaliciousOne: u sound like ur father

Heir2Throne987: did I convince u

SashaliciousOne: yes

Heir2Throne987: ☺

SashaliciousOne: i have another idea

Heir2Throne987: what

SashaliciousOne: bullets!

CHAPTER 9

■

David Hybrinski

Twilight washed the sky in pink and purple, and the sun sank behind the tree line bordering the softball field at Brandywine Hunt. The baseball diamond was set in a green field that had been mowed in swaths like a vacuumed rug, the red clay on the baselines had been newly raked, and the cinder-block dugouts freshly painted brown and white, courtesy of Browne Land Management. Multicolored plastic banners touting other corporate sponsors were tied to the PVC fencing, advertising Westtown Xpress Lube, Devon Family Practice, and Coca-Cola Bottling of Chester County.

The air was balmy, and everyone agreed they couldn't have asked for a nicer night for the quarterfinals of the Chesco Girls' Softball League. The Browne Batters were leading West Caln Chiropractic 9–8 in the seventh inning, with David's nine-year-old twin sisters, Jessica and Jennifer, playing first and second bases. The spectators cheered noisily and beat their feet, but David kept his head down, immersed in his thick paperback. It was 1,079 pages long with 388 footnotes, and he still didn't understand it completely, which was what he loved about it. He'd never read a book that was essentially a huge puzzle, with so much to hold his attention that he was able to screen out the noise around him.

"Way to go, Browne!" his father cheered, sitting to David's right. He'd come from work so he was still in his gray suit, with his tie loosened and his attention focused on the field. His father kept raking back his thinning hair with his fingers, making it greasy, and his fleshy features set in a scowl behind his prescription sunglasses. His father yelled almost constantly at the games, mostly encouragement except for the occasional *honey, look alive out there!* David's mother was helping the team in the dugout, distributing bottled water and orange slices.

"Go get it, Jessica! You got this, Jennifer!" David's brother, Jason, sat to his left, making a point of cheering for the twins separately. The twins were identical, so the only time most people could tell them apart was on the softball field, when they had their numbers on their shirts.

Jason nudged David. "Cheer for Jessica. She made a good catch."

David shouted, "Way to go, Jessica!"

His father turned to David. "So how was camp today?"

"Good." David didn't return to his book, since his father took it as a criticism when David read. It was why David would never tell him that he wanted to be a writer someday, as opposed to being the next Pete Sampras.

"Did you practice your overhead?" His father pressed his lips together unhappily.

"Yes."

"Hitting any better?"

"I will in time."

"You have to commit early. Make the decision early." His father frowned deeply, and David had learned not to talk back when his father gave tennis advice, even though his father never played the game. Suddenly his father leaned over, so close that David could smell the onions on his breath, from lunch. "Anything you want to tell me?"

"No, what do you mean?" David's mouth went dry, thinking about the gun. He had no idea how his father could've known. He thought of that line from his book, *My chest bumps like a dryer with shoes in it.*

"I heard you left camp early today." His father glowered. "Why are you hiding that from me?"

"I'm not." David wished he could tell his father about the gun, but no. Never.

"You didn't tell me."

"I forgot, it didn't matter."

"So did you miss practicing your overhead?"

"No, I practiced at our courts."

"You can't practice your overhead on a backboard."

David knew his father's eyes would be narrowing behind his thick sunglasses, sensing that David was lying but wrong about the reason. David tried to think of an answer. "I found somebody else to hit with. Mr. Forman was there with another guy, and they let me hit around."

His father glanced away. "Why'd you leave camp early? I heard you and Julian both cut out."

"Right, we did." David realized his father must have called the camp director to check his progress, something he did from time to time. Vince had had a dentist appointment, leaving the assistant in charge, which was why Julian had picked today to show David the gun.

"What for?"

David thought fast. "Julian didn't feel good. He said his stomach hurt and he felt woozy."

"What does that have to do with you?"

"He wanted to go home and he was going to ride his bike." David knew these weren't questions but criticisms, like many of the questions his father asked him, they came in disguise. "He keeps it at camp. On the weekends he goes to his father's and rides it home."

"So?"

David saw Jason opening his mouth, looking like he was going to interrupt but he didn't. A good decision. David felt a rush of affection for Jason, who picked up for him against their father, when he could. Jason was in a suit, too, because he was interning at a law firm in West Chester. David dreaded thinking about life at home after his older brother, Jason, left for college.

His father frowned. "You don't have to leave camp because Julian does. I pay good money for that camp."

"I know that, Dad—"

"Julian's set for life. *Set for life.* All that money behind him, he doesn't have to earn a g-d penny. You do. You're not in the same position, so don't slack when he slacks."

"He wasn't slacking—"

"Yes, he was. You didn't have to go with him. That kid is so spoiled."

"Dad, he's a nice guy." David didn't like his father criticizing Julian, because he didn't know him at all.

"He's had everything handed to him."

"He's still a nice guy." David recognized the rant. His father had a chip on his shoulder about money, which made no sense because everybody in Brandywine Hunt had money, including them. His father owned his own business, Hybrinski Optical, in a strip mall in Frazer.

"David, you don't have to do everything he does. Be a leader, not a follower. You follow him."

"I don't follow him." David got so sick of his father giving him grief.

"Then why'd you ditch camp?"

"I left early, is all. You got your money's worth."

"Don't smart-mouth me."

David fell silent.

"Why'd you leave early?"

"Julian said he felt sick and dizzy. He had to ride his bike home, so I told him I'd go with him to make sure he didn't fall or anything. I mean, he could've fallen in traffic. It's a long ride from camp." David saw his father's brow unfurrow, so he kept going. "I don't want him dead in the road, do you? Because I had to practice my overhead?"

His father didn't reply, turning away again.

David knew that his father would never say he was

sorry. Saying you were sorry meant you made a mistake, and his father could never admit a mistake.

"So how was Julian?" Jason asked, nudging him, and David realized his brother had believed the story about Julian being sick.

"He was fine. He was probably dehydrated."

"Right." Jason patted David on the back, a gesture that meant *you did the right thing*.

The crowd shouted and clapped, and David returned to the book. His favorite author was David Foster Wallace, a tennis player who loved books, kept his hair long, and wore a bandanna. David wore his red bandanna as his tribute to DFW, which was how he thought of him. DFW's book *Infinite Jest* was filled with insights about life and tennis, because tennis could really be cerebral. His father thought it was about *dominance*, but it was really about how you felt about yourself. Nobody understood that except for David and DFW.

"Jessica, way to go!" Jason nudged him again. "Dude, Jessica made another catch."

"Go, Jessica!" David watched the girls change sides, and the brown uniforms mixed with the red uniforms, coming together, then apart on the other side. Team sports were two armies opposed, but in an individual sport like tennis, it was you against yourself. David tested himself all the time, challenged himself to be more, and better. Someday he would do it as an author, too. He thought of his favorite line from *Infinite Jest*:

I am not just a boy who plays tennis.

CHAPTER 10

∎

Julian Browne

"Need a hand, Mom?" Julian entered the dining room, bracing himself for dinner. Last weekend was his father's weekend so tonight would be a cross-examination, not a conversation.

"No, honey, just sit down!" his mother called from the kitchen. "Dinner's almost ready!"

Julian sat down to a table that had been set with a platter of steaming roast chicken and fresh rosemary, next to a side dish of red potatoes with fresh dill. The herbs smelled great, and his mother had grown them in her garden, since she used only fresh herbs. She called herself a *perfectionist*, and it wasn't until Julian got older that he realized she was trying too hard to make everything perfect. And then he'd realized why.

Their house was the nicest house on Pinto Road, with three stories and seven bedrooms on the Alternate Second-Floor Plan, including the *master to end all mas-*

ters, according to the brochure that Julian had proofread himself. They had eight and a half baths with top-of-the-line, special-order Italian finishes, radiant floor heating under the marble tile, and Perrin & Rowe polished nickel faucets and trim. They had the optional Expanded In-Home Office Suite downstairs and a smaller Pocket TV Room/Study upstairs, also optional. The HVAC was zoned throughout, with the HEPA filtration system, and the floors were Resawn Oak, special-order. The dining room was a showstopper, 20′3″ by 16′8″, with the op-tional Coffered Ceiling, *conceived for the finest entertain-ing*. He worked in his father's office every summer and school vacation, where he had learned everything about the real estate business.

His gaze wandered outside, since windows sur-rounded the dining room on all sides, overlooking the wraparound deck, which came standard with the Main Line Model. Their backyard was landscaped with ter-raced gardens, a large pool, and a Pool House with the Optional Elite Guest Suite addition, for when his grandma visited. His mother also had an English Green-house and Potting Shed, which was a Luxury Option, which led to the Palm Beach Sunroom Addition, another Luxury Option.

Brandywine Hunt was the crown jewel of Browne Land Management, encompassing 410 luxury homes on eight hundred acres. The parcel used to be several horse farms, so the streets were named after horse breeds and the sections after local hunts. The minimum lot size was one and a half acres, and their street, Pinto Road, was in

Cheshire Hunt, the nicest section, where all of the homes cost between $1.2 and $2.3 million, had 5,500–8,500 square feet, two- to five-car garages, and three or four stories including the optional Two-Story Foyer. Browne Land Management had developed sixty-six residential and commercial properties in southeastern Pennsylvania.

Kiss my ass, Toll Brothers, his father always said.

Their dining room table was a walnut circle able to seat twelve, and did, back when his parents gave dinner parties. It was too large for Julian and his mother, who sat on the left side nearest the gourmet kitchen. Julian had asked his mother why they didn't just eat in the kitchen, but she insisted on the dining room, like his father had. She didn't want to change anything in case his father moved back in, but that was never going to happen and the only one who didn't know it was her.

"Spinach salad!" His mother entered the room with a large serving bowl.

"I was worried we weren't going to have enough food."

"Oh, you." His mother smiled, then put the salad down and served them both with tongs.

"Looks great." Julian's stomach grumbled at the delicious aromas, and his mother had made his favorite dinner, which she always did on the Wednesday nights after he'd come back from his father's weekends. Because that would be the first time they'd have dinner after he'd come back from his father's weekend. Julian's life was divided into his mother's weekends and his father's weekends, and none of the weekends belonged to him anymore.

"How was camp?" His mother picked up the carving

knife, which she would've just sharpened in the kitchen. *Like a true gourmet*, his father always used to say, back when.

"Fine." Julian thought of the gun, but would never tell her. She was only asking to warm him up. She always started with a few innocent questions before she got to the ones she wanted to ask.

"Is Vince treating you any better?" His mother carved two perfect slices of white meat from the chicken breast, and he offered his plate, then she served him some potatoes, too. His father always said, *the hostess with the mostest*, but he was really talking about her chest. His father had once called himself a *breast man*, an expression Julian had never heard before or since.

"He treats me fine."

"Oh, you said he was helping with your backhand or something?"

"He did." Julian shrugged, taking a bite of chicken, which practically melted on his tongue. His mother was an excellent cook, though Julian sensed she believed if she cooked well enough, or did everything else well enough, that his father would have stayed married to her, but Julian knew that wasn't true. His father had a slew of girlfriends, and none of them could cook for shit.

"So how's your backhand?"

"Fine. He only says that so we think we get our money's worth."

"*Exactly right.*" His mother smiled, turning on the charm. Everything he said for the rest of the night would be *exactly right*. She was softening him up to get the dirt.

"What did you do after camp?"

"Hit with David. He likes to practice." Julian ate, happy to answer her preliminary questions.

"Well, *my* lesson went great today." His mother smiled. She played golf, and it kept her in good shape, chesty with a thin waist and really nice legs, always tanned. She got manicures and pedicures, but Julian doubted his father noticed. No man was a *foot man*, unless it was a fetish. Julian had been learning about fetishes. He was starting to think he had one.

"What was so good about your lesson?"

"I was hitting really well. I could feel it." His mother beamed, and Julian thought she had the greatest smile. She'd been a cheerleader at the University of Delaware, and she still looked like one, with bright blue eyes and a short nose. Her hair was medium brown but she streaked it blond and wore it bouncy around her chin. She had met his father when she was playing in a local amateur tournament sponsored by Browne. His father always said that she was *the prettiest girl there who wasn't gay.*

"Good for you."

"What did you have for lunch, honey?"

"Hoagies from Wawa."

"Again?" His mother frowned. There was never anything to make a decent sandwich with at his father's house. He and his father always rolled in to the convenience store in the morning.

"It was fine."

His mother picked at her salad, and Julian knew she was getting ready to pump him for information about his father. She'd caught him screwing his assistant in his Porsche Carrera at the office. Their divorce had become final last year.

"So is your father still seeing that girl?"

"Which one?" Julian realized it was a mistake when he saw his mother cringe.

"Lindsay?"

"Oh, right, I think he's still seeing her." Julian ate more quickly, to finish sooner.

"Weren't you with him and Lindsay last weekend?"

"No." *Shit.*

"So were you guys alone?"

"No." Julian's father's girlfriends were always around, which was fine with Julian. His father didn't act like a father, but like a cool older guy who had a younger friend named Julian. His father didn't want to be a father anymore, if he'd *ever* wanted to. It worked for Julian, who didn't need a father anymore.

"So he goes out with other girls, in addition to Lindsay?"

"Right, I don't think they're *exclusive.*" Julian used his father's term.

"So which girl was he with?"

"Another one, I forget her name."

His mother set her glass down. "Julian. You didn't forget her name. Don't lie to me."

"I forgot her name, really." Julian wasn't lying, for once. He did forget the girl's name. He didn't forget how she looked in a bathing suit.

"Was it Brittany?"

"No."

"Courtney?"

"There's no Courtney."

"There's *always* a Courtney." His mother laughed. "Tell your father to hop to. Find himself a Courtney."

"Good one, Mom." Julian wished she could laugh it off more often, but she couldn't. They'd been married nineteen years, and his mother really loved his father, even though he'd turned into a selfish jerk after he became a successful developer. He'd developed into an asshole.

"Did you guys go *on the boat*?" His mother's expression soured because the boat drove her crazy. His father had bought it after the divorce, and Julian had overheard his mother talking about it on the phone with her friends, saying *since when did he start boating* and *who does he think he's kidding* and *he can't even swim.* They used to sign off, *man overboard!*

"Yes, we went on the boat."

"Again!" His mother rolled her eyes so hard the white showed.

"Don't start." Julian smiled, but they both knew she was going to.

"Was it an overnight trip?"

"Yes."

"How many nights?"

"Just one." Julian loved the boat trips because it was fun to dock in the small towns in New Jersey, Delaware, and Maryland. He always packed his binoculars.

"Not Friday night?"

"No, Saturday." Julian explained the binoculars by

telling his father that he had to bird-watch for an independent study. He even bought a *National Audubon Society Field Guide to Birds, Eastern Region* with a waterproof cover that he took everywhere. Julian had convinced his mother, too, and she'd bought him a membership to the Audubon Society, which encouraged junior birding. So he'd become Julian Browne, junior birder.

"Did he get you the adjoining room this time, at the hotel?"

"Yes." Julian stabbed his potatoes with a fork. The last time he'd stayed in a room on a completely different floor from his father, and his mother and her lawyer had thrown a fit, saying it was unsafe, that he was unsupervised, that he could even be kidnapped.

"Was it *right* next door?"

"Yes, it was adjoining."

"You swear? Don't lie for him."

"I wouldn't." Julian was almost finished with his meal. Thanks to the lawyers, he got to listen to his father and his girlfriend having sex. His father said *oh baby* in orgasm, a fact Julian never wanted to know.

"So where did you go *this* time?"

"The Eastern Shore."

"Maryland again?" His mother clucked. "I hope his girls are old enough to cross state lines. Your father will end up in jail."

Julian laughed, pretty sure she was kidding. If anyone was going to end up in jail, it would be him. He'd started by looking into the houses from the window of his hotel, but then he realized that he could leave the hotel without his father knowing, since Mr. Oh Baby was asleep next door. If Julian ever got caught at night, he'd tell his father he was looking for owls.

"Do you ever sleep on the boat? It sleeps six. Supposedly."

"No, and the town we stayed in was nice." Julian was thrilled they didn't sleep on the boat. He walked around the towns at night, looking inside the houses. If he got close enough, he could peek through the windows. Julian Browne, junior voyeur.

"Which town?"

"Chestertown. I saw a lot of mallards, but nothing special. The Eastern Neck National Wildlife Refuge is down there, but we didn't go. They have ospreys and eaglets learning to fly this time of year." Julian had done his research. "Dad said we can go next time. It's best in fall or spring for migratory birds."

"Like your father would ever go birding. So what's her name, really?"

"I don't know. I tell you, it doesn't matter. They're all the same, Mom."

"And how is that?" His mother held her water glass to her lips.

"You know, they're just women, younger women." Julian rose, picking up his plate. "May I be excused?"

"How much younger?"

"I don't know." Julian realized he was making it worse. "He introduces me, that's it."

"Where does he meet them? Where did he meet this new one?" His mother arched an eyebrow. "Is she from the same strip club as the last one? Amber or whatever her name was?"

"I don't know." Julian didn't add that they all looked like they were from a strip club. And they danced like that, too. *Oh baby.*

"Do they ever hit on you?"

"Of course not!" Julian burst into laughter. It hadn't happened, but he'd thought about it more than once.

"I want you to tell me if that happens."

"Mom, they never pay attention to me. They pay attention to Dad." Julian didn't add that the only girl he cared about was Sasha. She was his secret obsession. She was the one who started him being a voyeur. If there was one bird he wanted, it was Sasha Barrow.

"I bet they're all over him." His mother snorted. "Hot young girls on a boat, that's his fantasy. It's so juvenile!"

Julian flashed on his AIM convo with Sasha. He would do anything for her, and if she wanted bullets for the gun, he would figure out a way to get them. Now the two of them had a secret, from the others. Him and Sasha, together.

"Does he pay any attention to *you* on these trips?"

"I don't need him to."

"But you're with him every other weekend. It must be lonely."

"I'm fine." Julian had been standing with his dirty plate forever. "Now can I be excused?"

"Yes, but listen to me." His mother touched his arm, her charm bracelet jingling with the gold number-charms that his father had given her on their anniversaries. "You don't have to go if you don't want to. The judge said the custody schedule is optional at your age. It's a guideline, not the law."

"If I don't want to go, I won't." Julian used to look forward to his father's weekends, before he'd found the gun. If things started to heat up with Sasha, he'd stay home on his father's weekends.

"When school starts, you can't go boating on weekends. You'll have homework."

"I know."

"I just hate that this is your life now, back and forth all the time." His mother's pretty face fell, and three wrinkles popped on her forehead. Lately she'd been talking about Botox.

"Mom, I'm fine." Julian knew what she needed to hear. "And take it from me, none of those girls are as pretty as you—"

"Is."

"What?"

"Your verb agreement. 'None of those girls *is*.' Not 'are.' You'll never go wrong if you pretend 'none' is 'no one.' Think to yourself, 'no one *is*.'"

"Okay, no one *is* as pretty as you, or as cool as you, or as smart as you, and they can't do *anything* as well as you. Dad's crazy, and you're perfect."

"Really?" His mother swallowed hard.

"Perfect." Julian gave her a kiss on the cheek, and when he straightened up, his mother was smiling again.

CHAPTER 11

Kyle Gallagher

Mom, I'm gonna take the dog out." Kyle flipped the new red harness over Buddy's broad back. It had the dog's name with their phone number, a 610 area code that Kyle hadn't gotten used to. He'd joked with his mom, *We don't have to change Buddy's name, too, do we?*

"Thanks, honey." His mother looked up from the kitchen table, where she was paying bills. "You're so helpful."

"No problem." Kyle smiled at her, knowing she stressed over money. They were living on so much less without his father. She never even had to work before, so she'd volunteered at school and for the booster moms on the basketball team. But she never complained about what happened, always saying *it put life in perspective.*

"Don't be too long, okay?" His mother's expression turned serious. "You've been walking him a long time, every night."

"No, I haven't."

"Last night you were gone an hour, honey. I timed it. You were gone from 10:15 to 11:16."

"It was a nice night."

"I worry about you."

"There's nothing to worry about, Mom. It's safe out there." Kyle tried so hard not to make her worry. She never worried about herself. Only him.

"Where did you go?"

"Just to Pinto, around the big houses." Kyle started to leave the kitchen with the dog, who tugged ahead, his tail wagging.

"Someday we'll get back up there, honey."

"Mom, that's not why I walk there." The notion caught Kyle by the throat, and he stopped. "I don't care about the houses. Buddy likes a nice long walk, and it's cooler at night. Okay?"

"Okay." His mother pursed her lips, and Kyle wanted to reassure her but he didn't know what to say.

Kyle headed for the door. "Love you."

"Love you more!" his mother called back, which always made him feel bad, like he didn't love his mother as much as she loved him. Like his father. Kyle wondered if his father had loved either of them, really.

He left the house trying to shake off the feelings, walking down the flagstone path to the pavement. The air was cool, and it wasn't dark in the townhouse section because there was ambient light. At the other end of the street, one neighbor was rolling out a recycling bin, and another was walking a white poodle. He passed the other townhouses where the TVs were on, the news ending. People were talking and laughing inside, but he didn't want to hear the families, the way his used to be, or at least the way he thought they were.

Kyle turned right, letting Buddy tug him along, then took a left on Thoroughbred. He paused to let the dog pee and patted his jeans pocket, reassured that he had pickups. It was the rule of the development that you had to pick up after your dog with a special green eco-bag, and his mother wanted them to follow the rules to the letter, so as not to attract undue attention. It bothered Kyle that they acted like they were criminals, when the real criminal was his father.

Buddy did his business, and Kyle's gaze lifted to the townhouses around him, a cluster of three-story buildings with parking between them. The fronts were white and the shutters were black. They had to keep it that way because it was the rental section. Everybody got assigned to spaces, and needed special permission for more guests. It had been the same way at New Albany Mews, the development where they'd lived before. Kyle turned the eco-bag inside out, scooped up the poop, and knotted the bag.

Kyle walked on autopilot, wondering if it was really a fresh start to move to another development. Brandywine Hunt was just a bigger version of New Albany Mews. Like strip malls that had a McDonald's, a Taco Bell, and a Domino's, developments were just strip malls of people. The only difference was that here no one knew the truth about them. His mother told people only that she was divorced and that Kyle never saw his father, which was technically true. It turned out that she had worried for nothing, because nobody asked. They got what they wanted, which was to be left alone. And they were, especially Kyle.

He breathed in the night air, walking along. He tried not to think about his father or if they would ever visit him in prison. His mother never wanted to see him again, and Kyle didn't blame her, but it wasn't so easy for him. She'd divorced him, but Kyle couldn't divorce his father. And he still had so many questions, like why his father had done what he had, and how much of what the newspapers said was true. Their therapist had said that Kyle *needed closure*, but Kyle didn't know what he needed. He felt tangled, his emotions knotted together, inside.

Kyle walked past the houses without really seeing them. His father, Dr. Brian Hammond, wasn't the kind of guy who would do well in prison. He was a suburban pediatrician, not a badass. The thought of what could happen to him made Kyle sick, even though his father deserved it, no question. He could feel his anger simmering. He was so mad at his father. Sometimes he tried to tell himself that the jury had made a mistake, but his mother swore it was true. She'd even testified against his father. When she'd come home after, she'd cried as hard as Kyle had ever seen her cry. He couldn't stand the sight, the sound, any of it. She had doubled over at the kitchen table. Her face had turned red. She hadn't been able to catch her breath. If Kyle could tell mothers anything, it would be that. Never cry in front of your sons.

Kyle reached Pinto, where the houses were so much bigger, all lit up like a stage set. The lamps inside glowed yellow, and the big TVs flickered. He could see people going upstairs and walking around, but he couldn't hear because everyone had central air. Kyle didn't miss their old house but he missed their family, or what he thought their family had been. He missed who he was then. He missed himself.

He picked up the pace. He didn't know if he was walking away from something or toward something else, but he kept going. He thought of the bottle he had hidden near the recycling, but he didn't want to sneak a drink tonight. He was always worried his mom would smell it on his breath. She was finding them a new therapist, now that her insurance kicked in, but Kyle knew it wouldn't help. It hadn't before.

Suddenly he spotted a flash of light in the woods behind the houses, like a flashlight. He watched to see if it came again, but it blinked off. Buddy must have seen it, too, because he started to bark, facing that direction.

"Hello?" Kyle called out, feeling a nervous tingle. It seemed strange. No one was on the street, and the flashlight had come from deep in the woods.

Kyle told himself it was nothing. Maybe somebody was running on the track that encircled the development, which had a parkour course. But Buddy kept barking, like something was hiding in the woods.

"Hush, pal." Kyle turned back home, having problems of his own.

CHAPTER 12

■

Allie Garvey

Two Days Later

The white signs were hung on the cyclone fencing: BRANDYWINE HUNT PROPERTY, DO NOT ENTER. AUTHORIZED PERSONNEL ONLY. NO TRESPASSING. CONSTRUCTION SITE. Allie would've obeyed every one, even HARD HATS MUST BE WORN, but Julian ignored them. He led the way with Sasha, and David and Allie brought up the rear. The four of them followed the path through the cleared trees on the way to the construction site. Allie had never broken the law, and she was pretty sure that breaking into a construction site qualified, even if Julian's father *owned the site*, like he said.

Allie felt hot in the sun, and flies buzzed around her head. It was still warm even at five o'clock, and they had to wait until the construction workers left for the day. Julian had planned it all, digging up the gun, getting the bullets, and deciding on the location because it was *in the final phase*, on the *westernmost part of the property*, set off from the other houses. Julian said that if anybody heard gunshots, they would dismiss it as nail guns because the construction workers put in overtime when *time was of the essence,* which was *a term of art in the construction business.*

Allie trundled behind them, her sandals sticking in the mud. She'd taken a shower, put on a nice yellow sundress, and blown her hair dry, though it was frizzing. She had dressed up for David, but he had barely said two words to her, and if he shared her nervousness, it didn't show. He looked handsome in his tennis whites and the wide red bandanna around his forehead. She'd quit running, but she lost a pound riding her bike up and down Palomino Road, hoping to run into him.

David was in the back of her mind all the time. She'd fall asleep kissing her pillow, pretending she was kissing him, and it felt real except for the cat hair. She was so ready to lose her kiss-virginity to him, and she felt excited just walking close to him.

They headed toward the site, and Allie wished they had left the gun buried. She wouldn't have come today except that David had called her last night and asked. She'd felt such a charge hearing his voice. She hadn't heard anything from him before that. They had exchanged screen names so they could message each other. David had liked hers, which was AllieOop918. It had been Jill's idea.

"Watch your step, Sash." Julian pointed at the deep ruts in the mud.

"If I get hurt, can I sue you?"

"Good luck." Julian gave her a playful shove, and they passed yellow and red construction vehicles that read CASE and TAKEUCHI.

Sasha asked him, "Are those tractors or what?"

"A trackhoe, a backhoe, and a skid steer."

"How about this?" Sasha pointed to long green tubes that ran along the muddy ground like fabric snakes.

"Silt fencing to control the runoff. This section is going to be called Vicmead Hunt. It's only 'carriage houses,' which means twins. Marketing is everything."

Allie could tell that Julian felt proud, and David looked over at her with a sly smile. "Guess what, I'm reading that book you recommended. *Infinite Jest*."

"Really?" David smiled wider.

"Yes, and it's so thick!"

"I know, I love it." David chuckled, his eyes lighting up.

"I started reading it, and it's amazing." Allie warmed inside, happy that her trip to the library had paid off. Of course she wasn't the one who liked thick books, Jill was. Allie had just told David that to match him. She liked reading, but she was a slow reader compared to Jill, and *Infinite Jest* made her feel dumb because it had so many SAT vocab words.

"How far along are you?"

"I'm in the beginning. I just got it yesterday." Allie had gone to the library the day after David had told her about the book. She didn't want to say she was only at page fifteen because that sounded pathetic.

"I love the beginning." David grinned. "Hal Incandenza in the job interview."

"Right, yes." Allie remembered that Hal Incandenza was the character, but she couldn't tell if it was a joke name or a real name. She hadn't even known it was about a job interview until David said.

"What do you think of his writing?"

"The writing is so good, and he seems *so* smart." Allie thrilled to see David nod, and a lock of hair fell into his eye, which made him look gorgeous.

"He's a genius, officially. The year after he wrote *Infinite Jest*, he got a MacArthur genius grant."

"Wow." Allie hadn't even known there was such a thing as an official genius.

"He's won other prizes, too, like the Whiting Award. He published his first book when he was only twenty-four."

"Really?" Allie asked, though she remembered that David had told her that already, but she didn't mind. She could listen to him talk about David Foster Wallace all day.

"His father taught philosophy in college, and his mother taught English."

"Wow." Allie wished she could think of something to say other than *wow*, but she was starting to get nervous. She was walking right behind Julian's backpack, and inside were the gun and bullets. They were getting closer to the entrance of the construction site, and soon they'd be shooting the gun.

Julian led them to a double-wide gate in the fence, locked with a heavy chain and a combination padlock. He examined the padlock and thumbed the dials. "Gimme a minute."

Sasha stood next to him. "How do you know the combination?"

"They keep it the same on all the sites. It's 911 with a 0 in front, because you need four numbers." Julian unlocked the gate and opened one side with a flourish. "*Entrez*, milady."

"Awesome!" Sasha popped through the gate. "Where now?"

"We're going past the houses to the end of the site, by the woods. The turnpike's on the other side, and the traffic will drown out the gunshots. That's why these lots suck. Turnpike noise."

"Race me!" Sasha took off, sprinting away in her tank and shorts from cross-country. Julian bolted after her, his backpack bumping along, a sight that made Allie cringe.

"I wish he wouldn't run with the gun and the bullets."

"Nothing's going to happen." David chuckled, and Allie looked around as they walked along a gravel path. Houses and wood skeletons lined what was going to be the street. A few houses were wrapped in white paper that read KINGSPAN GREENGUARD NV HOMES. Porta-Johns stood on one corner, among piles of white pipes and lumber wrapped in plastic.

Allie watched Sasha and Julian finish their race at the end of the street. Julian hugged Sasha, laughing.

"She won." David's dark eyes narrowed in the sunlight as he looked up the street.

"Where did he get the bullets?"

"I don't know. Sasha wanted them, so he got them."

"But where?"

David shrugged. "I assume he bought them."

"Can you just do that?" Allie was getting close enough to see Sasha and Julian take out the newspaper with the gun and a small cardboard box, which probably contained the bullets. She shuddered. "You can't walk into a store and buy bullets at our age."

David didn't answer, and they passed a big white trailer with a door and windows, with a brown banner that read BROWNE LAND MANAGEMENT, then walked down the gravel street, rutted deeply, passing numbered signs that read LOT AVAILABLE. Boxy green drains stuck up out of the dirt among piles of boards that were broken and studded with nails. A rusty red Blosenski dumpster brimmed with drywall, boards, and trash. There was nobody around, but that didn't make Allie feel better.

"You okay?" David shot her a sympathetic look, and Allie would have been sorry she'd come except that she was standing close to him.

"I'm worried. Why are we even doing this?"

"Sasha wants to shoot."

"Why?" Allie kept an eye on Sasha and Julian, who had reached the wooded area.

"Because that's Sasha." David glanced over. "Julian says she has too much MAO, or not enough, I forget which. It means she likes risk."

"Oh great." Allie watched Julian and Sasha open a yellow box of bullets that read REMINGTON, then load the gun. "Do they even know what they're doing?"

"It's not rocket science. Do you want a turn?"

"No way. Do *you*?"

"No. I've shot a rifle. Relax." David patted her back, and Allie loved the warm weight of his hand. They reached the end of the street, where scraggly grass struggled to grow through the stones, silt fences, and construction debris. Allie heard the *whoosh* on the turnpike, but it didn't sound loud enough to hide gunshots.

David asked Julian, "Dude, where'd you get the bullets?"

"The job trailer." Julian snapped the gun's cylinder closed. "I've known Mac, the project manager on this job, since I was little. He keeps a gun and bullets in his desk. There's payroll checks and petty cash in the trailer. Sometimes people steal tools, copper piping, and scrap metal."

Allie felt more worried. "Won't he notice the bullets are missing?"

"No, I don't think he's ever used the gun."

"And the bullets go with your gun?"

"They're the same caliber." Julian had barely finished answering before he stood up with the loaded gun, aimed it at the woods, and started firing.

Pop pop pop pop pop!

Allie jumped, startled. She covered her ears, and David winced. Birds flew panicked from the trees. Leaves fluttered to the ground. A weird smoky smell filled Allie's nostrils.

Julian laughed, his eyes oddly animated. "Cool!"

"Let me!" Sasha burst into giddy laughter. She and Julian crouched, reloading. Allie edged backward, shaken, liked she'd been on a roller coaster.

David crossed to them, frowning. "You guys don't know what you're doing. Let me show you how to reload. Give me the gun."

Julian handed him the gun. "I thought you only shot a rifle."

"My uncle has a revolver, too. I know the basics. Look, here." David pressed the lever with his thumb, and the cylinder flopped open with the shell casings inside. "These are warm. Heat expands them, so they won't come out by themselves." He pressed the ejector pin in the center of the cylinder and pointed the muzzle skyward, so the shiny shell casings tumbled onto the grass. "See? You push this and they fall out the back."

"Cool."

"Now you can reload." David handed Julian the gun. "This holds five shells, which is pretty common. My uncle has it, too."

"Thanks, cowboy." Julian smiled crookedly while Sasha grabbed the gun from him, took some bullets out of the box, and reloaded, then stood up and pointed the gun toward the woods.

"I see a squirrel!"

"Don't you dare!" Allie heard herself shout, then couldn't believe it came from her.

"*What?*" Sasha whirled around, her face contorted with anger.

"Don't kill anything!" Allie shouted again. She'd seen something die, and she never wanted to see it again.

"I'll do what I want!" Sasha shouted back, facing the woods again and raising the gun.

Allie felt herself trembling. "Sasha, if you kill *any-thing*, I'll tell everybody about the gun! I'll *tell*!"

Sasha glowered at Allie, but Allie only stared back. She could see that Sasha hated her guts, but Allie stood her ground.

David pointed at a large tree. "Sasha, see that knot, halfway up the tree? Bet you can't hit it."

Julian put his hand on Sasha's arm. "Sash, shoot at the tree."

Sasha aimed for the knot and started blasting. *Pop pop pop pop pop!* Wood chips flew from the trunk, pitting it. Birds squawked in fright, and bugs flew everywhere. Sasha and Julian reloaded quickly, and Sasha fired another five shots. *Pop pop pop pop pop!* The shooting stopped abruptly, and the only sound was the *whoosh* of traffic on the turnpike.

"Let's go," David whispered to Allie.

CHAPTER 13

■

Sasha Barrow

What a *bitch*!" Sasha said to Julian. They'd left the construction site and were walking through the woods off Connemara Road to bury the gun. Allie was with David far behind them, but Sasha was so mad she could spit. "Who does Allie think she is? I don't even know why she's here."

"Because she's in the pact."

"Not anymore. She threatened to tell. If that's not a violation of the pact, I don't know what is."

"She didn't mean it. She'd never do it."

"She's a *loser*!"

"Losers don't tell, so let it go."

"You don't know that. Girls know girls." Sasha was mad at Julian, too. She wished she hadn't invited him over to her house tonight. She'd intended to reward him for the bullets. "Why did you take her side against me?"

"I didn't."

"You did, too. You said I should shoot the tree. That's taking her side."

"It wasn't about sides."

"Everything's about sides. You used to be on mine and now you're not."

"Yes, I am, you know that."

"I did until today!" Sasha eyed him, gritting her teeth as they walked along. Julian looked upset, which made her happy.

"I got you the bullets."

"So what? What's the point if you won't let me have any fun?" Sasha snorted. "Bullets are for shooting, and all I wanted to do was shoot. What *should* I do with the bullets? *Throw* them at the squirrel?"

"Sash, gimme a break." Julian sighed, stepping over a log. The underbrush was getting thicker. "She was crying."

"She had no reason to."

"Her sister died. David told me." Julian looked over, his expression reminding Sasha of a sad-face emoji.

"So? What does one have to do with another? What, I can't have fun because her sister died? Why'd you even invite her?"

"David did."

Sasha rolled her eyes, hard. "Ugh! Don't tell me he likes her. He could do *so* much better."

Julian moved a skinny tree limb aside so Sasha could pass. "Whatever, it was fun, wasn't it?"

"It was fun until she ruined it."

"I liked it more than I thought I would. It was easy."

"Ha! I was a better shot than you. I could've hit that damn squirrel, too."

Julian stepped over a rotted tree trunk, its wood crumbling. "It's better you didn't."

"Because Allie cried like a baby? Boo-hoo. People hunt every day."

"Not with a revolver."

"What's the difference what you shoot it with? It comes out dead either way." Sasha made her way through some vines, almost at the bent tree. "So what about the bullets? You really want to bury them?"

"Yes, I already dug the hole."

"I could take them home. Nobody will find them in my house."

"What about Bonnie and Clyde?"

"They ignore what they're not supposed to see, like my vibrator."

"Really?" Julian's eyes flared.

"Yes." Sasha didn't really have a vibrator, but she liked teasing him. Actually, she loved teasing him. She could do whatever she wanted with him. They started up the hill.

"Here's where the gun was." Julian pointed underneath the bent tree.

"Where's the hole for the bullets? I don't see one."

"Good, that's the idea. First let's bury the gun." Julian climbed to the bent tree, then set down his backpack, crouched, and moved the dried leaves and underbrush aside to reveal an empty hole, about a foot deep.

Sasha squatted next to him. "So tell me, where's the hole?"

"Don't be impatient."

"When did you dig it?" Sasha asked as David and Allie started up the hill toward them. Sasha looked away from Allie, barely able to contain her anger.

Julian caught her eye. "Tell you what, Sash. Stand up, walk ten paces north, and you'll find the hole for the bullets. The bullet hole."

"Which way is north?" Sasha popped up.

"Follow your nose. Directly ahead. And walk it off on your feet."

"Got it." Sasha walked straight, putting one sneaker in front of the other until she was ten paces away, then she knelt down and started moving leaves aside.

David stopped on the lower part of the hill, with Allie. "Julian, do you need help?"

"No, I'm done here." Julian put the gun in the hole and was already covering it up. "Sasha's digging where we're going to put the bullets."

Sasha looked over her shoulder. "This way, we know where they are in case we want to do it again. That is, if Allie doesn't object." Allie flushed, stung, and Sasha went for the jugular. "Allie, you're not in the pact anymore, after what you said. You should just *leave*."

Allie reddened and turned to go, but David took her arm.

"No, you don't have to."

"Yes, she does!" Sasha shot back.

David pursed his lips. "Sash, you're making a big deal out of nothing."

Sasha rose, angry. "It's not nothing when she threatens to tell."

David frowned. "You were going to kill a squirrel."

"What do you care? I have the right to do what I want!"

"Not really," David said. "You don't have the right to shoot in residential areas with illegal handguns. There's laws about hunting. Permits. Seasons."

"So what?" Sasha threw up her hands, looking at Julian to see if he would finally side with her.

Julian turned to David. "She's right, David. It doesn't matter what you shoot it with, it's dead either way."

David stepped back. "Julian, seriously? You think that was a good idea to go blasting away?"

"That's what we went up there for."

"No, it isn't," David shot back. "You guys were taking unnecessary risks."

"Like what?" Julian frowned.

"Like shooting so many rounds, and we left that tree shot up. They'll find the casings. They're going to know somebody was shooting up there. And why keep the extra bullets? Why not put them back in the trailer?"

Allie nodded, beside him. "I bet they put up security cameras now."

Julian smirked. "I think I'll know if they do that. I'll find out from my father."

Sasha couldn't believe Allie and David had joined forces against her and Julian. "Julian *owns* this place, Allie. Shut up because you don't know what you're talking about. Just shut up!"

New tears welled in Allie's eyes, but she said nothing.

David took Allie's hand. "Sasha, don't talk to her that way."

Sasha scoffed. "You're as much of a little bitch as she is."

"Fuck you, Sasha."

"Fuck you, too, David. I'm out of here." Sasha was sick of all of them. She'd seen where the bullets were buried and that was all she needed to know. She turned on her heel and started up the hill, breaking into a jog.

"Sasha!" Julian called after her. "Catch you later?"

"Forget it!" Sasha called back, charging up the hill.

CHAPTER 14

■

Julian Browne

Julian's mother entered the room with a tray holding a bowl of popcorn and root beer floats. She had gone to a lot of trouble, but all he could think about was Sasha. It was already past eight o'clock at night, and Sasha hadn't been home since they buried the gun and bullets. He'd been watching the house, and her room was completely dark. The only lights on were in Bonnie and Clyde's suite and the family room downstairs, which they kept on when Sasha wasn't home. Julian didn't know where she was, and it was driving him crazy.

"Movie night!" his mother said, setting down the tray. "How much fun is this?"

"Fun." Julian smiled, hoping it looked convincing. "Real butter and everything?"

"Nothing but the best for my baby!" His mother put a napkin in front of him, then a root beer float with a special long spoon. His parents used to entertain all the time, and his mother had shrimp forks, mother-of-pearl caviar spoons, and cake knives. She even had special ice cream dishes, gravy boats, soup tureens, and ramekins; Julian knew the names because she took the time to educate him. Now the only person she was entertaining was him.

"I just love that we get to spend this time together, truly quality time."

"Right." Julian glanced out the window, keeping an eye on Sasha's house. Their family room was cavernous with brown leather sectionals arranged opposite the fireplace and entertainment center, and on the left side of the room, they had huge Palladian windows. It gave Julian a great view of the street, and from this angle, Sasha's house. The light over her front door was on. He sensed she was punishing him for what happened with Allie.

"Have some root beer float. It's going to melt."

"Good point." Julian picked up the spoon and slurped some root beer float, which tasted absolutely delicious. "This is perfect, Mom. Thanks."

"I love that you still drink it with the spoon. You used to do that when you were little."

"This spoon seemed bigger then."

"I'm sure." His mother grinned broadly, so excited on these weeknights, when it was *her night* as opposed to *his father's night*, since Julian went to his dad's house on alternating Tuesdays and Thursdays, depending on if he had been there the weekend. His mother always tried to plan something special for them, which they had never done when his father lived at home. He secretly wondered if she felt she had to, in order to win him over in the battle of who he liked better, mommy versus daddy. Of course she won hands down, but he could never convince her of that and he understood why. His father offered motorboats, blondes, and no adult supervision. Because his father wasn't an adult.

"Which movie do you want to watch first?" His mother held up the two VHS tapes, her pick, *You've Got Mail,* and his pick, *The Big Lebowski.*

"We can watch yours first, Mom."

"No, we can do yours."

"Please, you love chick flicks." Julian glanced out the window, but the Barrow house was still dark and quiet. One of their neighbors was walking his malamute, but nobody else was on the street.

"No, we watched mine first last time, remember? I love a double feature!"

"What's a double feature?"

"Oh my, I'm dating myself. Oh well, somebody has to these days!" His mother laughed as she crossed the room, slid the tape into the VHS player, and picked up the remote, hitting a few buttons to get the tape running. She eyed *The Big Lebowski* box. "What's this about again?"

"It's great, I love it."

"Wait, you saw it already?"

"Yeah, I told you at the store."

"I didn't hear you. Don't tell me my hearing's going now, too."

"I saw it with Dad." Julian didn't add that his father

hadn't seen the movie with him, just dropped him off. "It doesn't matter. I want to see it again."

"I didn't want you to have to sit through something you saw already."

"But I love it. I want to."

"Okay." His mother returned her attention to the movie, which was starting. "So is that man the big Lebowski? He wears a bathrobe to the grocery store?"

"Yeah, he's a stoner."

His mother frowned. "You mean he smokes dope?"

"Weed."

"We called it dope, in my day."

"People call it weed now." Julian didn't explain that his father called it weed, even though he was from the same day. Nor did he tell her that his father smoked weed on the boat.

"But *you* would never smoke dope, er, weed." His mother shot him a look.

"No, I wouldn't." Julian didn't say that he'd tried weed for the first time when his father gave him some on a trip to Cape May. Julian had liked smoking with his dad and the blonde *du jour*. His father let him have beer, too, but Julian took it easy because beer made him fart, which would not be cool.

"Don't even experiment with it, okay?" His mother sat down on the couch. "They tell you that in school, right?"

"Yeah, in D.A.R.E., since middle school." Julian didn't add that the weed-and-beer combination made him throw up over the side of the boat. His father had laughed, and the blonde hadn't known what to do, though his mom would have brought him a ginger ale.

His mother frowned at the TV screen. "Does this glorify drug use?"

"It's a comedy; he's funny." Julian was so preoccupied he couldn't think straight. Sasha still wasn't home. She dated seniors like Jake Myers, Malcolm Hobb-Jacobs, and Zachary Pearlstein, major competition. Julian knew their cars, so when one of them dropped her off, he would know who.

"Jeff Bridges used to be so handsome! He really let himself go for this role!"

"He drinks White Russians. That's his thing. He drinks them all the time. He calls them his 'beverage.'" Julian didn't remind his mother that she had drunk plenty in her entertaining days, and she fell silent, watching the movie with growing disapproval.

"There are a lot of f-words in this movie, honey." His mother shook her head, clucking. "Why would your father take you to a movie that's so inappropriate?"

"I asked."

"It's not on you, it's on him. What's it rated?"

"Don't worry about it, Mom." Julian rolled his eyes, restless. This was going to end up with his mother calling her lawyer, then her lawyer calling his father's lawyer, who would talk to his father, which sucked. The movie went on without Julian seeing it, thinking of Sasha.

"Oh no, who are those guys?"

"Bad guys."

"Why are they hurting him?"

"They have him mixed up with another Lebowski. He's Jeffrey Lebowski, the Dude. They think he's a millionaire."

"Wait, are they *peeing on the rug*?" His mother threw up her manicured hands. "Julian, how can you like this movie? It doesn't make any sense."

"Let's watch yours then, okay?" Julian couldn't enjoy it anyway. Where the hell was Sasha? Who was she with? Was she having sex with one of those seniors? Seniors got it all the time, didn't they? They expected it! It made Julian crazy because he had loved her for forever.

"You mean stop watching it? Are you sure you don't mind?" His mother pouted prettily, like the cheerleader she'd been, and Julian realized that beautiful women always got what they wanted. Sasha sure did.

"I saw it already. See, it turned out fine."

"You sure?"

"Please put on your chick flick, Mom."

"Don't call it a chick flick. It's a love story. Men can enjoy love stories, don't you think?"

"Yes," Julian said, ironically in the circumstances. Suddenly he noticed a car pulling up in front of Sasha's house. Zachary Pearlstein's red BMW 325.

"Here we go! Oh, I love Tom Hanks. Isn't he just the best? I think he's so cute. And a nice person, a *good man*. He's been married to Rita Wilson for a long time, did you know that?"

"Excuse me, I have to go to the bathroom." Julian had to see what was going on at Sasha's house.

"Do you want me to put it on pause? I can wait."

"No, you keep watching." Julian fled for the powder room, which had a great view of the Barrows' house.

He hit the powder room and closed the door behind him, leaving the light off and parting the curtain to look out the window. Zachary and Sasha got out of the car holding cups of Rita's water ice. Sasha would have gotten the lemon with bits of rind, that's how well he knew her. Zachary put his arm around Sasha and walked her to her front door. Julian could see them clearly under the light. Zachary kissed Sasha, and she kissed him back, and Julian thought he was going to throw up.

His mother shouted from the family room, "Honey, you sure you don't want me to put it on pause?"

"No, keep watching!"

"Are you okay in there?"

"Yes!" Julian shot back, trying not to sound angry, though he wanted to put his hand through the window. Sasha was giving Zachary another long kiss, which had to be with tongues, then she let him go and went inside her house. It pissed Julian off that Zachary got to make out with Sasha when he was supposed to, this very night. It made him crazy, and he wondered if she'd kissed Zachary outside so he could see. Even though she toyed with him, he couldn't help the way he felt about her. She was his obsession, like in that song by Fine Young Cannibals. *She drives me crazy like no one else.*

"Honey?" his mom called out again. "You're missing the movie! It's so cute!"

"My stomach is upset! I'll be out in a little bit!" Julian flushed the toilet for show, let the water run so his mother would hear it, and returned to the window, but the scene at Sasha's house had changed. *Another* guy stood on Sasha's front step, and Julian had no idea who he was. It wasn't Zachary, and it must've been somebody on foot, but Julian couldn't make out any details because it was too dark. All he could see was the man's back, and Sasha opened the front door, threw her arms wide, and hugged the guy. Then the guy went inside the house, and Sasha closed the front door.

Julian didn't know what the hell was going on. Did Sasha have *two dates* tonight? Was this the ultimate move to drive him crazy? The Dude would have said, *This aggression will not stand, man.*

"Honey?" His mother knocked on the door, and Julian jumped to lock it.

"Mom, jeez, I'm coming out right now!"

"Why do you have the lights off? It's dark underneath the door."

"Mom, I don't need lights. I know where my dick is."

"No need to cuss, and you'll miss the seat if you pee in the dark."

"I'm not peeing! Mom, jeez!" Julian opened the door. "I said my stomach was upset. That means *I was pooping.*"

His mother's eyes flared. "Do you want me to get a Tums? Or some Kaopectate? Was it diarrhea?"

"No, I'm fine, really." Julian walked past her into the family room and looked out the window to see what was going on at Sasha's house. The light was still on in their family room, so Sasha was in there with that new guy.

"You're sure you're okay?"

"I'm fine. Let's watch the movie." Julian flopped onto the sectional, and so did his mother.

"But you missed the beginning."

"I'll figure it out."

"I can tell you, from the box. Okay, so Meg Ryan owns an independent bookstore and Tom Hanks owns a big chain bookstore and they talk on that computer thing you go on, AOL—"

Julian zoned out as his mother droned on and they watched the movie, and after about half an hour, he could see the new guy leaving Sasha's house. Sasha hugged the guy goodbye, then he walked down her front walk. Julian couldn't see his face or his features. The guy was a silhouette backlit by the portico light, but he was tall, so he could be older. Maybe in college.

Julian watched as the new guy took a left, then turned the corner. Who the hell was the man? Where was his car? Why did he park away from the house, to avoid being seen? Or did he walk to Sasha's? Did that mean he lived in Brandywine Hunt? Where? Julian knew the streets behind Sasha's house: Palomino, Hanoverian, Andalusian, and Welsh Cob Drive. It had been his idea to name them after horse breeds because it had been a horse farm.

"Julian, watch the movie. I think they're going to fall in love."

"Terrific," Julian said, forcing a smile.

CHAPTER 15

Bill Hybrinski

Darkness fell outside the kitchen window, and Bill Hybrinski eyed the calculator. He'd gone over his cost of goods, rent, payroll, utilities, inventory, and township, state, and federal taxes. He couldn't deny the obvious any longer. He'd have to go out of business.

Hybrinski Optical spreadsheets cluttered the table. He'd wracked his brain over what he could've done differently, but there was nothing. He was a member of the Pennsylvania opticians' guild and followed the Tips of the Trade. He'd painted his store blue (*a welcoming hue*) from beige (*avoid beige*). His frame displays were *innovative*, like the sportsman's display with the picture of Bambi and the sign KEEP HUNTING AND/OR FISHING FOR SUNGLASSES FOR YOUR OUTDOOR SPORT! He'd trained his staff to upsell lenses to polarized, antireflective, or Transitions. He'd trimmed his operating expenses by cutting out Vision Expo, audited his lab and frame statements to make sure he was credited for warranty items, and held sales to turn over his inventory. None of it worked.

Bill eyed the spreadsheets without really seeing them. It was the end of a dream, one he had grown up with. He was from Milwaukee and had worked in one of the Stein Drugs stores in high school, where he met Marty Stein himself. Bill admired Marty Stein the way other boys admired baseball players, and when Marty sold his chain to Walgreens, Bill decided that someday he would be Marty. Marty founded Stein Optical with sixteen stores and had just sold it to Eye Care Centers of America, almost four hundred stores in thirty-six states. Bill would've settled for a fraction of Marty Stein's success, but it wasn't to be.

"Hey, honey!" Marianne entered the kitchen with the twins. He thought of them as his girls, a yappy trio of double ponytails, Browne's T-shirts, and jean shorts. They'd had a softball game tonight against West Chester Automotive, but he'd missed it to work late, sitting in his empty store.

"Hey, Dad! Hey, Dad!" Jessica and Jennifer called out, their lips stained with cherry water ice. Twins didn't run in their families, so Jessica and Jennifer had been a surprise. Like life itself, a series of surprises that cost you money you didn't have.

"Hello, beauties! How was the game?" Bill tried to look happy when the twins scooted over, and he gave them big hugs. He kissed the tops of their heads, he could swear their hair smelled like strawberry shampoo and Big Macs.

"We won! Yay! Yay!"

"Yay! Yay!" Bill cheered. They always said *yay-yay* because there were two of them.

"We got you some fries." Marianne came over with a weary grin, her light brown hair in a ponytail. She had round hazel eyes, a fine nose, and a warm, omnipresent smile, which was the reason he married her. Marianne Dunn was simply the most positive person he'd ever met, always upbeat. *A born teacher*, she said. But her salary only supplemented his income, which supported the family, or used to. He didn't know how he'd tell her the truth.

"Thanks." Bill opened the French fry bag, which released a mouthwatering smell. He popped a fry in his mouth. "You guys feasted, eh? McDonald's and Rita's."

"How's it going?" Marianne bent over, kissed him on the cheek, then surveyed the bills scattered around him.

"Great," Bill answered, because the twins were here.

"Okay, girls. Go get showered and into your pajamas. Vamoose!" Marianne got them moving, and the twins hustled out of the kitchen.

Bill watched them go, thinking that parenthood was all about momentum.

"How'd the game go?"

"Jennifer got two hits, and the other one got one." Marianne smiled. "I forget her name."

"It begins with a *J*." Bill managed to smile back. They both called the kids the wrong names all the time.

"Want some coffee?" Marianne leaned on the wall and took off her sneakers.

"Love some, thanks." Bill closed the checkbook, and Marianne padded to the counter.

"Where's David?"

"Take a guess," Bill answered, more sharply than he'd intended. "Up in his room reading *Infinite Jest*, which is infinite, but not a jest."

"He's been in his room a lot lately. Or out riding his bike."

"He did that earlier."

Marianne poured some coffee beans into the grinder. "He's less plugged in, don't you think?"

"Nah, he's fine."

"Where's Jason?" Marianne turned on the grinder, and it churned noisily. When it stopped, she spooned the grinds into the coffeemaker.

"Working late."

"Poor thing."

"Lucky dog." Bill knew that came out wrong.

"What did you have for dinner?" Marianne poured water into the coffeemaker and hit BREW.

"Cap'n Crunch. Does that count?"

"Works for me."

Bill forced a smile. The aroma of fresh coffee filled the kitchen, a large rectangle ringed with oak cabinets and the island with a marble countertop. Top-of-the-line appliances and bay windows over the backyard. He'd never lived in a house this nice.

"So how bad is it?" Marianne gestured at the bills.

"Bad."

"How bad?"

"You need to sit down first."

"Tell me."

Bill took a deep breath. "I have to close the store."

"For real?" Marianne kept her expression of loving interest. She never let herself get down, no matter how bad things got.

"For real."

"You can't let any more people go?"

"No. I'm down to two, the doctor and me. I do everything I used to pay for. Yesterday, I cleaned the display cases."

"Maybe it's not that bad?"

"Honey, it is. It's over." Bill loved her so much it hurt, and it broke his heart that he had let her down. And the kids.

"But why?"

"My sales are down, almost half, for the past three quarters. I can't survive that."

"Won't they go back up?"

"I doubt it. The optical business has changed too much, honey. You've heard me complain. It used to be mom-and-pop stores like me, with a thousand square feet in a strip mall. I can't compete with LensCrafters and its eight hundred stores, with national advertising and one-hour service guarantees. They're driving customers to them. They do a billion in sales."

"But you're the neighborhood guy."

"There's no neighborhood anymore. Nobody lives in

Meghan's Run. We live in developments and we shop in strip malls and malls."

"But people still go to you. Everyone we know."

"That's not enough." Bill hated putting this on her, this way. "I'm losing entire families now, because of managed care. It happened overnight. I'm still trying to recover. I've told you about that."

"I didn't really understand. I didn't think it was that bad."

"Right." Bill knew he had hidden it from her. He hadn't wanted her to worry. "Okay, take Vanguard, the biggest employer around here. They deal with a company that packages eyecare benefits, like Davis Vision, for example. Their package includes glasses, contacts, and routine exams. Almost half of my customers are now members of that plan."

"Okay."

"I can either accept the plan or not. If I don't, the customers go elsewhere. So does the entire family."

Marianne frowned. "Then why don't you accept it?"

"I do, but it only pays me forty bucks for a routine eye exam. I used to charge seventy, and that's not unreasonable, at all. And I have more paperwork than I ever used to because I have to verify the benefits, enter it into the system, and make sure I get paid. They're always a slow pay." Bill couldn't sugarcoat it any longer. "I spend half my time managing my accounts receivable now. I don't have the money to hire anybody to do the paperwork."

"I can do that." Marianne smiled in an encouraging way, which only made Bill feel worse.

"Thanks, but no, honey. I know you could, but it wouldn't make a difference. I don't have the sales, the revenue. There simply isn't enough money coming in."

"So what can we do?"

Bill braced himself. "We have to sell the house. The mortgage is a killer."

"Bill, no." Marianne moaned.

"Honey, I'm sorry, but we have no other choice. We bought here when we were high on the hog. We have to move out and downsize."

"But what about the rent on the store?" Marianne walked to the table with the two coffees, putting one in front of him. She sat down with the other.

"What about it? I was talking about the mortgage, which is $2,450."

"I know, but how much is the rent on the store?"

"The business pays it, and it's $1,950. Lee's giving up, too."

"The mattress store is going out of business?" Marianne grimaced. "When did *that* happen?"

"A few days ago. I forgot to tell you."

"You didn't want to tell me."

"That, too." Bill met her eye, crestfallen. He had failed her and the kids. If his father wasn't already dead, he would die of shame. Bill's father had been a self-employed plumber, with pride to spare. *Always be your own boss,* he'd said.

SOMEONE KNOWS ■ 107

"So you're at the point of no return? The worst-case scenario?"

"Yes. Is this supposed to make me feel better?" Bill chuckled, but it came out like a hiccup.

"What I mean is, desperate times call for desperate measures." Marianne took a quick sip of coffee. "I have an idea."

"Your last idea was skip the condom."

"That's not funny." Marianne frowned.

Bill had to remind himself not to joke about that. Marianne worried that the twins would hear. Bill figured that, sooner or later, the twins would realize they were six years younger than David and put two and two together.

"Keep an open mind." Marianne leaned forward. "Scott Browne owns your strip mall, right?"

"Yes."

"So he's your landlord?"

"In a manner of speaking," Bill answered cautiously.

"So all you have to do is call Scott, get a meeting, and ask him to forgive a few months of rent—"

"Honey, no." Bill felt crushed. Scott Browne had turned out to be Marty Stein, not him.

"Bill, think about it."

"No."

"Why not?"

"It's not that easy."

"You don't know until you try. Everybody needs a hand, sometimes."

Bill shuddered. "Not me."

"You're too hard on yourself. It's why you're hard on the boys."

Bill sipped his coffee, which tasted bitter. He knew he was hard on Jason and David, but that was to prepare them. You had to be bulletproof to provide for a family. God knew, he was living that right now.

"Bill, all you need to do is call Scott. We're friends. We've been over to the house plenty of times, and they've been here."

"In better days."

"That doesn't matter. They got divorced. They don't throw those parties anymore. Times change."

"Tell me about it."

"The point is we're *friends*. Scott has to be feeling the pressure, too. If Lee *and* you are going out of business, where does that leave Scott's company?"

Bill felt his shoulders fall. "You want me to go to Scott Browne with my hat in my hand?"

"Such an old-time expression."

Bill knew it was his father talking.

"Scott's in a position to help us, and you know he wants to."

"No, he doesn't. Nobody in business wants to *help* each other. What do you think, it's a sharing circle, like school?"

"Don't be condescending." Marianne pursed her lips. "You're *kind of* in business with him."

"No, he's in business for himself, and so am I. I sign the check, and Browne Land Management is the payee. *I* pay *him*."

"How can it hurt to ask?"

"It's humiliating," Bill blurted out, feeling his face redden.

"You know what's *more* humiliating? Us losing everything." Marianne's eyes glistened, which killed Bill.

"We wouldn't lose *everything*, honey."

"We'd lose the *house*. *This* house, *our* house, our *home* that we worked so hard for. We live in Brandywine Hunt. We made it to the Radnor Hunt section. It's all we have to leave the kids. It's stability. It's a school district. It's their friends. Their bus route. My friends, my job— everything centers around this house."

"It's just a house—"

"No, it's not. What about Hybrinski Optical? Is it just a business?"

Bill blinked. He realized that the business meant everything to him, and the house meant everything to her.

"If you want to keep the business, you have to fight for it. Swallow your pride." Marianne touched his hand. "If Scott cut you a break on the store rent, would it help?"

Bill felt his heartbeat quicken. Maybe he could make magic happen. He would love not to throw in the towel. *Hybrinskis never give up,* his father used to say. "Possibly."

"Then please, ask him." Marianne took his hand. "Just do it."

"That's the Nike slogan, honey."

"And look where they are now, huh?"

■

CHAPTER 16

Barb Gallagher

B arb dragged the mattress upstairs with her best friend, Sharon Kelly, helping her, since Kyle wasn't home. Sharon was slim, pretty, and African-American, with her hair smoothed into a low ponytail, her dark eyes set wide, and a round face with an easy smile. Except for now, with the effort of moving the mattress.

"Is it too heavy?" Barb asked, worried.

"Nah. I just wish I'd changed after work." Sharon was a commercial insurance agent in Philadelphia, so she was dressed in a white oxford shirt with a navy blue suit. "Can I just ask, why didn't you have the delivery guy bring it up?"

"It cost extra. They call it white glove service. Are you sorry you dropped in?"

"No way." Sharon hoisted the mattress from the bottom, climbing the stairwell slowly. "I'm happy to help."

"Thanks, I appreciate it." Barb felt so grateful to Sharon, who was one of the few friends who had stuck with her, after what had happened last year.

"I'm just so glad you moved back."

"Me, too." Barb and Sharon had grown up together in nearby Meghan's Run, a quaint town that got swallowed up by strip malls and developments like Brandywine Hunt.

"Whatever." Sharon pushed the mattress upward with a grunt of effort. "Thank God it's only a single mattress."

"That would be me, from here on. Single all the way."

"You could meet someone. I know a girl at work who's dating someone she met online, if you can believe that."

"That's crazy." Barb yanked on the mattress. "Let's review. I live in the suburbs with a teenage son. I have a dead-end job. Oh, and lest we forget, my ex is in prison. Other than that, I'm marketable."

"You could be the bad girl." Sharon's dark eyes glittered.

"I was never the bad girl."

"I tried to teach you, but you failed." Sharon grinned crookedly. "Guess what I heard? Tom Whitfield is single."

"The day I go back to my high school boyfriend, shoot me." Barb groaned, hauling the mattress.

"Why? He was sweet."

"He was eighteen!" Barb had to admit to feeling a tingle. She'd been crazy about Tom back then. But still, you can't go home again. Then she realized she was trying. She reached the top of the landing. "You need a break?"

"No, I'm fine. Git 'er done."

"You sure you want to be at the bottom? I think the bottom is harder." Barb flashed on her first day at college. They'd gone to the University of Delaware with many of their classmates, since Meghan's Run was close to the state line. "You know, I think we had this same conversation when we moved into the dorm, remember?"

"Are you kidding? I don't remember yesterday, much less the first day of college."

"Let's go." Barb edged backward, and the mattress curved in the narrow staircase, then got wedged against the bannister. "Oh no, it's stuck."

"Damn." Sharon stopped, wiping her brow. "Just shove it hard around the corner."

"I knew you were going to say that." Barb muscled the mattress around the stairwell as Sharon inched up, and together they reached the hallway on the second floor, where they caught their breath. "I can't believe I'm starting over at my age. What's next, orange crates full of albums?"

"Honey, you can start over at any age. And you got rid of bad rubbish."

"That's true." Barb tried not to second-guess herself, but it came second nature. "I should never have married him in the first place."

"You loved him."

"I was blind."

"Let it go, girl."

"I can't, when I look at what it cost. *All* it cost." Barb sighed heavily, and the hallway felt tight, warm, and vaguely claustrophobic.

"Go. Move."

"Got it." Barb slid the mattress toward the spare room, and Sharon pushed from behind. They passed the family photos on the wall, which were few, since Barb hung only those with her and Kyle.

"You landed on your feet, and you did the right thing. That matters most of all."

"Remind me, so I feel good about myself."

"You blew the whistle on your sleazoid husband."

"I should've known it earlier."

"You couldn't have, he hid it from everybody. Give yourself some credit, please."

"I can't." Barb shuddered to remember that night, the beginning of the end. Brian had been working late so often that she suspected he was having an affair. It wasn't like him, but she'd felt him pulling away from her, spending more time at the hospital. He was a pediatric oncologist, and she understood that he was dedicated to his cases. He always brought the work home, withdrawn when he'd lost a patient. But their sex life had tapered off, even from married-people levels.

So one night when Brian said he was working late, Barb had driven to the hospital and gone upstairs to the pediatric oncology floor. It had been after visiting hours, and Barb had beelined for the nurses' station, staffed by a nurse she knew, Sandy, who looked up from her computer.

Hey, Sandy, Barb had whispered. *Is Brian here? I want to surprise him. I have some great news.*

Yes. Sandy's eyes had flared with excitement. *What's the surprise? Can you tell me?*

Not before I tell him. Are you the only nurse on duty?

No, Cheryl and Bob are both on. You know Bob but not Cheryl. She's new, young. Bob's showing her the ropes.

I see. Barb had suspected that Brian was showing Cheryl the ropes.

Just tell me, you're not pregnant, are you?

Are you insane? Barb had whispered, and they'd laughed.

I think they're down the hall, in 301. It's a little girl with spleen cancer, a two-year-old. The mom went downstairs for a coffee.

Thanks. Barb had headed down the hall, bracing herself to catch him with the young nurse. She'd hoped they could go to therapy and work it out. She hadn't wanted to break up their family. And she'd had to admit, she still loved him. Barb had walked down the hallway, passing rooms 307, 305, and 303. The door to 301 had been closed, but she'd cracked it open, peeking inside. It had been too dark to see what was going on, since the only light on was over the child's crib.

Barb's eyes had adjusted to the semidarkness, but there was no young nurse in the room, nor was Bob. Brian had been leaning over the crib, with the railing down. The toddler had been sound asleep, her head to one side, with tape holding her oxygen tube onto her tiny cheek. Brian had been whispering in her ear, and Barb had felt touched until she realized that the toddler's diaper was off and Brian's hand was between the little girl's legs.

Barb had screamed.

Sharon cocked her head. "You don't regret what you did, do you?"

"No," Barb answered, meaning it. That night, hospital security had come running, the police had been called, and Brian had been arrested on the spot. The police investigated, so did the hospital, and sedatives were found in thirteen of Brian's patients, resulting in child abuse, child endangerment, and sexual abuse charges. The newspapers had had a field day, calling Brian *Dr. Dirtbag*, and when the case had gone to trial, Barb had testified for the prosecution. The jury had convicted Brian, and he'd been sentenced to twenty-five years in prison.

"You did the right thing, honey."

"But Kyle's not doing well at all. He left everything behind. His friends, his team, his school."

"He'll make new friends when school starts."

"I think he's angry at Brian, but he misses him, too." Barb felt her chest tighten. "He misses who he thought he was, and I think he blames me for testifying."

"But he admires it, too."

"I know. He's torn."

"Welcome to motherhood. You're the safe one to blame. You catch it all. Moms are lightning rods with breasts."

Barb smiled, then it faded. "He hates the name change. He finds it confusing, which I get."

"I think it was a good idea."

Barb told Sharon something that Kyle had said last week: *Mom, it's different for me than for you. We moved to where you grew up, so you're home. I'm not. You drive around knowing all the roads. I don't. You went back to your maiden name, but it's your name. Gallagher is not my name. It never was.*

Sharon winced. "So what did you say?"

"I said, 'Honey, you're right and I'm sorry it turned out this way.'"

"And what did he say?"

"He took the dog out. He walks the dog all the time. The dog's going to be a skeleton if this keeps up."

"But what else could you have done after Brian was convicted? Stay?"

Barb sighed, pained. "I suppose I could've moved to a place that neither of us knew, then we'd be on equal footing. Both disoriented."

Sharon scoffed. "No kid needs a disoriented mother."

"Right, but . . ." Barb had to acknowledge the truth, which was less flattering. "But I really wanted to come home. I wanted to lick my wounds. I thought of myself."

"Aw, honey, that's okay." Sharon made a sad face. "You're allowed to take care of yourself. Brian was your *husband*. It was your *marriage*."

"Still." Barb felt a wave of guilt, then tried to shake it off. "Let's get this mattress where it belongs."

"Okay." Sharon pushed, Barb pulled, and they reached the spare room at the end of the hallway, a small rectangle with a window. They dragged the mattress inside and let it flop on the floor, next to the metal frame. Sharon grinned. "We did it!"

"Thanks for the help."

"Anytime." Sharon gave her a big hug. "I'm proud of you."

Suddenly Barb heard the door opening and closing downstairs. "*Now* he's home?"

"Perfect timing." Sharon laughed, and Barb led her into the hall and downstairs, where Kyle was dropping his keys into the basket on the hall table.

"Hi, Mom. Hi, Sharon!" Kyle smiled, looking up, with the dog dancing around his sneakers. He looked oddly happy, dressed in his oversized T-shirt and gym shorts, with his slides. Barb didn't know why he was smiling so mysteriously.

"Good to see you, honey!" Sharon gave him a big hug, which he returned.

"Where were you?" Barb asked, intrigued.

"It's a long story." Kyle tried to avert his eyes, still smiling.

"I got time." Barb folded her arms.

"So do I," Sharon added slyly.

Kyle rolled his eyes, still smiling. "I put out the recycling and I saw a calico cat stuck in a tree, in front of the neighbor's house. So I got it down and brought it to the owner."

"You rescued a cat?" Barb asked, surprised. "That was a nice thing to do. How did you know who it belonged to?"

"It had a tag."

"So where's the owner live?"

"On Pinto Road."

"The *million*-dollar houses." Barb shot Sharon a meaningful glance.

Sharon winked. "Movin' on up."

Barb smiled. "Kyle, how did you get there with a cat?"

"I walked. How do you think I got there?"

Barb ignored his back talk. Kyle was hiding something,

but it seemed good, not bad. "You walked all the way to Pinto Road? With a cat?"

Sharon looked incredulous. "A *cat* let you carry it around, just like that? A *stranger*? Hell, Felicia won't even let *me* carry her. She bites me."

Kyle rolled his eyes again, good-naturedly. "It was a friendly cat. I think it was scared from being in the tree. Why are you guys asking so many questions?"

Barb answered, "Why are you making us? Why don't you just tell us what happened?"

"Agree, something else *definitely* happened." Sharon turned to Kyle. "Honey, I've known you since you were born. I can tell by the look on your face. You can run, but you can't hide."

"Sheesh, all that happened was I returned a cat!" Kyle headed into the kitchen, but Sharon and Barb followed him.

Sharon asked, "Who did you return it to?"

"The owner." Kyle went into the refrigerator, hiding his face.

"Who's the owner?" Barb and Sharon asked in unison.

"A girl," Kyle answered, but when he closed the refrigerator, his face was flushing.

"A girl!" Barb sensed they had struck pay dirt. "Your age?"

Sharon snorted. "*Obviously!* Is she pretty, Kyle? What's her name?"

"Argh." Kyle tried to get out of the kitchen, but Barb and Sharon blocked his path, like a Wall of Moms.

Sharon snorted. "Kyle, who is she?"

Kyle shook his head, exasperated. "Sasha Barrow."

"Oh, yes!" Sharon burst into laughter. "She sounds foxy!"

"Kyle, that's great!" Barb felt happy for him. She couldn't remember the last time something good happened. "You met a pretty girl! Does she go to the high school? What grade?"

Sharon started clapping. "Did she thank you? Kyle and Sasha sitting in a tree K-I-S-S-I-N-G."

"Good night, Sharon! Good night, Mom!" Kyle laughed, scooted between Barb and Sharon, and headed for the staircase with Buddy trotting behind him, tail awag.

Sharon kept singing, "Then comes Kyle Junior in the baby carriage!"

"Sleep tight!" Barb called to Kyle as he went upstairs, her heart light. If Kyle got a girlfriend, things were looking up. She couldn't be happy unless he was, and now she had hope.

Sharon chuckled. "I think we handled that well, don't you?"

CHAPTER 17

■

Linda Garvey

Linda Garvey gazed at her reflection in the bathroom mirror without recognizing herself. Her own eyes stared back at her, less blue than they used to be. She felt diluted, *washed out*. She'd cried herself away and now she was gone. She raked her fingers through her short hair, but her natural dark roots had taken over. She had new lines under her eyes, jowls, and cracks in the corners of her mouth. They were called laugh lines but she hadn't laughed in forever. Suddenly she flashed on the last time she'd laughed.

Jill had asked for a sandwich, and Linda had run into the kitchen and made her favorite, Muenster cheese and tomato with mayo. Linda had brought the sandwich and a glass of homemade iced tea into the family room, but she'd tripped over the cat and dropped the plate. The sandwich fell open on the rug.

Well done, Mom! Jill had laughed.

Have a nice trip? Mark had laughed, too.

I'll help! Allic had hurried over to unpeel the bread from the rug, and the cat had licked up the mayonnaise.

That was her secret plan! Jill had said, and they'd all laughed again.

Linda felt a stab of pain at the memory. She eyed the woman in the bathroom mirror, feeling weirdly separate from her. The therapist had talked about *de-realization*, where you felt like a cardboard cutout of yourself. Linda thought that she didn't look like herself because she wasn't herself. She hadn't been back to the therapist in a while, and the therapist was calling to get her on the schedule, at least to check her meds, one of the messages had said.

Linda didn't think that she needed therapy because what *agonized* her wasn't losing Jill but everything that Jill had gone through, so much suffering every day. The pain that child had endured, the visits to the doctors, the needles, the tests, the *struggle* of Jill's life, one that no child should have to endure, for *life. For* life. Linda knew that her pain was truly *for* her child, and now that Jill had died, only *now* could Linda allow herself to experience that pain. Because until now, Linda had been one hundred percent busy being everything that Jill needed, a mom, a nurse, a cheerleader, a therapist, a bestie, and now Linda could just kick out the jams and she finally had.

She blinked, and so did the woman in the mirror. She eyed her reflection, or whoever's reflection it was, wondering how long she was going to feel this bad. She was sleeping so much these days. She tried to feel better but something kept pushing her back down again. She was too exhausted to live.

Her eyes teared up, and she leaned on the sink for support. She felt so much pain that she wished for another pill, even though they made her so useless. She didn't know who she was if she wasn't Jill's mother. She couldn't accomplish a single thing. She couldn't even get out of bed. She barely washed or fed herself.

Tears blurred her vision, and she thought about Allie. She knew that helping Allie was beyond her. Mark would have to take care of Allie, and Linda could leave Allie to him for a little while longer, until she could get past this, or over it, or through it, or magically emerge on the other side, like herself, a mother to at least one daughter, the one left but lost.

"Lin, what are you doing?" Mark asked, appearing in the bathroom behind her in his T-shirt and boxers. He didn't have his glasses on, and he blinked, squinting against the bright light.

"I woke up." Linda looked at Mark blankly, trying to remember the last time she had really looked at him. Now he was looking at her like she was crazy.

"You're naked."

"I was asleep."

"But the AC is on. It's cold."

"I'm fine." Linda knew it was a ridiculous thing to say.

"It's the middle of the night. Why are you up?"

"I woke up," Linda repeated, since she couldn't say why she slept or why she woke up anymore. "It's nighttime, right?"

"Yes. It's 4:17 A.M."

Linda thought it was so like him. A precise man, super-reliable, and kind from the day they'd met in college. They had been leaving Wright Hall after Business Accounting. Funny she should remember that and she couldn't remember so much else.

"Come back to bed." Mark took her arm, and Linda allowed herself to be led into the bedroom, slipping into the cool darkness.

"How's Allie? Is she okay?" Linda went to her side of the bed and sat down.

"She's fine, don't worry about a thing."

"You're taking care of her, right?" Linda needed to make sure, to hear him say it, to tell her.

"Of course."

"I woke up before but you weren't there." Linda got the Valium bottle from the night table, shook one out, and drank from the water bottle. She eased down on her side, her head in the pillow, and Mark covered her with the sheet.

"I was at a meeting tonight, for Jill's 5K. Remember, I told you, everyone's excited about seeing you."

"I can't go." Linda had already told him.

"Lin, you have to."

"I can't possibly."

"Fran's expecting you. She's looking forward to seeing you. Jim tore his rotator cuff. That's why she hasn't been to visit." Mark got into bed, and Linda turned to face him, but couldn't see him in the dark.

"Say I can't come, she'll understand. It's the drugs,

we need to change the dosage again, it's too much or maybe too little—"

"I called the doctor. We have an appointment next week. All I'm asking is that you go to Jill's 5K. You don't have to do anything else."

"But it's the day she died, it's *the day*." Linda couldn't understand why she had to explain. "Can't you move it?"

"No, I told you, it was the only weekend I could get the permit for, and they have to have police and an ambulance, by law. The Fourth of July is coming up, and if we wait until August, everyone will be on vacation."

"But on the day? The *very day*?"

"Make lemons into lemonade. It's a memorial run. It's a tribute to Jill, a celebration. Don't you want to celebrate her life? That we loved her, that we had her for as long as we did? She was a blessing, you know that. A blessing."

Linda couldn't ignore the judgment in his voice, feeling worse. She didn't want to celebrate her daughter's life on the anniversary of her death, and she didn't want to celebrate her by *running*. She wanted to stay in bed and sleep. She was in too much pain. Jill had wanted to live, not become a 5K, but Mark had set a goal after Jill died, to *make sure it didn't happen to another child*, to make sure *Jill didn't die in vain*, when Linda knew that really, truly, that was exactly what had happened. Jill died for nothing. Like Allie said, *Jill died for air*.

"You can do it, Lin. I'll help you."

"How is Allie? Are you taking care of Allie?"

"You asked me that already, and I told you. She's fine, she's great, she's enjoying the summer."

Linda could only pray that Allie was okay and that Mark was in charge. She felt her eyes close, and Allie's sweet, round face emerged out of the darkness, but Allie wasn't smiling. She was crying on her bed, calling *Jill, Jill*, and Linda hugged her while they both cried.

Linda turned over miserably, curling up as tears slid from underneath her eyelids. She wasn't herself anymore. She needed to be gone for a while longer, until she got to be herself again and the dosages got fixed and the pain stopped and she came back from the darkness into the light.

"I'm trying, Allie," Linda whispered, just before she fell asleep.

■

CHAPTER 18

Daphne Barrow

D aphne sank into the magnificent four-poster bed, which was covered with a thick duvet, a brocade coverlet, and shams with gold tassels. She breathed deeply, inhaling the perfumed air of the suite. Her gaze wandered over the crystal lamps, provincial antiques, and heavy brocade curtains flanking the doors to the balcony. The curtains were open, but Daphne had been to Paris three times this month, so she didn't bother to look.

She wanted to shower and change for the conference, so she slid off her Roger Vivier pumps and set them side by side on the cotton mat beside the bed. She slipped her stocking feet into a fresh pair of terry-cloth slippers with the hotel crest on them, even though she still had her pantyhose on. Rugs were a source of bacteria in hotels, even one as world-class as the George V.

Daphne unfastened her gold Rolex and set it atop the night table, followed by her *pièce de résistance*, a Jean

Schlumberger sunflower-yellow *cloisonné* bracelet. She wore it with a silk ecru blouse and a Chanel suit in gold tweed, albeit from last season. She was striking, tall, and lithe, with her hair in a trademark blond chignon, accessorized with heavy gold earrings. She was often mistaken for a model, at least when she was younger. Daphne was a partner in the International Arbitration Group at Lovell Wheeler, some forty-five lawyers in New York, Los Angeles, London, Paris, Berlin, Rome, Beijing, and Dubai.

Daphne realized she had forgotten to call her daughter this week, so she picked up the handheld, pressed in the country code and number, and waited until it was finally answered. "Sash? It's Mum. How are you?"

"I was asleep. Um, er, it's, like, six o'clock in the morning."

"I'm in Paris, and it's the only chance we'll get to speak." Daphne disliked Sasha's sleeping in. It wasn't a formula for success. "Darling, you mustn't spend your summer laying about."

"I'm not."

"I thought you had arranged to give riding lessons at that therapeutic barn, whatever it's called."

"Thorncroft, but—"

"So why aren't you doing that? You need those volunteer jobs for your applications."

"The camp doesn't start until next week, so I—"

"Why not go over, introduce yourself, help out? You can clean tack or muck stalls."

"Mom, you woke me up and now you won't even let me talk—"

"Seriously, darling?" Daphne felt her anger flare. "Now, please, there's something you must do. I've been getting emails from Dr. Garvey about a 5K run for his daughter."

"You mean Dr. Garvey, like, Allie Garvey's father?"

"I assume so. I'm on the planning committee because he needed a lawyer to draft the waivers. It's today, and he needs help. Go to the clubhouse, find him, and ask him what he needs. Be there at seven-thirty."

"In the *morning*?" Sasha sighed heavily. "That's, like, in an hour."

"Do stop whinging." Daphne abhorred whinging. Or *whining*, as Americans called it. "Now, darling, I have to go. Have fun. Love you, goodbye and—"

Sasha ended the call.

Daphne hung up, cross. She had no clue how she'd ended up with such a selfish, entitled daughter. She would have hoped she'd be an excellent role model for Sasha, but evidently not.

No one knew how difficult it was to be a mother.

CHAPTER 19

■

Allie Garvey

It was a beautiful morning, and the clubhouse buzzed with volunteers hurrying to set up for the 5K, unloading cardboard boxes of blue caps and T-shirts, bottled water, and waiver forms. It was only seven-fifteen in the morning, so the only other people there were the planning committee, a group of moms and a retired guy. A bright blue banner reading STARTING LINE hung over the entrance, and blue Jog For Jill signs covered the doors and windows. A long white tent had been erected over registration tables draped with matching blue tablecloths. Three Chester County police cruisers and a red boxy ambulance were parked at the driveway, where the paramedics stood around drinking coffee.

"It's the big day!" Allie's father spread his arms wide, standing in front of the tent. "Doesn't everything look great, Linda?"

"So great!" Allie answered for her mother, who clung

to Allie's arm like a much older woman. The Garveys had on their blue Jog For Jill T-shirts with their shorts, though her mother was wearing jeans that looked baggy on her. Allie felt a pang, not having realized how much weight her mother had lost, and some of the volunteers remarked it when they said hello to her, welcoming her with big hugs.

Allie's father rubbed his hands together in delight. "We're going to raise a lot of money today! My colleagues are coming in force. Morty said his office is entering as a team, and Shawn's dental techs are, too."

"That's great, Dad." Allie understood why he'd been so busy, now that she saw what it took to stage the 5K. But she also understood why her mother hadn't wanted to come, since Jill had died a year ago today, at 3:32 in the afternoon. Allie was mentally counting down, but she didn't want to make her father feel bad. Luckily, she'd be home by then.

"So what do you think, Linda? Aren't you impressed?"

"Totally, Dad," Allie answered again, because her mother merely nodded, her lips pursed and her features barely visible in her oversized sunglasses and her blue Jog For Jill cap. Her mother had to be on her meds, but they were making her act strange, disconnected from everything.

"Allie, check this out." Her father pointed at the cardboard boxes. "Everything was donated by local businesses. We didn't have to spend a dime, so all of it goes into the pot for CF."

"How do you raise the money, Dad? Like, do the runners get sponsored?"

"No, we do it with the entry fee. It's thirty-five dollars a person, and the corporate teams have pledged to make a matching contribution. I think we're gonna get two hundred, maybe even three hundred people. We blanketed the area with flyers, not just in the development." Her father looked up at the sky, grinning at heaven itself. "Not a cloud, not a single cloud. And it's not even hot."

"We couldn't have asked for better weather!" said one of the volunteers, scurrying past with a box.

"Linda, look at this." Her father grabbed her mother's arm in his enthusiasm. "Linda? Yoo-hoo?"

"Yes," her mother said quietly, from behind her sunglasses.

"Look at the people who gave their time to make this happen. Not just our friends, but people from the development." Allie's father gestured to the volunteers. "Lin, it's a tribute to Jill, it truly is. I hope you see it that way. With everybody working together, we can cure this awful disease, and no other kid will have to go through what Jill did. No other family will have to go through what we did."

Her mother pursed her lips harder.

Allie put her arm around her. "Mom, it's okay," she said quietly, and some of the volunteers looked over.

"Linda, this 5K is *a great thing*." Allie's father touched her mother's arm again. "This is our silver lining. We can make sure that Jill didn't die in vain. We can give meaning to what happened to her, to all of us."

"No," her mother whispered. "No, we can't, Mark."

"Honey, don't be that way."

"Don't tell me how to be. Don't tell me how to mourn my daughter."

"Honey, this isn't the time or the place."

"That's why I didn't want to come. You made me. You're *sick*."

"Mom." Allie recoiled, shocked. Volunteers were sneaking glances at them, and suddenly Sasha Barrow was running toward them. Her blond ponytail swung, and she had on a blue Jog For Jill T-shirt, which made Allie want to barf.

"Dr. Garvey?" Sasha called out, reaching them. "I'm Sasha Barrow, Daphne's daughter. She's out of the country and sent me over to help. I'm going to run, too."

"Terrific." Allie's father recovered with a smile. "This is my wife, Linda, and daughter Allie."

"Hi, Mrs. Garvey, and I know Allie. Hi, Allie." Sasha grinned in a way that was convincing, to everyone but Allie.

"Hi, Sasha." *Kill any squirrels today?*

Allie's father rubbed his hands together. "Well, Sasha, I'm sure we can put you to work. Allie, why don't you get Mom some water, and you guys can sit at the registration table. Fran's coming at the end, they're driving in from New York."

"Okay, Dad." Allie led her mother through the volunteers, found her a folding chair to sit on, and got her a bottle of water, which she opened for her. "Here we go."

"This is *not* a silver lining," her mother said under her breath.

"Dad didn't mean it the way it sounded." Allie sat down next to her mother and put her arm around her back.

"It's a terrible day. It's too sunny." Her mother turned to Allie, her lips still pursed. "I'm not myself. I don't feel like myself. I'm sorry, honey. For everything. I'll be better soon. I'm trying."

"It's okay." Allie felt her throat thicken.

"You know I love you."

"Yes, I love you, too." Allie felt tears come to her eyes, but blinked them away. God forbid Sasha saw.

"When is Fran coming, again?"

"At the end."

"He's the sick one, not *me*!" Her mother raised her voice, and Allie's gut tensed.

"Mom, please."

"Okay," her mother said, turning away, and Allie let it go. Allie's father, the volunteers, and Sasha hustled back and forth, and in time, the runners and spectators arrived, registered at the table, and went to the starting line, milling around.

Allie noticed there weren't very many runners, certainly not the two or three hundred that her father had been predicting, and it never got better. She counted only forty-eight, including Sasha. Two police cruisers departed, leaving only one and the ambulance. Boxes of T-shirts, caps, flyers, and waivers remained unopened. Stacked pallets of bottled water were untouched. It was an obvious failure, and Allie felt terrible for her father. She would have gone over to comfort him, but didn't want to leave her mother. She felt torn between two unhappy parents.

At race time, her father made a speech that Allie couldn't hear, gesturing to Allie and her mother, but wisely not calling them over. The tiny crowd of spectators clapped, her father fired a starting pistol, and the runners took off, sprinting down Thoroughbred Road, rounding the corner, and disappearing from sight.

Her mother touched Allie's arm. "Go tell Dad I want to go home."

"Mom, really?" Allie asked, nervous. "He can't leave now. It just started."

"Tell him. I can't do this."

"Okay. Stay here." Allie got up and went over to her father.

"Hey, honey, having fun?"

"Yes." Allie felt terrible for him, knowing he was putting on a brave face. He had worked so hard on the 5K for months, and things were about to go from bad to worse for him.

"I realized I forgot the trophy. I left it at home."

"It's okay." Allie patted his shoulder. "Dad, Mom's having a hard time. She wants to go home."

"We can't." Her father frowned, his fake smile shaken.

"She wants to leave now, Dad."

"Too bad."

Allie felt stung. "It's not her, it's the meds. They make her weird. She just told me, 'I'm not myself.'"

"I got her an appointment next week." Her father

took off his cap, palmed his balding head, then put his cap back on.

"She said she was sorry, Dad. I'm just saying she needs—"

"Enough." Her father looked into the distance, where the runners had gone. "The problem with the turnout was unfortunate. They tell me Will Smith made a surprise appearance at the mall this morning, to promote some new movie. It was on the TV news and the radio. Everybody must be there. We caught a tough break." Her father shrugged. "I don't know what happened to Morty or the girls from Shawn's office. Something must have come up. Still, this is a great crowd. Enthusiastic, that's what counts. Positivity. People working together, helping each other. Helping these kids, eradicating this awful disease." Her father brightened, giving a thumbs-up to a passing volunteer. "And your friend Sasha ran, too. That was nice of her."

Allie couldn't stand her father saying nice things about Sasha, especially today.

Her father turned to the finish line, with its blue banner that read YOU JOGGED FOR JILL! "Sasha's a nice girl. She lugged some heavy boxes. She's on the cross-country team. Quite the athlete, that one. Very fit."

Allie blinked, trying not to feel criticized. "I would've helped, but I was taking care of Mom and she really wants to go."

"She has to wait."

"She can't."

"She has to. Tell her."

"Fine." Allie turned on her heel, crossed back to the table, and sat down next to her mother, on the hard plastic chair. "We can't go yet. It won't be much longer."

"Then Fran will take me home when she gets here. I don't want to ride with your father."

"Mom, really?"

Her mother didn't reply, sitting stiffly upright, and Allie tried to watch, trying not to think about Jill. This time last year, they were getting her sister chipped ice that wouldn't give her any comfort. Jill had been dying, and they all had known it, trying to stay strong. Trying to be there for Jill. Allie didn't want to let her go, but wanted her free from her suffering.

The runners reappeared, racing toward the finish, and in the lead was Sasha, her ponytail flying, her arms pumping, and her legs churning. Allie watched aghast as Sasha crossed the finish line, her arms flung wide and her smile ear to ear. The sun shone on her blond hair, and the sky was so blue it hurt. Somewhere, way up above, was Jill. Gone, one year ago today.

Everybody clapped for Sasha.

Allie's father among them.

CHAPTER 20

∎

Scott Browne

Scott stood near his office window, pressing the hand-held phone to his ear so nobody could overhear his conversation. He was on the phone with Tiffany, one of the girls he'd been seeing, and it wasn't a conversation he wanted his secretary to overhear. The office was open on Saturday, since real estate was one of the businesses that got more active on weekends, not less.

"Scott, when are you gonna pick me up tonight?" Tiffany purred. "I can be ready at five."

"I'm ready now." Scott chuckled, but he wasn't kidding. He'd already played nine holes and he had an hour to kill before this afternoon's meetings. He wouldn't mind sneaking out for a nooner.

"I'm *always* ready for you, baby. I'm at the pool. Come over. All I have to do is take off my bikini."

"Your bikini?" Scott's mouth went dry. Tiffany sunbathed without her top, which drove him crazy. She was one of the few dancers with natural tits. The woman's body was proof of heaven.

"The black one I wore on your boat, remember? You said you liked it?"

"I *love* it." Scott felt movement in his golf shorts. *Fore!*

"My skin is soft and warm, and I have oil *all over me*." Tiffany laughed in a throaty way, and Scott headed for the door, almost running into his secretary, who was standing in the threshold, waving to get his attention.

"Scott, sorry to interrupt—"

"What?" Scott covered the phone with his hand, not bothering to hide his irritation. He did hide his erection, however.

"Mr. Hybrinski is here to see you."

"Who?" Scott asked, momentarily confused. All the blood had left his brain, taking the express train south. He couldn't hold a single thought in his head except Tiffany, topless.

"Bill Hybrinski. He said you told him to come by this morning."

Shit, of course. Scott sighed, realizing he was getting done out of doing Tiffany. "Sure, send him in."

"Will do." The secretary vanished.

"Tiffany, bye," Scott whispered into the phone, then hung up.

"Hey, Scott!" Bill entered the office, wearing a white shirt, pressed khakis, and a nervous smile that Scott recognized immediately. It was how everybody looked when they were about to ask him for something. He'd seen it a million times before because everybody wanted something from him, money, a loan, a job, a favor, a discount, a donation, a recommendation, a leg up, whatever. Scott resented it, since he'd never asked anybody for anything, having built Browne Land Management from the ground up. He was a self-made millionaire because he knew that success wasn't something you asked for, but something you earned.

"Great to see you!" Scott masked his feelings and extended his hand, and Bill pumped it heartily.

"It's been too long!"

"It sure has." Scott couldn't remember the last time he'd seen Bill or his wife, Marianne. Julian had brought David on the boat recently, but otherwise the Hybrinskis were in Scott's ex-life, like mulch.

"How have you been, Scott?"

"Terrific! How about you and Marianne?"

"Can't complain."

"Please, sit." Scott sat down, gesturing at the chair opposite the desk.

"Thanks. This is a great office." Bill took a seat, looking around with a wistful expression, and Scott suppressed an eye roll. Bill was feeling sorry for himself because he had to ask for a favor, when it should be the other way around. *Try being the guy who everybody wants something from.*

"Thanks, but we're outgrowing the space already. The plan was to be here for the next three to five, but it looks like we'll be out by the end of the year."

"Business is that good?"

"And then some," Scott answered, rubbing it in. "We're moving to Chester Springs Corporate Center. It's part of the plan."

"That'd be great." Bill smiled, more nervously. "You seem pretty busy today."

"I am."

"Thanks for taking the time to see me."

"For an old friend like you? Not a problem." Scott watched Bill squirm, for shits and giggles.

"Well, I guess I should get to the point."

Scott kept his mouth shut. He wasn't going to make it easy. If Bill wanted something, he could ask.

"Long story short, my business isn't doing that well."

Here it comes. Scott feigned surprise, but he visited that strip mall from time to time to check, and anybody could see that Hybrinski Optical was circling the drain.

"The chains and managed care are killing me."

Excuses, excuses, excuses. Scott linked his fingers in front of him, but said nothing.

"And you already know Lee, from the mattress store, is going belly-up."

"I expect that from him."

Bill cringed. "But Lee worked hard. Really hard."

"Business is business, Bill. You don't get an A for effort. It's about results."

"But Lee's results were good for a long time, then came Dial-A-Mattress. He couldn't compete."

"Gimme a break." Scott knew they weren't talking about Lee or the mattress store. "What kind of businessman are you if you can only make money when there's no competition?"

"I guess, uh, you're right."

"You didn't come here to talk about Lee, did you?"

"No." Bill swallowed visibly.

"Well?"

Bill shifted in his chair. "So, anyway, uh, I hate to ask, but I was wondering if you could forgive my rent for six months."

"You in a hole?"

"Frankly, yes."

"What's the plan?"

"What do you mean?" Bill frowned.

"What's the plan to get you out of the hole? Or is the plan good-money-after-bad?"

Bill paled. "Well, uh, I'm thinking that six months will get me ahead of the game."

"Face the facts, Bill. Your business is dying, and a transfusion isn't gonna keep you alive. It'll just make you stagger longer until you fall down dead."

Bill's mouth dropped open.

"The truth hurts, buddy. Anyway, of course I'll 'forgive' the rent. Technically, I'll delay the payment by making an addendum extending the lease. For three months, not six. Otherwise I can't square it with my lender."

"Okay." Bill blinked, stunned.

"Let me give you some advice."

"Uh, okay."

Scott looked Bill in the eye. "If you don't have a plan, you're not a businessman, you're a gambler."

■

CHAPTER 21

Sasha Barrow

Sasha lifted the last cardboard box onto the truck, wiping her brow. She was so happy the stupid 5K was over. It had taken up her whole morning, but at least she had won, which would look good on her college apps and shut her mother up. Otherwise, it was a total flop. A volunteer told her they wouldn't break even after they paid for the ambulance, and Sasha had spent more time than she wanted to around Allie's wacko family.

"Sasha, thanks so much!" Allie's father scooted over, moving fast on his short legs.

"No problem, Dr. Garvey! I'd better be going home now."

"Not yet, you have to get your trophy." Dr. Garvey frowned. "I left it at home, and it will only take a minute. We can stop by the house, and I'll give it to you."

"No, that's okay." Sasha waved him off, edging away.

She couldn't stand another minute with nerdy Dr. Garvey. "I'll get it another time."

"No, please, I called the newspaper, and they said if I send them a picture of you holding the trophy, they might run it. It will get us some good publicity for CF."

"But I don't want to impose." Sasha suppressed an eye roll. "I can get the trophy another time."

"It's not an imposition. Come with me." Dr. Garvey motioned to her, quick-stepping to a brown Honda. "You won't get to see Allie, though. She and her mother went out to lunch with our friend Fran, doing some catching up. Hop in."

"Okay, thanks." Sasha climbed in the car, and they left the clubhouse and steered through the development in silence, since she didn't care enough to make small talk and Dr. Garvey had no social graces. He drove like three miles an hour. They could've gone faster on a turtle. The Garveys were a nerdy turtle family.

"So you won. I'm sure your mother will be very proud. I'll be sure to email her and tell her how much you helped. Where did you say she was again?"

"Paris, I think."

"Well, that's exciting! Paris is supposed to be one of the most beautiful cities in the world. Have you ever been?"

"Yes."

"I haven't." Dr. Garvey pulled into his driveway, turning off the ignition. "So they're not home yet. I don't see Fran's car."

"Okay." Sasha felt relieved that she didn't have to see

Allie or her mother, who'd looked so weird at the 5K, sitting at the registration table behind big sunglasses and not smiling even once.

"We'll get the trophy and take a picture outside, so they can't tell it wasn't taken at the race." Dr. Garvey got out of the car, and Sasha followed him up the front path to the house, which was a smaller version of hers. He unlocked the front door, and just then the phone started ringing inside the house. Dr. Garvey perked up. "That must be the reporter!"

"Reporter?"

"Yes, she said she'd call! This'll be great!" Dr. Garvey hurried into the house, and Sasha entered after him. He took the call in the kitchen, leaving Sasha to stand awkwardly in the house, looking around.

The layout was the same as Sasha's, with the kitchen connected to the family room, and the décor of Allie's house was exactly what Sasha expected. Flowery stenciling everywhere, tacky furniture with pillows that said BLESS OUR HOME, and no good art. Family photos covered the walls, and Sasha eyed them, not surprised to see that Allie had been fat when she was little, too. Her sister, Jill, had been the pretty one, which sucked.

"Sure, I understand completely," Dr. Garvey was saying into the phone. "I'm delighted you'd consider interviewing me. We need all the publicity we can get. It will help a very worthy cause, curing CF in our lifetime and saving children's lives."

Sasha sighed, standing around with nothing to do. She couldn't believe she was wasting a beautiful Saturday in Allie Garvey's cheesy house getting a rinky-dink trophy.

"Yes, I'm available right now. But please, excuse me for a moment." Dr. Garvey covered the receiver with his hand. "Sasha, the trophy is upstairs in our bedroom. I think I left it on my dresser, on the right. Can you go get it so I can do this interview?"

"Okay." Sasha headed for the staircase, thinking that only a weirdo like Dr. Garvey would send her up to his own bedroom. She climbed to the second floor and took a left at the top of the stairs, knowing that the master would be on the left and the kids' rooms to the right. The layout in her house was the same, the parents separated from the kids, so the parents could have sex and the kids could get high. Or vice versa.

Sasha entered the master bedroom, where the weirdness continued. The bed was messy and unmade, the hamper overflowed with dirty clothes, and the air smelled stale. She turned up her nose, thinking the Garveys needed better cleaning people. The trophy stood on the nearer bureau, so she crossed the bedroom, took it, and left. She was heading down the hallway when she heard shouting coming from downstairs.

Sasha stopped at the top of the stairs. The sound traveled up the stairwell. Curious, she listened in.

"Mark, hang up the phone. Hang up!"

"Fran, please, this is an interview about the 5K—"

"You will not avoid me for one more minute! How dare you let her get this way! She's lost weight! She's a wreck! She needs help, can't you see that?"

"Aunt Fran, please, he's trying his best."

Sasha recognized Allie's voice. So it was a juicy fight between Dr. Garvey, Fran Somebody, and Allie. Sasha didn't know where Mrs. Garvey was. Sasha eavesdropped, wanting to hear what happened.

Fran was saying, "Allie, your father's in denial, you said it yourself! He's pretending your mother is fine when she obviously isn't! She needs psychiatric help, this instant! Probably inpatient! She's in the car, crying her eyes out!"

"Fran, you have a lot of nerve interfering—"

"Dad, Aunt Fran—"

"*I* have a lot of nerve, Mark? *You* have a lot of nerve! You've let her *languish*!"

"I have not! I got her to a therapist! She's on meds! She's going to talk therapy! What more do you want?"

"I want it to *work*! She's a zombie! She looks like a ghost! Her clothes are *swimming* on her! Are you *blind*?"

"Aunt Fran, Dad, please don't fight—"

Upstairs, Sasha started to feel bad. A normal fight was one thing, but this was worse. It sounded like Allie's mother was a mess and Allie was freaking out. Sasha's mother wasn't around much, but at least she wasn't a basket case. Meanwhile Sasha couldn't go downstairs in the middle of a family fight. She stayed still, unsure of what to do next.

"Fran, I've done everything for her! Everything!"

"You've done everything but *help her*! Can't you tell she's sinking? She's circling the drain!"

"She's grieving! Everybody grieves differently!"

"She's going under, Mark! What were you thinking today, forcing her to go to a *fun run* on Jill's anniversary? Are you insane? What mother would want to do that?"

"What mother *wouldn't*? It's a celebration of our daughter's life!"

"Mark, you're failing her!"

"I'm *failing her*?" Dr. Garvey exploded. "Fran, who are *you* to tell me I'm *failing her*? Do you know what I *do* around here? I'm the husband *and* the wife! I'm the father *and* the mother! I go to work every day, I make sure there's food in the house! I get the laundry and dry cleaning done! I make sure the lawn gets mowed, the bills get paid! *I do it all!* I've been doing it all for a year! All she does is sleep, eat, and cry!"

"Mark, her daughter died!"

"So did *mine*!" Dr. Garvey shouted, his voice breaking.

"Dad, Aunt Fran, stop!" Allie burst into tears, running up the stairs.

Oh, shit. Sasha realized Allie was coming. Sasha edged backward, clutching the trophy. Her instinct was to run back into the master, but that would be weirder. There was no time anyway. Sasha froze.

Allie reached the top of the stairs and saw Sasha. Allie gasped, startled. Her eyes went wide. Tears streaked her cheeks. "What are *you* doing here?" she blurted out, shocked.

"I had to get this." Sasha hoisted the trophy. "Sorry—"

Allie turned away, fled to her bedroom, and slammed the door closed.

Sasha flew down the stairs, through the front door, and out of Allie's house. She didn't stop running until she got home.

She threw the trophy in the garbage.

CHAPTER 22

■

Julian Browne

There were six tennis courts at Brandywine Hunt, maintained in excellent condition, covered every winter and the nets put away so the tape didn't get dingy. They were Har-Tru, so their surface was soft green stone, which complemented the green coating on the cyclone fence. The courts were set off on the far side of the pool and snack bar, with the clubhouse. Julian and David hadn't had to wait for a court because it was hot and nearly everybody was at the pool. They'd been playing for less than an hour, but Julian was getting frustrated. He couldn't concentrate. He gritted his teeth, watching the ball sail out-of-bounds.

"Sayonara!" David called from his side of the court. "That's the match!"

"Son of a bitch!" Julian banged his racket on the court. It was his new Head titanium graphite but he didn't care if it broke. "I want a rematch!"

"Not today, bro! You're off your game."

"Bullshit!" Julian noticed the old couple on the next court looking over in disapproval. He wasn't supposed to use profanity on the property. Most people knew who he was, and he couldn't disgrace the family name, which was a *brand*. "I want a rematch!"

"No way! I won in straight sets. You're officially humiliated."

"Come on, David!"

"Stick a fork in it, my friend!"

"But I know what I'm doing wrong! I got it now!" Julian knew he sounded ridiculous, since what he was doing wrong was everything. He'd been driving himself crazy wondering where Sasha was, because he hadn't seen her in her bedroom, nor did he see her leave.

"Let's just hit around!" David lobbed a shot over the net, but Julian let it bounce.

"I don't need charity!"

"Be cool, dude." David pocketed the second ball, came forward to the net, and rested his hands on the tape. "Then let's call it a day. Get a swim."

"I don't want to."

"I do. We played an hour. Come on, let the kids play." David gestured at two kids sitting on the other side of the fence, waiting for a court.

"Fuck 'em."

"That was us once." David motioned to the kids, and they scrambled to their sneakers, picking up their rackets and a can of balls.

"We were cooler than that."

"No, we weren't. Let's go." David chuckled, and Julian examined his racket, happy to note he'd damaged its rim. He hustled to collect the balls on his side, picked up his racket cover, and walked to the gate.

"Hi, guys." David opened the gate for the kids. "Have a good game."

"Yeah, don't suck out loud," Julian added, and the kids laughed nervously, heading on to the court, unzipping their racket covers, and opening the zip-top on a new can of balls with a satisfying hiss.

"I love that sound, don't you?" David closed the gate, with its sign BRANDYWINE HUNT TENNIS COURTS. NO SKATE-BOARDING. PROPER FOOTWEAR REQUIRED. MINORS MUST YIELD TO ADULTS ON WEEKENDS AND WEEKNIGHTS.

Julian flopped onto the silvery wooden bench, which was real cedar. His father always specified cedar benches instead of all-weather in the upscale developments. Julian wished he could turn off his developer brain, but he couldn't. He wanted to have his own land development business someday. His father wanted him to work for Browne Land Management, but Julian knew that would be a mistake. He would never be anything but the boss's son if he did that. Julian wanted to be the boss.

"You okay?" David sat next to him, wiping his forehead with his bandanna, in a loop like a noose.

"I sucked hard. You were in the *zone*."

David smiled crookedly. "The true opponent is the player himself. If you read *Infinite Jest*, you'd know that."

"It's too long."

"The Bible is long."

"*Infinite Jest* is not the Bible. It's a normal book."

"The word you're searching for is *novel*, my friend. Allie's reading it."

"Allie has the hots for you. I don't."

"What's going on?" David twisted open a bottle of water. There had been stacks of Deer Park outside the clubhouse, for free.

"I'm so pissed about Sasha." Julian couldn't shake his mood.

"Because she made such a stink about the squirrel thing? You're not pissed at me, are you?" David gulped some water.

"No. I get it, no worries. You felt bad for Allie."

"Right." David shrugged. "That 5K for her sister was this morning. I saw some flyers in the trash. I would've run in it, but my dad had chores for me."

"You like the underdog." Julian's mother always called David *sensitive*.

"So what's going on with Sasha?"

"She's seeing somebody, somebody older. Like, a man. He's really tall, like, over six foot five."

"How do you know?"

"I noticed some guy at her house. He wasn't any of the guys she usually sees. He didn't drive a car, so he must live in the development. I mean, it's driving me crazy. She drives me crazy."

"You know she sees other guys. She's got a lot of dates."

"But a new one, now? Who's he? I *know* the other guys. Now there's another one, just when I thought we were getting closer."

"Closer, you and Sasha? Why?"

"Because of the gun," Julian answered, lowering his voice. "I got the bullets for her. Now there's a new guy? What the fuck?"

"You don't know who he is?"

"No, and she gave him a big hug and brought him inside." Julian felt his jealousy flame. "I was, literally, in the family room with my mom, watching a movie. All I did was look out the window, and there was Sasha with *him*."

David tucked a strand of hair behind his ear. "You should ask her out."

"You think?" Julian asked, uneasy. "I've been waiting until I get a car."

"Don't wait. Like you say, she sees a lot of guys. Sooner or later she's gonna pick one, like, a boyfriend. You're gonna get shut out."

"I couldn't take that." Julian felt his stomach turn over. It was his worst fear that Sasha would go on without him, leaving him behind. And he'd spend the rest of his life watching her.

"Take a shot. Go for it."

"I should." Julian had always thought his ace in the hole with Sasha was who he was. He'd told her his father was grooming him to take over Browne Land Management, even if it was *a classic case of nepotism*, as he overheard one of the office workers say.

"It can be you. Why not you?"

"But what do I ask her to do? And what, do I ask my mom to drive us? That's so lame."

"Whatever, you don't have any choice." David paused. "Dude, you should ask her out on your dad's boat."

"Whoa. Why didn't I think of that?" Julian brightened.

"That's the way to go. The other guys have a car, but they don't have a boat. That would be cool."

"Right." Julian nodded, getting excited.

"Remember when you took me? That was awesome."

"Yes!" Julian had taken David, and they'd had a blast, fishing and drinking beer. His father hadn't brought a girl or offered David weed, which was smart. David might have told his parents, and they weren't cool.

"You go to the boat and spend the whole day. You said he brings girls, so he won't be in your face. It could even be overnight."

"That's true!" Julian fast-forwarded to an inn at the Eastern Shore with Sasha. He could knock on her door, she would let him in, and they could have sex, finally. He wished he wasn't a virgin, but he would tell her he wasn't. He shoved David in the arm. "You're a genius!"

David grinned. "So is Sasha why you played like shit?"

"You don't understand! I'm obsessed."

David sipped water. "I'm not into her."

"How could you *not* be? She's unbelievably beautiful."

" 'Pretty girls have pretty ugly feet.' "

"When did you see her feet? And who cares?"

"It's the first line from *The Broom of the System*. He also said tennis is 'chess on the run,' which is so true, and you—"

"We were talking about Sasha."

"She's bitchy, dude." David shrugged. "I don't like it. She says mean things all the time."

"Dude, if I were alone with her, like, really alone, like, after a few beers on my father's boat, I guarantee you, we would *not* be talking." Julian gave David another shove, his mood improved. "Hey, I almost forgot, my dad called me this morning about your dad."

"Why?"

"My dad told me he and your dad worked out a deal."

"What deal?" David frowned, setting down his water bottle, and Julian realized that David must not have known.

"Uh, my dad's working with your dad."

"What do you mean, 'working with' him?"

"I didn't get the details." Julian was sorry he brought it up. David looked upset. Man, he *was* sensitive. "I think your dad called my dad and asked him to do something for his store."

David blinked. "Like what?"

"I don't know. Maybe your dad was having a problem? Either way, no biggie. My dad was happy to spot him a few months."

"Oh, no." David grimaced, flushing.

"Dude, no worries, we're cool." Julian tried to get past the moment, definitely awkward. "You're my best bro."

"Still." David looked away.

"Come on." Julian clapped him on the shoulder. "Let's go to my house and swim."

"I gotta go home." David picked up his racket, turning away.

CHAPTER 23

∎

David Hybrinski

D avid walked down the driveway to the backyard, sorting out his thoughts. He'd assumed his father's business was doing fine, but things started to make sense, like that his father had fired the lawn guys and started mowing himself. Or cleaning the gutters instead of calling the roof guy. And his mother was buying store-brand peanut butter instead of the crunchy Jif. Maybe Hybrinski Optical was in trouble. David felt guilty that he'd talked back to his father at the twins' game the other day.

You got your money's worth.

David lifted the magnetic lock on the gate and entered the backyard. In a better mood, he would've found the scene idyllic. Two acres of grassy lawn bordered by his mother's flower garden, and a kidney-shaped pool with a corkscrew water slide the twins loved and a hot tub nobody used, now that the novelty had worn off. His

SOMEONE KNOWS ■ 157

father was on the riding mower on the far side of the yard, and his brother, Jason, was skimming the pool in his Ray-Bans and gym shorts.

"Jase, I did that already," David said, walking over. It had become his Saturday chore to clean the pool, after his parents let go of the pool guys.

"I figured." Jason shrugged. "Dad told me to do it again."

"Why?" David looked at the water, squinting hard. "It's perfect."

"I know. He asked me to do it."

"What's his mood?" David and his brother routinely shared intel on their father. If he was in a good mood, they tried to keep him happy. If he was in a bad one, they stayed out of his way. David wondered how well he really knew his father, after what Julian told him.

"Honestly, he's happy as shit. God knows why." Jason shrugged.

David knew why, but didn't tell Jason because his father was already looking over.

"Here, let me do that." He held out his hand for the skimmer. "You're, like, rowing. It's not an oar, it's a skimmer."

"Dude, thanks. This is so boring." Jason handed over the skimmer, and in the background, their father cut the ignition, then got off and walked toward David with a smile.

"How was tennis?" his father called out, and David and Jason exchanged glances, since *how was tennis* wasn't his father's typical greeting.

"Great." David smiled, and his father took off his sunglasses and wiped his face with a meaty hand. Little pieces of dirt, what his mother called *schmutz*, were stuck to the sweat on his father's face.

"David, you don't have to clean the pool. Jason can do it." His father gestured at the skimmer. "Give it back to your brother."

"That's okay, but I already did it. Did you know that?"

"Yeah, but I got clippings in it from the mower."

"I'll do it again."

"No, Jason can. Jason, you do it." His father grabbed the skimmer from David and handed it to Jason. "Jase, why did you give it to David to do? I asked you to do it."

"I didn't give it to him. He offered to do it."

"I asked you to do it. So you do it."

"Fine." Jason started skimming the pool.

David's mouth went dry. "Dad, I can do it. It's my job."

"It doesn't always have to be your job. Jason can help out around here."

"I don't mind." Jason kept skimming.

David couldn't let it go, for some reason. "Dad, I don't mind, either. It's my job. I'll clean it."

His father pursed his lips. "I said, let Jason do it. He can help out around here."

"He does," David said defensively.

"You do it every morning. You do the recycling and trash. What does he do?"

"He works, he has to work."

"He lives under my roof, so he can pull his own weight."

Jason shot David a warning glance behind their father's back.

"Anyway, David, I have plans." His father wiped his hand on his chest. He had on a white Lacoste shirt, and his fingers left a faintly grim print. "I got three tickets to the Phils next week. Wanna go?"

"Really?" David didn't get it. His father had never asked him to go to a Phillies game before. The Hybrinskis didn't do things together. His mother did things with the girls, like a separate family. The boys didn't do anything.

"What's your problem? Your father bought tickets for the game. You wanna go or not?"

"Sure." David turned to Jason. "Jase?"

His father interjected, "No, it's just us. You and me, David."

"Oh." David couldn't remember the last time he'd gone anywhere alone with his father. Jason looked away.

"Yes, but you can ask Julian."

"Julian?" David asked, now entirely confused. "But you don't like Julian."

"I never said that."

Jason burst into laughter. "Dad, you hate Julian. You say it all the time."

"Who asked *you*?" David's father snapped, whirling angrily around. "Because I didn't hear it if they did."

"Dad, chill." Jason put up both hands, edging away with the skimmer hooked under his thumb.

"David, as I was saying, I thought it might be fun to take you and Julian."

David didn't know what to say. "I don't know if Julian is free that night. He might have plans."

"Give him a call. Ask him."

"Okay, I will."

His father gestured at the house. "Go ask him."

"Right now?"

"There's no time like the present. If you want to make something happen, you have to make it happen. Call him and see if he's free."

"But I don't know if he's home yet."

"Only one way to find out." His father gestured at the house again, and David felt angry.

"Dad, we never go to games."

"So? We can't now?"

"Why do I have to ask Julian? Why don't we just go? With Jason."

David nodded toward Jason, who was heading away, retreating to the shallow end of the pool.

"What's the matter with you?" His father looked at him hard, eye to eye, and David realized that he was taller than his father. He could take him. Suddenly he was tired of making his father happy or making sure he didn't piss him off, especially since the first time his father had ever asked him to go to a Phillies game was after he had borrowed money from his best friend's father.

"I don't want Julian to go," David said firmly. "I want Jason to go."

His father snorted, recoiling. "What is this bullshit?"

"That's what I was thinking," David said, speaking his mind without thinking twice, for the first time. "I'm trying to figure out why, all of a sudden, you want to be best buddies with Julian when you hate him."

"What are you talking about?" His father scowled, and David felt resentment bubble up inside him, because he'd been keeping it down for so long. It sucked if Hybrinski Optical was in bad shape, but his father made it hard to feel sorry for him.

"You know what I'm talking about."

"Why don't you tell me, big guy?"

"Julian told me that you asked his dad to let you off the hook for the rent, for the store."

"*What* did you say?" His father's dark eyes flared.

"You never liked Julian before. But his dad gave you money and all of a sudden, you screw Jason for Julian?" David saw the pain flicker across his father's face, and the guilt came back. "Dad, listen, I get it, if you're having money trouble—"

"I'm not having money trouble!"

"You must if you're asking Julian's father for money."

"I *didn't* ask him for money!" his father shouted.

"Then for a loan—"

"I didn't ask him for a loan!"

"Then whatever you asked for, to cut you a break on the rent, whatever, and that's what I mean, I didn't know it was that bad—"

"That's none of your business, faggot!" David's father pushed him so hard that he lost his balance, his arms pinwheeled, and he fell backward into the pool. Cold water buried him. Air bubbles slipped from between his lips. His sneakers hit the bottom of the pool, and he pushed off, kicked to the surface, and gulped air, his hair plastered to his forehead.

Jason's mouth had formed a grim line, and his father stalked to the house.

The word filled David's ears, flooding them.

Faggot.

CHAPTER 24

■

Kyle Gallagher

Kyle took a shot, letting the basketball fly. He knew it was a swish as soon as it left his fingertips. The ball arced through the air and dropped through the hoop, and he felt a surge of good feeling, for the first time in a long time. He'd decided to shoot hoops since it was nice out and his only other choice was food-shopping with his mother. There were six courts in the development, surrounded by a green cyclone fence and set off by evergreens to minimize the wind. Kyle couldn't believe how nicely they were kept.

Kyle chased his ball down, dribbled, and shot a layup. He was feeling great since he'd met Sasha Barrow, the most beautiful girl he'd ever seen. He hadn't believed it when she'd opened the front door and was so excited to see the cat that she'd given them both a big hug. It had been so long since he'd hugged a girl that all his senses exploded, and she smelled like vanilla, and her bare arms felt soft, and she had the most beautiful smile, crazy white like in a toothpaste commercial.

He went after the ball, dribbled it, and took another shot. The ball circled the rim and went in. He hadn't realized how much he'd missed basketball, his shoulders and upper arms aching, but in a good way. He loved the slap of the basketball against the court, and the feeling of the pebbled grain on his fingertips. He was relieved to find that he hadn't lost his mojo completely.

Kyle took another shot, *swish*, thinking of Sasha, who had offered him a Coke and popcorn from the microwave. They'd talked in the kitchen, and she asked him all kinds of questions, which he answered without telling her too much, and she would be in his class at high school. She didn't mention a boyfriend, which was awesome.

Kyle took a jumper, and the ball went in. Sasha could have any guy she wanted, but she'd said they *should get together sometime*, and he'd said, *yes, totally*, and they'd exchanged numbers and screen names so they could IM each other. He would IM her as soon as he got home and ask her out. No reason to wait. He couldn't stop thinking about her. Maybe he would like it here, after all. If she lived in the same development and went to the same school.

Kyle kept to his side of the court, taking shots while a group of dads played on the other side. They looked over at him, sizing him up. None of the dads was very good, but they had truly awesome sneakers. It was like a shoe store over there.

"Nice shot!" said one of the dads, and another one clapped. They stopped playing and came to mid-court. "Hey, pal, what's your name?"

"Kyle Gallagher." *Swish.*

"Ross McKnight." The baldest dad came over, with the Penny Hardaway Nikes. He extended a hand, and Kyle shook it. "Good to meet you. I live on Hanoverian."

"Hi." Kyle held his ball as McKnight gestured to the man next to him, who was an older Indian-American with bristly gray hair and old Air Jordans.

"Ray Patel," the man said. "Hiya, son." Patel extended a hand, and Kyle shook it, hiding his reaction to the word *son.*

The skinniest dad grinned. He had the cool white-and-silver Scottie Pippen Nikes. "I'm Ron Berman, and you're a phenom."

"Nah," Kyle said, but it reminded him of the newspaper headlines back home. He hadn't minded being called a phenom. And he had wanted those Scottie Pippens.

"You could probably give us a few pointers. Say, what's Rodriguez doing wrong?" Berman pointed. "He's the fatso with the beard and the midlife crisis."

"No, that's okay." Kyle laughed.

"Tell me, I wanna know!" Rodriguez called out, having missed the foul shot. He wore Dikembe Mutombos. "What'd I do wrong?"

"In a word, *pizza,*" one of the dads interjected, and the others laughed.

Kyle said, "Mr. Rodriguez, you released the ball too late, that's all."

Berman folded his arms. "Kyle, you wanna play for us? The game is today at four."

"What team?" Kyle asked, confused.

"You live here, right, Kyle?"

"Yeah. On Paso Fino."

"So that's legit." Berman grinned, turning to the others. "He lives in Brandywine Hunt. He can play on the team."

Rodriguez cocked his head. "Kyle, how old are you?"

"Fifteen."

"You're kidding!" Rodriguez's mouth dropped open, a pink circle buried in his beard.

Berman's eyes went wide. "You're fifteen? You look twenty! What are you, six five? Do you go to Bakerton?"

"I will next year. My mom and I just moved here."

"From where? Did you play?"

"Columbus," Kyle answered, hoping it would suffice.

"Is that near Akron?"

"About two hours away."

"My nephew keeps talking about some kid out there, a phenom with a funny name. You heard of him?"

"LeBron James? He's awesome." Kyle knew about LeBron James. Everybody did, back home. His mom had taken him and some of the guys to a game once, to see LeBron play.

Rodriguez folded his arms. "Berman, focus. It's an adult league. They're going to challenge him when they see how good he is."

Berman scoffed. "So we make an argument. It's a case

of first impression. There's no precedent. Are we not law-yers?"

"Are we not men?" Patel said, and they all laughed.

Berman looked over. "Ross, you were here when the league started. Did they say anything about minors?"

"Not that I remember. I think he's eligible. He lives here." One of the younger dads came over, tucking the ball under his elbow, and they clustered around, discussing the pros and cons.

"We didn't submit him in advance of the game—"

"—so we submit him now—"

"—he needs a shirt—"

"—I got one in the trunk—"

"—they're gonna challenge him—"

"It's a fucking development league." Berman winked at Kyle. "Sorry about the language."

"I've heard it before." Kyle shrugged happily. It was nice being around dads again.

"Oh man, this is excellent!" Berman clapped his hands. "We might actually win! Kyle, you in?"

"Sure, but I have to ask my mom," Kyle answered, and they all burst into laughter, and one of the dads patted him on the back.

"Good answer. You were raised right."

Another dad said, "Kyle, is your mom single? *I'll* ask her."

The other dads laughed, but not in a gross way, and Kyle thought it wouldn't be the worst thing for his mother to meet a nice dad. Maybe starting over was this easy. Join a dad team. Rescue a friendly cat. Meet a beautiful girl. Life could change for the better.

"Excellent!" Berman clapped him on the shoulder. "You want a ride, Kyle? I'll take you home."

"No, thanks. I have my bike."

"Okay, hurry, go ask her. Gimme your phone number, and we'll call in an hour."

Kyle gave it to him, excited. He jogged off the court with his ball, jumped on his bike, and pedaled home, his heart pumping. It was a short ride, and he steered around the corner in no time. He waved to an older neighbor like he was Mr. Brandywine Hunt. He spotted his mother's car, so she was home from shopping, and Sharon's Honda was there, too. Kyle dismounted on the fly, running with his bike to the door, leaving it against the wall, and hustling inside, since the front door was unlocked.

"Hi, Mom! Hey, Sharon!" he called out, hustling toward the kitchen with the ball.

His mother looked up from the nook, where she was sitting with Sharon, and something was wrong. His mother had been crying, her eyes watery and puffy, and crumpled tissues sat next to a Kleenex box and a glass of water. Sharon turned to face Kyle; her expression was pained.

"What's the matter?" Kyle asked, his mouth dry. Buddy came over, wagging his tail.

"Your father," his mother answered, her voice soft. She pushed back a strand of hair.

"What?" Kyle set the ball down, stricken. It was his worst fear. "He's not . . . dead, is he?"

"I *wish*." His mother snorted. "He gave an interview from jail to the *Dispatch*. Now everybody knows about us. Reporters from Philly got our number and address. They've been calling for the past hour. See for yourself." His mother slid a paper across the table, a faxed copy of a newspaper article from home, with a headline that made his stomach drop. DR. BRIAN HAMMOND "DR. DIRT-BAG" TELLS ALL, EXCLUSIVE JAILHOUSE INTERVIEW, SOON AN EPISODE OF *DATELINE* ON NBC-TV.

"Oh, no." Kyle controlled his reaction because his mother was so upset. This couldn't be happening. He had just met Sasha. He had just had one good day. Sadness washed over him. And shame. Everybody would know what his father had done. The newspapers had called his father Dr. Dirtbag and said he fingered *cancer kids*. Kyle put his hand on her shoulder, reading the article:

> . . . *Dr. Brian Hammond, 47, once a trusted and respected pediatric oncologist at New Albany General, is serving twenty-five years in prison for twelve counts of unlawful sexual conduct with a minor, gross sexual imposition, and sexual battery* . . .
>
> . . . *Dr. Hammond was found guilty of sexually abusing twelve female patients between the ages of nine months to seven years old* . . .
>
> . . . *the crimes took place on hospital grounds and were discovered by his wife, Barbara, nee Gallagher, who reported her husband to local authorities* . . .
>
> . . . *civil lawsuits brought by outraged parents bankrupted Dr. Hammond and have cost New Albany*

General over seven million dollars in negligence law-
suits . . .

. . . New Albany General has been found liable
for negligent supervision of Dr. Hammond and with
respect to security procedures . . .

. . . Barbara Gallagher divorced Dr. Hammond
and returned to her hometown of Bakerton, Pennsyl-
vania, with their son, Kyle.

His mother sniffled. "The reporters faxed it to Sharon, since we don't have a fax."

"How did they know? How did they find us?"

"Your father gave them an earful, all of it lies, like that
I lied on the stand to ruin him, and he only pleaded
guilty because his lawyer coerced him, and he's unjustly
accused. The Philly newspapers are going to print everything, that we moved here, that we changed your name,
that you're going to Bakerton High in September."

"I'm so sorry, Mom." Kyle sank into a chair, and his
mother's expression showed a familiar anguish, her eyebrows sloping down like a collapsed roof, her cheeks
slack, her mouth downturned, her lips trembling.

"No, *I'm* sorry. I'm so sorry this is happening all over
again, and to you."

Sharon interjected, "You guys will get through this.
Don't talk to the reporter, and that will shut it down."

"That won't shut it down, Sharon." His mother
reached for a Kleenex and mopped her eyes, leaving reddish streaks. "The mistake I made was coming back

home. It was too easy for Brian to figure out. I should've gone somewhere else entirely, like California."

"No, that's not it." Sharon patted her hand. "Don't blame yourself."

"He knew I'd come home. We should move again."

"Mom, we just got here," Kyle blurted out, before he could even understand his own feelings. "I played basketball," he started to say, and his mother looked at him like he was crazy.

"We can't stay here, we can't. Do you know what they're going to do to you? This reporter is going to run a story if I *don't* speak to him and he's going to run a story if I *do* speak to him, and there's other reporters where he came from, and a TV show—"

"But *we* didn't do anything wrong, Mom. We have to stop running."

Sharon interjected again, "Barb, Kyle's right. You turned Brian in. You testified against him—"

"That's why they want to talk to us. He says I lied, and they want my side of the story. They're not gonna let up." His mother's eyes filled with tears, and she turned to Kyle. "Honey, this is killing me, for you. I could handle it for myself, but I hate to see you so hurt, trying to start over. We have to go. Right away. I could do this, but it's you I worry about."

"I'll be fine, Mom, I don't want to move again—" Kyle started to say, but he could see she had made up her mind, and he had lived this nightmare already. He had become the son of Dr. Dirtbag. Not Hammond, not even Gallagher. Sasha wouldn't give him a chance now. He wasn't going to play basketball with dads. School would be a nightmare. He would make zero friends. The teachers would look at him funny. Everyone would be gossiping about him. He'd been through it before, and now it would be worse. Because the Gallaghers were frauds, and his father had busted them.

CHAPTER 25

∎

Sasha Barrow

S asha came out of the shower, toweling off her hair, her bathroom thick with steam. She bunched the bath towel on the rack and slipped into her robe, glad to be done with the drama at Allie's house. Sasha had felt bad for Allie, and her mother had been crying in the car when Sasha had run from their house. It made Sasha grateful for her own mother, who totally had her act together.

Sasha left the bathroom, went to her desk, and got on her computer. She logged on to AOL Instant Messenger, and her Buddy List came up immediately. Julian was already online and messaged her first:

Heir2Throne987: hey sash i was about to IM u

SashaliciousOne: we shld have fun tonite

Heir2Throne987: totally

SashaliciousOne: lets meet @ the tree

Heir2Throne987: k when

SashaliciousOne: half an hour

Heir2Throne987: pick u up

SashaliciousOne: no meet me there & tell the others

Heir2Throne987: who

SashaliciousOne: david & allie u lamo

Heir2Throne987: why

SashaliciousOne: youll see

Sasha jumped up and hurried to her closet to decide what to wear.

CHAPTER 26

∎

Julian Browne

Julian could barely control his excitement after Sasha's IM. He had been about to ask her out on his dad's boat, but now she was asking him out, sort of. He would've preferred to be alone with her, but he would take what he could get. He checked his Buddy List for David, but he wasn't online, so Julian picked up the phone and called him.

"Hybrinski residence," said a male voice, and Julian realized it was David's father.

"Oh hi, Mr. H, this is Julian. Is David there?"

"Sure. How are you doing, pal?" Mr. H's tone warmed up, and Julian wondered how much it had cost his father for Mr. H to call him *pal*.

"Great, how are you, sir?"

"Terrific. How's the tennis going? I hear you and David played today."

"He beat me in straight sets, so if you ask me, it went lousy."

"Ha ha ha!" Mr. H laughed as if Julian had said something super funny, showing social skills that would drive anybody out of business.

"So is David around?"

"Sure, he's up in his room. I'll get him. You take care, pal."

"Will do." Julian waited while Mr. H covered the phone and called David, and a moment later, there was a click and the extension was picked up. "David?"

"Hey, Julian," David answered, and there was another click.

"Dude, guess what?" Julian couldn't wait to tell him. "Sasha invited us to meet her at the tree in half an hour."

"What?" David sounded preoccupied, but he had probably been reading.

"Sasha wants to meet us at the tree in half an hour. You and Allie, too."

"Why?"

"For fun."

"What kind of fun?"

"I don't know; does it matter? Let's go."

"I don't want to."

"What? Dude. Come on, it'll be fun." Julian could hear David sounded bummed. "What's the matter with you?"

"My dad sucks."

"Dude, so what?" Julian figured it was about the store rent, but he didn't want to bring it up again. "For real, you gotta come. I'm begging you. Sasha wants you and Allie to go. I don't know if she'll go if you guys don't."

"Julian—"

"Please do it for me." Julian got an idea. "If you go, I'll read your book."

"No, you won't. You say you will but you won't."

"No, I will." Julian felt desperate. "I might not get another chance with Sasha if this new guy steps up his game. Don't let me down, not now."

David sighed. "All right."

"Dude, thank you. I swear I'll read your book."

"You're not gonna. You don't have to read it."

"I will," Julian said, but he wouldn't. Nobody in his right mind would read a thousand-page book. "And you have to ask Allie."

"Why me? Why not you?"

"She likes you."

"What if she's busy?"

"Allie? What could *she* have going on?"

CHAPTER 27

■

David Hybrinski

F *aggot.*
  David lay in bed, the word reverberating in his ears. His father had never called him that before. David knew he'd meant it from the way he said it, like he'd been holding it back for a long time. His father always said that David was *gay for David Foster Wallace.* And once he'd even called Julian his *boyfriend.* His mother had shot his father a stern look, one she used for her students.

David tried not to cry. Once when he was little he'd cried and his father had said *stop or I'll give you a reason to cry*, and his hand had moved to his belt buckle. The twins cried whenever they wanted. Jessica cried when water ice stained her My Little Pony shirt and Jennifer when her gerbil ate its babies. But the Hybrinski men didn't cry.

David wondered if he was gay. Secretly he'd been asking himself that question for a while. He didn't have a girlfriend, but he went out with girls and had gotten pretty far with them. Melissa, Jodi, Abby, Hanna, all of them were cute, popular, and crazy about him. He was a virgin, but he was only fifteen, and David Foster Wallace had been a virgin at fifteen, too. David knew because he had read it in one of DFW's tennis essays. Still, he wondered if you could be gay and not know it. There were a lot of things that people didn't know about themselves. For example, his father didn't know he was a jerk.

David opened his eyes, and his gaze went to his bulletin board, where he'd thumbtacked photos from *Tennis* magazine, which they used to get before his parents canceled all their magazine subscriptions. Another clue to their family finances that he had missed. So maybe he'd just missed the clues about himself being gay. Maybe there *were* clues he didn't want to see.

The photos were of Pete Sampras, Andre Agassi, and Arthur Ashe, and older greats like Rod Laver and John Newcombe, an Australian with a cool handlebar mustache. David had vowed to grow one of those mustaches someday. Did that mean he was gay? Was he gay for handlebar mustaches? Next to the tennis greats on his bulletin board were photos of DFW cut out from *The New York Times*. David loved David Foster Wallace, but did that make him gay?

David scanned the wall and realized that there wasn't a single picture of a woman. Why? Julian was so in love with Sasha, and the other guys on the team had girlfriends and pictures of models on their locker doors. Troy Burkett loved his poster of Farrah Fawcett in the red bathing suit. *You can see her nips,* Troy always said excitedly. But David had to admit that Farrah Fawcett's nips didn't excite him.

His troubled gaze found the last photos on his bulletin board, group shots of the tennis teams. He was standing next to Julian because they'd always been doubles partners. There were two pictures of him and Julian, after they'd won juniors doubles under sixteen, each holding a handle of the silver trophy.

David loved Julian like a best friend, but he wasn't gay for him, was he? He didn't feel that way. He wasn't attracted to him. David wasn't attracted to any other guy, either. David wondered if Julian was his *boyfriend*, like his father had said. David had dismissed that, until now. His father had called him a faggot, and David thought *Maybe I am.*

David felt miserable, deep inside. His father made jokes about gay men who came into the store, calling them *fruity* and *light in the loafers.* If David was gay, his father would make jokes about *him*. And maybe hate his guts.

He wiped his eyes, realizing he had a secret. He was getting used to being a phony. He was phony about having a happy family, because they didn't. After the twins were born, his mother got involved with them and left him and Jason with his father, on their own sucky little island.

David didn't want to think anymore. He got up, went to his computer, logged on to AIM, and looked for Allie.

CHAPTER 28

Allie Garvey

Allie lay on her side, watching the clock on the nightstand, an electric Westclox that glowed so bright at night that she had to cover it with her panties. It was seven minutes after five o'clock, which was ninety-five minutes after Jill had died, one year ago. Allie had cried so much that her eyes actually burned. She was still in her Jog For Jill shirt, and the late-day sun came through the window. She had been so shocked to see Sasha upstairs, and Sasha looked like she felt sorry for her, which was even worse than her laughing her ass off.

Allie's father was downstairs, unable to deny anymore that her mother was in bad shape. Aunt Fran had said her mother was *having a nervous breakdown* and wouldn't even come in from the car. Her father had gone out to talk to her, and Allie had watched from her bedroom window, horrified that her mother had refused to speak to him. Her father had pounded on the car window, *honey, what is it, what did I do*, but Aunt Fran had shouted at him, yelling that her mother *needed to be admitted inpatient somewhere,* then she'd gotten in the car and driven away, leaving her father standing in the driveway.

The neighbors had peeked out their front doors to see what was going on, and Mr. Selig across the street abandoned his riding mower and hurried inside his house. Allie had watched, trying not to cry as her father had shuffled inside, stunned.

Their house had fallen quiet and still. Half her family was gone. Her sister was dead. Her mother was crazy. Her father was probably sitting at the kitchen table, his glasses off and his hands over his face, hiding from someone, maybe himself. He was an orthodontist, used to straightening what was crooked, but families were always crooked, or at least the Garveys were.

Allie wondered if David was online, so she went to her computer, and logged on to AOL to find that he'd messaged her.

She wiped her eyes.

CHAPTER 29

∎

Allie Garvey

Allie entered the woods, walking next to David. It had come as a surprise when he'd IMed her to meet the others by the tree, and she'd put on a sundress with purple flowers and twisted her hair into a topknot, which turned out like a fancy updo. Plus she had on her sandals with ribbons that crossed at the ankle, which made her feel like a ballerina. She'd left the house quickly, telling her father she was going to Sasha's. He'd been sitting in the kitchen like she had expected, but she'd fled out the door.

"Hey." David took her hand with an easy smile, in his red bandanna, white Lacoste polo, and long shorts.

Allie's heart pounded, and she felt a surge of happiness. He must like her if he held her hand. They walked through the woods together, with David moving branches aside for her. His hand felt so good, except for his palm. "Your hand's scratchy."

"It's calluses from tennis."

"Oh." Allie kicked herself for saying something so dumb. "Anyway, I'm on page forty-three of your book."

"You made progress." David smiled again.

"I'm slow, though." Allie stepped over some old leaves, not to mess up her sandals.

"Slow but steady wins the race." David looked over. "I saw there was that 5K today for your sister. How'd it go?"

Allie forced a smile. She wasn't going to tell him everything, or even *anything*. She wanted to change the subject. "So why did Sasha want us to come tonight?"

"For fun."

"Oh." Allie prayed that Sasha didn't tell the others about the fight at her house. The Barrows, Brownes, and Hybrinskis were such normal families compared to hers, which was a mess. Allie didn't even know where her mother was. *Inpatient somewhere.*

Allie heard talking as they approached the tree, and when they came through the clearing, she could see Sasha and Julian sitting on the ground on a blue cotton blanket. Julian was digging up the gun, and Sasha was watching, drinking from a water bottle.

"Hey, guys!" David released Allie's hand, and she guessed he didn't want to show the others how he felt about her. She told herself it was okay. It could be their secret.

Sasha waved in a surprisingly friendly way, grinning. "Hey, David; hey, Allie! Let's get this party started!"

"Agree!" David called back, and Allie smiled, too, but

she was unsure. Sasha seemed like she was in a great mood, but Allie didn't trust her. She wondered if Sasha felt sorry for her or if she was finally being accepted, maybe because David liked her. That would be awesome.

"What are you guys up to?" David asked, and Julian looked up from the gun, slapping him high-five with a dirt-covered hand.

"Fun and games, bro."

"That's what I thought." David chuckled, sitting down on the blanket.

"Thirsty?" Sasha offered David a bottle from a tote bag, and David took a sip.

"Vodka, no chaser? Ugh. Next time, mix it with Gatorade."

"You're welcome." Sasha handed a bottle to Allie, who accepted it, hiding her reluctance. "Don't worry, Allie. Nobody can smell it on your breath or anything."

"Thanks." Allie sipped the vodka, which tasted horrible, like the alcohol she put on zits. She made a face but didn't complain.

"The 5K was fun today. Your dad did a great job."

Allie blinked. "Thanks. Congratulations."

"That's why I was at your house, to get the trophy. Your dad left it upstairs."

"Oh." Allie held her breath, waiting for Sasha to say something about the fight, but Sasha was looking at her with shining eyes, wearing the coolest black sundress. Her hair flowed to her shoulders like a sheet of gold in the sunlight through the trees.

"Oh, that's right, you won, Sash. Impressive." Julian opened the newspaper. "I saw it on the TV news. You got good PR, Allie."

"It went really great," Allie lied, but it came easier with the horrible vodka.

"It was a fundraiser, right?" Julian took the gun out of the newspaper, setting it aside. "For cancer?"

"Cystic fibrosis." Allie remembered when she used to call it *sis*. She had been little then.

"I bet if I ask my dad, Browne would make a contribution."

"That's really nice of you." Allie felt a rush of gratitude. She took another drink of vodka, but it still tasted terrible. She felt less nervous. Maybe they would become friends. Sasha was being nice to her, Julian was making a contribution, and David was holding her hand. She could feel the warmth of his body beside her, and their bare knees touched as they sat side by side on the blanket.

"Drink!" Sasha held up her bottle. "Ready to play?"

"Play what, crazy?" Julian grinned.

"Spin the Bottle!" Sasha laughed.

Julian's mouth dropped open. "I didn't know that's what you had in mind."

"You should have." Sasha downed more vodka. "You guys will play, won't you?"

"Totally," David answered quickly, and Allie felt her face flush with excitement. She couldn't believe that David wanted to play Spin the Bottle with her. All three of them were looking at her like she was supposed to answer.

"Yes, but I never did it before," Allie blurted out, tipsy.

"Really?" Sasha asked, laughing, and Julian joined her.

"I haven't, either." David touched her back, and Allie felt the warmth of his hand. The sensation was almost electric, and she took another drink from the bottle, then another.

"Julian, why are you digging up the gun?" David watched Julian brush it off.

"Sasha wants it."

Sasha grinned. "Don't worry, Allie, I'm not going to kill anything. I'm not going to even shoot it. I just want to see it."

Julian laughed. "She's a gun nut now. She loves it. It turns her on."

David took another drink. "Right, whatever turns you on."

"Doesn't it turn *you* on?" Sasha held the gun, pushing a button and opening the chamber that was supposed to hold the bullets. "This is so cool. You can see how each hole is perfectly drilled, like, perfectly round, for the bullets to go in."

"It's called ballistics." Julian moved over and was digging up the bullets with a stick.

"How do you know?" David laughed. "From *Law & Order*?"

Julian smiled, digging away. "Detective Browne on the case."

"Like Encyclopedia Brown." Sasha smiled, drinking.

"Never heard that before." Julian dug the bullet box

from the hole, then set the empty bottle in the middle of the blanket. "Now everybody sit on the blanket, one on each side."

"Okay." Sasha crossed her pretty legs, but her dress came up. "Wooo!"

"Settle down, Sash." David resettled on the blanket, with Allie catty-corner to him. A soft breeze blew through the trees, and the last sunlight of the day made a moving pattern of light and dark on their beautiful faces. Or maybe the vodka made it look that way. No matter, they were the cool kids, she was hanging with them, and David Hybrinski wanted to kiss her.

"I have an idea!" Sasha picked up the gun. "Why don't we play Spin the Gun instead?"

"Spin the Gun?" Julian looked at her like she was crazy. "Woman, what's the matter with you?"

"If you don't know, you're about to find out." Sasha giggled, the boys laughed, and even Allie joined in.

Julian snorted. "A bottle spins easier than a gun."

"How do you know? Anyway, how far do you want it to go?" Sasha burst into giddy laughter, and so did the others, since everybody knew Julian wanted to kiss Sasha, who plucked the bottle off the blanket and replaced it with the gun. "Okay, who wants to go first?"

"I will!" Julian spun the gun, which got caught in the blanket, its muzzle aimed at Sasha.

"Oh, too bad!" Sasha laughed, and so did Julian and Allie.

"Do it, dude!" David called out, so Julian leaned close to Sasha, put his hand on her cheek, and started kissing her.

"Way to go!" Allie realized that was probably a dumb thing to say, but she was so excited. She was getting ready for her turn, with David.

Suddenly they heard a shout from the top of the hill, and they all looked up to see someone was coming toward them, a tall silhouette. It looked like a man, but Allie couldn't see his face because it was getting dark. Julian picked up the gun and hid it behind him.

Sasha rose, waving at the man. "Kyle, what took you so long?"

CHAPTER 30

■

Julian Browne

J ulian realized who the silhouette was because Sasha was so happy to see him. It was the new guy that Sasha had hugged at her doorstep. Julian gritted his teeth so hard his gums stung. Sasha must have invited Kyle because she wanted to play Spin the Bottle with *him*.

Sasha called out, "Kyle, hurry! You're late! We already started!"

"Started what?" Kyle called back, his voice deep. He climbed down the hill toward them.

"Our party!"

David sat straighter. "Who's this dude, Sasha?"

"He's new," Sasha answered over her shoulder. "He saved my cat. He'll be at school in September."

"He's a *hunk*," Allie blurted out.

Julian struggled to control his emotions. Kyle was just Sasha's type. A dumb jock with big shoulders, cut biceps, and swollen forearms. It was getting dim under the trees so Julian couldn't make out the guy's face, but he wasn't about to let anybody move in on Sasha. His father taught him *you have to fight to win*, and if Julian had to fight for Sasha, so be it.

"Kyle, I even brought a beverage for you!" Sasha dug her hand in her tote bag and produced another water bottle.

"A *beverage*?" Kyle called back, laughing.

"It's not water." Sasha giggled.

"I didn't think so." Kyle reached them, accepting the bottle from Sasha. "Thanks."

"Welcome to our gang. Guys, say hi to Kyle!" Sasha giggled again, and Julian couldn't believe the way she was acting.

"Kyle Gallagher." Kyle twisted open the bottle and took a swig.

"Julian Browne." Julian glanced at David, hoping he would remember their conversation at the tennis courts about Sasha's new guy. But David was smiling at Kyle, which made Julian even angrier. David could be such a jocksniffer.

"I'm David Hybrinski."

"Allie Garvey." Allie smiled.

Sasha giggled, touching Kyle's arm. "I think I drink too much. I mean, *drank*."

"I think you did, too," Julian said pointedly. "So, Kyle, what are you doing here?"

"I invited him," Sasha answered, her eyes still on Kyle.

Julian let it go. Kyle was playing the cool jock role, big easy grin, dumb look in his eyes. No way was he good enough for Sasha. "Are you new or something?"

"Yeah."

"Where are you from?"

"Ohio."

"Where in Ohio?"

"Columbus subs."

"My dad has developments there." Julian knew the nice neighborhoods. "Dublin? New Albany?"

"Julian, don't brag." Sasha shot him a look, and her body was facing Kyle's in a way Julian didn't like at all. "Kyle is my hero. He rescued Bootsy."

"Really." Julian couldn't shake the challenge from his tone and didn't want to try.

Sasha hung on Kyle's arm. "Kyle, come and sit down. We were just playing Spin the Gun."

"What?" Kyle squinted in the direction of the gun, and Julian realized that he had forgotten about it and scooted over, blocking it futilely.

Sasha laughed. "Julian, are you trying to hide the gun? Come on, put it back on the blanket."

"Wait, was that really a *gun*?" Kyle asked, incredulous. "Is it *loaded*?"

"No, of course not." Sasha giggled. "But isn't it cool? I wanted to show it to you."

"No way," Julian said, frustrated. He was losing control of the situation. "Sasha, he's not supposed to know about the gun. Kyle, forget you saw it."

"Don't be ridiculous, guys!" Sasha tugged Kyle downward and sat beside him on the blanket. "I told him about it. He saw it. You're being silly, Julian."

"I can't *unsee* it, dude." Kyle scoffed. "What are you doing with it? Where did you get it?"

"Julian found it, that's why he's freaking." Sasha's dress slipped up, showing her perfect thigh. Julian noticed Kyle looking over, too.

"I'm not freaking." Julian tried to recover.

"Are you serious?" Kyle took a swig of vodka. "You're playing Spin the Gun?"

"It works better than a bottle because it doesn't go far. Watch!" Sasha grabbed the gun, returned it to the blanket, and spun it. The muzzle got caught in the blanket and pointed at Kyle. Sasha leaned over, grabbed Kyle by his shoulders, and kissed him hard on the lips.

Julian's heart pounded in his ears. He had spent a lifetime watching Sasha but he'd never watched her making out with another guy, right in front of him.

Kyle burst into laughter as Sasha let him go. "Well, hello, Sasha!"

"Let *me* spin," David said out of the blue.

"Go for it, David!" Sasha clapped. "Who do you want to kiss? Allie or me?"

"Take a guess!" David drained his bottle, then spun the gun, but it ended up with the muzzle pointing at Julian.

Julian recoiled, putting up his hands. "Don't even think about it, dude."

David snorted. "Dude. So not happening."

"No!" Sasha waved her hands. "That's not the rules. You have to kiss whoever it lands on."

"The hell I do." David laughed.

"Damn right." Julian laughed, too.

"Julian, are you afraid to kiss David?" Sasha asked, her eyes narrowing.

"Sasha, stop it!" Julian felt hurt. Sasha had played him. "Why are you being such a bitch?"

Allie drank more vodka. "Guys, she's just joking around."

Sasha giggled. "Julian, don't get all mad. Just kiss him! It's the rules!"

Julian felt his temper give way. "Sasha, since when do you care about rules? You weren't supposed to tell anybody about the gun. You told Kyle."

"You're not mad about the gun," Sasha shot back, but Julian was too angry to stop now.

"Sasha, we don't even know this guy. We can't trust him knowing about the gun. How long have you been dating him?"

"Dating?" Sasha burst into laughter. "What are you, my *dad*?"

Julian let it go. "How long have you known him?"

"I know him."

Julian turned to Kyle. "For how long?"

"I'm not gonna tell anybody about your stupid gun," Kyle said, his tone matter-of-fact.

"How do I know that? We're all friends. We don't even know you." Julian got an idea. "If you want to hang with us, you have to prove yourself."

"I'll hang with whoever I want to hang with."

"You can't hang with us or with Sasha unless you prove yourself."

Sasha perked up. "Prove himself to me? Like how?"

Julian didn't miss a beat. "He has to do what we all did, way back when. He has to play Russian Roulette."

"Russian Roulette?" Kyle repeated in disbelief. "You guys played Russian Roulette?"

"Yes," Julian answered without hesitation. "We all did. It's the price of admission. Right, Sash?"

"Yes." Sasha started laughing, turning to Kyle. "Kyle, we played Russian Roulette to hang together, and this is where we played it. It's, like, our initiation. If you want to hang, you have to play, too. Right, David?"

David caught Julian's eye, then turned to Kyle. "He's right. We all played it. If you wanna hang, you have to."

Kyle snorted. "I don't want to hang that much."

Sasha put her hand on Kyle's arm. "Take a chance. We all took a chance. Even Allie."

Allie didn't say anything.

"Here, dude. Let's play." Julian grabbed the box of bullets, took one out, loaded the gun, and spun the barrel. "Now it's got a bullet. That's how we played. It's your turn to play."

"I don't want to." Kyle recoiled, aghast.

"Play, for Sasha." Julian thrust the gun at him. He was hoping to send a message to Sasha, that this guy wasn't good enough for her.

"No." Kyle edged away.

"Not even for me?" Sasha said, stroking his arm.

"Is this a joke?" Kyle looked at Sasha, and Julian felt his heart pound. The only way his trick worked was if Kyle *didn't* agree. The last thing Julian wanted was Kyle to prove that he liked Sasha enough to play Russian Roulette for her.

"It's no joke, dude." Julian bore down. "Make a decision."

Kyle brushed Sasha's hand away, getting to his feet. "I'm out of here. You guys are nuts."

"Pussy." Julian hid his happiness. His gamble had paid off. He had fought and won.

"You don't like me, Kyle?" Sasha pouted prettily. "I thought you did."

Kyle frowned. "It's not that, it's that I can't decide right now, on the spot—"

"Bullshit." Julian withdrew the gun. "I'll tell you what, Columbus. I'm calling your bluff. I'll let you think about it overnight. We get back together tomorrow night, all of us."

"I'll bring vodka," Sasha added.

"Right, you bring vodka," Julian repeated. "Kyle, we meet here nine o'clock tomorrow night."

Kyle shook his head. "Go to hell."

Sasha pouted. "Kyle, don't go!"

Julian rose. "Tomorrow night at nine o'clock. If you're here, you'll do it. If you won't do it, don't come."

Kyle edged away, then broke into a jog up the hill, disappearing into the darkness.

Sasha turned to Julian, angry. "Julian, you took it too far. What if he did it?"

"I knew he wouldn't. Anyway, look." Julian opened his hand, revealing a single bullet sitting in his palm, its brass casing glinting darkly in the twilight. "I palmed it. I didn't really load the gun. Still, it shows you he's a pussy."

"Oh my God!" David clapped his hands together. "Dude, you had me going! I was totally fooled!"

"Me, too!" Allie burst into nervous laughter. "That was so scary! I believed you!"

Sasha wasn't laughing. "You did that to scare him off."

Julian wasn't about to deny it. "And he got scared off, didn't he?"

"You don't know that yet." Sasha jumped to her feet, brushing off her dress. "He could still come tomorrow night."

"I doubt that."

"I don't." Sasha picked up her tote bag and yanked the blanket away angrily, unsettling them. "Tomorrow night at nine, we'll see what happens."

"Okay, we'll see, Sasha."

Sasha turned, hurrying up the hill into the darkness.

"Dude." David looked over at Julian. "What if he comes back tomorrow night?"

"He won't." Julian gave David the bullet. "Put this back in the box and bury it. I'll bury the gun the way it was. If he comes back, we'll tell him we buried it loaded with a bullet."

"Okay." David took the bullet and dropped it in the box. "You going to be here tomorrow night?"

"Yes, and so are you." Julian wrapped the gun in the newspaper. "Let's bury this thing. It's getting dark."

David went over to the empty hole, dropped the bullet box inside, and covered it with dirt.

Allie shook her head. "I don't think we should come back tomorrow night."

Julian buried the gun. "Then don't."

■

CHAPTER 31

Allie Garvey

D ad, where's Mom?" Allie asked, entering the kitchen. She felt raw and achy from the vodka last night, having her first hangover. Her head hurt, and her stomach felt queasy. She didn't understand where her mother was because her parents' bedroom was empty.

"Come, sit down. I was waiting for you to get up." Her father sat hunched over at the kitchen table next to a cup of black coffee and the thick roll of the Sunday newspaper, still in its plastic cover. He would normally have read it from front to back by now. He was unusually dressed up on a Sunday morning, even for him, in his pressed white shirt and khaki pants.

"But where is she?" Allie didn't want to sit down. She didn't like the look on his face. He looked very grave, like he used to with Jill when something was really wrong. His forehead wrinkled, and there were dark circles under his eyes.

"Mom's in the hospital. I was about to go visit her. I'll be gone most of the day and evening."

"She stayed overnight? Why?" Allie had so many questions she didn't know where to start. She tried not to get upset because that was the last thing her father needed. She'd learned that from the years with Jill. Allie was supposed to not ask questions, not talk back, not act out, and not be. Just *not*. Her parents would say, *Allie, could you just not?* But this was too much.

"She's in the psychiatric wing at Bryn Mawr Hospital."

"Dad, you mean, she's in, like, a *mental hospital*?" Allie felt so shocked, she couldn't even process it. She'd known her mother was depressed, but she hadn't thought she was *that* depressed. It terrified her to think of her mother in a mental hospital. Allie didn't know anything about mental hospitals. Except *One Flew Over the Cuckoo's Nest*. They had to read the book for summer reading last year, and she'd seen the movie, too. It scared her out of her wits. They did electroshock on Jack Nicholson and he turned into a zombie. Allie felt terrified for her mother. Nurse Ratched was so mean to the mental patients. Now Allie's mother was one.

"It's not a mental hospital, exactly. It's the psychiatric department of a regular hospital—"

"But, Dad, why does she need to be in a *mental hospital* overnight? What's the matter with her? Is she crazy? Does that mean she's *crazy*?"

"No, she's depressed." Her father blinked, pursing his lips. "She's clinically depressed."

"What's the difference between depressed and clinically depressed?" Allie didn't understand. Maybe *clinically depressed* meant you went to a clinic, like a mental hospital. "Does that mean she's crazy? Are they going to give her electroshock? They're not going to do that to her, are they? Please don't let them do that to her. You know that movie—"

"Allie, it's not like in the movies, and don't get ahead of yourself. They're going to do what they need to do, and—"

"When's she coming home?"

"She's going to be there for a while—"

"*What?* Why? How long?"

"Honey, please stop interrupting me. The doctors don't know. Maybe a month or two. It's open-ended."

"Dad, no! The *whole summer?*" Allie felt her gut twist for herself, and for her mother. She flashed on the fight yesterday between her father and Aunt Fran. "Does that mean Aunt Fran was right about Mom? Was she right, Dad?"

"We don't need to get into that."

"But I don't get it. I don't understand. How did Mom go from depressed to *crazy?* Why does she need to be in a mental hospital for *the whole summer?* Was Aunt Fran right?"

"I thought we could take care of her at home." Her father frowned deeply. "I thought we could handle it ourselves."

"But she was sick enough that the doctors are keeping her! They *committed her* to a mental hospital, is that what you're saying?"

"They didn't *commit* her, per se, and we gave it a try at home, but I guess it didn't work. I thought the 5K would help her. She was looking forward to it."

"Dad, that's not true. She hated the 5K." Allie didn't know if he was lying to her or to himself, but either way, she couldn't believe it had come to this, that her mother was in a mental hospital.

"She wanted to go when it was in the planning stages—"

"Maybe before, but when she was there, she hated every minute. I *told* you she wanted to go home, but you didn't take her." Allie felt tears coming to her eyes, afraid that her mother might never come out of the mental hospital, that she might lose her mind completely. "She only went to the 5K to make you happy. Because you made a big thing over it, and you made it about Jill. She *had* to go or it would've looked weird. It would've embarrassed you and our family."

"I thought it would do her good. I thought she would get better with time. I thought she *was* getting better." Her father looked up at her directly, his eyebrows sloping down behind his glasses, and Allie could see he was upset, but she was starting to lose control.

"Dad, she wasn't getting better, and even I knew that, even I could see that! I told you that, that she was depressed, and now look what happened! She was worse than I thought, and Fran was right, Dad! She was *right*!" Allie felt tears spilling from her eyes, beginning to cry. "And now Mom is so sick that they made her stay."

"I thought I was doing right by her, and I did get her to a therapist, and I got her the medication she needed."

"But she was sicker than that, Dad!" Allie blurted out between sobs. "How did Aunt Fran know and you didn't?"

"Fran comes in from the outside." Her father rose, still frowning but oddly shaky, resting his fingers on the table. "Fran didn't see her day to day, like I did, and I didn't notice how bad she was—"

"You didn't *notice*, and now Mom's crazy?" Allie blamed her father, but she realized she was at fault, too. "I should have done something! I should've made you take her to the therapist or something. Whatever needed to be done! I should've made you do it or done it myself, like Aunt Fran did!"

"You can't do that, honey, that's not your job. You're a kid."

"I'm not a kid . . . I'm a teenager!"

"You're not an adult."

"So *what*?" Allie shouted back, crying full bore. Her nose filled with mucus, congested. "What difference does that make . . . whose job it is? You're the adult, but you didn't do . . . the adult job! Sometimes the kid has to do the adult job!"

"No, no, no, that's not right!"

"I should've found a way . . . to take her home myself! The 5K put her over the top, Dad!"

"Enough!" her father shouted, throwing up his hands. His face turned red, and the veins in his neck bulged.

"What do you want me to say, honey? I'm sorry? Okay, I'm sorry. I'm sorry, I'm sorry, I'm sorry! I'm out of sorrys, okay? I can't always make it better. I can't always make everything better!"

"Could you not make it *worse*?" Allie shouted at him through her tears, then rushed out of the kitchen and ran upstairs to her bedroom.

■

CHAPTER 32

Julian Browne

Julian pushed his banana pancake around in the syrup. Sasha wasn't answering his IM and he'd called her twice, but the housekeeper had told him she was out, which she wasn't. She was in her bedroom but she must be mad at him, after last night. All he'd done was show her the truth, which was that Kyle was totally lame.

"You're not hungry?" His mother sipped her coffee, peering over the rim of the cup. She had on her bathrobe and wacky reading glasses, so she looked like a hippie professor.

"I'm full." Julian forced a smile, since she had made his favorite pancakes.

"I hate that I have to be gone all afternoon. What are you going to do?"

"Swim, play tennis." *Call Sasha.*

"Tonight is bridge night. I tried to get them to move it, but you know how that is. A foursome."

"It's okay, I might be doing something with Sasha or David."

"Good, just be home by eleven." His mother returned her attention to the Sunday paper, spread out on the table between them. "Well, this is interesting."

"What?" Julian asked, but he didn't really care. She was always pointing out Dear Abby columns about divorce and children and ex-husbands, like mom propaganda.

"Hmm, I think this person lives in the development."

"What person?"

"It's a woman who's living under an assumed name, or her maiden name. Her ex-husband was a doctor who went to jail for fondling little girls, his own patients. Can you imagine?"

"No," Julian answered idly, wondering if he'd over-played his hand last night.

"What's the matter with people? His name is Hammond, but they call him 'Dr. Dirtbag.' His wife turned him in to the police, then moved here from Columbus, Ohio. *Here*, on Paso Fino. Yikes. I doubt your father will like that very much."

"Right." Julian half-listened, wondering if he'd ever get Sasha on the boat now.

"She has a son your age, too. He's going to the high school in the fall. What a shame." His mother clucked. "His name is Kyle."

"What, a new kid named Kyle? From Columbus?" Julian got up to see the newspaper.

CHAPTER 33

■

Sasha Barrow

Sasha checked her Buddy List, but Kyle still wasn't online. His screen name, Buckeyezzz716, was grayed-out at the bottom of the list.

"Sasha, telephone!" Bonnie called her, from the base of the stairwell. "It's Julian!"

"Tell him I'm still out!"

"He's been calling! He says it's an emergency!"

"Okay," Sasha called back, rolling her eyes. She had punished him long enough. She picked up the phone. "I'm so mad at you for what you did to Kyle."

"You're about to thank me."

"What do you mean? I would *never* thank you."

"Sash, he's not who he says he is. Did you see the newspaper today?"

"What are you talking about?"

"Whatever Kyle told you about himself, it's a lie. He's

not who he said he is. His father was a doctor, and he's in jail for molesting little girls. His patients."

"What?" Sasha didn't believe him. "Julian, you're making this up."

"No, I'm not. Look online. You can read it for yourself. He's not only a loser, he's a lowlife. Whatever he told you was a lie."

"Come on."

"I'm not kidding, it's real. My mom checked at the office. He uses a fake last name. His real last name is Hammond."

"Hold on." Sasha logged on to the Internet, searched *Dr. Dirtbag*, and skimmed for details that Kyle had told her about the night she'd met him. New Albany was his old high school, and he'd played basketball there. One article had a photo of Kyle Hammond, and it was a picture of him, Kyle Gallagher. "Oh my God! You're right."

"I told you. He's a jerk, a loser, a liar. His father's in jail. He played you."

"He didn't *play* me," Sasha shot back, embarrassed. She'd never been played by a boy. She *played* boys. "I want to get him back. How can I get him back?"

"Go tonight. Hope he comes. We'll prank him."

"Totally. We'll prank the *shit* out of him."

CHAPTER 34

David Hybrinski

Hey, Mom," David said, coming into the kitchen where his mother was cleaning up after breakfast. He'd missed it on purpose. He couldn't stop thinking about what his father had called him. He had taken Allie's hand as an experiment, but he wasn't attracted to her. It had kept him up all night, but he had to admit, the only person he had been attracted to last night was the new kid. Kyle Gallagher.

"What's up?" His mother rinsed a dish and loaded it in the dishwasher.

"What's the matter with Dad?"

"Nothing."

David didn't know if she knew about the money trouble. "He seems like he's in a bad mood."

"Not really." His mother rinsed another dish, quickly. She had to get the twins ready to go. They had an away softball game today, and she already had her brown uniform on. The insulated cooler sat open on the island, the top unzipped.

"Mom, something's going on with him, I can tell."

"He's fine." His mother closed the dishwasher door and headed to the refrigerator, opening it. She never stopped moving, and David wondered if all moms were blurs.

"He wants to take me and Julian to a ball game. He's never done that before."

"That's nice." His mother got water bottles from the fridge, and they reminded David of last night. The vodka. Kyle. Maybe David only *thought* he was attracted to him because of the alcohol. Maybe David wasn't a faggot. Kyle had made eye contact with him, more than once. Maybe Kyle was a faggot. David felt confused and angry.

"Mom, Julian told me that Dad asked his father for a loan. Do you know if that's true? Did he tell you that?"

"What?" His mother's face fell. "I don't think this should be your concern."

"But it is, because Julian's my best friend. He told me. What do you want me to do?"

"I want you not to worry about it. It's our concern."

"Mom, I'm fifteen."

"That's my point. You're only fifteen."

"Just tell me."

His mother glanced toward the door, as if somebody were listening, but nobody else was home and the twins hadn't come downstairs yet. "Julian's father has agreed not to charge your father rent for three months, then we're going to take it from there."

"How much is the rent?"

"That's *not* your concern." His mother met his eye, giving him one of her teacher looks.

"Mom, don't you think I have a right to know? Julian is my best friend—"

"I know that, and we're friends of the family."

"You're only friends of the family because of me. You know the Brownes through me."

"What are you talking about?" His mother waved him off. "That's how we know everybody. Our friends are all from you kids. That's how it works."

"But it makes it weird between him and me. It's like I owe him something. Like he's my boss now or something."

"Don't be ridiculous."

"How am I supposed to act with Julian?"

"Be nice to your best friend, like you would anyway."

"But what if I wouldn't be?" David was thinking about last night, when Julian had pulled that prank with the gun. It wasn't funny, and now Julian wanted to keep it going tonight. Plus it was at Kyle's expense. And David didn't know how he felt about Kyle.

"David, you'll understand when you get older." His mother zipped the cooler closed. "You don't know the pressure Dad is under, and the money doesn't mean anything to Julian's father. He didn't mind it at all. Three months' rent is nothing to Scott Browne. He has developments all over Pennsylvania. You think he cares about the rent on Hybrinski Optical? And it means so much to us."

"What does it mean? Why do we need it?"

"That's not your business." His mother snatched

napkins out of the holder, and it fell over. "We wouldn't have asked if it weren't necessary."

"How necessary?"

"You think you're old enough to know, then *act* old enough to know. We could lose the house. *This* house. *Our home.*"

David's mouth went dry. He hadn't realized it was that bad.

"That's right. It's not your father's fault, it's the economy. It's the chain stores and the mall, and people lose their houses every day. We couldn't get another mortgage, not with the way the business is, so we couldn't even stay in the school district. You like your house? You like your school? You like your friends? You want things to stay the way they are?"

"Yes," David answered, since she was glaring at him, waiting for an answer.

"To get what you want, you do what you have to do. Did your father want to ask Scott Browne to forgive the rent? No, he did not. He's a proud man. We're doing what's right for this family." His mother stopped when she heard the twins bumping down the stairs, then she stepped closer to David. "All you have to do is be nice to your best friend. Will you do that, for your family?"

The phone rang on the wall, and his mother lifted the receiver from its cradle. "Hello? Hi, Julian. Hold on, he's right here."

CHAPTER 35

∎

Kyle Gallagher

Kyle kept his head down as he walked Buddy, hiding his face. He felt the worst he'd felt in his entire life. The interview with his father had been in the newspaper this morning, and his emotions were all over the place. He let Buddy sniff a tree, and the old lady neighbor watched him from her window.

He turned away, feeling people's eyes on him, whether they were or not. Everybody on their street got the newspaper, and they would all know his story, sooner or later. His mother had spent the morning crying, finally taking the phone off the hook because so many reporters were calling. They'd figured out the last name was bogus. Sharon stayed over to keep her company and talk her out of moving again.

Kyle quickened his pace when he reached the corner. Neighbors were emerging, pulling into the driveway after church or heading out for errands. He kept moving, tugging Buddy along, out of the neighborhood, away from where the houses were close together. Ordinarily he would've gone to the left, heading for the fancy houses like Sasha's, but now he turned right. He'd seen her AIM messages asking him if he was angry at her, so she must not have read the newspaper yet. He'd been so weirded out by her friends trying to get him to play Russian Roulette, but he knew it had been a joke. They weren't the type of kids who played Russian Roulette.

He broke into a jog, and Buddy trotted along, panting. Kyle felt himself running quicker, away from the neighbors, the news story, his mother and Sharon. He caught sight of the basketball courts and hustled toward them. They were empty, and he could just be by himself, alone with his thoughts. He had to get his head right. He kept trying to, but he couldn't. He felt so disgusted and furious at his father.

Kyle ran and ran, almost at the courts. He flashed on how many times he had heard his mother cry at night, how many phone calls with Sharon, how many phone calls with the lawyers. He'd watched her get sadder even as she said she was getting stronger. She never complained about what she was going through, only what Kyle was going through.

He beelined for the courts, heading off the sidewalk and onto the grassy border. She was the best mom anybody could ask for, and no matter what Kyle did, he could never get her to stop worrying about him, and he was realizing more and more that *he* himself was the problem, that he was a burden to her, that she could get through anything if she didn't have to worry about him.

His chest heaved, his thighs burned. He could never outrun anything that had happened. No matter how hard he tried, no matter what he told his mother, she'd always worry about him, and when she'd asked him if his father had ever touched him, Kyle had lied. He had lied to the therapists and the lawyers from the court, too. He'd told them all that his father had never done anything to him when he was little.

But that hadn't been the truth. Kyle remembered that his father had. They were memories, but they were real. Kyle had been little, but he knew what his father had done. He tried not to remember, but he couldn't help it. The thoughts kept coming back, and Kyle would sneak a drink from the bottle he hid by the recycling. It had helped him sleep. It had helped him keep the memories away.

Kyle reached the trees around the basketball courts. He found himself falling to his knees. His hands covered his face. His knees hit hard dirt. His forehead buried in pine needles. Buddy came over panting hard, his tail wagging.

Kyle started to cry, his body wracked with hoarse, choking sobs.

He had lied, but he couldn't forget.

Ever.

■

CHAPTER 36

Allie Garvey

The sun sank behind the houses and trees, painting the twilight sky a weirdly hot pink. Allie spotted David waiting for her at the head of the trail, and it made her forget about everything else. He looked so tall and strong, wearing a white polo shirt and gym shorts with slides, and no red bandanna. His hair was tucked behind his ears. She couldn't believe that a boy like David liked her. She felt lost, confused, and alone, except when she was next to him. She hoped he'd hold her hand again and try to kiss her. She felt her lips almost tingling.

"Hi." Allie reached him, and David took her hand, the way she'd hoped. Her stress floated away as soon as he wrapped his palm around hers. She'd never liked any boy as much as she liked him. She didn't know how you knew for sure, but she had to believe this was her first love.

"Hey, you." David grinned crookedly, and they held

hands as they walked together into the woods. "Like your dress."

I even love his voice. "Thanks. Sorry I'm late."

"No worries. Glad you decided to come."

"I wanted to see you," Allie heard herself say with a giggle. She didn't even know where that had come from. Beside him, she felt like she was on a cloud.

"Hey, now." David grinned again.

"I wish they wouldn't play the prank, though."

"Don't worry about it. I doubt very much that Kyle will come."

"I hope he doesn't."

"Sasha's not as hot as she thinks." David lowered his voice like he was confiding in her, which gave Allie a thrill.

"You don't think so?"

"No."

"I don't think Kyle will come, either." Allie squeezed David's hand, telling herself to go with the flow. It felt so good to forget everything at home. She could swear her lips were tingling. She pressed them together.

"Where'd you tell your parents you were going?"

"Um, my dad's out," Allie answered, faltering. She didn't want to think about her father right now. She didn't want to think about her parents at all. "How about you?"

"Julian's." David moved a branch aside for her, and Allie spotted the bent tree ahead. It was dark underneath, and its leaves blocked what was left of the daylight. Julian's white polo shirt and Sasha's blond hair made bright spots in the dimness. They were sitting together, drinking.

"Kyle's not there," Allie said, relieved. Now she didn't have to worry. She could focus on David. She couldn't wait to make out with him. She felt so sexy and pretty and flirty. She didn't feel like herself at all.

"See, I told you." David smiled at her, and they approached the bent tree together.

"Just in time!" Sasha rose, hoisting two large Evian bottles full of red liquid. "Gatorade and vodka, coming right up! Liter bottles!" She thrust a bottle at Allie. "Here, Allie, have some fun for a change."

"Don't mind if I do!" Allie grabbed the heavy bottle, tilted it back, and chugged the alcohol. It tasted sweeter, but she didn't care. She knew she shouldn't drink, but she didn't care about that, either.

"Whoa, somebody wants to party!" Sasha cheered. "You go, girl!"

Allie drank another big gulp, then another. She felt the lukewarm alcohol rushing down her throat. She swallowed it as fast as she could. She wanted to get wasted. She wanted to get *trashed*.

"Allie?" David said, laughing. "Slow down, girl. Leave some for me."

"Do it!" Sasha clapped. "Go, go, go, Allie."

"Chug!" Julian joined in, clapping.

"Woo-hoo!" Allie stopped drinking, swallowing her last gulp. She'd downed a full third and hoisted the bottle high, showing off. "Ta-da!"

"Way to go!" Sasha grinned, a pretty white smile in the murky gloom under the tree.

"My turn." David reached for the bottle.

"Go for it." Allie passed it to him, sitting down.

"Come here, you." David sat down with the bottle and put his long arm around Allie. Her whole left side touched his body, and she felt something she'd never felt before. *Chosen*. David had *chosen* her over everyone, even Sasha. He wanted to be with her. He wanted to kiss her. She slid her arm around his waist, hugging him close, as if they'd been together forever.

"This is so great," Allie heard herself say, and David chuckled, a deep sound that she could hear resonate in his chest.

"You're easy to please."

"Obviously, if she's with you." Julian laughed, leaning back on his elbow.

Sasha sat down beside Julian, drinking. "I think they make a nice couple."

Allie loved the sound of that, feeling loose enough to speak her mind. "I'm glad Kyle's not coming. I'm glad we're not pranking him."

"I'm not. He's been pranking *us*." Julian sat up, newly animated. "Didn't you see the news? Kyle isn't who he says he is. His father is a child molester, in prison for molesting his own patients. Little girls. *Babies*."

"Are you kidding?" David took another swig from the bottle and passed it to Allie, who accepted it and took a slug.

Julian was saying, "Dude, for real. Gallagher isn't even his real last name. It's Hammond."

Allie only half-listened. She didn't care what they were talking about. She took another big gulp, then another. She wanted this buzz to last forever. She wanted to make out with David. She wanted to do whatever he wanted.

"I swear, it's true." Julian snorted. "He's using an alias to hide his real identity. He's a poser and now he's busted. My mom can't even believe they got into Brandywine Hunt. My dad will be *so* pissed."

"Are you joking?" David leaned over, and Allie took another swig, then passed him the bottle and resettled her arms around him. He had an amazing body, a trim waist with no fat and real abs. She could feel how strong his back was under his shirt. She realized for the first time that backs were unbelievably sexy. She held him tight.

"It's disgusting." Sasha shook her head, holding her bottle. "He's a disgusting liar, and his father is a pervert. He molested little girls in the hospital. Does it get worse than that? Gross!"

Allie didn't pay attention, her brain fuzzed. She felt so relaxed and so good, warm against David, whose hand moved to stroke the bare skin of her thigh. His tennis calluses felt cool and manly, and it made her tingle all over. She wondered when they were going to start making out. She waited for him to kiss her.

David chuckled. "I thought *my* father was bad."

"Same here!" Julian burst into rueful laughter.

"That's nothing," Allie heard herself say, but she

didn't want to think about her father now. She couldn't think straight anyway. "My father's worst of all."

Sasha waved them off. "At least you *see* your parents. I'm never in the same time zone as mine." She raised her bottle in a mock toast. "To Bonnie and Clyde, the mom and dad who Mom and Dad bought me."

Suddenly David lowered his face to Allie's, and his mouth was on her lips. She felt herself tilt her head back, not knowing how to kiss him because she'd never really kissed a boy, but she let it happen. His mouth was so soft and warm, and she felt his tongue flickering inside her mouth. She kissed him back, let her body do what came naturally. She breathed in his smell of spicy cologne, excited that he had put it on for her.

His hand slid up her thigh and under the hem of her dress. She didn't stop him because she wanted it, too. She wanted to lose herself in this feeling, forgetting everything else. Nothing mattered but him and her. She felt like she was melting under his weight and warmth, and she loved being kissed and held by him. Happiness spread throughout her entire body.

Julian was making out with Sasha, lying on top of her on the ground, and Allie started to feel water dropping on her. She looked up from David's arms, and all she could see was his handsome face, in front of inky branches swirling like shadowy spin art. A drop of water splashed on her cheek.

"Is it . . . *raining*?" Allie murmured, too buzzed to tell.

"Only drizzling. I'll cover you." David kissed her

again, and Allie kissed him back, letting herself go, sur-
rendering to the feeling. His hands were everywhere, up
her dress and on her breasts, and Allie loved all of the
sensations. She didn't know how long they made out for,
only that it was a long time, but still not long enough
because she never wanted it to stop, ever, ever, ever. She
became aware that someone was calling to them, and
that Sasha and Julian were talking.

David broke off their kiss and looked up. Allie looked
over in a fog, but it was too dark to see much. She didn't
care anyway. She wanted to keep making out. She clung
to David. They were boyfriend and girlfriend now. They
were together.

"It's *on*, David," Julian whispered. "Act like you don't
know about his dad."

Sasha stood up, waving. "Kyle, I'm waiting for you!"

■

CHAPTER 37

Allie Garvey

Hey!" Kyle came down the hill, a tall, dark figure in a light T-shirt. He was with a yellow dog, wagging its tail.

"Kyle, what kept you?" Sasha called to him. "You're super late!"

"So what?" Kyle called back, laughing.

"Son, have you been drinking?" Sasha put her hands on her hips, like she was angry.

"Totally!" Kyle reached Sasha, and Sasha gave him a big hug.

"Hi, Kyle!" David called out, shifting away from Allie.

"Kyle, you don't have to . . ." Allie said, but she couldn't finish the sentence. She felt so dizzy, she couldn't even hold her head up. She couldn't think, numb and wasted. She was totally trashed, just like she'd wanted to be.

"Whoa, Sasha?" David said, laughing, and Allie

looked over to see that Sasha was kissing Kyle now, not Julian.

Julian flicked on a flashlight and shone it on Sasha and Kyle. "He has to play the game, remember?" His tone darkened. "We played the game, now he has to."

"I'm not playing your stupid game, dude." Kyle let go of Sasha, his eyes narrowing. "Get that light outta my face."

Julian moved the flashlight. "Sasha, tell him he has to play. That was the deal."

"Oh, right. You have to play, Kyle." Sasha let Kyle go, sitting down, and Kyle eased down next to her. The dog nestled beside him, chewing a stick.

"Kyle," Allie started to say, but her head rolled off to the side. She clung to David. Her thoughts kept sliding sideways. Her mouth felt soft and fuzzy. She could barely keep her eyes open.

David clapped. "Julian's right. You have to play, Kyle. We played, so you have to play."

"We left the bullet in yesterday." Julian passed the gun to Kyle. "Take it and spin the cylinder, but don't look at it. That's how you play."

"Whatever, dude, I know this is a joke. I know it's not loaded." Kyle took the gun, spun the cylinder, and closed it, rolling his eyes. He put the gun to his temple and squeezed the trigger.

Orange flame burst from the gun. The sound was loud as an explosion. Kyle slumped over sideways, his head misshapen and dark. His hair and T-shirt were drenched with blood. His body lay perfectly still, a gruesome, motionless shadow. The dog sprang aside, barking.

Allie screamed in horror.

Everything happened at once. David grabbed Allie by the wrist. He yanked her to her feet. She kept screaming. She could barely stand. David was yelling but suddenly Allie couldn't hear anything. She reeled, almost falling.

Someone picked up the flashlight, maybe Julian. Someone picked up the bottles, maybe David. They were shadows. Allie couldn't see. Her eyes blurred with tears. She didn't know what was happening.

Sasha was crying, too, covering her mouth. Julian grabbed Sasha, pulling her to him. The dog barked at Kyle.

David pulled Allie away. They ran crashing through the woods. Allie burst into tears.

Julian took the lead. Allie began to be able to hear again, faintly. Somebody was saying *oh my God, oh my God* over and over. It was her. Tears streamed down her cheeks. She felt sick to her stomach. David kept her running.

Julian charged ahead but Sasha passed him, bolting between trees. David pulled Allie forward, faster than she could go, his legs longer, his stride wider. Branches and leaves scratched her arms and legs. Rain fell harder, splashing cold on her head and bare shoulders.

"Hurry, Allie!" David said. "Run!"

Julian's chest heaved. "I got the flashlight!"

"I got the bottles!" David panted. "Everybody go home! Don't tell anybody!"

"Right!" Julian called out, frantic. "Go, go, go!"

Allie ran breathless, crying, horrified. "Call 911—"

"No, he's dead!" Sasha spat out, edging away. "Go home!"

Julian darted ahead. "Go to your room, don't say anything! Don't tell anybody! Don't *say anything*!"

Sasha ran off through the woods.

"David, bro!" Julian clapped David on the shoulder. "Get rid of the bottles!"

"I will!" David squeezed Allie's hand. "Allie, go home! Don't tell anyone!"

Allie sobbed, her chest heaving. They were almost out of the woods. The rain fell even harder. She slipped in mud and almost fell.

David took off, dragging Allie, who cried all the way.

CHAPTER 38

Barb Gallagher

I'm worried." Barb glanced at the clock on the stove. It was almost eleven, and Kyle had gone out around nine. She was sitting with Sharon in the kitchen. Barb sipped her coffee, which had gone cold. "He should've been home by now."

"He's out with the dog."

"Where, for so long? And it's raining." Barb frowned, looking out the window.

"I tell you, he's probably waiting it out. It came on quick."

"But this is the longest he's ever been out." Barb got her mug from the table, took it to the sink, and rinsed it. "What if something happened?"

"What could happen in a development?"

Barb didn't have an immediate reply. She crossed to the refrigerator and opened the door, staring at the contents without really seeing anything. It was what Kyle would have done if he was home. That boy was either eating or deciding what to eat. "You hungry?"

"We just had Chips Ahoy."

Barb closed the refrigerator door.

"Maybe he's with that girl, the one with the cat. Sasha . . . Barrow?"

"After the news about his father today?" Barb didn't think so. "And he said he was going for a walk."

"So he lied."

"He doesn't really lie."

"Doesn't *really* lie?"

"Well, he never has. I really don't think he has." Barb met her best friend's eye, uneasy. Sharon knew Kyle almost as well as Barb did. She was his godmother. "And Buddy doesn't like cats."

"We teased him about her. Maybe it embarrassed him, so he didn't want to tell us." Sharon frowned, looking out the window. "I bet he's waiting it out. Typical summer shower, comes and goes fast."

Barb opened the base cabinet, tugged out the thick phone book, and thumbed to the B's. She ran her fingernail down the names until she found Roger Barrow on Pinto Road. "I think I'll call."

"If he's there, he'll kill you."

"Only after I kill him." Barb picked up the receiver, pressed in the number, and waited for an answer.

"Barrow residence," a woman said stiffly.

"Hi, my name is Barb Gallagher, and my son, Kyle, is a friend of Sasha's. He brought your cat home Friday?"

"Oh yes, hello."

"Are you Sasha's mom?" Barb couldn't tell from the woman's voice if she'd read the news story, but she was keeping a civil tone.

"No, I'm Bonnie, the housekeeper."

"I'm calling because Kyle's not home, and I wonder if he's with Sasha."

"No, he's not here."

"Is Sasha there?"

Bonnie paused. "Yes."

"Do you think I could speak to her? I'd like to know if she has some idea where Kyle might be."

"Sorry, I believe she's gone to bed."

"Can you check?" Barb didn't know any teenager in bed at eleven o'clock. "It would put my mind at ease."

"I'm sure she's gone to bed." Bonnie's tone sounded final, but Barb wasn't taking no for an answer.

"Well, if I can't find my son, I'll call back or maybe stop in. I see you live on Pinto."

Bonnie paused. "I'd rather you didn't. It's late."

"Then can you ask her? Please, I'm just a worried mother." Barbara hoped the housekeeper could relate. "Do you have children, Bonnie?"

"Hang on, and I'll see if Sasha is awake." Bonnie set the phone down with a *clunk*.

Barb covered the receiver with her hand. "Sharon, am I being too annoying?"

"No, you're the perfect amount of annoying. Who's Bonnie?"

"The housekeeper."

"She must live in." Sharon put her index finger to her

nose and turned it up. Barb uncovered the receiver when she heard Bonnie get back on the line.

"Ms. Gallagher, Sasha has no idea where Kyle is. She hasn't seen him since he brought the cat home."

"Okay, thank you. I appreciate it, good night." Barb hung up, her heart sinking. "So much for that. He could be at the basketball courts. Maybe he went back down there. He could be waiting for the rain to pass." Barb opened the refrigerator door. "I should go look for him."

"Okay, I'll go with." Sharon rose. "It'll do us good to get out."

Barb couldn't shake the feeling that something had gone wrong. "You know, it just sucks."

"What does?"

"Everything." Barb hung on the refrigerator handle. "I never could've guessed that my husband was doing—"

"Of course you couldn't, he hid it from you, and we've been over that."

"But it proves that *anything* can happen. Really, the strangest things really *do* happen. Do you know what I mean? I'm speaking from experience because it did happen to me, and to Kyle. It ruined our lives."

"Only if you let it."

"I'm trying not to, but my ex is the gift that keeps on giving. We were doing great until this happened. Well, maybe not great." Barb hesitated. "You know, I think Kyle might be drinking."

"How do you know?"

"I smell it on him from time to time, after his walks. I asked him once. He said no."

Sharon frowned. "Where does he get it?"

"I don't know. I only keep wine in the house now. I never leave an open bottle anymore."

"Don't sweat it. I told you I caught Susie last month with a flask. Can you believe that, a *flask*, of all things?"

Barb closed the fridge door. "Let's go."

■

CHAPTER 39

Allie Garvey

Allie lay in bed, a soggy mess. Her head thundered, her mouth tasted terrible. Her nose was clogged, and used Kleenexes lay crumpled around her. She looked at the clock beside the bed and realized it wasn't her Westclox. It was Jill's clock. She was in Jill's bedroom. She must've stumbled in by mistake. She hadn't been in here since Jill died.

Allie looked around the darkness. She tried to think through the fog in her brain. Tears spilled from her eyes, and she reached for Kleenex. She couldn't believe that Kyle was dead. The gun wasn't supposed to be loaded. It was supposed to be a prank. Somebody must have loaded it. She guessed it was Julian. She told herself that it was a nightmare, because that was how it felt, but it wasn't. Kyle was dead. She had seen him *shoot himself.*

Suddenly she heard the sounds of her father coming home. The front door opening and closing, the jingle of his car keys in the bowl. She hadn't heard his car because Jill's room was in the back of the house. And there was no talking so it sounded like he was alone. Which meant her mom was still at the hospital.

Allie didn't know whether to stay here or to run back to her own room. She started to get up, but felt like she might throw up. She turned her back to the door, pretending to be asleep. She heard her father's steps on the stairwell. She fought the impulse to go to him, bury herself in his arms, and tell him everything. Maybe they could still help Kyle, her father would know what to do, he was sort of a doctor. Maybe there was a chance to go back to when the worst thing that happened was they hadn't cured cystic fibrosis.

Allie curled into a ball and covered her mouth so as not to cry. Her thoughts flew through her brain, charged with panic. She couldn't tell her father about Kyle. David had told her not to. They had all agreed not to. They would get in trouble. They'd handed Kyle the gun. They'd told her it wasn't loaded. Her fingerprints were on the gun. All of their fingerprints were. They would get caught. They would go to jail. They were *murderers*.

Allie tried to calm herself. Her father was coming down the hall. She couldn't tell him. He couldn't take another bad thing happening. He might have a nervous breakdown, too. She had to keep it inside. She had to act normal. She lay still.

"Honey, are you in *here*?" Her father opened the door. "Are you awake?"

"Yes," Allie answered, after a moment.

"Are you okay?" Her father was walking over, his footsteps creaking on the floor.

"Uh, yes." Allie pressed her lips together not to say anything more, not to tell.

"This was a tough day. I know you miss Jill. We all do." Her father patted her shoulder.

Allie's eyes filled with tears. She squeezed them shut.

"Your sister wouldn't want you to be sad, you know. She'd want you to think of the happy times we had together. She always looked on the bright side, didn't she? And next year, the 5K will be better. We'll grow it as a tribute to her."

Allie couldn't speak or she would tell him everything. She had to keep it inside.

"So, anyway, Mom's going to stay at the hospital a while longer. But don't worry, everything's going to be all right. We'll be fine. We Garveys are made of sterner stuff." Her father leaned over and gave her a kiss on the cheek. "Love you."

"Love you, too." Allie tried not to cry. She wasn't made of sterner stuff. If she was, she would have stood up to the others. She would have told them not to play the prank. She would have stopped them. She would have told Kyle. Kyle would still be alive.

Allie was struck by a wave of guilt so deep she almost burst into tears. Julian must have been the murderer. Or maybe Sasha was, since she'd been so mad at Kyle. David would never do such a thing, but even so they were all guilty. She wanted to tell her father, but she had to keep it inside. She pressed her lips together, tight as a seal.

Jill's mouth had looked like that at the viewing. Her lips had been stuck together, with wax. Allie had looked close, in horror.

"You'll feel better in the morning, honey. Good night."

Allie nodded because she couldn't speak. She knew she wouldn't feel better in the morning. She knew she wouldn't feel better, ever.

■

CHAPTER 40

David Hybrinski

David sagged against the tile wall, crying in the shower. Hot water lashed onto his back, but he didn't make it cooler. He'd been shaking since he hit the house, his knees weak. He'd hurried straight up the stairs, calling to his mother that he'd gotten caught in the rain, and she'd called back *okay*, with the twins in the family room. He'd raced to his room and jumped in the shower.

He folded over, his face in his hands, almost squatting, trying to erase every single image from his head at the same moment that he tried to remember, tried to understand, tried to process what happened. Kyle was dead. David had seen it. It happened right in front of him. Kyle had put the gun to his temple. There was an explosion. Smoke. Blood.

David had seen Kyle's face go completely slack, his features edged in the shadow from the flashlight. David thought he had seen that much but maybe he hadn't. It was dark. Maybe he imagined it, he didn't know, but whatever he had seen was gruesome and he could swear he had smelled *brains*.

David covered his face, pressing his finger pads into his eyes, trying not to see. He thought of gouging his own eyes out, but the scene was in his mind's eye, so even that wouldn't help. Kyle falling over, dead. It was impossible. It hadn't happened. But David could smell the smoke clinging to his hair. He reached for the knob with trembling hands and made it hotter, feeling the temperature rise, the water whipping his back. He deserved it. All of it.

David felt terrified to think of what would happen next. The police would come knocking at the door, and they would all be arrested. They would go to jail for murder, they would get caught. He remembered Julian asking him to throw away the bottles, and he had seen the Guptas' green recycling bin and tossed the bottles in. He realized they would have his fingerprints on them, and he didn't know if the police would check the fingerprints, and his fingerprints would be on the gun, and they were all going to jail now that Kyle was dead, and they deserved whatever punishment they got. David thought of what his parents would say, how heartbroken his mother would be, and Jason, and the twins, and his father would beat him to death.

Faggot.

He cried harder, knowing now it was true, because he remembered Kyle coming down the hill to see them, the sound of his voice, the way he walked, and he had a white shirt on, or maybe it was yellow, David couldn't remember anything before the gunshot. The vodka had made him goofy, but he couldn't lie to himself anymore. He remembered liking the sound of Kyle's voice, cool, offhand, a little drunk.

And David hadn't felt anything when he'd kissed Allie, not really. He knew that she had a crush on him, but he was using her, experimenting on her, trying to see if he felt anything after what his father had called him. David realized that he really was gay and he'd lied to Allie and every girl he'd ever kissed and every girl whose boobs he'd touched or anything he had done before. It was all lies, all of it. And he'd lied to himself because what had gotten him excited was Kyle. And now Kyle was dead.

David wondered if he had wanted Kyle dead, if he wanted to kill that part of him that didn't want to be gay, because being gay meant the rage of his father, the disappointment of his mother, and the end of his friendship with Julian, which could mean that his family could lose their house, since Julian's father had given them money.

All you have to do is be nice to your best friend.

David felt distraught that he had made that bargain, that he had gone along with Julian's prank tonight, that he hadn't stood up to him.

He pressed his hands against his face, trying to stop his crying, his nose thick with mucus. He almost couldn't breathe, and he wondered if you could suffocate this way. He deserved to, he felt so guilty, guilty as sin, guilty as hell, and he didn't deserve to live, not another minute, not another second.

David sank to the tile floor, hugging his legs, then pressing his face into his knees, letting the water scorch his back, enduring the pain and the guilt and the shame, crawling into a fetal position.

David sensed he was being reborn, becoming a new person, the horrible person he would be for the rest of his life.

■

CHAPTER 41

Barb Gallagher

K yle, Buddy!" Barb called out the window as she drove. Sharon did the same on the passenger side. Rain spattered on her face and shirt. They cruised around the block, then headed toward Thoroughbred Road. Raindrops pelted the windshield and pinged off the hood of the car.

Barb cruised past the lovely homes behind the squared-off hedges, manicured lawns, and mulched beds of peonies, their frilly heads drooping in the pounding rain. She spotted the husbands and wives through the picture windows, going upstairs or into the family room, carrying a tray, drinking a beer. Before she would've looked on them with envy, but now she knew better. Any one of those wives could be surprised by something her husband was doing, and any one of those husbands could be surprised by his wife. God knew what the kids were up to.

Sharon called out, "Kyle! Buddy!"

"Kyle, Buddy!" Barb left their neighborhood. "This is the way to the basketball courts."

"Good, let's go."

Barb cruised ahead, taking a right turn and then a left to the complex at the center of the development. She could see it at a distance, the clubhouse, tennis courts, basketball courts, and a skate park, each set off in its own area by evergreen trees. Lights illuminated the tennis and basketball courts, which were empty.

Sharon was looking, too. "Kyle, Buddy!"

"Kyle, Buddy!" Barb headed toward the basketball courts, where she steered into the lot. "Let's walk around."

Sharon and Barb got out of the car, opening their umbrellas, and they walked around the courts, calling and looking. No luck. The rain poured down, and drops ricocheted off the basketball courts.

"Where could he be?" Barb asked, raising her voice over the rain. They hurried back to the car, their sneakers and ankles getting wet. They jumped in, stowing the dripping umbrellas at their feet.

Sharon looked over. "Is there a security office we can call?"

"I don't know." Barb started the ignition. "Let's try the high-rent district."

"The promised land," Sharon said, but she wasn't smiling.

Barb cruised past the houses, too nervous to enjoy the curb appeal, though it was obvious. They were massive, three stories with extra wings, au pair suites, and rooms over garages that held three and four cars. The roofs were real slate, the gutters were real copper, and the fieldstone covered all four sides of the house, not just the façade. Everybody had a pool in the back or beside the house, surrounded by privacy fences that began at the edge of the garage.

Sharon called out, "Kyle, Buddy!"

"Kyle, Buddy!" Barb took a hard right around the corner, and her attention was drawn by red-and-white flashing lights deep in the woods.

"Do you see that?" Sharon asked, her tone darkening.

"It's the police." Barb felt an instinctive tingle of fear. She hit the gas, speeding to the end of the street, momentarily confused. "I don't know how to get there from here."

"Take a left on Connemara." Sharon pointed, and Barbara veered around the corner, accelerating to the end of the street, keeping her eyes riveted on the lights deep in the woods, which sloped down.

"There must be a road down there, on the other side."

"Or something's going on in the woods, and the cops are parked on the other side."

Barb shouted out the window, "Kyle, Buddy!"

"Stop the car!" Sharon yelled suddenly, and Barb slammed on the brakes just as a familiar yellow blur leapt into her high beams.

"It's Buddy! Buddy!" Barb put the car in park, flung open the door, and jumped out. The dog leapt into her arms, jumping up on her, panting frantically. His harness was on, trailing the leash. Dark blotches covered his muzzle and streaked his ruff.

"Buddy, what did you get into, you nut?" Barb guessed what had happened. Buddy must've run off. He always did when he got a scent. He must've gotten into something. Deer poop, mud, whatever. Kyle must be trying to find him. He must have called the police. He would be worried sick about the dog.

Sharon gasped, pointing. "Barb, your hands! Look at your hands! Is Buddy hurt?"

"No, he's fine!" Barb looked down, and her hands were illuminated by the high beams. Rain washed her palms. The water off her hands ran pink. It was blood, not mud. She felt around in Buddy's fur, frantic to see if he was injured. He wasn't. It had to be *Kyle's blood*.

"No!" Sharon shouted. "No, no, no!"

"Kyle!" Barb screamed at the top of her lungs, whirling around toward the police lights.

"Oh my God!" Sharon caught Buddy by the collar. "Let's take the car! It'll be faster!"

"Kyle!" Barb ignored her, racing toward the woods in the downpour. She ran across the grass, almost tripped running down the hill, and crashed into the woods. Her shirt caught on a branch. Limbs scratched her arms and legs. She ran forward, putting up her arms to break the vines and branches.

"Kyle!" Barb shouted again, tears flooding her eyes, desperate, terrified, not knowing if Kyle would make fun of her and not caring. She ran through vines, leaves, and branches, fighting her way forward. She tripped on rocks and logs but kept going to get to the lights.

"Help, help!" Barb hollered, over and over until she

heard the cops' voices deeper in the woods, then the mechanical crackling of walkie-talkies. Flashlights shone her way through the trees and branches, their cones of light zigzagging, trying to find her.

"Help, Kyle! Kyle!" Barb saw the cops coming closer, hustling through the woods to her, and she barreled forward, down a hill, powered by momentum and terror.

"Ma'am, ma'am!" the cops shouted, and in the next moment they shone their flashlights on her.

"My son, I'm looking for my son! His name is Kyle!" Barb kept going forward, but two cops held her and tried to stop her.

"Ma'am, please—"

"Where's my son? Is he there? What's going on?" Barb couldn't see the cops' faces, only the outlines of their caps, lit from the red-and-white flashing lights. Their badges glinted in the darkness, and their radios crackled at their utility belts.

"Ma'am, please, don't go down there," one cop said, holding her, and then Barb couldn't be stopped. She slipped past him, running downward. Cops holding flashlights formed a ring at the bottom of the hill, and one of the flashlights shone on the ground.

"Kyle!" Barb screamed in horror. Kyle was lying sideways on the ground. Blood covered his face and matted his hair. His head was horribly cratered. His Buckeyes T-shirt was black. He was so still. Barb didn't understand what she was seeing. She didn't know what happened to his head. It couldn't be.

Barb made a sound she'd never made before, it wasn't

even human, and the cops surged toward her, trying to keep her away, pushing her back; it took four of them, dropping their flashlights, calling *ma'am, ma'am, please!*

Barb cried, fighting them, pummeling them with her fists. She had to get to her son, protect him from the rain, save him somehow.

"Kyle!" she screamed to heaven.

CHAPTER 42

Sasha Barrow

S asha lay in bed in the darkness, the covers up to her chin. Her room was quiet and still. She had cried all the tears she could cry, or all she wanted to. *Crying doesn't do any good*, her mother always said. Sasha wished her mother was here, or her father, because they were lawyers and they would know what to do. Because she knew something that Julian, David, and Allie didn't. She could have left a bullet in the gun, by accident. She had been in the woods yesterday, late at night. She could have killed Kyle.

Sasha tried to rewind Saturday in her head, to understand what happened. She should be able to figure this out, but she couldn't think. She felt hungover. She kept hearing the *boom* of the gunshot. Flame had burst from the gun, right at Kyle's head. It had been so awful.

A tear slid from underneath Sasha's eyelid, but she wiped it away. She had to keep it together. They had all thought the gun was unloaded, and so had she. She hadn't realized that she might have accidentally left it loaded, *might have* left, until it actually went off. She might not have, too. It might not have been her fault. It probably wasn't. She was an organized person. She got things done. She didn't make mistakes. She had tons of extracurriculars. Her grade average was 4.1. She was going to make National Honor Society and already ranked first in her class.

Sasha tried to think back in time. She hadn't been alone Saturday night. She had been with a boyfriend she kept secret from everyone, even Bonnie and Clyde, who would have told her parents. His name was Luiz Carvalho and he went to Penn, from a super-rich family in Rio de Janeiro. He was gorgeous, sexy, and smart. A man, not a boy.

Sasha loved seeing Luiz. He lived in an entirely different world, even bigger than college, hanging out with other rich Latin Americans from New York. He'd taken her to private casino nights and VIP dinner clubs in Philly and Manhattan. She'd lost her virginity to him, and he'd taught her everything. He told her she was good, and she felt like she'd gotten another A.

Sasha tried to stay focused, thinking back to last night. Luiz had called her, saying he was free, and he'd picked her up around the block, away from the house, the way he always did. She'd told him about the gun because she wanted to go shooting. It would be fun. He had a car and could take her anywhere she wanted, to shoot. So they'd gone to the woods to get the gun. But he'd had other things in mind. He'd kissed her against a tree, so hard that she'd felt his teeth pressing into her mouth, like he would *bite* her. His hips grinded into hers, making her feel his erection, parting her legs with it, letting her rub against it, teasing her until she was begging him to make love to her.

Sasha felt her eyes close, and a tingle shuddered through her body. When Luiz had had enough, and so had she, they'd dug up the gun and the bullets. He'd had a penlight on his keychain, and they'd used it to see in the dark. She'd loaded the gun, showing off. He'd never held a handgun, and she'd felt like *she* was the adult, for once. They'd been about to leave when they'd heard women walking a dog at the top of the hill, where Luiz's Porsche had been parked.

Sasha hadn't wanted to get caught with the gun, and Luiz hadn't wanted to get caught with *her*. They'd unloaded the gun quickly, put the bullets back in the box, reburied the bullets and gun, and run from the woods the other way. Sasha hadn't checked to make sure the gun was unloaded. She hadn't been paying attention. It had been dark. They'd had only the penlight. They'd had to hurry. But still, they'd probably unloaded the gun completely.

Sasha bit her lip. She hadn't told Julian, David, or Allie about Luiz and the gun. She was supposed to have kept the gun a secret. She was supposed to have kept *Luiz* a secret. She wasn't about to tell them now that Kyle was dead. Maybe it wasn't her fault. She thought she'd unloaded the gun and put it back the way she'd found it, and she probably had. She never messed up. It was like when you thought you left the water running, but you didn't.

Sasha never left the water running. She wasn't that kind of person. It *definitely* wasn't her fault.

Tears welled in her eyes, but she blinked them away.

CHAPTER 43

∎

Julian Browne

Julian's bedroom was dark, and his mother thought he'd gone to sleep, but he was sitting at his computer, having messaged Sasha to call him. Across the street, her bedroom was dark, but she wasn't asleep, either.

Julian had never felt more focused. He hadn't drunk as much as the others had. He'd wanted to keep his wits about him. He had to make sure they didn't get caught. It would ruin his life, his father's business, and the Browne brand. His mind was clear, and he knew what to do.

His phone rang, and Julian picked up right away. "Sasha, are you okay?"

"No, it's just so *awful*." Her voice sounded soft and shocked, and Julian imagined her curled up naked in bed, talking to him in the darkness.

"I know, it's so sad."

"What the hell happened? How did a bullet get in the gun?"

"I don't know." Julian loved the sound of her voice. She sounded so sweet and feminine. He started to get hard. His hand strayed to his shorts.

"You said the gun was empty when you buried it. Didn't you check it?"

"Sasha, none of this matters now. I have a plan—"

"Of course it matters. I want to know what happened, and I think you know."

"I don't." Julian didn't like the change in her tone, which turned accusatory.

"You *have* to know. It's your gun. You didn't do it on purpose, did you?"

"No, of course not." Julian's boner stalled.

"You know you were jealous of him, and the prank was your idea—"

"No, are you crazy?" Julian moved his hand away. He had to focus anyway. "Listen, I have this figured out. We have to stay quiet. No one knows we were there. No one knows we know him. The cops are going to find him alone with a gun. They'll think he shot himself because of the news story about his father."

"Don't forget he returned my cat. His mom called here looking for him, but Bonnie told her I was asleep."

Shit. Julian had forgotten. "It better not be a problem."

"Julian, if anybody's the problem, it's *you*. The Russian Roulette thing was your idea, and it's your gun. You got us into this."

"You wanted to prank him, too, Sash. You were the one who told him about the gun in the first place. You invited him to meet us."

"I can't believe you're trying to blame this on me."

"I'm not," Julian shot back, but the conversation wasn't going the way he planned.

"You were in charge of everything, Julian. If you didn't do it on purpose, then you did it by accident. You're careless, and you know it. You always lose your keys, and your backpack, too. You're arrogant, and that's how Kyle ended up dead. Anyway, I don't want to get caught, so we shouldn't hang out for the rest of the summer."

"*What*? No." Julian felt a wrench in his chest. It sounded like she was breaking up with him, and they hadn't even gotten started.

"Yes. We need to chill. Lay low."

"I don't agree." Julian couldn't lose Sasha. "We should act natural. Hang out, like normal. I was going to see if you wanted to go out on my dad's boat."

"No, I don't want to get caught. I can't get caught."

"Sasha, I can't not see you all summer."

"You don't want to get caught, do you? We could go to prison. Julian, grow up."

"Come on, Sasha." Julian felt like he was begging her. "So you're saying we're not gonna be . . . friends anymore?"

"You were supposed to be looking out for me. Instead you got me mixed up in this awful thing."

"I'm sorry." Julian could hear her slipping away from him. He didn't know what to do. Sasha had so many other guys. She could have anybody. He would never get back in with her now.

"Whatever, just don't say anything to the police."

"I know that. I figured that out. That was my plan."

"Well, good, because it's completely obvious. We all need to keep quiet."

"Except our fingerprints are on the gun."

"What do you mean?"

Julian blinked. "Like you told Allie, when you made her touch the gun. Our fingerprints—"

"I was jerking her chain. Don't you know anything? Our fingerprints aren't on any record. They can't match our fingerprints to anything." Sasha snorted. "God, I pranked you."

Julian didn't laugh. He felt miserable. He couldn't speak, but Sasha was taking over.

"I'm not worried about Allie. She's too chicken to say anything, but you have to talk to David. Call him and tell him to keep his mouth shut. He'll do it if you ask him to. He's in love with you."

"What?" Julian didn't know what she meant.

"David will do whatever you want, the same way *you'll* do whatever *I* want, and for the same reason."

Julian recoiled, his mouth going dry. "Sasha, no, that's not true. David's my friend."

"Oh my God, boys are so dumb. You're oblivious, Julian."

"No, you're totally wrong. That's ridiculous. That's *crazy*." Julian knew she was wrong. She *had* to be wrong. She had to be wrong, didn't she?

"Whatever, you're in love with me, you can't deny that. Are you looking at me now? I can't tell, your room is dark, but I know you watch me. I've seen you."

"You have?" Julian looked over at her window, stricken.

"Of course. If you can see me, I can see you. It's a window, not a door, you idiot."

"Why didn't you say anything?" Julian reeled, busted.

"Because I like it. And it doesn't matter, you're my neighbor."

"Your *neighbor*? *That's* what I am to you? I'm your *neighbor*? Like *Mr. Rogers*?"

"Have a great summer. Goodbye." Sasha hung up.

Julian couldn't bring himself to say goodbye to Sasha. He didn't know what to do. He hung up the phone, put his head down on the desk.

His life was over.

CHAPTER 44

David Hybrinski

David crouched on his bathroom rug, stretching the phone cord so he could close the door. Everyone was asleep, and he'd been waiting for Julian to call him. David was getting more and more nervous, so he called Julian, who finally answered.

"David, yo."

"Julian, why didn't you call?" David whispered into the phone.

"I was talking to Sasha. How are you?"

"How do you *think*?" David could barely keep it together.

"Calm down."

"Are you crazy? After *that*?" David tried to talk in code, in case anyone happened to wake up. It was unspeakable, what they'd done.

"Dude, take a breath. Chill."

"I can't. How can I? How can *you*?" David didn't understand how Julian could be so calm, or so cold. It was weird.

"We have nothing to worry about."

"What are you talking about? We have *everything* to worry about!"

"Dude, focus. Nobody knows we were there. Nobody knows we even know him. Nobody saw us. It's dark now, I covered up the hole."

"When did you do that?"

"Before you and Allie came. I took the gun out and covered the hole back up. I didn't want him to know where it was buried. Now listen to me—"

"I can't, I can't." David struggled to stay in control. "We're in so much trouble, dude."

"No. It's going to be fine. Don't tell anyone and don't IM it. We have to chill. The police are going to think it's a suicide."

"Why would they think that? We were there."

"Don't say that. They won't know that. They're going to find a kid with a gun in the woods. He shot himself because his pervy dad was in the newspaper."

"But our fingerprints are on the gun. Remember, Sasha made Allie touch it?"

"Fingerprints only matter if they have a match in the computer, like on TV, don't you know that?"

"But I smelled his . . . *brains*." David sniffled, trying not to cry.

"You didn't smell anything. Don't be so dramatic."

"I'm not," David said, defensive.

"Don't say anything to anyone. Don't tell your parents. Act normal. Get it together. You're going to get us in trouble."

"We should be in trouble. We killed him."

"*Never* say that again." Julian's voice hardened. "He killed himself. We weren't even there."

David raked his hand through his hair. He'd never heard Julian sound like this. "We can't get away with this."

"Dude, we shouldn't talk for a while."

"What do you mean?" David asked, surprised.

"I think we should cool it for the summer, at least."

"What?" David couldn't believe the way Julian was acting, like he didn't even know him. "What about camp?"

"I'm quitting. I'm gonna get my mom to go down to the shore early. We all need to separate."

"You're going to separate from *Sasha*?" David didn't think it was possible.

"Yes, I told her. It's for the best. If you shut up, we'll be fine."

"No way, they'll figure it out." David felt more panicky as Julian got calmer. "They'll know; someone will know—"

"No, they won't."

"Why are you acting so—"

"Excuse me if I don't want to go to jail. Maybe you do."

"Of course I don't! Why would I?" David felt tears come to his eyes. "I'm scared! I'm fucking scared!"

"If you shut up, nothing's going to happen."

"Something *already* happened."

"Don't be such a pussy. We can't do anything about it

now. Don't say anything. Don't ruin me or our business. If Browne goes bankrupt, so do you. My dad can't give your dad money he doesn't have. So shut up."

"Okay."

"Promise me, bro."

"I promise." David took it like a blow. He realized it was never going to be the same between him and Julian. No friendship could survive what they had done. He held back his tears. "Okay, I get it. What about Allie?"

"She's nobody. Freeze her out."

"Like you're doing to me?"

"Whatever, dude. Have a nice life."

CHAPTER 45

Allie Garvey

Allie slid out of Jill's bed, left the bedroom, and headed down the hallway to her own room, closing the door quietly. Her head hurt, and she felt sick to her stomach. She hadn't slept a wink. She went to her desk, sat down, and opened her computer, blinking against the brightness.

The clock on the screen said 2:17 A.M. She knew the others had to be awake, too. She felt a part of them now, in the worst way possible. They had all done a horrible thing. They were responsible for it. They caused Kyle's death. Tears came to her eyes, but she wiped them away.

She logged on to the Internet, then AOL Instant Messenger. Sasha and Julian weren't online, but if they had taken her off their Buddy Lists, she wouldn't know if they were online. David was online, and he was the only one she wanted to talk to. She knew he'd be feeling

as awful as she was, and he liked her. He might be hoping
to hear from her.

AllieOop918: hi will u call me?

NetProphet182: i dont know u leave me alone

Allie blinked, bewildered. Maybe she'd messaged the
wrong person. She checked the list, and NetProphet182
was David's screen name. It was him.

Allie heard the sound of the AIM door, cyber-closing.

CHAPTER 46

Barb Gallagher

B arb sat next to Sharon in old-fashioned wooden chairs in Chief Holtz's office, at the township police station. They had fallen into an exhausted silence, having given their statements, then the chief had told them to wait here. The police suspected suicide, but the cause of death wasn't official yet. Barb knew it had to be true because it was the only thing that made sense. She knew he was hurting. She knew he'd been drinking. She should've seen this coming, especially after the newspaper article. She couldn't blame anybody but herself, not even her ex. Barb would never, ever forgive herself.

The fluorescent lights hurt her eyes. Her shirt and shorts clung to her, clammy. Her sneakers were soaked and muddy. Buddy slept under her chair, the traces of Kyle's blood almost gone from his ruff and muzzle. Kyle always called Buddy *self-cleaning*. Barb would have cried at the memory, but she couldn't cry anymore.

Barb's heartbroken gaze took in the chief's office, with its old wooden desk cluttered with sports paraphernalia, an antiquated computer, and a calendar from a local plumbing company. The air smelled of stale cigarette smoke, though she doubted smoking was allowed. Either way, she didn't care. She was trying to neither think nor feel.

She didn't want to live anymore, truly, and she'd said that to Sharon, sobbing, hysterical, brought to her knees when they'd zipped Kyle into a body bag in the pounding rain.

No, no, no, Sharon had said, crying, too, full bore.

I never should've let him go tonight, I should've known he'd be upset—

—no, you couldn't know that—

—yes, I could, the newspaper article—

—but you didn't know he could get a gun—

Chief Holtz entered the office, a taciturn type in his late fifties. A paunch strained the buttons of his blue shirt, and his jowls bracketed his lips, which were fleshy. His eyes were a weary blue-gray behind stainless-steel bifocals, his nose was bulbous, and his chin grizzled salt and pepper after the long night. He closed the door quietly behind him, meeting Barb's eye with surprising tenderness.

"Ms. Gallagher, Barbara, can I get you another water?"

"No, thank you."

"How about you, uh . . ."

"Sharon," Sharon supplied. "No, thank you."

Chief Holtz lumbered around the desk and sat down

heavily, sliding some paperwork aside and folding his hands on top of an old-fashioned green blotter. "You have my deepest sympathies on your loss."

"Thank you," Barb said, numb with shock. She had to keep it together. She had to hear what she was being told.

"As you know, this is a small county, so we only have the one medical examiner. That's why it took so long. I have the autopsy results, not the report. They gave us priority on account of the press attention."

"I understand." Barb didn't want to even think about the reporters already out front, having smelled blood. Literally, her son's blood. Kyle, her only child. Her big baby boy, oversized, eleven pounds. It took her twenty-one hours of labor and every drug they could give her.

How did you pass that thing? one of the nurses had joked.

With great difficulty, Barb had shot back, and they had laughed.

Chief Holtz cleared his throat. "I'm sorry to have to tell you this terrible news. The coroner has found that the cause of death was a gunshot wound to the victim's temple, self-inflicted. The manner of death was suicide."

Suicide. Barb imagined the bullet blasting through her son's brain, destroying everything in its path, the blood vessels, soft tissue, neurons, all the things that somehow comprised his thoughts, memories, and his very soul. All that was *him*.

Chief Holtz blinked, waiting for Barb to say something, but she couldn't speak. She was remembering when Kyle was thirteen years old. He'd been five foot seven and having a growth spurt. She'd put cocoa butter on the bright red stretch marks that went sideways across his back. He'd never once complained about growing pains. He was always in the ninety-seventh percentile for boys ages two to twenty, and last year, he'd gone off the chart. He'd grown two inches since September. She couldn't keep clothes on him. He was always wearing floods and belly shirts. She couldn't find anything tall enough that wasn't too wide. And good luck with jeans.

Sharon interjected, "Chief Holtz, is the coroner sure?"

"Yes."

Sharon shifted forward. "How does he know? How can you tell that he wasn't murdered?"

Barb wanted to know, but couldn't ask. Sharon would understand this instinctively. Sharon would have anticipated it. Sharon would know that Barb wanted to know everything but couldn't speak right now.

Chief Holtz cleared his throat again, in a deliberate way. "The wound, obviously. The pattern of the wound. It was a close-contact wound, with stippling typical of a suicide. In addition, there was what we call blowback on the victim's right hand, which indicates that he fired the gun himself. Gun residue was also present on his right hand, and we're testing to double-check. In addition, there were no defensive wounds on his body. That is, no signs of a struggle to suggest the victim was in a fight with another person. For example—I'm trying to put this in layman's terms—there was no evidence that another person put the gun to the victim's head." Chief Holtz hesitated, though he was speaking slowly. "Finally, we searched the area and the woods, and there was no evidence that he was with another person, though that might've been compromised by the rain. We will double-check after the storm. Unfortunately, it's going to be a nor'easter."

Barb listened. She sat very still while Chief Holtz kept talking.

"Oh, I should mention, the initial blood screening shows the presence of alcohol in his blood. Toxicology tests were performed but we won't have those results for a while. Finally, we considered the circumstances, such as the adverse publicity in today's newspaper. It suggests an explanation for why the victim would do away with himself." Chief Holtz turned to Barb. "You did say earlier that he was in therapy, for depression."

Sharon interjected again, "But she was told that he wasn't at risk."

"It's not an exact science, is it?" Chief Holtz sighed. "I'm so sorry. This is one of the most heartbreaking cases I've ever experienced."

Barb believed that this was one of Chief Holtz's most heartbreaking cases. He looked so sad. His tone was sincere. He had a family photo on his desk, a wife and two sons. This was heartbreaking. Her heart was broken to death.

Sharon shifted in her seat. "But, Chief, what about the dog? Kyle loved that dog. If he went to the woods to commit suicide, he wouldn't have brought the dog. He would have worried the dog would run off. It could have gotten hit by a car."

Barb felt it ring true. Sharon was right. Kyle loved Buddy. He would have worried about Buddy. He never let him off the leash. He always worried he'd get hit by a car. He never would have left him alone, outside, in the rain.

Chief Holtz shook his head. "I remind you, there was alcohol in his blood. He wouldn't have been thinking clearly. He didn't behave the way he normally would. He could have acted impulsively."

Sharon sighed. "But where did he get the gun? We told you, Kyle didn't have a gun."

"It's an illegal gun. It's one of the most common revolvers. Its serial number was scratched off, typical of a gun you buy off the street."

"But *here*?" Sharon asked, skeptical. "I grew up in Bakerton. It's not easy to buy a gun around here."

"We've changed since then. Street guns are available in the county, and it wouldn't take much doing."

"But he didn't have a car, so he couldn't drive anywhere."

"Did he have a bike?" Chief Holtz didn't wait for an answer. "And we have public transportation. Believe it or not, I've seen cases where street guns have been delivered to the buyer." He paused. "It's also a possibility that he bought the gun in the Columbus, Ohio, area and brought it with him."

Barb closed her eyes. She could have missed the gun.

Kyle had cleaned his own room. He'd packed himself for the move. He had insisted on it, and she'd thought he was being responsible. Maybe he'd been hiding the gun. There were kids on his old basketball team who weren't from New Albany. He could have bought the gun from them, or somebody they knew. Or at an away game.

Sharon leaned back in her chair. "How much would the gun cost? Where would he get the money for a gun?"

"A few hundred bucks?" Chief Holtz turned to Barb. "Did he have that sort of money?"

Barb nodded, stricken. She had given him the money because he'd done so many chores, packing boxes for the move, all the heavy lifting. She'd looked for reasons to give him money, to make him feel good after everything had gone to hell. She never would've thought he'd buy a gun. She should have, considering what he'd been through. The therapist had told her he wasn't at risk, but she was his *mother*. She was supposed to know him better than anybody else. She'd thought she had. She loved him more than anybody and anything else. More than the sun, the moon, the stars, her life. He was her baby boy, still growing. He was only fifteen. She would never, *ever* forgive herself.

Barb blurted out, "I thought things were bad, I didn't know they'd get worse, I was so wrong, I should have known."

"Honey, don't do this."

"But I *should* have." Barb couldn't even finish the sentence, there were so many things she should have done, so many things she didn't do, so many things she would've done differently that she couldn't even begin to list them all, she could go on and on and on, and all of it, every decision, every action, inaction, mistake, and misstep had led to this moment, and Kyle was dead.

Chief Holtz linked his fingers on his blotter. "Do you have any other questions?" he asked, his tone gentle.

Barb had a question, but it wasn't one Chief Holtz could answer.

Why go on?

CHAPTER 47

Allie Garvey

It was August, so it got dark outside after dinner, leaving the family room gloomy, but Allie didn't turn on a lamp. She slumped in a chair in front of the TV, watching music videos. She and her father had just eaten, and he was cleaning up in the kitchen. She'd had mashed potatoes with no butter and chicken breast with no skin, since the doctor said only bland foods. If she ate normal food, she'd get cramps and have to go to the bathroom. Her father had taken her to a gastroenterologist who diagnosed her as having ulcerative colitis. Allie was consumed with guilt about Kyle. Literally, consumed. She was eating herself alive, from the inside.

A TV commercial came on for Blockbuster, and the volume went too loud, but she didn't bother to lower it. She wasn't listening anyway. She was thinking about Kyle. During the daytime, she'd get flashes of him walking down the hill to them, or of the gun against his head, or the blood drenching his shirt. She'd hear the gunshot and smell smoke in the air. At nighttime, she'd replay what happened like a horror movie. She slept badly. She was tired all day. She never left the house. She told her father it was because she couldn't leave the bathroom, but that was an excuse. She lost thirteen pounds and weighed 135, which was the thinnest she'd ever been. She couldn't keep weight *on*. She sealed her secret inside.

Suddenly her father dropped a pan in the kitchen, and Allie startled. She was nervous all the time. She expected the police to come knocking on the door any minute. She was terrified of getting caught. She'd read in the newspaper that the police ruled Kyle's death a suicide, but she still worried they would figure it out. She'd jump whenever the phone rang. Once she was driving with her father and a police car passed. She started shaking.

An ad for *Law & Order* came on TV, and she stiffened. It seemed like all the TV shows were about murders, the whole summer. *NYPD Blue, Homicide*. The TV cops always caught the bad guy, and Allie was the bad guy. She still didn't know how the gun got loaded, but she suspected Julian. He was jealous about Sasha, and he was cold that way. She felt sick to her stomach, keeping his secret. By shutting up, she was helping him get away with murder.

Another TV commercial came on, showing a smiling mom serving a platter of watermelon, and even that reminded her of Kyle. She felt so bad for Mrs. Gallagher, who'd been in the newspaper after Kyle died. There was a picture of her, and she had a nice smile. She'd moved out of Brandywine Hunt and stayed in the area, but the newspaper didn't say where.

Allie thought about her every night, wracked with shame. She knew how heartbroken Mrs. Gallagher must feel because she knew how her mother felt after Jill died. Her mother was still in the hospital, and she and her father visited her there, but she wasn't getting better. Allie used to worry that Mrs. Gallagher would end up in a hospital, too. Allie cried at night, knowing she was responsible.

"Honey, ready to go?" her father said, coming into the room, his car keys in his hand. He was still dressed from work, in his pressed white shirt and slacks, though he'd taken off his tie.

"Where?"

"Let's go get your school supplies." Her father jingled his keys, but Allie looked away. She dreaded going back to school because it felt like coming out of hiding, and she would see David and Sasha. She knew they'd avoid her, but it would still be weird. David never spoke to her again or messaged her. She thought of him all the time, but what had happened to Kyle made David a terrible memory. She didn't return *Infinite Jest* because she didn't want to let it go, but she couldn't read it, either. Oddly, the library fines added to her guilt, even at a nickel a day.

"I don't want to go, Dad. Can we do it another time?"

"No, honey. School starts next week. You keep putting it off. Your mother told me to take you. She said you like this. You love to get school supplies, she said." Her father smiled in an encouraging way, and Allie flashed on the annual trip to Staples with her mother. Allie had her mother all to herself for those trips, and they both loved school supplies, for some reason. They would take forever choosing highlighter colors, pencils with novelty erasers, and the correct point size for pens. Allie loved thick points, and her mother liked fine-point.

"I don't really, I don't want to."

"She said you like to get a new backpack. Every year that's your big thing. So let's go get a backpack."

"I'll use the one from last year, okay?"

"She says you never want to do that."

"I'm fine with it."

"Honey, let's go. Let's go, really. It's back-to-school time. Look, everybody's doing it." Her father gestured at the TV, which showed a happy family skipping into a Staples store. His eyes were worried behind his glasses, and Allie felt bad for him because she knew he was trying so hard, working all day and taking care of the house and her, but she couldn't help him, or herself.

"Dad, they run those commercials in June."

"Still, come on, honey. You have to go outside. You never even go outside anymore."

"I don't have to."

"Honey, enough with the television." Her father tried to take the remote control out of her hand, but Allie yanked it away.

"Dad, please. I'm not watching television. I'm resting."

"Well, enough with the resting. Let's go. Come on out." Her father clapped his hands together.

"What if I have to go to the bathroom?" Allie shuddered to think what it would be like to have colitis at school. Diarrhea city.

"They have a bathroom. Honey, I'm not gonna let you do this."

"Do what?"

"Wallow in misery."

"I'm not *wallowing in misery*."

"Yes, you are," her father snapped, grabbing her hand, but she pulled it free.

"Dad, stop." Allie felt disturbed. Her father had never been physically rough with her, ever.

"Get up or I'll get you up."

"Why can't you just leave me alone?"

"Because we have to get school supplies." Her father tried to catch her eye, leaning over, but Allie stared at the TV.

"Dad, please, leave me alone."

"No. Get up. No more wallowing."

"Why, are you worried I'm like Mom?" Allie shot back, regretting the words as soon as they slipped past her lips, and her father's face fell instantly.

"Honestly, honey, that's *exactly* what I'm worried about. You have to fight this wallowing you've been doing. You and me, we can't fold up the tent. We can't pack it in. We have to keep on keeping on. That's why you have to get up. Not because of a backpack."

Allie swallowed hard, surprised that he was being real with her. It felt adult. "But I don't want to."

"I don't care if you want to. I'm your father, and I know it's best for you. You have to get out of the chair and come with me. You're going to be fine, and so am I, and your mother's going to get better, and she's going to come home soon."

"No, she isn't."

"Then all the more reason. Honey, think of it like a tooth. If I pull a tooth in my patient's mouth, the others don't have to go, too. Every tooth has its own roots. That's us, you and me. We stay rooted in the gum, even though the others go. We're our own separate teeth."

"We're not teeth, Dad," Allie said, though she got the analogy. Her mother and Jill were the missing teeth in the Garvey gums. "You're in denial."

"It's not about denial, it's about survival. Maybe you need to be in a little bit of denial to survive. We have to survive, and you know how we survive? By putting one foot in front of the other."

"Dad, no."

"Don't think. Just *do*. Now get the fuck up."

"Did you just *curse*?" Allie asked, so surprised that she finally looked up at him. His eyes were burning, his lips pursed hard, and his jaw set with determination. He was an orthodontist on a mission, and she felt a pang of guilt, knowing he was trying to help her. She needed help because she didn't know what to do or how to live anymore. She didn't want to come out of hiding to go to the store, school, or anywhere. She loved him so much, and maybe he was right. She wanted him to be right.

"I'm not gonna let you sink, like I let your mother sink," her father said, his eyes newly wet behind his glasses. He held out his hand. "I'm your life preserver."

Part Two

—TWENTY YEARS LATER—

It is not the least bit coincidental that adults who commit suicide with firearms almost always shoot themselves in: the head. They shoot the terrible master. And the truth is that most of these suicides are actually dead long before they pull the trigger.

> —David Foster Wallace,
>   Kenyon Commencement Address, May 21, 2005

The tears I shed yesterday have become rain.

> —Thich Nhat Hanh, "Message,"
>   *Call Me by My True Names: The Collected Poems*

CHAPTER 48

■

Allie Garvey

The morning sun rose in a cloudless blue sky, and Allie walked toward the green Gardens of Peace tent on the gravesite. Fifty mourners clustered underneath, holding red roses with droopy heads. An older priest stood before bouquets of white lilies and red gladiolas, and an enlarged photo of the deceased rested on an easel.

DAVID PAUL HYBRINSKI read the caption, and the photo was a candid of David at a tennis court, showing him from the waist up. He was grinning, resting his hand on the net and dressed the way Allie remembered, in his red bandanna and white polo shirt. He looked in his early twenties, so maybe the photo was taken at college.

Allie's gut clenched as she approached, and she felt a deep wave of dread. She eyed the photo, and David's warm brown eyes gazed back at her, telegraphing why she'd fallen for him, twenty years ago. Now she tried to see behind them. He had to have been miserable but hiding it, like she'd been, ever since the night Kyle died. He had to have felt the same guilt, and she sensed it was why he'd committed suicide. His obituary hadn't specified how he had done it, and she knew that newspapers followed rules about reporting the details. Allie had a guess, because he had killed himself on the twenty-year anniversary of Kyle's death.

She walked forward, her heels clacking on the asphalt. She'd kept the secret about Kyle because she hadn't wanted to get caught, back then. Now she didn't know what she wanted. She knew only that she couldn't go on this way. She'd never considered suicide, even as low as she got. Her punishment was to live with the shame and to wonder forever. To this day, she didn't know how the prank had gone so lethally wrong.

She drew closer to the mourners, who were divided into two groups, one on the far side of the casket, facing her, and the other on the near side, their backs turned. Then Allie spotted Sasha and Julian, who were standing together on the far side, and she could see them clearly. Her reaction was visceral; her gut twisted as if being wrung.

She reminded herself to breathe slowly, in and out. Sasha looked strikingly beautiful, with her fine blond hair swept into a chignon, fancy gold earrings, and a black dress that looked like Chanel. She wore only light makeup, but she stood out, naturally stunning. Julian was next to her, tall and gym-trim in a well-tailored dark suit with a print tie. His hair was finely cut, and his thin lips pursed unhappily. His face had grown longer, but he looked predictably successful.

Allie approached, suppressing her emotions. She'd long suspected that Julian had loaded the gun, but Sasha was also a possibility. She'd never believed for a second that David would have done such a thing. It had haunted her, and at night she imagined each step leading to Kyle's death, visualizing someone opening the cylinder, loading the bullet, and firing the gun. She blamed herself for Kyle's death, and now David was dead, another unimaginable thing she could take credit for.

Allie reached the closer group of mourners. The priest was speaking, but she tuned him out, her thoughts racing. Something about seeing Sasha and Julian in the flesh made her doubt her suspicions. They looked like two normal people. How could they have murdered someone? Was she crazy to suspect them? But hadn't Julian seemed jealous of Kyle? Hadn't Sasha been angry that Kyle had tricked her? They had all known where the gun was buried, and the bullets, even David. Could his suicide mean *he* had killed Kyle? He was incapable of such a thing, wasn't he? And why would David have wanted to hurt Kyle?

Allie flashed to Sasha and Julian sharing the vodka, passing Kyle the gun, racing away through the woods. She had thought about it so many times, but even she had to admit her memories had been eroded by time and emotion. She remembered them talking, shouting directions as they ran away. She remembered them not being as hysterical as she was, but she could have been wrong.

She'd learned since that memory could be warped by trauma. She'd never shaken the gruesome image.

Allie wished she could run to Sasha and Julian, grab them, and shake the truth out of them. It took nerve to come to the funeral if David had killed himself over a murder one of them had committed. She even tried to give them the benefit of the doubt, wondering if they had come for the same reason she had. Maybe they'd felt drawn here by a guilty conscience, too. David's suicide could have provoked in them the same reaction it had in her. An urge to return to where it all began. To each other, after twenty years. To a reckoning.

Allie caught a glimpse of the casket, which was polished walnut with bronze handles. It was so hard to believe that David was inside. He'd become a freelance writer, and she'd read articles he'd posted online from literary journals like *Granta*, *GQ*, and tennis magazines. He would reference David Foster Wallace from time to time, and she'd felt so sad when David Foster Wallace had himself committed suicide. She could imagine how devastated David would've been.

She'd never spoken to David after what had happened that summer. He wouldn't look at her if she saw him in the hallway at school. He had taken all AP classes, like her, but was always in the other section. He'd dated a lot and stopped hanging with Sasha, who'd become prom queen. The *Bakerite* had published where seniors were going to college, and Sasha went to Wake Forest and David to Amherst, like his idol David Foster Wallace. Julian had gone to NYU.

Allie had gone to Penn, where she buried herself in her classes, getting great grades even though she made only a few friends. She struggled with colitis, and lost more weight. Girls in the dorm assumed she had an eating disorder. The song "Fucked Up Girl" was popular, and Allie identified. She graduated *magna cum laude* and met a law student, Larry Rucci, an outgoing Italian-American from North Jersey, who was chubby, laughed easily, and asked her out. They made a classic pairing of opposites, got married, and now, five years later, were foundering. Opposites don't attract, they divorce.

Allie always thought of David as her first love, and that the night ended in such a horrific way burned him into her consciousness. The best night of her young life was also the worst, and kissing David would always be linked with killing Kyle. She couldn't disentangle the two because she couldn't tell her therapist about David without also telling him about Kyle. She hadn't even told her husband about Kyle, or David. Their therapist said Allie had *intimacy issues*, and they were why her marriage was in trouble. No shit, Sherlock.

A tall man shifted in front of her, giving Allie a view of David's wife and family. She recognized them from photos on his Facebook page, since his settings were public. He'd married a painter named Martine Jocose, an artsy redhead whose delicate features were today masked by oversized designer sunglasses. She'd had gallery showings in New York, and they'd lived in Williamsburg. Suddenly Martine moved the handbag she was clutching in front of her, and Allie caught a glimpse of her pregnant belly. It took Allie by surprise, since David hadn't mentioned it on his Facebook page. She felt sympathy for Martine, raising their baby on her own, and for David, who would miss out on becoming a father.

The rest of David's family stood next to Martine, and Allie recognized them from Facebook, too. His father, a stocky, spectacled man with wisps of salt-and-pepper hair, stood stoic with his arm around David's mother. She held a Kleenex to her nose, her eyes spilling over with tears, her eyebrows sloping down, and her expression etched with deep grief. David's brother, Jason, was next to her, somber in a dark three-piece suit, and looked like an older, corporate version of David. His pretty twin sisters stood on Jason's other side, distraught as the priest finished his prayer.

Everyone said a final amen, then it was time for the goodbyes, and everyone placed a rose on the casket, ending with David's parents. They stepped up together, and his mother set a rose down, murmuring through her tears, "David, I don't understand, I don't understand."

The mourners reacted with sniffles, and Allie felt her heart wrench, the pressure building inside her. She couldn't stand to see David's mother suffer, wracking her brain about why David had done it, when Allie knew at least one reason. She couldn't be sure that it was the only reason, and she wondered if anyone committed suicide for only one reason.

Suddenly David's father looked away, and he scowled deeply. He pointed to the right, his arm a straight line of accusation and his anger so sudden, swift, and undisguised that the mourners turned to see what was the matter. Even the priest turned around, and a tall, thin man in a black suit was walking toward them. He had dark, good-looking features, but he was grief-stricken, his head down, eyes puffy, and his expression drawn. He was obviously a mourner who'd come late, and Allie didn't understand why David's father was getting so angry.

"Get out of here!" David's father shouted at the mourner. "You're not welcome here! You have no business here! No business!"

The mourner stopped in his tracks. His eyes flared in defiance. "I have every right to be here! David would've wanted me here!"

"*I* don't want you here! No, no, no!" David's father erupted, letting go of his wife and storming off toward the mourner, wagging his finger. "Get out or I'll throw you out! I'll *throw you out*!"

Allie's mouth dropped open, aghast. The mourner started walking toward the casket again. David's father charged toward him, shouting. Jason ran after his father. The funeral director and his assistants raced to intervene. It looked as if a fight was about to break out. The funeral erupted in chaos. The priest and mourners surged forward to see what was going on. Allie moved to the front of the crowd.

"Dad, no!" His father ignored him, continuing to advance on the mourner.

"You have no business here! Get out! Right now!"

"I have every right! He was my boyfriend, whether you like it or not! We loved each other!" The mourner kept advancing, on a collision course with David's father.

"Get out! Get out right now!"

"This is a public place!" the mourner yelled, and as soon as the two men got close enough, David's father lunged at the mourner, clamping down on his shoulders and tackling him. Jason leapt into the fray, yanking his father backward. Funeral assistants rushed to restrain the mourner, then pushed him back toward the street.

Allie felt dumbfounded, trying to process what was happening. The mourner was David's *boyfriend*. She'd had no idea from his Facebook page that David was gay. She'd had no idea from his kiss, either, way back then.

Meanwhile Martine had collapsed, sobbing. David's mother led her from the scene. David's boyfriend was being ushered off in tears. David's father headed after his wife, flustered and infuriated. Jason looked stricken, and the twins hurried crying to the limos.

The priest looked this way and that, bewildered. The funeral, completely disrupted, ended. Some of the mourners talked among themselves, their heads bent together, and others dispersed, placing their roses atop the casket before they left. The funeral director dismantled David's photograph and easel, and his assistant ushered mourners to their cars.

An elderly mourner turned to Allie, her hand at her chest. "Goodness, what a scene! I couldn't hear much, but Bill's not himself. How could he be? I assume we'll still go back to the house in Brandywine Hunt, don't you? For the reception?"

"I guess," Allie said, trying to recover.

"Good, I'll see you there."

"I wasn't . . ." Allie started to say, then stopped. She hadn't known David was gay, and it had obviously caused drama in his family. She wondered if it had something to do with his suicide. "Yes, I'll see you there."

Allie felt a hand on her arm and looked over, startled to see that it was Julian.

"Wanna catch up, instead?" he asked with a tight smile. "I know a place we can talk privately. Sasha's coming, too."

"Yes," Allie answered without hesitation. It was a conversation she had waited twenty years for.

■

CHAPTER 49

Barb Gallagher

B arb stood alone at Kyle's grave, near the top of the hill at Gardens of Peace cemetery. She still couldn't believe he was really gone, even now. She could remember the stretch marks on his back, from growing by leaps and bounds. It was hard to believe he wasn't growing anymore. He stopped growing twenty years and three days ago, exactly.

It seems like yesterday, Barb thought, though she knew that was a cliché. She felt like he'd grown up *in the blink of an eye*, too, another cliché. She decided that clichés ring true for a reason. She knew because she'd lived them. Kyle would be fifteen forever, in her mind. She was fifty-five. She'd put on a nice outfit from Chico's, because she dressed up whenever she went to visit his grave. She wanted to look nice for him. It was the least she could do, since she had failed him, in the end.

Suddenly Barb heard shouting behind her, at a distance. She turned around and saw a commotion at a funeral in the new section of the cemetery, closer to Scattergood Road. A fight had broken out among the mourners. Some men were shoving each other, and others were trying to break up the fuss. It was too far away for Barb to hear or see much, and it wasn't her business.

She turned away. She came here often enough to witness more than a few family fights at funerals. Last month, the police had to be called to the columbarium to break up a scuffle, and two mourners had been taken in handcuffs to police cruisers. It happened more than people realized, and Barb understood why. She would have thrown a *fit* if her ex-husband had been allowed to attend Kyle's funeral. He hadn't been, since the prison officials wouldn't give him bereavement leave. He was rotting behind bars, which was fine with her.

Barb bent her head and linked her hands in front of her. She scanned Kyle's grave now that she had finished tending it, and it looked nice and neat. His memorial plaque was bronze, recessed in the green brushy grass. It read KYLE GALLAGHER, BELOVED SON, which Barb thought he would have liked. It was simple but did what needed doing, like Kyle himself. He did what needed doing, like packing boxes, unloading groceries, cutting the grass. Even on the basketball court back in Columbus, he'd done what needed doing. A three-pointer in the clutch, a foul shot, even a dunk. He'd had more than one buzzer-beater in his high school career. That was her Kyle.

He was always in the back of her mind. She would see Kyle as a baby, grinning to show his first tooth, his gums wet with drool. Or Kyle as a little boy, shooting a foul shot in a jersey that hung to his knobby knees. Or Kyle as a teenager, wrestling on the kitchen floor with their old yellow Lab, Buddy. The poor dog had died a year after Kyle, and Barb told herself it wasn't from a broken heart. But she couldn't deny that for months after Kyle's death, Buddy would go to the pantry and sit in front of the cabinet where they kept the leash. Barb would take him out, but he'd pull her back to the house and plop down in front of the cabinet again. The dog seemed to think that sitting there would bring Kyle back. Some nights, Barb folded her hands and prayed that Buddy was right.

She let her eyes fill with tears. She knew not to hold them back, though they didn't bring her to her knees like they used to. The pain was still fresh, and the grief. She never got over it, though she'd gone back to work and resumed her life. Sometimes she felt like she was sleep-walking, but she couldn't end it all, like Kyle had. Sharon made sure of that, anyway. They met every other week for dinner or a movie, and Barb watched Sharon's son and daughter grow up and clapped at their high school and college graduations, weddings, then their children's christenings, thinking every time, *This could've been Kyle, too. Should've been Kyle, too.*

Barb still felt so surprised that he'd committed suicide. It just didn't seem like something he would do, no matter how unhappy he was. It was Buddy that made her question it, too. She couldn't imagine him taking the dog with him if he was going to kill himself. It didn't square. But the autopsy report and blood tests showed the police had been right. Kyle had had alcohol in his blood, and that was why he hadn't thought about Buddy. The case was closed. She had to face the facts.

Still, all the what-ifs kept her up at night, to this day. What if she'd made a stink about his drinking on the sly? What if she'd found him a therapist sooner? What if she'd known how down he was? Since then, she'd gone to therapy, where they told her she was *beating herself up*, but she knew it was her fault. She blamed herself for not seeing the signs. She'd let Kyle down. She should have known. She should have stopped him. A mother is supposed to protect her child, and she had failed to.

Barb wiped her tears away. Every time she came, she apologized to him. She begged him to forgive her. But Kyle was silent. It wasn't he who blamed her; she blamed herself. She was her judge and jury, and she deserved the punishment she'd given herself. She was behind bars, too. She was serving a life sentence.

It wouldn't end until the day she died, too.

CHAPTER 50

Larry Rucci

A re you sure Allie's not there?" Larry asked, confused, the phone to his ear. He was trying to reach
his wife to tell her he'd been called out of town. She was
supposed to be meeting with a special ed lawyer, Jeff
Sherrod, in King of Prussia. Larry knew Jeff, so he'd
called Jeff's office, but evidently Allie wasn't there.

"Totally sure," answered Jeff's secretary, Gloria. "Jeff's
on vacation in Hawaii. I don't have Allie or anybody else
scheduled for today."

"I swear she said she had a meeting with him this
morning."

"You must've misheard."

"Right," Larry said, relieved to arrive at a conclusion
that saved face. "Okay, thanks, Gloria."

"Have a good day."

"You, too, goodbye." Larry ended the call. He'd
called Allie three times, but no answer. He hadn't both-

ered leaving a message because she never listened to them. He'd texted her, too, but no text back. It was odd, but not *that* odd. Allie could be so remote, and Larry was coming to the reluctant conclusion that his marriage sucked.

Larry's gaze wandered restlessly around his office, in a corner with a prestige location on the twenty-third floor, with a great view, indirect light, diplomas, plaques, and awards, and photos of him glad-handing every CEO, VP, CFO, COO, or GC in a variety of target-rich environments like shareholder conferences, CLE seminars, and meetings. Larry loved connecting with people. It brought in business, and felt natural and good. But no matter how hard he tried, he couldn't connect with Allie, and he was her *husband*.

He eyed the Philly skyline, with its mirrored spikes and shiny ziggurats piercing a cloudy gray sky. He was supposed to grab a flight to Detroit because a client needed hand-holding, and nobody held hands like Larry. Everyone at Dichter & O'Reilly said so, and he was on his way to becoming department head. He was well-liked, but more than that, he *tried*. He tried the most with Allie, despite everything she did to push him away, to *distance him*, in yet another phrase of their marriage counselor's. They quoted her like the Bible now.

He got up, gathered his laptop, and grabbed some fresh legal pads. He shoved them into his logo messenger bag, then took a bunch of pens because he would lose five for every one. The only pen he ever managed to hold on to was the gold Cartier pen Allie had given him for his last birthday. He had an hour and a half to make his flight, and it would take twenty minutes to the airport from Center City, more when it was starting to drizzle, like now.

He shouldered his messenger bag and left his office, waving to his secretary. "Monica, will I make the flight?"

"Not this time. Did you reach Allie?"

"No, bye." Larry kept going, hiding his surprise. He hadn't realized that Monica had overheard him. He wondered how many times she'd asked him the same question over the years. His work wife was more available than his real wife. It was beginning to exhaust even him.

Larry headed down the hallway, troubled. He kept a professional smile in place, nodding at the associates as he passed them, making a point of using their first names, a salesman's habit. He'd sold knives, vacuum cleaners, and insurance to pay for college and law school. Now he sold the law, the firm, and himself, and everybody bought except the buyer he wanted the most. His own wife.

Larry caught sight of his outline in the stainless steel of the elevator doors. His was indistinct, blurry even to himself. His eyes looked like dark holes in a skull. His black curls piled on his head like a poodle. Allie always said *at least you're my poodle*, an unfortunate turn of phrase in retrospect. He was reasonably fit in his gray suit with his fancy silk tie, and he'd trimmed down since he met Allie. She never ate much because of her stomach issues, so the duration of their meals never matched. He'd lost forty-seven pounds, thinking that would make her happy, more attracted to him, maybe he wouldn't have to *reach* for her all the damn time, but that hadn't helped, either.

The elevator door slid open, and Larry climbed inside, greeting the associates he knew, *hey, Josh, how's the new puppy, good, good, yes, housebreaking is tough*. He put his head down after he said his hellos, wondering if Allie was having an affair. It didn't seem likely, because she was so absorbed in work and not the sexually freewheeling type. Still she had plenty of opportunities and was undeniably attractive, with pretty blue eyes, thick wavy hair, a great body, and an even greater smile, even if it had to be coaxed out of her, like the sun breaking through an Allie-cloud. Larry always tried to make her laugh, the court jester of husbands.

Larry's thoughts brewed as the elevator descended. Their marriage counselor had said he was *codependent*. Maybe so, but he thought husbands were *supposed* to be codependent. His father always told him, *happy wife, happy life*, and Larry believed him. Wasn't that the exact *definition* of codependency? Larry was trying to have a happy wife and a happy life. Why was it so damn hard? He was a good husband. A good provider. Fun to be with. Everybody loved him. He never cheated, not once. Thought about it, but didn't do it. Frankly, women didn't think of him that way. He was friend-zoned until he became husband material. He sensed it was because of his weight, and even after he got thin, he acted like a fat guy. He *thought* like a fat guy. Women could smell it, and it wasn't sexy. He didn't mind. He loved his wife and his job. That was his life, until they'd have kids.

He stepped off the elevator, crossing the busy lobby, waiting on his way to the exit door, nodding hellos to everybody on the way out, but no first names or small talk downstairs, everybody was in a hurry, rushing out to quick lunches. He was thinking of his parents, who had the greatest marriage ever, the two of them from Queens, both Abruzzese from Chieti, so alike they could've been related. The family joke was they probably were, since he had two aunts who married two brothers.

He pushed through the glass exit doors and stepped outside to noontime rush in Center City. Walnut Street was only wide enough for colonial traffic, so it clogged easily. He hoped he could get a cab, but it wasn't looking good. Alternatively he could walk to 30th Street and take the airport train, but he was cutting it close. He stuck his hand out but there were no cabs in sight, and it was drizzling.

Larry realized he'd forgotten his umbrella, preoccupied. He was always running his cases, firm business, and Allie in the back of his mind, especially when she wouldn't return his calls. He always worried that something bad could've happened, because bad things happened. Not to him, because the Rucci family had the best luck on the planet. His mother won the lottery all the time, only hundred dollar increments, but still. And when the Ruccis were running late, the train would be delayed, the same with planes. Larry believed that the flight to Detroit would be delayed because things usually went his way. Allie never felt that way because her sister,

Jill, had died, and it had really affected her. They talked about it in therapy all the time.

He kept his arm out, hoping to get a cab uptown, and his cell phone rang in his pocket. He kept one hand stuck out while he took his phone from his pocket with his other hand, glancing at the screen. ALLIE, it read. "Hi," he said, picking up.

"Hey, how are you? I see I missed your calls. I was in a meeting."

"Oh, with Jeff?" Larry asked, taking a flier. He wanted to see what she would say. If she was lying to him or if he was mistaken, which was possible.

"Yes, he says hi. We're talking settlement, which is great."

Larry felt a wrench in his chest. She was lying. He swallowed hard, his arm stuck out like an idiot, trying to flag down a cab that wasn't coming. The drizzle turned to rain.

"I'm in the car now. I thought I'd pick up some groceries out here. The parking is easier. Anyway, I gotta go. What did you call about?"

"Where are you, really?" Larry asked directly.

"I told you, I'm driving in the subs."

"No, you're not. I know you're not. I spoke to Jeff's secretary. He's on vacation." Larry couldn't stop himself now, even if he wanted to. The truth was out, and he was speaking from his heart. "Allie, are you having an affair?"

The line went silent.

"You're having *an affair*?" Larry repeated, shocked.

"No."

"Then where are you? Why are you lying to me? Why can I never reach you? What *is* it with you?" Larry felt wetness in his eyes and tilted his head down, hiding his face. He wasn't supposed to be crying on the streets of Center City. He was a litigator with a logo messenger bag.

"I can't explain now, I'm driving."

But Larry knew he'd caught her in a lie. "What's the matter with *us*? Why aren't you happy? Why aren't you ever going to be happy, no matter what I do? Allie, I'm miserable, I'm telling you now. *Miserable.* I'm doing the counseling, I'm trying everything, I fight with *I*-words, I'm trying to reach you, but I give up. I give up. It's not supposed to be this hard." Larry's throat thickened. "I think we should get a divorce. I think I *need* a divorce. I'm going to Detroit. I'm going to be there a week. When I come home, I'll move out."

"Larry, no, please, you don't."

"Yes, I do. I want a divorce." Larry confirmed the truth of the words as he said them. He had to give up on *happy wife, happy life.* He had to make himself happy. He couldn't be happy loving somebody who never loved him back. Who wouldn't even tell him the truth.

"Larry, you don't mean this."

"I'm tired of chasing you, I'm tired of trying to get you interested, keep you interested. I don't know what I don't have that you want, but I'm done. I love you, honey, but I'm *done.*" Larry held his breath to see what Allie would say, hoping she would beg him to reconsider. He'd never said *divorce* before because he hadn't realized how strongly he felt, but he felt it strongly, *so* strongly that he didn't even bother to flag down an empty cab three lines of traffic away.

"Larry, I'm sorry, I want to talk about this, but I can't right now—"

"Is that *it*? Is that all you got, babe? Seriously? Do you know how *woefully inadequate* that is? You can't talk—"

"But I really can't—"

"Then neither can I!" Larry hung up, angry. Tears blurred his vision, but Allie hadn't been crying at all. She never cried unless she was talking about Jill. She never even cried in therapy, where he blubbered like a baby. He was sick of having emotions for them both.

The rain fell hard, spattering his jacket. The cab was pulling over, and he hurried across the street, flagging it down. He still had a chance to make the flight.

Larry Rucci was a lucky guy.

He just didn't feel like one right now.

CHAPTER 51

■

Allie Garvey

Allie hung up, bursting into tears. A sob hiccupped from her lips. Larry had never said *divorce* before. Her marriage was really ending. It broke her heart. She couldn't believe it. He'd sounded so fed up, so sick of her. She couldn't blame him. She didn't deserve him. Marriage counseling hadn't worked, and the fucked-up girl had become a wife with issues. Stomach issues, anxiety issues, intimacy issues. She'd lied to him about where she was because she hadn't been able to tell him about David.

Allie wiped her eyes. Tears spilled down her cheeks. Her nose filled with mucus. She gripped the steering wheel, fighting for emotional control. She was following Julian in his gray Mercedes, and they were almost there, where he'd said they'd meet Sasha. She passed a sign that read BAKERTON NATURE PRESERVE, DONATED BY JULIAN BROWNE LAND MANAGEMENT, in front of a grassy pasture surrounded by a jogging path. There was a parking lot next to the street, and Julian steered into it and parked under a tree.

Allie fumbled in her purse for a Kleenex, wiped her eyes, and willed herself to stop crying. She turned in to the lot and spotted Sasha sitting on a park bench next to a tan car, smoking. Allie blew her nose, parked, and took a moment to compose herself. She couldn't get out of the car like this. She cleared her throat and checked her bloodshot eyes in the rearview. She looked like a wreck, but she couldn't worry about that now. She got out of the car.

"You okay, Allie?" Julian emerged from the Mercedes with a concerned frown.

"Yes, thanks." Allie sniffled.

"Right." Julian patted her on the back. "I miss him, too."

"Thanks." Allie blew her nose, realizing that Julian thought she was crying because of David.

"Here, look around. There's nothing as restorative to the soul as nature." Julian gestured around the preserve. "It's pretty here, isn't it?"

"Yes, really."

"My company placed this parcel under the conservation easement, and we opened it to the public in May. It's our mission to preserve open space." Julian slid a business card from his wallet and handed it to her with a smile.

"That's nice." Allie read the card, though she had known about Julian's company from Facebook.

"Come on, let's sit down." Julian touched Allie's elbow.

"Hi, Sasha." Allie forced a smile, and Sasha smiled back.

"Hey, Allie. Good to see you, and don't let Julian tell you he's anything but a ruthless businessman, bent on world domination."

"Very funny." Julian sat down next to Sasha, smiling. Then it faded. "Well, these are terrible circumstances in which to see you again. It's a damn shame that David's gone."

"I know." Allie felt her emotions well up again, though she controlled them. She had to focus. This would be her one and only chance to talk to them. "It's awful."

"Just awful." Sasha picked a piece of tobacco from her lower lip, without marring her neutral gloss. "So, Allie, what did you grow up to be?"

"I'm a child advocate." Allie wanted to talk about David, the funeral, and Kyle, but she held fire for now.

"What's that?"

"I help kids with special needs get the programming they need in school. The parents hire me, and I know special ed law and how to navigate it."

"So are you a lawyer?"

"No, but I work with the special education lawyers on behalf of the kids." Allie realized there was no room on the bench for her, so she remained standing, still the outsider with the cool kids. "How about you, Sasha? What do you do?"

"Publicity in the fashion industry, I freelance. I started with an internship at Fendi in Milan and did some modeling there and in Rome. I just got back from Grasse, for a piece about the fragrance business. I go to Paris tomorrow, then on to Nice." Sasha smiled in a pat way. "I love it, and you learn so much from travel. It opens your eyes. Americans need to travel more."

"Wow," Allie said, though up close, she could see that Sasha had changed. She was beautiful, but seemed brittle, more world-weary than world traveler. It didn't show on Facebook, but in person, that happy, confident spark Sasha used to have was gone. Sasha had been salutatorian, headed for law school like her mother, but she'd dropped out of college. Allie guessed it was because of Kyle, no matter what Sasha said now.

"Anyway, Allie." Julian cleared his throat, as if he were starting a business meeting. "It was good to see you at David's funeral. Sasha happened to be in town. I didn't expect that shit show with the boyfriend."

"Awkward." Sasha blew out a cone of smoke, which smelled unusually acrid, like French cigarettes.

"Did you guys know David was gay?" Allie asked.

"I didn't." Julian reached over to Sasha, and without his asking, she handed him her cigarette and he took a puff.

"Me, either."

"Julian, did you stay friends with David, afterward?" Allie didn't explain what she meant by *afterward*. They knew.

"No. Different schools, all that." Julian took another drag on the cigarette. "We never spoke, and neither did Sasha and I. It was for the best. It's why everything turned out fine."

"You think everything turned out fine?" Allie asked, taken aback.

"Of course, don't you? It's all good, right?"

"Totally." Sasha tilted her chin upward. "Allie, don't you think so? We didn't do anything wrong."

"*I* think we did something wrong," Allie shot back, incredulous. "We killed Kyle."

Julian's eyes flared, and he frowned. "What are you talking about?"

"What are *you* talking about? How did a bullet get in the gun?"

"I have no idea." Julian shook his head. "I didn't know the gun was loaded. All I know is I didn't load it and neither did Sasha."

Sasha nodded.

Allie thought they might be crazy. Or lying. Or both. "Then what happened? If you didn't load the gun, who did?"

"I have no idea." Julian shrugged in his fancy suit, the padded shoulders shifting up and down. "Anything is possible. It was an old gun buried in the ground. Anybody could have found it. Maybe the owner of the gun came back and loaded it."

"Possible," Sasha chimed in. "Or some other kids found it and loaded it. They could have known about it before we did, for that matter."

"Really, guys?" Allie eyed them, not disguising her skepticism. "On the same day we agreed to play that stupid prank?"

"Whatever, I didn't load it." Julian's manner remained businesslike. "And you know what, David could have."

Allie glared at him. "Why would he?"

SOMEONE KNOWS ■ 303

"He was the only one of us who knew about guns, remember? His uncle had handguns and rifles. He taught us how to load the gun."

Sasha sucked on her cigarette. "I remember that, too."

Allie wasn't having any. "David didn't have any reason to want Kyle dead. He only met him the night before."

Julian nodded. "What if he had a crush on Kyle? David got married and had a boyfriend, too. He was obviously conflicted about his sexuality. It's possible that David had feelings for Kyle and decided to kill those feelings. Then what if he felt guilty about it, all this time? And that's why he killed himself."

Sasha nodded. "That's totally possible."

"David got a crush on Kyle in a single night?" Allie asked in disbelief.

"Well, *you* fell for David that fast." Julian's eyes glinted in the sun. "I could tell, and Sasha could, too. You were all over him."

Allie flushed, feeling shamed. "That's hardly likely."

Julian raked back his hair. "I knew David better than you, Allie. Sasha and I both did."

"I understood him," Allie said, though she couldn't be sure how much she truly understood about David, how much she remembered, and how much she projected. She hadn't known he was gay, but then, they hadn't, either.

"There's another possibility." Sasha opened her palms, the cigarette between her slim fingers. "Maybe David left the gun loaded by accident. That's possible, too."

"This is bullshit." Allie couldn't stand to hear them

blame David, a convenient excuse now that he was dead. "I don't believe you. I think *you* loaded the gun, Julian. Or you, Sasha. Or you did it together—"

"Whoa." Julian's eyes flared open. He recoiled, frowning. "Are you seriously accusing me of murder? I shouldn't even dignify that with a response, but just so we're clear, once again, I didn't load the gun, either intentionally or unintentionally."

Sasha glowered, an icy blue stare. "Allie, come on, I didn't load the gun, either. I told you. We didn't *kill* Kyle. How can you even say that?"

"Julian, you were jealous of him, and, Sasha, you were mad because he made a fool of you."

"He *didn't* make a fool of me," Sasha interrupted. "I would never kill anybody, and neither would Julian. We're not the kind of people who kill people, Allie. Any more than you are. Did *you* load the gun?"

"No, of course not."

"How do I know *you're* telling the truth?"

"You know I am. I was afraid of the gun. It scared me."

"Of course it did." Sasha snickered. "You were afraid of the big scary gun because you're so sweet and nice."

"And you were *excited* by the gun," Allie shot back, angry.

"You're damn right I was! You wanna know why? Because it was *fucking exciting*!" Sasha raised her voice. "*That's* why I don't live here anymore. That's why I left Wake Forest. All the girls were from suburbs like Bakerton. Their lives were small and so were their minds. Like yours, Allie."

"Look, there's no need for that." Allie tried to get back on track. "I just want to know what happened."

"We can't know, it's too late." Julian puckered his lower lip. "Kyle and David are dead. Allie, you need to let it go."

"Let it go? Come on. If you didn't load the gun, don't you wonder who did?"

"I wondered in high school," Julian answered coolly. "But not anymore."

"Why? What stopped you from wondering?"

"Time. Maturity." Julian shook his head. "I can't even remember what happened that night, for sure. My memory's in bits and pieces. It skips, which is typical after something that upsetting. It's called 'traumatic memory,' I read about it online. The brain remembers some things but forgets others. The latest thinking is that it forgets things in order to remember others."

"Wow." Sasha nodded, impressed. "Traumatic memory. I bet that's true because there's a *lot* I don't remember from that night."

Allie suppressed an eye roll. "Sasha, how do you know that you don't remember things, if you don't remember things? I remember a lot."

"I don't," Julian interjected. "Anyway, traumatic memory is different for everyone. I read that, too. Everyone's brain chemistry is different. Like, I still can't remember who handed Kyle the gun."

"Really?" Allie asked, skeptical. "You did, Julian. You handed Kyle the gun."

"No, I don't think so." Julian shook his head again. "I remember David did."

Sasha nodded. "I remember David handing him the gun, too."

"No, *Julian* did, and David was with me." Allie felt like they were gaslighting her. "Julian, you had the gun. The gun was your thing, not David's."

Sasha shrugged. "To tell you the truth, I can't swear to anything that happened that night. It has to be because of traumatic memory, and I was drunk. So were you, Allie. You really went for it. You were totally out of it."

"She's right, Allie." Julian frowned. "I was, too. I remember feeling my eyes were blurry, and it was so dark—"

"And raining," Sasha interrupted.

"Yes, pouring." Julian looked over at Sasha. "See? I totally forgot that."

But Allie hadn't forgotten. She'd been wasted that night, but still. "The weather isn't the point."

Julian sighed. "Look. Allie, I know you're upset, and I used to be, too. It's awful what happened. It's a tragedy, for sure. But I can't explain what happened. I don't know, and neither does Sasha. You have to be satisfied with that. It doesn't matter anymore."

Allie recoiled. "It does to me, and I bet it does to Kyle's mother. Don't you think she's still grieving? Don't you think she'd want to know that Kyle thought it was a prank?" She turned to Sasha. "Sasha, what about you? Kyle played Russian Roulette for *you*. Don't you feel guilty?"

"*I'm* not why he did it, Allie. His father is why." Sasha

dropped the cigarette butt and ground it out with her Louboutin. "And if you ask me, I personally think Kyle hoped the gun was loaded. He was depressed. His mother said so in the newspaper. He *wanted* to kill himself."

"I don't think that," Allie shot back.

"*I* do." Sasha frowned.

Julian interjected again, "We'll never know. We can't know the answer to that."

"Oh, come on." Allie raised her voice. "David didn't think Kyle wanted to kill himself."

"How do you know?" Julian asked, blinking.

"He was upset that night. Did you ever talk to him about Kyle?"

"I told you, no."

"Then why do *you* think David committed suicide?"

"Hello, were we at the same funeral?" Julian snorted. "David was a closeted gay man with a pregnant wife. He never became a novelist like that author he idolized. And by the way, did you know that his idol committed suicide, too? They come in clusters."

Sasha looked over. "You mean he was triggered."

Julian nodded. "Be realistic, Allie. What happened twenty years ago has nothing to do with David's suicide."

"Then how did David kill himself? Do you know? I'll bet he shot himself."

Julian pursed his lips. "I heard he did, but that doesn't prove anything."

"I think it does." Allie felt horrified and validated, at once. "He shot himself, twenty years to the day later. I'm sure he was haunted by what we did. I wonder if he told his wife or his boyfriend. He was sensitive."

"My mother used to say that." Julian laughed.

Sasha chuckled. "Julian, we're not *sensitive* enough." She waved her hand airily and knocked over her handbag, which tumbled off the bench, spilling makeup, cigarettes, and a pill bottle. "Oh, shit." She jumped off the bench and collected the pills, with a label that read XANAX. Julian helped her, and Sasha set her purse back on the bench. "Thanks, Julian."

"No worries." Julian smiled.

Allie tried to pick up where she'd left off, but she was distracted. She flashed back to the night Kyle died. She heard the gunshot. She saw Kyle falling over. She smelled the blood. She remembered the four of them running away, panic-stricken except for Julian. "Julian, do you remember that afterward, you asked David to throw away the bottles?"

"No."

"Did you ever ask him if he did?"

"No."

"What did you do with your flashlight?"

"I don't remember."

"You thought to clean up, isn't that surprising?"

"No, I'm good in an emergency." Julian smiled slyly. "That's why I make the big bucks."

Allie let it go, turning to Sasha. "Sasha, you ran. Why?"

"I was a runner. It seemed obvious."

"Did you decide, right then? Had you planned it?"

"No, and I didn't decide, I *reacted*." Sasha's eyes went

flinty, her mascaraed lashes touching. "Is this an interrogation? Are you playing lawyer?"

"Sorry." Allie dialed it back. She didn't know what to think. Either they were lying or she was dead wrong. She couldn't push it or they would leave. She had no one else she could talk to about Kyle. "Let's start over a second. Assume *none* of us loaded the gun, even David, and we'll never know who did. What about Kyle's mother? Where does that leave her?"

"I don't know." Julian shook his head. "I don't know her. Do you?"

"No, but I wish I could help her. If we wanted, we could tell her that Kyle didn't really commit suicide. That we were there—"

"Are you *insane*?" Julian interrupted. "Are you saying you're going to tell her?"

"No, I'm not, but I think about her. She was one of the first people I looked up on Facebook. She keeps her privacy settings high, but her profile picture used to be an old yellow Lab. I think it was the dog Kyle had with him that night. I used to stare at the dog picture and feel so ashamed. Can you imagine how awful she feels to have lost her son? I can."

"Because of what happened to your mom, after your sister died?"

"That's only partly why," Allie answered, caught off-balance. So Julian knew. Sasha probably did, too. Allie's mother had never fully recovered from her depression and had been in and out of the hospital until she died of pancreatic cancer, when Allie was in college.

"Allie, it wouldn't help Kyle's mother to know that he played a prank that went wrong." Julian pursed his lips again. "You wish you could alleviate your guilt, but it's not right to do that to Kyle's mother. She's suffered enough. Be real. You're being selfish."

"I'm not saying I would tell her, but it's the truth." Allie felt confused and frustrated. She couldn't let it go, not after so long. "We've kept the truth a secret for twenty years. It's made me sick to my stomach. Literally. There have to be options."

"Correction. We don't know the truth. We can't even agree on what happened. We all remember it differently, and that makes sense because we were under the influence."

"We know some of the truth. We know we were *there*." Allie was saying what she'd needed to say for so long. She heard it pouring out of her to two jerks who didn't care in the least. "What happened to Kyle changed my life. It changed me. I function on the outside, but not inside. I can't tell anyone, and I can't go on this way."

"That's your problem." Julian met Allie's eye, his expression softening. "You have to accept that we'll never know more. A terrible thing happened to us, but there's nothing to be done. Move on."

Sasha nodded. "Allie, he's right. You're obsessed. You need to get past it, like us."

"Allie, I should go." Julian rose. "I'm late to a meeting. Take care."

Sasha stood up, smoothing down her elegant skirt. "Bye, Allie. Bye."

"Goodbye." Allie turned on her heel, went to her car, and left the parking lot without looking back. She knew they'd talk about her after she was gone, but she didn't care.

If she hurried, she could make it to the reception.

CHAPTER 52

■

Sasha Barrow

Sasha watched Allie drive away and began to panic. "Julian, do you think she'd tell Kyle's mother?"

"No. She's not gonna do anything." Julian patted her shoulder, his expression melting like it used to, and Sasha knew he was still crazy about her.

"How do you know that? She said she couldn't take it anymore. If she tells the mother, the mother could tell the cops."

"She won't tell the mother because it would upset her and Allie knows it." Julian went to his car. "Sash, I'm sorry, I have to go. I'm late."

"But she's out of control."

"Sash, don't worry." Julian opened his car door and got inside.

"How can I not? She knows everything."

"What's happened to you? You used to be so cool. Relax."

"I can't!" Sasha felt so anxious, her heart thumping, her pulse racing.

"Sash, even if she went to the police, we'd deny everything. There's no proof. It's just her word against ours. Two against one." Julian closed the door and slid down his window. "Sasha, she's nothing."

"She's not nothing. The cops aren't nothing."

"We're talking the Bakerton Police Department, not Interpol. I know them. Browne sponsors their baseball team." Julian rested his hand on hers. "Listen, why don't you stay at my place tonight, instead of a hotel? We can talk it over. Go out to dinner."

"Maybe I will," Sasha answered, leaving her hand in place. She knew he'd ask, and Julian was better than the chain hotels out here. She didn't have family here anymore. Her father had moved to Singapore, and her mother to London. They'd divorced a long time ago, amicably, of course. Everything about her family was amicable. It just wasn't intimate.

"It's 981 Cobblestone Trail Road. I'll call Francie, my farm manager, and she'll let you in. I'll be home as soon as I can."

"Okay." Sasha forced a smile, and Julian reversed out of the space, leaving her feeling panicky. She went to her car, climbed inside, and rummaged in her bag to find her Xanax. She popped one dry and eased back into the driver's seat. It wouldn't take long for the pill to work its magic.

She pulled down the visor to check her makeup, frowning at her reflection. Her skin wasn't as pretty as it used to be, and she knew it wasn't only from smoking, because every model she knew smoked. She was thirty-five, which was eighty in fashion years. Her crow's-feet were deeper, and new wrinkles creased her forehead. She thought of what Julian said.

What's happened to you? You used to be so cool.

Sasha flipped the visor up, realizing that Julian was right. What had happened with Kyle had changed her. She used to party in high school, but never like this. She used to drink, too, but she hadn't used. She'd had goals, back then.

She thought back, with regret. She'd wanted to be a fashion designer, not a publicist. She'd dreamed of owning a fashion empire, but she didn't earn enough to support herself, without her trust fund. She jetted from city to city, show to show, and man to man, surrounded by artists, models, and photographers. It looked like a party, but she was getting too old to be a party girl, and she had nothing to fall back on. Her parents disapproved of her lifestyle. She'd never achieved anything near either of them. She hadn't accomplished anything.

Sasha used to win, but no longer. She'd lost something. She'd lost everything. Her direction, her drive, herself. When Julian had called her about David's suicide, it had shaken her up. All of the memories had flooded back. She couldn't stop thinking about Kyle.

The Xanax was kicking in, and Sasha began to feel calmer. She could acknowledge that her life was going nowhere, but it didn't upset her. Her panic about Allie ebbed away. Sasha would be on her way to Paris tomorrow, beyond anybody's reach.

She eyed the grassy field through the windshield, watching the leaves moving in the breeze, and the shifting sunlight and shadow on the mowed grass. It was so strange to be in Bakerton again. The Pennsylvania terrain was burned into her brain, the hills and trees just like Brandywine Hunt, in the woods.

Sasha's thoughts floated on a pharmaceutical cloud, back in time to that Saturday night with Luiz, when they'd had sex, then loaded and unloaded the gun. She'd decided that she *definitely* didn't leave a bullet in the gun. She'd become absolutely sure over time. She was pretty sure now. She'd run into Luiz last year, and he owned an export business with offices in New York and Rio. The sex had been phenomenal. Again.

Sasha would love to talk to him again. He was even good at phone sex. He'd speak to her in Portuguese. She picked up her phone and scrolled through the names, numbers, and country codes.

She pressed CALL.

CHAPTER 53

Julian Browne

BROWNE LAND MANAGEMENT read the sign, and Julian drove into the parking lot, took the space next to his father's blue Maserati Quattroporte, and got out of the car. Browne had expanded over the years, taking over the Chester Springs Corporate Center, a modern tan brick complex with a lunchroom, a gym, and a day care center, which had been his father's idea, since his latest wife had a little girl. The marriage, his father's fourth, was already on the rocks. Had probably started on the rocks. Julian retained his primacy as the first son, having gotten in on the ground floor, family-wise. He never bothered getting to know his father's wives because they were like booster rockets that soared in the early stages, then fell back to earth after fulfilling their purpose. To get his father up.

Julian hustled into the entrance, the proverbial spring in his step since he was in love with Sasha all over again, even though he had everything he wanted sexually since he'd moved beyond voyeurism. He could see that what happened with Kyle had changed her. She'd lost her direction and her self-confidence, but he still couldn't wait to see her later. The whole mess with Kyle hadn't changed him at all, except for the better.

He entered the building and strode along the air-conditioned hallway past a framed lineup of Browne properties, blueprints, and awards like Best Single-Family Home; Best Architectural House Plan, Condo; Best Architectural House Plan, Townhome; Best Builder Marketing Campaign; Best Builder Direct Mail Piece; and many others except Best Builder, which Toll Brothers won every year, driving his father crazy. One day, Julian hoped Julian Browne Land Management would win.

He reached his father's suite at the end of the hall, stopping at the secretary's desk. "Hey, Karen, how are you?"

"Good, thanks, Julian. He's waiting for you. Go on in."

"Thanks." Julian opened the door to find his father on his phone as he stood at the floor-to-ceiling window, surveying the artificial lake on the north side of the campus. He always wore a pressed shirt with a striped Dunhill tie and a tailored Brioni suit, and his jacket would be hung on a wooden hanger on the back of the door. He'd gained weight, but it only made him look more prosperous. His hair was thick and black, silvering only at the temples, and his eyes remained intensely brown. He had crow's-feet, but he was always sunburned, so he looked healthy, not old. He'd had his teeth veneered, and his latest wife wanted him to get *injections*. He hung up the phone, and Julian knew he was up to his usual hijinks, since he was using one of his burner phones, which he called his boner phones.

"Hi, Dad." Julian sat down opposite his father's desk, a polished sheet of glass stacked with papers and a laptop.

"You're late." His father frowned, setting the boner phone on the desk with three other cell phones.

"Sorry, I was at a funeral."

"Explain these T & E expenses from last quarter. Because they're *way* out of line." His father tossed a stack of printouts toward Julian, and on top was a spreadsheet of travel and entertainment deductions from Julian Browne Land Management.

"How did you get my T & E numbers?" Immediately Julian burned with a familiar resentment.

"That's not your business."

"Dad, literally, it *is* my business. Julian Browne Land Management is my company."

"Correction. It's a wholly owned subsidiary of my company. It's part of the Browne family of companies, and if you think Tim's not going to give me numbers when I ask for them, you're out of your mind. I hired him before he had hair on his dick. I practically raised that boy."

Julian ignored the irony. His father wasn't the one who raised him. "Why did you ask him for numbers?"

"What difference does it make?"

Julian let it go. He had bigger fish to fry. "Dad, regardless of whether it's a wholly owned sub, I'm President and CEO. I run the company."

His father lifted an eyebrow, standing over him, hands on hips. "If you run it well, I'll *let* you continue to run it."

"I *am* running it well."

"Not recently. Your sales are down this quarter, twenty-eight percent. Last year overall, down five percent. That's a bad trendline. Your Sandy bubble has burst."

Julian tensed. "Dad, those expenses are legit."

"Almost $23,000 last quarter? When your sales are down? What the hell are you doing? What'd you spend the money on?"

"Travel and entertainment? What do you think?" Julian couldn't believe he had to explain it to his father, who'd lived and breathed T & E, *even more than T & A,* as he always said.

"Gimme the details."

"What, are you the IRS now?"

"If you file a return with a number this far out of whack, the IRS is gonna knock on the door. Your door. Then, *my* door."

"Please, we both know enforcement is at an all-time low."

"So says every smartass who gets audited." His father pressed his fleshy lips together. "How's it legit?"

"I take people out to eat. It's not cheap. I take them on the boat. I get party trays, first-class. Lobster, stone crab claws, shrimp. Booze, top-shelf. The whole nine, like you."

His father's eyes narrowed. "Girls?"

"No, it's not that kind of sell."

His father sniffed. "My preppy son keeps it classy."

"It's not that, either." Julian had heard that before, many times. "Building is specialized there after Hurricane Sandy. There's a lot you don't know about it."

"Oh, I'm a rookie at this real estate stuff." His father scoffed.

"Dad, building down the Jersey shore has unique issues, and I'm also flipping foreclosures, which entails remediation. You have to deal with water damage, mold—"

"Who are you *entertaining*?"

"Contractors and their subs, other builders, water-damage guys, mold-removal guys—"

"Those are your *vendors*." His father looked at him like he was crazy. "They're supposed to blow *you*. Not the other way around."

"Dad, that's not how it works down there. I need the best contractors, carpenters, and remediators to put my jobs first. The good guys are in high demand. You have to woo them or you can't get them. Everybody and his brother's calling himself a contractor. They moved from Delaware and Connecticut for the work. The hotels are full. It's a gold rush."

"It *was*, but it's over now."

"Not completely. The news stories aren't on the TV and in Philly newspapers, but some residents are still out of their homes. Others are suing their insurance companies for open claims. The grant payments are a joke.

FEMA lowballs the residents. The money gets held up. It's a nightmare for them, but for me, it's an opportunity."

"One man's ceiling is another man's floor." His father's forehead eased, so Julian continued.

"I entertain the insurance guys, the FEMA types, guys from Community Disaster Loan, Individual Assistance guys, DHS, Department of Emergency Management, Community Affairs, Jersey Economic Development, mortgage finance agencies, you name it. It's a governmental clusterfuck."

"And you want to make sure they fuck *you*." His father chuckled, and Julian joined him.

"Exactly, and I have to keep the lawyers happy, too."

"What lawyers? Government lawyers?"

"Yes, and the ones who get the Sandy people paid, who handle the claims. Private lawyers and public interest do-gooders. I need to stay in front of them so they recommend us when the check comes in."

"Sandy people? Is that what you call them?"

"Do you realize that five billion dollars in federal and state funds were disbursed for Sandy relief? Three billion was sent directly to the municipalities to be distributed to the residents. And that doesn't even consider the payout from insurance companies."

"It *is* a gold rush." His father eased into his ergonomic chair, a black Aeron.

"So you see, any T & E is well worth it. I want to parlay my experience with Sandy. I want to build and remediate after hurricanes and floods all across the country. There's gonna be more, every year, and why not expand into post-disaster building and remediation in five to seven years? It's a niche, and it's national."

"Okay, son."

Son. Julian warmed. "Not so crazy after all?"

"Not just another pretty face." His father grinned. "How'd you figure all this out again?"

"I got lost," Julian answered, and they both laughed, because they loved the story. He'd gotten lost in Mantoloking, New Jersey, and seen for himself the devastation and chaos after Sandy. He'd jumped on the opportunity, started building and flipping, making a killing. He'd bought a second home and didn't come to Bakerton unless he was seeing his mother. He'd gotten out from under his father's thumb, literally and figuratively, by running Julian Browne Land Management, even though it was *technically* owned by Browne. Hurricane Sandy was the best thing that ever happened to him.

"So you have a plan."

"Yes, for world domination." Julian smiled, thinking of Sasha. He couldn't wait to get home. She would be waiting for him. It was a dream come true.

"Better cut me in, Julian. I knew you when."

No, you didn't, Julian thought. "How so?"

"We could go into mold removal together, as partners. I have the capital, and we could get into water damage and fire damage. We could *package disaster relief.*"

"Maybe." Julian felt his father's shadow slip over him,

but he didn't want to deal now. Sasha was waiting. "Let's talk about it another time. I have to go."

"Sure, no rush." His father started scrolling through his boner phone.

"Hey, Dad, let me ask you a question. I'm having a problem with theft on one of the sites. You know anybody I could use down there, with a carry permit?"

"You mean, like, security?"

"Yes," Julian answered, since it was code for dirty work.

"I'll ask Mac. He'll know somebody. Remember him? The PM on Brandywine Hunt? He did Phase IV by the turnpike."

"Oh, right." Julian remembered. Mac was the project manager he'd gotten the bullets from twenty years ago, so they'd come full circle.

"Julian." His father set his phone aside, and a new grin spread like melting butter. "I'm wondering if you really think you sold me that bullshit."

"What?" Julian asked, his mouth going dry.

"Do you really expect me to believe that you're sucking up to these contractors because they're so *good*? I know why you're doing it."

"Dad, I don't know what you mean."

"Don't kid a kidder. You know *exactly* what I mean. You're cultivating your go-to guys who'll cut the corners you want. Their work isn't so shitty it can't pass inspection, and if it is, the inspector takes a boat ride, too. Nobody's the wiser, not before the mold starts, and the homeowners can't afford to sue you." His father spread his big palms open. "Maybe your guys skirt the OSHA regs on mold. Or ignore the code when you want, and you'll reward them. Not just a blonde on a boat, but cash. Kickbacks. Am I right?"

"You're right," Julian admitted nervously.

"I knew it!" His father burst into laughter. "I'm *proud* of you. You *need* your own guys. I have my own guys. What do you think Mac is?" He leaned over again. "Come on, tell me, what do you *really* need Mac for? It's not theft from a job site. You could handle that yourself, easy. It's bigger, isn't it?"

"Yes." Julian had to admit that, too. He'd been worrying about Allie. If she told Kyle's mother and it got to the cops, Julian would be ruined. The publicity alone would kill his business. He wasn't about to take any chances.

"Okay." His father nodded. "I was thinking of going down the shore tonight anyway. How about I meet you at Mac's, at seven o'clock?"

"Sure, thanks." Julian hadn't planned on his father being there, but no matter. His father would want to keep a lid on things, too. He wouldn't want the Browne brand damaged, either. Julian rose to go, and his father started texting.

"Women," he said to himself, chuckling.

CHAPTER 54

∎

Larry Rucci

Larry let himself into the house, having missed the flight. He was in no shape to hold the client's hand, anyway. He felt too down after his call with Allie. He slid out of his damp suit jacket and dumped it on the chair. He dropped his messenger bag by the door and tossed his keys onto the console table, where they landed with a clatter. He had to move out. He'd told Allie he was leaving, though it was killing him. The marriage counselor had said, *stand in your own truth*. Larry's truth was he loved her, but she couldn't love him back the way he needed her to.

Larry looked around the family room, trying to remember when they'd been happy here. Early on, picking out the furniture, with Allie choosing the patterned fabric for the couches, which he thought was fussy. She'd loved the mahogany end tables because they were antique, though he was never drawn to the colonial vibe.

The lamps were crystal, also not his taste, and he realized there was no trace of him in the living room. Not that he'd minded, he'd gone shopping with her and wanted to make her happy. That had been his marriage, trying to make her happy and not succeeding.

Larry went to the kitchen, opened the refrigerator, and got himself a can of beer. He took a slug, and it tasted terrific, reminding him of days up at the lake, early on with Allie. They would picnic and make out. He loved it, and so did she. Back then, she had been his best friend, but no longer. He was better friends with Kwame, a partner of his. They'd have late-night talks at a conference table cluttered with trial exhibits and empty Styrofoam cups. Kwame had just gotten divorced and had never been happier, which was why Larry had blurted it out today to Allie, on the phone. He had to wise up. Life was too short.

Larry took another slug of beer. Now they wouldn't have a baby. They'd been trying for a year, with no luck, and he knew that had made everything harder for her. She was the one who had to take her temperature and do all that happy horseshit, and the doctor thought she was too stressed to get pregnant. They'd even gotten her colitis in remission. He hoped a baby would make them stronger as a couple, and Allie would have been a great mother. He'd seen her with his nieces and nephews. She remembered their birthdays, favorite foods, and the names of their stupid stuffed animals.

He gulped his beer. Allie was the same way with him. She kept track of his blood pressure, triglycerides, and all that. She accepted him without judgment or demand. She loved him the way he was, even the way he used to be, when he was fat. She took care of him without being loving to him all the time, if that made sense, and it showed him that she was a warm, good person, inside. That she wasn't cold, just closed, sometimes. That was why he'd fallen in love with her.

Larry remembered the day he'd decided to marry her. It wasn't a romantic moment, or a magical night or vacation sex. It was something she had done that touched him so deeply, something important to him. It had happened when he was in law school, and his mother had called the apartment from Pennsylvania Hospital because she'd fallen and broken her collarbone, shopping in Philly. Allie had taken the call, but she hadn't been able to find Larry or his father. So she'd gone to the hospital herself, stayed with Larry's mother in the ER, and taken her back to her apartment in Center City. Larry remembered going to Allie's after class and hearing the two of them laughing in the bathroom, behind a closed door. He couldn't imagine why his mother was in the bathroom at his girlfriend's place.

He'd knocked on the door, mystified. *Allie? Mom? What's going on?*

Don't come in! his mother had called back, giggling.

Right! Allie had chimed in. *Girls only!*

What are you doing? Larry had asked.

I'm giving your mom a bath, Allie had called back. *Before her painkillers wear off.*

Why? Larry had asked, surprised.

His mother shot back, *Because I wanted one after that dirty hospital, why do you think?*

Larry swallowed hard at the memory, then pushed it away. After that, his mother always said, *Allie's a keeper.* It was the only time his mother had been wrong. He wasn't keeping the *keeper.* He didn't relish explaining it to his family, either. All he really wanted was a family of his own, and he didn't want to think about the family he could have started with Allie.

He left the kitchen and trudged to the stairway with his beer, ascending on autopilot. He reached the second floor and walked down the hallway with a heavy tread. He couldn't believe it was really the end. How could he have been in such denial? He was a good lawyer, trained to examine the facts, highlight the relevant ones, then spin them into a narrative. How had he ignored so many relevant facts in his own life?

He went to his closet, took his suits on their hangers, and laid them on the bed, then rummaged underneath for a garment bag and put them inside. He slid his suitcase from the bottom of the closet and threw in his shoes. He grabbed the tie tree that Allie had given him for Christmas, to organize him. He went to his dresser, pausing at the wedding photo, wondering if he should take it. It was the only one they had, and it struck him as significant that it was on his bureau, not hers. Jesus, he was the dumbest man alive.

"You'll miss me when I'm gone," Larry said, to no wife in particular. He really wondered if she would miss him. She might not have married him in the first place if he hadn't been so persistent. He grabbed assorted cuff links from his leather tray, which had also been a gift to organize him. He went into his drawers, took some underwear, socks, and tossed them into the suitcase. He went back into the T-shirt drawer for shirts and jeans, but the suitcase was full, so he zipped it closed.

He grabbed his backpack from the closet and went to the bathroom to get his toiletries. He grabbed his electric toothbrush and his Dopp kit, then realized he would need some refills for his razor. Using a real razor was Larry's thing. His father had been the same way, using a mug and a brush. His grandfather had been a barber, and all the Rucci men used real razors.

Larry opened the cabinet under the sink and started rummaging around, spotting Allie's boxes of Tampax. Every time she would get her period, she would get them out with the same teary smile. He knew she felt responsible, considering herself *the problem* they couldn't get pregnant, even though the doctors hadn't said that. Larry had tried to make her feel better, just last week.

It's both our problem, honey. If we can't have a baby, it's our problem.

Larry didn't want to think about it now. Maybe it was for the best that they hadn't gotten pregnant. He rummaged around, felt for the razors, and pulled out his hand, but in his palm wasn't his razor pack at all. It was a plastic pack of Allie's birth control pills, probably one of her old ones. He was about to toss it back in the cabinet, then took a second look.

The prescription label was on the side. The date was current, for this month.

Larry didn't understand. He slid the pill pack from the plastic sleeve.

Allie had taken a pill yesterday.

CHAPTER 55

Allie Garvey

Allie drove along Scattergood Road, her jaw set. She was going to the reception. She would introduce herself, see what she could learn, and play it by ear. She wasn't going to tell his family, but she was going to find out what she could. What they had done twenty years ago had killed David, as surely as it had killed Kyle.

She switched into the fast lane in light traffic. Scattergood Road was Bakerton's main thoroughfare, and she passed strip mall after strip mall, some new developments, and ahead on the right was Gardens of Peace. Allie glanced over reflexively, noticing that there were cars parked near David's graveside, not far from the road. She wondered if they were cemetery employees, but they didn't appear to be.

On impulse, Allie switched back into the slow lane and drove into the cemetery, cutting her speed as she cruised to David's grave site. There were two cars parked there, and three men standing at David's grave, a rectangular mound of fresh earth.

Allie peered through her windshield and recognized one of the men as David's boyfriend, who'd been thrown out of the funeral by David's father. He must have come back, with friends. She cut the ignition and watched the men, a forlorn trio. She didn't know whether to intrude, but it occurred to her that if David was going to confide in anybody, he might've chosen his lover. There was only one way to find out.

Allie got out of the car, approached the men, and waved at them. The boyfriend had clearly been crying, but the other two, dressed in casual clothes, eyed her hard. They looked younger than she was, and they closed ranks, protectively flanking David's boyfriend as she approached.

"We're allowed to be here," one of the friends said. "This is a public place."

"I know, and I'm so sorry about what happened." Allie swallowed hard. "My name's Allie Garvey, and I was at the funeral. I'm a friend of David's from school."

"Why are you here?" The one friend folded his arms, frowning.

"I just wanted to talk to David's boyfriend. I cared about David, and I wanted to say how sorry I am."

The two friends exchanged glances.

David's boyfriend nodded, sniffling. "Thank you, that's very nice of you. I'm Ryan Safir."

"Allie Garvey," Allie repeated, and if he recognized

the name, it didn't show. "You have my deepest condolences."

He nodded. "You knew David from Amherst?"

"No, Bakerton High School. We lived in the same development."

"So you go way back." Ryan forced a sad smile, and Allie could see that he was in agony.

"Ryan, do you think we could talk a minute, alone?"

"Okay," Ryan answered, glancing at his friends. "Do you guys mind?"

"Not at all. We'll be in the car."

"Thanks." Ryan nodded, and his friends left.

Allie tried to think of what she could say without showing her hand. She didn't want to upset Ryan any further. "I don't know where to start. I just—I'm so sorry about what happened. I was so sad to hear this. David was such a wonderful guy."

"He really was."

"I'm sure this is so much for you to deal with, this loss. He was so young, and so interested in life, in books, in tennis, and well, I was really crazy about him," Allie found herself saying. She hadn't planned it, but the words were coming out with a force of their own. "David was my first crush, really, my first love."

"Funny, mine, too." Ryan laughed, but it came out like a sob.

"Can I just ask—I mean, how long did you know him for?"

"About three years. We were lovers that long. We met in a bar. I know, it's a cliché."

Allie smiled, liking him, and Ryan didn't need encouragement to continue.

"I live in the West Village, and I knew he was married, living in Williamsburg, so I guess I knew what I was getting into. I hoped he would leave her, but when she got pregnant, he didn't want to do that to his son. He knew it was a boy."

"Oh, that's so sad."

"And I knew his troubles would return, and they did."

Allie paused. "What troubles, if I can ask? I mean, we lost touch, but I always thought about him."

"He was an artist at heart. Such a good writer. But it was hard." Ryan wiped his eyes, leaving a pinkish streak. His skin was fair, but his eyes and hair were dark. "David had a really good heart and he struggled, he really struggled, so hard."

Gently, Allie asked, "How?"

Ryan hesitated. "Oh, I guess he wouldn't mind, he wasn't private about it. He struggled with depression, and he had a drinking problem, and he'd been to rehab twice but he relapsed both times. He started missing meetings, and last week, it got really bad, so I guess I really wasn't surprised when, you know, he did it. I think it was his way of telling the truth, finally."

"How so?"

"I have a studio in upstate New York, in the country. It's beautiful up there, along the Hudson, that's where we would go." Ryan smiled, but it vanished quickly, too fragile to stay long. "He would tell his wife he had an assignment out of town, because he did so much travel writing, and he got hired by the chamber of commerce up there, to write about the area. So it worked out." Ryan swallowed hard. "I had to run out to a client's that night—I'm a graphic designer—and when I came home, I found him. He did it at my place. Our place."

"Oh my, that must've been horrible." Allie touched his arm, and Ryan seemed to steady in her grasp.

"It was. It was horrible, *horrible*. It was the *most horrible thing* I'll ever see, in my whole life." Ryan looked away, taking a deep breath. "And the *fact* of it, at first I thought, like, what is this about? Is he angry at me? Why did he do this *here*?" Ryan rubbed at his forehead. "And then I was like, maybe he's trying to save his wife from seeing it. But in the end, I think he wanted to make a statement about us. That we were together, this was our place, and there was no hiding it anymore. No lies anymore."

"I can see that," Allie said softly, giving his arm a squeeze.

"I didn't want to disrupt his life. I wanted him to live the way he wanted to live. I knew he would find his own truth when he was ready, and it would be his decision, not mine."

"Of course."

"His family didn't know about me, or us. They found out when I called them to say that he was dead."

"Oh, no."

"I know, and I understand how bad David must've felt, too. How hopeless. My friends are angry at him, but I'm not. I know when he would get so low, he would talk about wanting to kill himself. And when he drank, too. I'm sure his family's not surprised, if they're being honest with themselves. He was estranged from them, even his brother. He just had Martine, and she didn't know about me, either. She couldn't have been surprised that he finally went through with it, after the second relapse. He was so depressed, it's an awful disease."

"My mother had it, after my sister died," Allie heard herself say.

"Then you know." Ryan looked sympathetic, his eyelashes still wet. "He used to tell me about growing up with his dad, and the pressure, like, his father wanted him to be a major tennis star, and he was obviously homophobic. David said that ever since high school, he couldn't get things right. Like, he felt like he didn't deserve to be happy."

Allie couldn't speak for a moment, hearing the echo of the way she felt, too. She felt like she didn't deserve to be happy after what they had done to Kyle. She could never tell Larry why, and she was getting the idea that David could never tell Ryan why, either.

"I'm so sorry I'm going on and on. I mean, you must think I'm crazy, I don't even know you. But we both love David, so we do know each other, don't we?"

"Yes, we do." Allie gave him a hug, though she wasn't the huggy type. It felt like something had broken free inside her, and tears came to her eyes, which she couldn't quite explain. "So David had kind of a double life?"

"Girl, it's not that uncommon in our community."

"Even now, in Philly?"

"Even in *New York*. Not everybody's ready to come out, and I don't judge. It took me a while, and I had girlfriends."

"Oh, that's so sad. What a loss of such a wonderful human being." Allie hesitated. "I don't mean to pry, but I assume he didn't leave a note."

"No, nothing like that. He didn't need to."

"I'm surprised he had a gun."

"We kept it for protection. Up where the studio is, it's rural. Not exactly Fire Island, if you follow me. I've been the victim of a hate crime, right in town. Two men jumped me. And the house is so far out in the boonies, we weren't taking any chances." Tears filled his eyes. "God knows, I'm so sorry I had it now. Between the drinking and the depression, I should have known it was trouble."

"Don't blame yourself."

"I do."

"I understand completely." Allie gave him another hug, already thinking about what she had to do next.

CHAPTER 56

■

Sasha Barrow

Sasha turned into the gravel driveway, impressed by Julian's farm, which was as nice as anything in the Hamptons. Grassy pastures flanked a long, tree-lined driveway, which ended in a large white clapboard home with black shutters. There were several matching outbuildings, a large chicken coop, and a massive white barn with a copper windvane in the shape of a foxhunter.

Sasha hadn't thought that Julian would be *this* successful, and he still wasn't married. She could have him if she snapped her fingers, and he'd marry her, move her in, and buy her whatever she wanted. But her answer was the same as twenty years ago. There was still something weird about him, something she couldn't put her finger on. Hard pass.

She drove up the long drive to the house. It would be nice to stay here for a night, and if she was finally going to have sex with Julian, she'd take another Xanax and enjoy herself. Of course, he couldn't excite her the way Luiz did, but she hadn't been able to reach him and had left him a message to call back. Given Luiz's high-flying schedule, she wasn't optimistic.

Sasha reached the house, and a smiling woman emerged, waving her hand as she walked toward the car. She must have been Julian's farm manager, wearing a sweaty polo shirt, tan britches, and cloppy Dansko clogs. Sasha wondered if horsewomen owned a mirror, but whatever. She was here to chill, and the Xanax had done the trick.

Sasha pulled over, parked, and grabbed her Birkin full of makeup, cigarettes, and pill bottles, like a go-bag for bad girls. "Hello, I'm Sasha Barrow," she said, getting out of the car.

"Welcome. Francie Fitzgerald, the property manager." Francie pumped Sasha's hand with vigor. "Julian said you'd be in town for the night. Sorry about your loss. I understand he was a friend of yours and Julian's."

"Yes, it's so sad."

"Come with me." Francie led her to the door, her clogs clumping on the gravel, and Sasha made her way with difficulty, since her Loubs weren't made for country life.

"It's beautiful here," Sasha said, since everything was beautiful on Xanax. *Xanax* was beautiful.

"Thanks. Julian restored the property, and his company won an award for most authentic colonial representation." Francie opened the front door. "I just went food-shopping, so the refrigerator's stocked, and white wine's chilling, if you're in the mood."

"Who isn't?" Sasha said, smiling.

"The guest bedroom is made up, I'll show you." Francie checked her iPhone. "I'll be here for twenty more minutes, turning out the horses. I leave after that, so if there's anything you need, can you let me know by then? By four-thirty?"

"I don't think there's anything I need. Feel free to go."

"Let me show you around quickly." Francie shepherded Sasha into an entrance hall with white wainscoting, a brick floor, and copper light fixtures, then a living room that was equally tasteful, with navy couches, a navy and orange Heriz on the floor, and a lovely watercolor over the stone fireplace.

"By the way, that's a Wyeth. Andrew. Julian also collects N.C., and they're in his study. I'll show you."

Sasha started to lose focus. "Francie, do you mind if we don't tour? It's been a long day."

"Not a problem. Let me show you to your room." Francie walked her past the kitchen, a pocket TV room, and down a long hallway with closed doors.

They reached the end of the hall, and Francie showed Sasha a large bedroom, which was predictably lovely, with pine furniture and a panel of deep-silled windows overlooking the pasture. The bed was king-sized, covered with a flowery sheet and duvet that Sasha recognized as a Porthault pattern. On the nightstand was a bottle of white wine on ice, with two large wineglasses on a silver tray.

"Wine, how nice!" Sasha entered the bedroom, setting her handbag on the bed. "Thanks."

"It's Vermentino, his favorite. Sure you don't need anything?"

"Nothing, thanks."

"Okay, bye," Francie said, leaving. "Holler if you change your mind."

"Okay," Sasha called back, though she'd never *hollered* in her life. She poured herself a glass of wine, kicked off her shoes, settled into the comfortable bed, sipping the wine, which tasted deliciously cool and dry.

She pulled her purse over to check her phone and see if Luiz had called her back. She rummaged inside her purse but couldn't find her phone. She took out the pill bottles and her makeup kit, finding her phone and checking the screen. Luiz hadn't called, but there was a lineup of Instagram notifications she skimmed. The mellow vibe of the Xanax and wine washed over her.

Sasha took another sip, resting her head back in the deep pillow. The guest room was obviously feminine, so he must have had girls here, but maybe it was for show, like it was for her. Also the wine setup was a routine. Sasha realized she hadn't seen any personal pictures around the house. It seemed weird, and when she'd looked Julian up on Facebook after he called her, she hadn't found the same woman in any of his photos, all taken at cocktail parties with professional types.

Her gaze wandered to the windows, and Francie was turning out four horses, leading two in each hand. Sasha wondered about any woman who would spend her life with farm animals, surrounded by manure and flypaper.

Such an earthbound, mundane life. Everything that Sasha's wasn't. She couldn't finish the thought because her brain was becoming muddled, pleasantly so.

She dozed, and when she woke up, the sun was lower, sending a shaft of sunlight into the room. She checked her phone again, but Luiz still hadn't called. The house was still and quiet. Outside the window, the horses were grazing in the pasture, flicking their tails. She reached for her wine, drained the glass, and poured another, hearing the sound of the front door.

"Honey, I'm home!" Julian called out, laughing.

CHAPTER 57

■

Julian Browne

Julian hustled down the hallway, alive with anticipa-tion. Sasha was waiting for him in the bedroom. She was his dream girl, his whole life. The sight of her had brought it all rushing back. He reached the bedroom and entered it on fire. "Sasha—"

"Julian, hi!" Sasha's eyelids were at half-mast, and her smile was sloppy. But oh well.

Julian crossed to the bed, cupped her cheek, and kissed her deeply. She tasted deliciously of his favorite wine, and he loved the feel of his mouth on hers, his tongue prob-ing. Sasha kissed him back, reached up for him, and pulled him on top of her, parting her legs in her skirt. Julian couldn't believe it was finally going to happen. He fleetingly thought he wanted to film this scene, but he didn't want to stop.

Julian pulled up her skirt, feeling the strength of her slender thighs as she lifted her hips to meet him. She moaned deep in her throat, which spurred him on. He undid his belt buckle, but suddenly a cell phone started ringing, with a techno ringtone he didn't recognize.

"Oh, hold on, that's Luiz." Sasha rolled out from underneath Julian, who propped himself up, his belt dangling and his mouth hanging open.

"Sasha, wait, who's Luiz?"

"A guy I wanted to see, so I left him a message with your address—"

"What *guy*?"

"Um, my Latin lover?" Sasha started to take the call, but Julian grabbed the phone from her hand and pressed END.

"You invited another man to my house?"

"Yes, and he's fucking awesome." Sasha lost focus, and a sexy grin spread across her face, but Julian realized it was for Luiz, not him. Outrage flared in his chest.

"Who *is* this guy?"

"He's this *gorgeous* Brazilian, he was my first. He *deflowered* me." Sasha giggled, but Julian gritted his teeth, flashing back on that night in the woods, when he'd thought Sasha wanted to play Spin the Bottle with him, but she'd invited Kyle. It was happening all over again. She was choosing another man instead of him, right in front of him. She had done that his whole life, and he had watched from the window. He felt blind, raging fury.

Sasha's giggle fizzled. "Please give me my phone."

"No." Julian kept her phone at bay, but it started ringing again. He jumped up, holding the phone in the air while the awful ringtone stopped. Sasha lunged for the phone but wasn't steady enough. She almost fell off the bed, but Julian caught her, held her close, and set her back on the pillows. It was then that he saw the truth. Sasha was too unstable not to blab about Kyle. After all the love he'd offered her, she would ruin him.

"Julian, please?" Sasha held out her hand for the phone.

"I'm sorry, I don't want you to talk to that guy. You know how I feel about you. You always have."

"Julian, you don't own me. You can't own me."

Yes, I can. "I know, I'm sorry." Julian picked up the wine bottle and poured himself a glass, then refilled hers and handed it to her. "Take a sip. Let's toast to being old friends."

"Old friends."

"Old-friend zone." Julian sat on the bed, with difficulty, since he was still hard. Or maybe the thought of what he was going to do made him hard. He knew he was a freak, with the cameras in the room. All he had to do was flip a switch hidden beside the headboard, and they'd be on film. The bedroom was wired for audio, too. Julian was still a voyeur, but he wouldn't film what was going to happen to Sasha.

"Sorry." Sasha made a pouty face, then sipped her wine.

"What are these anyway?" Julian picked up the pill bottle and read the label. "Xanax. Can I have one?"

"Sure, take two."

"Will you join me?"

"No, I'm good."

"Suit yourself." Julian opened up the pill bottle and took out two, but palmed them and only pretended to put them in his mouth. "Here's to us."

"To us." Sasha drank some wine, but Julian sipped his wine, let his hand fall, and dropped his pills out of view.

"What else do you have?" Julian scanned the labels on the pill bottles. "Ativan? Ambien?"

"Ativan for anxiety and Ambien for when I fly. But you can't mix Ambien with Xanax. They're both antidepressants."

"Right, everybody knows that." Julian picked up the bottle of Ativan. "Can I have one?"

"Go for it, I'll join you this time."

"Right, totally." Julian opened the bottle of Ativan, turning his back to Sasha, and blocking her view with his body. Quickly he took an Ativan from the bottle, swapped it for the Ambien, and pretended to take a pill, turning toward her. "Here's yours," he said, dropping the pill in her drink.

Sasha giggled. "Good idea!"

"I'm full of them." Julian smiled. He didn't really want to kill Sasha, but he had no choice. It had been the same with David, who had drunk-dialed Julian last week, blubbering over Kyle. David had been feeling worse as the twentieth anniversary approached, and he'd wanted to come clean, especially since he had a baby on the way.

A kid changes everything, David had said when Julian had gone to talk to him, meeting him at David's cabin in the Hudson River Valley. They'd talked and drank, and David got drunker and drunker, almost nodding off.

He'd told Julian he'd thought about suicide and even told Julian where he kept a gun. Julian had gotten the gun and shot David in the head with David's own hand, so the blowback would be on his fingers. Then Julian had left the cabin, and since no one had known he was there, no one looked for him after he'd gone. Getting away with murder was empowering, and practice made perfect.

"I'm so shhleepy." Sasha slurred her words, leaning back against the pillow.

"Rest, baby." Julian shifted toward her. "It's been a long, hard day."

"It really has." Sasha closed her eyes, and Julian reached for her wineglass, dropping in another Ambien.

"Here, Sash, have more wine. It'll help you feel better." Julian brought the wineglass to Sasha's lips, and she tilted her head back while he poured some into her mouth. It trickled down her lips, but Julian kissed her quickly.

Sasha giggled, drowsy.

"Rest, Sash." Julian watched her eyes close and her body relax. Her head tilted to the side, and a strand of her lovely hair fell across her brow. She was so beautiful, even now. He took her hand, holding it in his, and he began to enjoy the experience of watching as her breath slowed down. He'd been watching her live, for so long. Now he'd watch her die.

He watched her chest rise and fall, slower and slower, shallower and shallower. His loving gaze traced the shape of her breasts in her silky dress, the line of her bra, which was so thin he could detect the outline of her nipples. He knew what her breasts looked like, so there was no need to disturb her now. He didn't want to touch, he wanted to see. Over the years, he'd watched the videos she posted online and kept tabs on her. He knew everywhere she'd traveled, everything she'd done.

Julian moved her hair from her face, watching her die. He finally had Sasha all to himself, and no other man would ever have her, after him. Her breaths grew fainter. Her chest moved up and down, more and more slowly. She grew very still.

Twenty minutes later, he noticed her chest stop moving. She was completely still. Julian knew she was gone, but not for him, because he would always possess her. They'd shared this ultimate moment, joining them together, forever.

Julian checked Sasha's neck for a pulse. He got none. He left her wineglass and pill bottles, then picked up the pills he had dropped and his wineglass. He left the room and hurried to the kitchen, tossing the pills down the garbage disposal, washing and drying his wineglass, then bringing it and the dishtowel back to the bedroom. He restored his wineglass to the tray and used the dishtowel to wipe Sasha's cell phone and pill bottles clean of his fingerprints.

Julian pulled his cell phone from his pocket, pressed 911, and waited for the emergency dispatcher to pick up.

"This is 911. What is your emergency, please?"

"Oh God, please send an ambulance, right away! I think my friend overdosed! This is Julian Browne, at 981 Cobblestone Trail Road. . . ."

■

CHAPTER 58

Larry Rucci

Larry sat on the bathroom floor, holding the birth control pills. Allie had gotten them filled just last month, while they were supposedly trying to conceive. She'd hidden them in the back of the base cabinet, where he'd never be expected to go. She must've stayed on the pill this past year. Meanwhile she'd made a show of marking the days she was ovulating on the calendar, taking her temperature, even checking her mucus, which he used to joke about.

Is it snotty enough? Larry would ask. *Ovulation sex!*

Well, the joke was on him. Evidently, his wife didn't want to have a baby. Or didn't want to have a baby with him. Either way, she wasn't going to get one.

Larry swallowed hard. All this time, he'd thought their problem was that they couldn't conceive. He couldn't have felt more stupid. He put the birth control pills back, keeping her secret for her. He didn't even understand why he was doing it, except that he didn't want her to be unhappy.

Happy wife, happy life.

Larry grabbed his Dopp kit, toothbrush, and razor, and left the bathroom. He stuffed the toiletries in his backpack, zipped it up, then picked up his bags, loped his backpack over one shoulder, and left the bedroom without looking back. He didn't want to cry anymore. He just wanted to end his marriage. He wanted to put himself out of his misery. He climbed down the stairs, picked up his keys and messenger bag, and left the house, slamming the door behind him. *When one door closes, another one opens,* his mother used to say.

He walked down the front stoop and headed down the street. He'd always loved Davidson Street, one of the most charming streets in Center City, right near Fitler Square. It was lined with three-story townhouses, all authentically two hundred years old, their marble stoops worn with use and their red brick façades soft and saggy in places. He and Allie had been lucky to buy here, and Larry assumed Allie would stay. She could have the house. He'd give her whatever she wanted. He was done.

Ginkgo trees lined the block, their leaves fluttering in the breeze, pretty in summer. In autumn, they shed stinky berries that Larry would usually end up tracking into the house, to Allie's consternation.

There's a bootscrape out front for a reason, his beloved wife would say.

Larry sighed, hoping that going forward, his every

thought would not concern Allie. He beelined toward his car, an Acura he'd been lucky enough to get a spot for, so he could park indefinitely with his resident sticker. He was no longer a resident. He chirped open the trunk, put his gear inside, got in the car, and started the engine.

He drove away, feeling something inside him turn off, like a big switch had been thrown. The love switch. He wasn't in love anymore. He had maxed out. Her reserve, her secrecy. Now her lies. He was done. He was fresh out of luck, and maybe finally out of love. The two things that had always defined him.

Larry turned right, then took another right, driving north toward the center of town, thinking about where to go. One of his favorite hotels was the Rittenhouse, so he headed in that direction. They had a great restaurant where he took clients and a great bar in the lobby, with a happy hour. He was determined to get happy.

He navigated the one-way streets of Center City, traveling west on Walnut, along Rittenhouse Square, which was beautiful this time of year, its old-school wrought-iron fencing surrounding shrubbery, flowers, fountains, and a wacky statue of a goat. Larry found himself thinking of dumb stuff like that, instead of his wife's birth control pills. Ex-wife's.

He took a left around the square, then a right into the entrance to the Rittenhouse, pulling up in front. A tall doorman in a classy gray uniform approached him with a professional grin, and Larry remembered his name was Joe. Larry was the kind of guy who remembered names. Allie, on the other hand, could meet somebody five times and never remember their name. He'd been the one at the cocktail party, whispering in her ear, like her assistant.

"Hey, Joe," Larry said, getting out of the car. "Good to see you again. How are you?"

"Terrific, you going to be an hour or two?"

"No, a couple days. You don't need to leave it out front."

"You got it!" Joe said, and Larry handed him the key with a twenty. Another doorman held open the glass door, and Larry went to the desk and checked in, giving his Amex and ID to the young clerk, who, if she was surprised to see an address only five minutes away, was professional enough not to say anything.

"Miss, if somebody could unpack the car and take the stuff to my room, that would be terrific. I'm going to grab a drink."

"You got it, Mr. Rucci," the clerk said, smiling, and Larry thanked her, turned around, and headed to the bar off the lobby. He opened the doors, realizing that he was entering the bar as a single man, a first in recent memory. He plastered on a smile and reminded himself that he was a litigation partner with a trim waistline, a working dick, and an excellent sense of humor, at least until he'd found the birth control pills.

Larry waded into the noisy crowd, thick with men and women in suits, ties, and dresses, their hair moussed, dyed, or plugged, everybody yakking away. The air smelled of freshened perfume and expense accounts. Everybody looked younger than him.

Larry threaded his way through the crowd, slid onto

a barstool, and rested his elbows on the old-fashioned marble bar. He sat in front of the bartender's supply of sliced lemons, limes, and maraschino cherries, which reminded him of Allie, too. She loved maraschino cherries.

He waved at the bartender, a young guy whose neck was blanketed with tattoos. Larry had no tattoos, so he doubted he'd ever get laid again. "I'll have a beer," he started to say, then caught himself. "No, make that a double malt."

"You got it!" the bartender said, and Larry wondered if everybody here was taught to say *you got it*, and if so, it was fine with him. *A divorce? You got it!*

Starting over? You got it!

"Hi," someone said in his ear, and Larry looked over to see a young woman standing there, smiling. For a split second, he almost looked behind him. But she was talking to him.

"Hi," Larry said back, recovering his composure.

"I think I've seen you at the Litigation Section meeting. You were on a panel."

"I'm always on a panel," Larry said, because it was true.

"I know how you feel. I'm in the Young Lawyers Section."

"Good for you. I'm in the Half-Dead Lawyers Section."

"Ha!" the young woman laughed, then extended her hand. "Lacy Dalrymple."

Lacy is a name? Larry thought, but didn't say. He shook her hand. "Larry Rucci."

"Lacy and Larry! Funny!"

Funny. Larry felt uncomfortable, since he was more

used to Allie and Larry. Luckily, the bartender set his drink down, and he took a gulp.

"I think you did a CLE program, too."

"That I did."

"It was about client relations. I bet you're great at client relations."

"I'm a 'people person,' my wife says," Larry blurted out, feeling his face go red. *Jesus Christ, help me. I have no idea how to talk to this fetus.*

"I can tell."

"Thanks, I think. By the way, I mean my ex-wife." Larry felt a lawyerly impulse to correct the record. "I'm newly separated."

"That's obvious." Lacy grinned. "You still have your ring on."

"Oh, right." Larry looked at his own hand, stricken. He'd totally forgotten. His ring was practically a part of him. "I guess I should take it off, but I don't want to lose it, here, in a bar." *Shut the fuck up, Larry. Shut up.*

Lacy sat down next to him, setting her red wine on the bar. "Want some company?"

"Sure," Larry said, trying to get his act together. He gulped his whiskey, which burned his throat. He tried not to choke. He'd already established himself as a happy-hour rookie and newly minted single guy. He noticed that Lacy had on a wedding band plus a major sparkler, one which Allie never would've worn. She didn't want him to spend the money on her, saying she *didn't deserve a big ring.*

You deserve a ring as big as a meatball! Larry had said.

"Larry, what firm are you at again?"

"Dichter & O'Reilly." Larry realized that she was trying to make conversation with him, but he didn't know if it counted as flirting. She was married, and it had been so long since anybody had flirted with him. The only back-and-forth conversations he'd really had with young women were job interviews, so he tried to tell himself he was interviewing Lacy for a position. "So, Lacy, where do you work?"

"Morgan Lewis. I'm an associate."

"In what section?"

"Labor. I'm in labor. That's the joke."

Larry laughed, trying to think of what to say next. *Where do you expect to be in five years? What's your greatest strength? What's your greatest weakness?* None of those were good questions at a bar, but Lacy started talking, telling about her practice, then launching into funny stories about the partners she worked for, some of whom he knew, and they started trading stories, then gossip, and ordered another round of drinks, and Larry finally relaxed, whether it was because of the booze, the pretty young girl, or the fact that his heart was so broken he had nothing left to lose. And when it was time, he found himself asking Lacy if she wanted to go upstairs.

She answered, *I do.*

Larry managed a smile, trying not to think of his wedding day.

CHAPTER 59

■

Allie Garvey

Allie hurried down the hall past the plaque that read BARTON DINNERSTEIN, ESQ., ATTORNEY-AT-LAW. She'd thought about seeing a lawyer for so long, but David's funeral felt like a catalyst. She remembered reading Dinnerstein's name in the newspapers, so she'd looked him up online and he'd agreed to see her for a consultation. He had graduated from Brandeis University and Yale Law, and had practiced law for forty years.

His office was lined with stuffed bookshelves, and a gray file cabinet that squatted next to the door with accordion files stacked on top. More accordion files were piled on the floor, topped with yellow legal pads, xeroxed cases, and black notebooks. The desk was cluttered with files, legal pads, and an old laptop, and behind the wall of paper sat Barton Dinnerstein. He was in his late sixties and his frame was so compact that his gray suit hung on him. He was balding, with black reading glasses, and his hooded eyes were a sharp blue.

"Hi, I'm Allie Garvey," she said, from the threshold.

"Please, come in." Barton smiled and stood up as Allie entered the office, shook her hand, then eased into his chair. "So, Allie, sit down, please, and tell me what I can do for you today."

Allie sat down opposite him. "So it's hard to explain," she began to say, then stopped. She felt her face flush with shame.

"My dear, please continue, I've heard it all."

"It's just . . . hard. Is everything we say confidential?"

"Yes, unless you're about to commit a crime. Are you?"

"No, but I think I may already have. I feel like I did. I don't know where to start."

"Begin at the beginning." Barton linked his fingers on his papers.

"Well, um, it began twenty years ago, with me and three kids I knew from Brandywine Hunt." Allie hesitated again. "I'm not going to name them, if that's okay."

"Names and identities are privileged. But do what makes you feel comfortable."

Allie began, telling him about seeing Sasha in the woods that very first day, and in time, the words came easier, then the sentences, memories, and feelings. She even told him about her flashbacks and how she would lie awake visualizing what had happened. Tears came to her eyes, and Barton passed her a box of Kleenex but didn't interrupt her. She finished telling him about David's funeral and her talk with Ryan, because even though she didn't know if that was legally important, she couldn't stop talking until the end.

"Well." Barton met her eye, his lined expression grave, as she finished. "I can see why this affects you so deeply."

"It does, and I want to know what I'm guilty of. I feel like we killed Kyle, and I don't know if we should go to the police or tell Kyle's mother. I feel like a murderer. I've felt like one for the past twenty years. Or like an accomplice, because even though I didn't know the gun was loaded, if someone else did, I'm protecting a murderer by keeping it secret."

"Let me explain the law." Barton pursed his thin lips. "Under the Pennsylvania Crimes Code, the crime of murder requires an intentional killing. You did not kill anyone intentionally. You did not know the gun was loaded, and you believed it was not. Legally speaking, you made a mistake of fact, which negates the requisite *mens rea*, or intent to kill. Your mistaken belief was bona fide, reasonable, and about a relevant fact. Therefore, you are not a murderer."

"Thank God." Allie sensed that she was in good hands. Barton emanated a professorial calm, and she felt close to him, having told him a story she'd never told anyone else, not even Larry. Barton didn't seem to judge her, nor did he seem to absolve her. He merely informed her, so she listened quietly.

"You're not chargeable with attempted murder, nor are you an accomplice or co-conspirator, by the same rationale." Barton cleared his throat. "Under Section

2503, voluntary manslaughter, an intense passion to kill is required, also absent here. Section 2504 is involuntary manslaughter, but even with respect to that, you aren't chargeable. Nor is there reckless endangerment, under Section 2705. It is not reckless to be handling what you believed to be an unloaded gun." Barton tented his fingers. "The only other relevant statute is Section 2505, causing or assisting a suicide, but you're chargeable under the statute only if you intentionally caused a suicide by assisting or by deception, which you did not do."

"By *deception*?" Allie shuddered. "What if one of the others loaded the gun and tricked Kyle? Are they guilty then?"

"You mean if one of the others was a 'bad actor,' as the law says?"

"Yes." Allie didn't know the term, but she got the gist. "Would he deny it?"

"Yes. They both already did, to me."

"Then the answer is no. The relevant inquiry is whether any bad actor would be charged with anything at this point, and the answer depends on what the district attorney can prove beyond a reasonable doubt. The district attorney would not charge the bad actor because he couldn't *begin* to prove that the bad actor loaded the gun."

"So the district attorney doesn't charge what he can't prove?"

"Precisely." Barton smiled. "You're a quick study."

"Thanks." Allie's mind raced, now that she was getting solid answers to questions she'd had for so long. "Is that because we waited twenty years? Or would that still have been true, back then?" She tried to clarify her thoughts. "I mean, if I had come forward back then, and the bad actor had known the gun was loaded, would he have been charged with a crime?"

"No, he would not have, even back then, because he was a juvenile. A juvenile would not have been certified as an adult, under these facts." Barton paused. "An adult who played a conventional game of Russian Roulette, that is, with a gun that the players knew was loaded, would probably be charged with reckless endangerment of another person, or REAP, under Section 2705. Even so, REAP is only a misdemeanor of the second degree. The penalty would be a fine, and he'd probably be sentenced to six months in jail."

"What if the police found out what we did, now that we're adults?" Allie wanted to ask every possible question. "What if I went to the police now, suspecting that a bad actor had loaded the gun? What would the police do?"

"Assuming hypothetically that you could *prove* the bad actor loaded the gun or knew it was loaded?"

"Yes."

"*Nothing.*" Barton shook his head slowly, puckering his lower lip. "The authorities would do nothing. The district attorney cannot go back twenty years and certify the bad actor as an adult because the statute of limitations on reckless endangerment has run. It's only two years for misdemeanors." Barton leaned forward, linking his fingers. "By the way, you would not be found liable in civil court, either. The linchpin of any wrongful death suit is whether you knew the gun was loaded, which you didn't. This, even leaving aside the fact that you were under the influence. You are simply beyond the reach of the law, and so are your friends. Period."

"So it's over?"

"Yes." Barton pushed up his glasses.

Allie fell silent a moment. "I know I'm supposed to be happy about that, but really, I'm not. It was wrong what we did, morally wrong, and I feel horrible about it. I feel guilty."

"I understand. I'm Jewish. We specialize." Barton smiled, then it faded. "Allie, teenagers make mistakes. You did, and so did the others. So did the young man who died. Kyle. He played the game of his own volition. His judgment might have been impaired, but he put the gun to his own head. He might not have believed it was loaded, but it was. His mistake of fact cost him his life. That is a tragedy, but it is not a crime, or a civil wrong."

"It *is* a tragedy." Allie nearly shook with profound sadness. "So what do I do? I'm still hiding the truth. I'm still keeping the secret. It still feels wrong. It feels unjust."

"My dear, *that* is the problem." Barton lifted a graying eyebrow. "This matter is beyond the reach of the law. Interestingly, if we don't have a law that was broken, we don't have a clear path to justice. Conversely, because you don't have a crime, you don't have a punishment."

Allie blinked.

"Let me explain," Barton said, evidently reading her expression. "This isn't a typical case, in which you go to the police, give them information, and they arrest the bad guy. A young man is dead, but there is no punishment under the law. That's the good news for you *and* the bad news."

Allie nodded. It was a lot to digest, but she followed him.

"Punishment serves many purposes. Punishment expiates guilt, identifies a wrongdoer, and protects us all. It channels and confines vengeance. There is a minimum and maximum to every prison term, and after that sentence is served, we call that 'justice.' Correct?"

"Yes."

"But what result, in the absence of a legal wrong? What result, in the absence of punishment? What is justice then?"

"Right." Allie felt as if she and Barton were reasoning together, aloud.

"You find yourself in a morass. The law can't tie it up in a bow for you, and neither can morality. Your friends are content to let it lie. You are not."

"Yes." Allie felt it strike a chord. "I want to know the truth."

"But the truth may *not* be knowable, after so long. You may have to find a way to make peace with that. I suggest that you are missing the relevant point." Barton raised a finger. "I think that because you were not given a punishment, you have been punishing yourself. Is that a fair statement?"

"Yes." Allie knew it was true.

"But if you had gone to the authorities twenty years ago, you would not have been punished for twenty years." Barton's hooded eyes flared with new intensity.

"You wouldn't have gone to jail for even a *day*. You wouldn't have been found civilly liable for even a *penny*. Yet you've given yourself a life sentence. Your friend who committed suicide gave himself a *death* sentence. Is that justice? No."

Allie hadn't thought of it that way.

"The law is about apportioning responsibility with precision. The criminal law calibrates it *by degrees*. Simply put, the punishment you gave yourself does not fit the crime. It is far too excessive. That is not justice. Justice demands proportionality."

All of the hours Allie's mind had been filled with this, she had never before thought of it that way.

"Justice also demands that you consider your role in context and in relationship to the others, not in isolation. You are the least culpable of all, Allie. You did not load the gun. You did not supply the bullet. You did not supply the gun. You did not hand the decedent the gun. It was not your idea to play Russian Roulette or a prank. You didn't encourage the others to play. On the contrary, you *discouraged* them from so doing. You wanted to call 911 afterward, even though it was futile, but they told you to run. Is that fair to say?"

"Yes," Allie answered, feeling somewhat better. "But what do I do, going forward? I can't just shake it off."

"You have a guilty conscience and a good heart. Ironically, they are conspiring against you."

Allie hadn't thought of herself as a good person in so long. His words felt like a salve.

"It is not a legal problem, but a moral one. Where

does moral guidance come from? For myself, I look to my religion. Are you religious?"

"No, not really." Allie didn't add that ever since Jill died, she lacked faith.

"I normally don't discuss my religion with clients, but allow me an analogy." Barton paused, pursing his lips. "This set of facts is akin to an accidental killing, in that you took part in something in which someone was accidentally killed. So the question becomes, how can you shoulder this responsibility, this *burden* you feel, for this accidental killing? In fact, accidental killing is as old as biblical times. The example given is someone chops down a tree with an axe, but fatally injures another by accident. God recognized that such a person, if they were righteous, would feel lifelong guilt. That person would feel that they deserve to be rejected by other people."

Allie felt that way *exactly*.

"However, God didn't want them to feel rejected. He loved them still. So He commanded Moses to establish Cities of Refuge, where people who had accidentally killed others could live. He wished them to take refuge among those who had the same feelings and who bore them not as a secret, but *shared* them as a community. God's intent was that these people would heal each other over time, through loving-kindness." Barton's expression softened, falling into deep lines. "There is a lesson there. You can find happiness in your future, but not alone. Not in isolation, as you have been."

Allie found her heart lifting with hope. Tears came to

her eyes. If she'd had a defining moment twenty years ago in the woods, she was having another one now.

Barton motioned to her hand. "I see that you're married, so you have someone who loves you."

"Oh, no, not anymore." Allie felt a wrench in her chest at the irony. "My husband wants a divorce. My marriage is over because of this. I never told him what I told you today."

Barton paused. "Perhaps you can reconcile your differences now. Reconsider telling him. Let what I told you about the City of Refuge help you decide."

Allie felt her heart beating harder. "One last question. Should I tell Kyle's mother? She's still in the area. If I tell her, do you think I'm helping her? Or will it reopen an old wound? Do you think she'll call the police? Then what do I do?"

"If she calls the police, call me. As I say, there's no legal action that can be taken against you at this point, criminally or civilly. Now, as for your threshold question, of whether to tell her." Barton met Allie's eye directly. "I'll answer that question with another question."

"What is it?"

"If you were Kyle's mother, would you want to know?"

CHAPTER 60

∎

Barb Gallagher

The grocery store wasn't busy, and Barb pushed her shopping cart along, stopping at the lettuce and trying to choose between romaine, Bibb, mâche, mesclun, and good old-fashioned iceberg, wrapped in plastic and shipped from God-knows-where. Every time she saw a head of iceberg, she thought of Kyle because it was his favorite. She used to try to talk him out of it, thinking it wasn't dark enough and had less nutrition.

It tastes like water, he would say. *It's a drink and a vegetable, combined.*

Barb picked up a head of iceberg, remembering her visit to the cemetery that morning. She still hadn't decided whether it made her feel better or worse to go, but she couldn't *not* go. She was all Kyle had, and she would always be there for him, even now. She felt as if she were keeping in touch with him, filling him in on the things that would've interested him, like LeBron James. Kyle had been a fan of LeBron from his prep school days and predicted he would be an NBA superstar.

Barb smiled at the memory now, cruising past the red, green, and yellow peppers. Since Kyle was gone, it fell to her to follow LeBron's career, which she did avidly. She was certain she owned more LeBron James jerseys than any other middle-aged woman on the planet, all of them bought in Kyle's memory. When LeBron joined the Cavaliers in 2003, she'd gotten a team picture, taken it to the cemetery, and shown it to Kyle. She'd bought her second and third LeBron jerseys in 2009 and 2010, when LeBron won back-to-back MVP awards. When LeBron left the Cavs in 2010, she told Kyle the bad news, even though she knew he would be downhearted. Keeping Kyle abreast of LeBron James was practically a full-time job.

Barb eyed the zucchini, wondering if she had the energy to bother grilling some. She kept going. She remembered one of her happy days visiting Kyle at the cemetery, which was when LeBron had come back to the Cavs in 2014. She could barely wait to get to the cemetery to celebrate. She'd showed Kyle the newspaper as if he'd been sitting across the kitchen table. She wasn't the only one who talked to the dead. Once she saw an elderly woman singing "The Best Is Yet to Come" at the cemetery. Barb was the last person to judge.

She walked along the aisles of the grocery store, but her thoughts were back in the cemetery that day. She'd been about to leave a LeBron jersey on Kyle's grave when a groundskeeper told her that Gardens of Peace didn't permit toys, trinkets, or keepsakes on the graves. The management wanted to preserve the natural beauty of the cemetery, so only real flowers were allowed, except in winter when grave blankets or artificial flowers were permissible. But they had to be silk, not plastic, and potted plants were allowed only before Easter.

Gardens of Peace? More like Gardens of Rules, Barb had told him, but he'd given her a dirty look.

Barb cruised the carrots, but didn't bother with those, either. When she had Kyle on her mind, she felt as if she had him with her, and sometimes she could feel his presence. She smiled to herself because if Kyle were here, she would've been buying everything, not in produce, but in snacks. He'd hound her, and she always gave in. Back then, her food bill was ten times bigger.

A fine mist of chilled water sprayed from the sprinklers over the display case, and Barb startled. So did a woman about her age, coming toward her in the opposite direction, with a baby in the front cart. The baby giggled, and when they all got sprayed again, Barb couldn't help but smile. "Guess we got our shower for the day!" she said to the woman, who joined her, laughing.

"We sure did!" The woman was tan with feathery gray hair, silver earrings, and a trim figure in a tank top and yoga pants. She leaned forward, beaming at the baby. "What do you think about that, Josh!"

The baby giggled again, and when Barb came alongside them, she could see that it was an adorable little boy with dark curls, big brown eyes, and a perfect smile.

The woman said to Barb, "I think he liked it! Isn't he the cutest thing?"

"He sure is," Barb answered, meaning it. The baby's eyes were so bright they danced, and he looked directly at her and smiled. Barb smiled back. "Hi, honey!"

"He likes you!" the woman exclaimed, delighted.

"Aw, you're an angel," Barb said to the baby, whose eyes widened. He pumped his pudgy fists in excitement.

"Isn't he something! My first grandchild, and I cannot *tell* you how wonderful it is! I could just eat him up! I have him two days a week and I love it! Do you have any grandchildren?"

"No," Barb answered, and her heart sank. This was the first time anyone asked her if she had any grandchildren. It snapped something inside. She'd always wondered what Kyle's children would have looked like. He'd been so handsome. She'd wondered if they'd have been as athletic, as smart, as kind, or if they'd have been shy like him. Now women her age were becoming grandmothers, a joy she'd never know.

And she'd just finished two decades of the question *Do you have any children?* She could never deny that Kyle had lived, so she always answered, *I had a son, but he passed away.* People would redden, go silent, or say with sympathy, *Oh, I'm sorry; how did your child die?* Barb would have to say the word she dreaded, *Suicide.* Which just about killed her, every time. Because people expected to hear cancer, a car accident, even drugs. Anything but suicide. For anything but that, they'd have sympathy. She worried they judged her, or worse, they judged Kyle.

"You'd better tell those kids of yours to get busy! You can't wait forever! Being Grandma is the *best*." The woman's eyes lit up, a happy blue. "You know the way you love your child? Well, you love a grandchild even more!"

"I'm sure that's right." Barb plastered on a smile. God knows she'd seen enough bumper stickers. I ♥ MY GRAND-CHILD. WORLD'S BEST GRANDMA. I'M SPENDING MY GRAND-CHILDREN'S INHERITANCE. I LOVE MY GRANDDOG.

Barb lost focus a moment, wondering if grief went on and on, and if she would ever get over this heartache. She not only would never have a grandchild, she'd never have a granddog. Sharon always wanted her to get another dog, but Barb couldn't. She had no love left to give. She was an empty vessel.

"You know why grandchildren are so great? I'll tell you why, but it's not a popular view. People say it's because you can send them home at the end of the day, but that's not how I feel *at all*." The woman bubbled over with enthusiasm. "It's because you can give *all* the love you have, with none of the worry about spoiling them. You're *supposed* to spoil them! You know what I mean?"

"Yes, but I should go, take care." Barb tried to keep smiling, but she couldn't. She turned around, abandoned the cart, and left the market.

CHAPTER 61

Allie Garvey

Allie sat in her car outside Barton's office. The events of the day were catching up with her, washing her with fatigue. It was all too much, processing David's funeral, her conversation with Sasha and Julian, and now with the lawyer. She couldn't decide what to do about Kyle's mother, and it hardly seemed possible that it was only this morning that Larry had said he wanted a divorce. Somehow that was the least significant event of the day, which told Allie something. She'd kept her husband at a distance and now she'd lost him.

She looked through the windshield of the car, watching the traffic on Lancaster Avenue. Everybody was racing home from work, and it struck her that the last place she wanted to go back to was Philly and the house she used to share with Larry. She'd taken him for granted and trashed her marriage, and she didn't need to see an empty house to remind her. And she realized she'd never really thought of the place as home, no matter how much furniture she'd stuffed it with—just as she never truly came to see the marriage as hers.

Allie was only fifteen minutes from Brandywine Hunt, but ever since the night Kyle died, she'd never felt the same about the place. It was no longer *home*. She felt so dislocated from it altogether, and from herself. She wondered if you could have a self if you didn't have a home. Growing up, she'd felt like the development was her neighborhood, but after Kyle's death it became the location of the worst thing she had ever done in her life, a crime scene. Although in truth her sense of dislocation had probably begun after Jill's death, Kyle's death had severed her location utterly. Since her mother died, her father lived there alone, a shell of a man in a shell of a house.

He'd thrown himself into his work, practically doubling his hours as an orthodontist, and he'd done more with less, since Invisalign had cut into his business. There were even chain orthodonture clinics, as dental medicine had corporatized, like everything else. He'd stopped the Jog For Jill 5K, which never caught on. Cystic fibrosis still killed children, and families still grieved. Research made advances, and Allie would read the headlines in the newspaper, her heart leaping with hope, even as she felt anger that they hadn't come soon enough for Jill.

Tears came to her eyes, and Allie realized that her father had been there for her, as much as he could be. She would have to find a way to tell him she was getting divorced. It would kill him because he adored Larry. Everybody adored Larry. Her father was closer to Larry than to her, and Allie didn't have to be a psychiatrist to figure out that she was the one with the issue, not them. She had enough issues for the entire family. But she had to change that, starting now. She picked up her phone, scrolled to her favorites, and called her father's cell.

He picked up after one ring. "Allie, how nice to hear from you!"

"Hi, Dad," Allie said, her throat suddenly thick. Something about the sound of his voice broke down whatever wall she usually hid behind. "I just want to say hi."

"What's the matter?"

"Everything's fine," Allie managed to say.

"No, what's the matter? I can tell."

"Nah, I'm fine," Allie tried to laugh it off.

"It doesn't sound like it."

Allie typically would've persisted in denying the truth, but she couldn't bring herself to do that anymore. "Honestly, Dad, things aren't going so well. I'm actually in the area. I had a funeral."

"Oh, no, is that why you're upset?"

"No, there's a lot, well, uh, Larry and I might be getting a divorce."

"Oh, no!" Her father gasped. "That's terrible news!"

"I know." Allie fought tears, hearing the shock in his voice. "I'm sorry, Dad, I'm really sorry, it's all my fault, everything."

"No, honey, not you."

"Dad, I made so many mistakes with him, and he was a good husband, a great guy, but he couldn't take it anymore. He couldn't take *me* anymore." Allie felt herself give way to tears. "Dad, I don't blame him, *I* can't take me anymore, I'm so sick of myself, I'm sick to death of myself."

"Honey, where did you say you are?"

"Fraser."

"Okay, so why don't you meet me at home in an hour? I'll be there. We'll have dinner. Hotdogs, like we used to. Remember? You used to love them?"

"Dad, you were the one who loved the hotdogs, not me."

"What?" Her father paused. "That's not how I remember it. I only ate them for you."

"I ate them for *you*!"

"Honey, go straight home. The key is under the pot, you remember."

Allie didn't, having blanked out so much about the house. She hadn't been there much since her mother's death. She always sensed her father preferred to come in town anyway, to mingle with Larry, her in-laws, and the boisterous extended Rucci family, who brought the fun on the holidays, birthdays, and other occasions. Allie wondered if every crappy family married into a good one.

"So will you meet me? I'm almost finished here. I'll be there in an hour."

"Okay," Allie agreed, reluctant.

"I have to go now."

"Okay, love you."

"Love you, too, honey. Go home."

"Okay, bye." Allie hung up, with his lovely word resonating in her chest.

Home.

CHAPTER 62

Julian Browne

Julian sat on his couch, being interviewed by Detectives Moran and Garcia while official activity whirled around them. According to police protocol, Julian's house was considered a crime scene because an unattended death had occurred on its premises. The ambulance had gone after the paramedics had examined Sasha, saying *no heart activity*, upon which Julian had shed appropriate tears. In truth, he felt them. He'd killed her, but he missed her.

The detectives and county coroner had arrived, ushering Julian from the bedroom and asking him to wait in the kitchen. Crime techs had photographed every room, the coroner examined Sasha's body, and the detectives collected and bagged as evidence her purse, pill bottles, and the wineglasses and bottle. Sasha's body, zipped into a black vinyl bag, was rolled out of the house on a gurney.

Julian had called Francie, and she'd come back to the

376 ■ LISA SCOTTOLINE

house, shocked and upset. Detective Moran and Detective Garcia had interviewed her first, in his study, intentionally out of earshot. He'd hung in the kitchen, unworried. He knew everything she'd say would support his story. He'd gotten every detail right, even the two wineglasses. When the detectives were ready to interview him, he was confident.

Detective Moran conducted the questioning, and Detective Garcia took notes. They both wore lightweight sport jackets and dark polo shirts, and Detective Moran was senior, in his forties with graying hair and a salt-and-pepper mustache, bright blue eyes, and a businesslike way about him. They knew who Julian was, and regarded him with the mix of envy and admiration that men show more successful men. He'd seen it growing up, for his father. It was serving him well today, because it was clear that the detectives did not suspect foul play.

Detective Moran was saying, "So we'd like to obtain an initial statement, primarily to capture the sequence of events earlier in the day, or days, leading up to present."

"Well, it's only today. This morning, I met up with Sasha at the funeral of a friend of ours from high school. His name was David Hybrinski. We all grew up in Brandywine Hunt. Sadly, he died by suicide."

"I'm sorry."

"Thank you. Sasha had flown in from Paris this morning, rented a car, and come directly."

"Was the funeral local?"

"Yes, at Gardens of Peace on Scattergood. I hadn't seen Sasha since high school, but I messaged her on Face-

SOMEONE KNOWS ■ 377

book when I saw his obit, and she was going to be in town, so she came."

"She must have been jet-lagged."

"Probably." Julian hadn't thought of that. It worked in his favor.

"Was she employed?" Detective Moran met his eyes directly, and Julian kept his game face on, while the other detective took notes in a skinny notebook.

"She was a freelance fashion publicist. She travels. She doesn't live here anymore."

"What was her state of mind at the funeral?"

"It was upsetting at the graveside because there was a family fight. The father of our friend threw his boyfriend out of the funeral."

"That's too bad." Detective Moran grimaced.

"It upset her."

"Is that how you would describe her state of mind?"

"Yes. She was upset after the funeral. Shaken, I guess. Her flight to Paris wasn't until tomorrow, and she planned to stay at my house. I asked Francie, with whom you spoke, to let her in before she left for the day." Julian edited out the meeting with Allie at the nature preserve. The last thing he wanted to do was put the police in contact with her.

"Had Ms. Barrow stayed here before?"

"No, never. I haven't said a word to her in decades, until today. I was doing an old friend a favor, putting her up. An old *neighbor*." Julian smiled inwardly. *Payback was a bitch.*

"So what did you do after the funeral?"

"I had a meeting with my father at his offices."

Detective Moran brightened. "My family and I live in a Browne development, Charleston Mews."

Julian flashed a professional smile. "I know it well. I worked on that project, one of our best. Two hundred homes around the reservoir. Love it."

"We do, too."

"I'll tell my dad." Julian rode the goodwill. He had earned it, after all.

"Where did you go after the meeting?"

Julian tried to look sad again. "I came home."

"What time did you get home?"

"Around six."

"Now tell me, how did you come to find the body?"

"I went to the guest bedroom and found her. It was just awful. At first I thought she'd fallen asleep, but then I saw the pills." Julian paused, pursing his lips as if he were maintaining emotional control. "I was going to do CPR but it was clear she was already dead. That's when I called 911."

"Were you aware that she used drugs? Do you have any personal knowledge about that?"

"No."

"What about alcohol? Do you know if she abused alcohol?"

"I have no idea."

"Where did the wine come from? There was a platter with two glasses."

One of which was clearly unused. "I always ask Francie to set out a hospitality plate for guests, white wine and fruit. She did that, turned out the horses, and went home." Julian paused. "I assume she told you that."

"Yes. Now, do you know how much alcohol Ms. Barrow consumed?"

"No, I didn't look at the bottle. I was so shocked when I saw her that way, I didn't think of it."

"As far as her state of mind earlier today, was it your impression she intended to commit suicide?"

"No, not at all." Julian shook his head. *Dumbfounded.*

"Did she say anything about suicide? Any words to that effect?"

"No, and if you want my opinion, I don't think it was intentional. I think it was by accident. I know she was upset after the funeral, but she wasn't suicidal, and as I said, she hadn't seen David in a long time, as far as I know."

"Do you know if she was in a romantic relationship?"

"No, but I don't think she was."

"So no boyfriend?"

Julian thought of Luiz. "Not that I know of."

"Was she ever married?"

"I don't think so."

Detective Moran paused. "Did you have a romantic relationship with her?"

She was the love of my life. "No, we were just friends."

"May I ask if you are in a romantic relationship?"

"Not really, no one steady." Julian knew they'd never find the hidden camera in the bedroom, and if they did, it wasn't illegal.

"Do you know if she had any relatives, friends, or associates in the area?"

"No idea. She told me today that her parents live out of the country."

"Do you have any idea if she had any friends who would know about her state of mind?"

"No." Julian edited out Allie, again.

Detective Moran smiled in a pat way, leaning back. "I think we have what we need, for the time being. Thanks for your time."

"Thank you."

"We'll be doing an autopsy, routine blood testing, and an initial toxicology scan. We'll need you to come to the station in a day or two. We'll go over your statement, make sure we have the details right, and have you sign off."

"Not a problem." Julian sighed. "I wonder when the funeral will be. Did you notify her family?"

"Yes, we reached the mother. The contact information was in the wallet. We normally wouldn't have moved so fast, but the press jumped on the story." Detective Moran hesitated. "I think because it involved you."

"I get it. It's gossip." Julian frowned, not completely for show. News vans with microwave towers were parked on the street in front of his house, and reporters stood at the curb smoking, talking, and filming B-roll of the horses. He didn't like the publicity, and neither did they.

"Your house will be released tomorrow. You might want to stay elsewhere tonight. I assume finding a place to stay isn't a problem for a builder." Detective Moran chuckled, and Julian did, too.

Ha ha ha. "Luckily, I have a house in Jersey, and I can stay there tonight."

"Good." Detective Moran rose, brushing down his slacks. "I have your cell number, and I'll give you a call if need be."

"Here, let me walk you to the door." Julian got up, led the way, and opened the screen door. "Thanks again, and let me know if there's anything else you need."

"Thanks for your cooperation. Again, our condolences." The detectives left the house, walked to an unmarked black Explorer in Julian's driveway, and started the ignition.

Julian waved goodbye, looking every inch the responsible Chester County citizen.

■

CHAPTER 63

Allie Garvey

Brandywine Hunt had expanded since Allie had been here. Studying the map at the development's entrance, it took her a minute to get oriented. The original development was now at the center of the property, and Thoroughbred Road, which used to be the outermost road, was now somewhere in the middle, with other roads radiating out like rings on a suburban sequoia.

Allie followed signs to Thoroughbred, passing the new McMansions, but the road had been rerouted. She realized she was approaching the section that had been the construction site where she, Sasha, David, and Julian had gone to shoot that night. The memory came back to her. She hadn't thought about the details of that night in so long, since it was buried by the horror of the night Kyle died.

She took a right turn, heading in that direction, since she had time before her father got home. The late-day sun hung low in the sky, tarnishing the rich greens of the grass and the pinks and oranges of the daylilies and coreopsis borders. She took a right turn, realizing that ahead lay the road they had walked down when it was being paved. The houses became smaller as she reached the street where the cyclone fence, gate, and job trailer had been.

The sun angled right through her windshield as she drove west, and she put down the visor, driving between lines of neat townhomes with vinyl clapboard façades and blue shutters. The townhouses were exactly the same, personalized only by different flowerpots, hand-painted mailboxes, or cute family signs.

Allie cruised ahead, remembering that she had walked here beside David, so excited to be with him walking next to her, hanging back with her, like they were a couple. She knew that he hadn't loved her, but he had liked her and been kind to her, especially that night.

She drove to the end of the street and saw that the woods hadn't been developed. It was exactly where it used to be, but thicker and more overgrown. She pulled up to the curb, parked, and lowered the window, feeling all of those sensations she felt so long ago, with David at her side. She smelled the freshness of the air and heard the noise of the turnpike, fainter now, the tree barrier fulfilling its corporate purpose.

She got out of the car, leaving the door open, looking at the woods, and somehow being in that same place transported her back to a time with David at her side. She flashed on standing beside him while Sasha and Julian got ready to shoot the gun. She remembered David going to help them load it—or at least she thought she remembered that, because these memories hadn't come to the surface of her consciousness ever, but being in the spot brought it all back. She remembered being worried about the gunplay, and that David had been so nice to her when Sasha started shooting, when she'd tried to kill something. A rabbit? A bird? No, a squirrel.

Allie could hear the gunshots ringing in her ears. *Pop pop pop pop pop.* She'd never heard gunshots before. She hadn't realized how loud they'd be, how profoundly unsettling. She didn't want to see anything get killed, not since Jill had died. She remembered fighting with Sasha, then there were more shots. *Pop pop pop pop pop.* And they reloaded. Julian had shot, too. *Pop pop pop pop pop,* she could hear the gunshots right now, she remembered them, they came five at a time. *Pop pop pop pop pop.*

Something occurred to Allie that never occurred to her before. Sasha had shot two rounds of bullets, and Julian had shot one. She and David hadn't shot at all, and David had said the gun held five bullets. If Sasha and Julian had shot three rounds of bullets, and the gun held five at a time, that would mean they'd used fifteen bullets. They'd never fired the gun again, except the night that Kyle had been killed.

Allie found herself wondering how many bullets had come in the box. Julian had said he hadn't loaded the gun. Sasha had said the same thing. Allie realized that there might be a way she could find out.

Allie's heart beat faster. As far as she knew, the box remained buried where they'd left it. She'd never gone back to dig it up. She doubted any of the others had, either. It would've been like murderers returning to the scene of a crime. Maybe they did that in the movies, but in real life, she couldn't imagine it.

Allie turned on her heel, walked back to the car, and started the engine.

She was going back to Connemara Road, where it all began.

CHAPTER 64

■

Larry Rucci

Larry lay in bed while Lacy showered in the hotel bathroom, having answered a question he'd had for some time. *What's it like to have sex with another woman?*

Surprisingly, the answer was *Meh.*

He couldn't explain it. He should have been thrilled, psyched, sated. He was in a hotel room with a big-screen TV, a king-sized bed, and a minibar stocked with Scotch and condoms. He was allegedly living the dream. Allegedly. Kwame would've high-fived him. Larry had just done what men talked about, dreamed about, obsessed over—sex with a beautiful young girl, free and unencumbered, no demands and no future, five different positions, three orgasms, two condoms, thirty-seven flavors, whatever.

But he didn't feel good. On the contrary, he felt vaguely nauseated, whether from the Scotch, from the fact that he hadn't eaten, or from what he'd done. With

Lacy, it wasn't sex, it was a workout. She wanted everything, this position, that position, her on top, him on top. *Do cowboy! I love cowboy!* she had said at one point.

I'm a lawyer, not a cowboy, Larry had thought, but didn't say. With Allie, he would have said it. They used to laugh in bed, early on. He'd loved to make her laugh.

Lacy was a marathoner with a lean body, muscular arms and legs, and small breasts because she had two percent body fat. After they were done, she'd jumped up, bounded into the bathroom, and turned on the water. Meanwhile Larry lay panting like a heart patient.

A shaft of sunlight shone through the sheer curtains, and he watched dust motes bump into each other in confusion. Everything had happened so fast. He'd slept with Lacy before he'd even unpacked. He still had his wedding band on. He was still Allie's husband. He'd set a land speed record for adultery.

"Hi, pal." Lacy emerged from the bathroom fully naked, strutting around. She had zero problem with him seeing her body, which was new for him. Allie was self-conscious when she was nude, and Larry felt the same way. There was a fat guy stuck in his head, and it was why he pulled up the sheet to cover his paunch. Also he was hiding his underwear, since they were plaid boxers. Single guys wore the tight black underwear that Kwame did, like bicycle shorts. Tommy Bahama? Or was it Tommy John? Larry made a mental note to get some and give himself a hernia.

"So how are you?" Larry asked, trying to make post-coital conversation.

"Oh, *I* know what you're asking." Lacy dropped the wet towel on the foot of the bed.

"You do?" Larry had no idea what she meant. He was worried about the wet spot her towel would make. Allie had trained him not to do that. *No wet towels on the bed.* She was right. He got it. Lacy didn't.

"Sure. I have your number. I read you like a book."

But we just met, Larry thought, but didn't say. Meanwhile she was *completely* shaved, a look he wasn't ready for. To tell the truth, he wasn't a fan. Bottom line, vaginas weren't any prettier than dicks.

"You guys are all alike."

"We are?" *Arg.*

"Yes." Lacy slipped into her thong, which reminded him of a slingshot. Surprisingly, it wasn't lacy.

"How are we all alike?"

"Oh. You want an evaluation, like those emails you get after you buy something online. 'Would you like to rate your experience?'"

"That wasn't why—"

"Or like the evaluation sheets they hand out after your panel, with a one-to-five scale. 'Number One, Unsatisfied. Number Two, Adequate. Number Three, Pleased. Number Four, Very Pleased. Number Five, Exceeded My Expectations.'"

Larry tried to laugh it off. "I was just being nice."

"Nice?" Lacy put on her bra and a white silk T-shirt that skimmed her flat tummy. Larry had never had a stomach that taut in his life. Her belly button was a pierced frown.

"Yes, nice. Asking how you are. Getting to know you."

"Oh, I see. So you want the section at the end of the form. 'Please leave any comments to help improve our programs in the future.'"

"No, not like that." Larry thought the joke was getting old.

"I've got to go. I'm late for my train."

"Okay." Larry thought they might get dinner, but evidently not.

"You're not used to this, are you?"

Larry chuckled, busted. "No, I'm totally not. I told you. I'm a divorce virgin."

"But you fooled around, didn't you?"

Larry blinked. "No."

"Come on. You can tell me." Lacy smiled slyly.

"No, I never cheated on my wife."

Lacy waved him off. "It's generational."

"Thanks."

"You look like you're judging me. I can tell by that look on your face."

"No," Larry said, meaning it. He didn't know how to make his face look less judgmental.

"I've gotten this before. You're not used to a woman having the same sexual needs as a man."

"You think I'm sexist? I don't think I'm sexist." Larry was starting not to like Lacy.

"You were surprised that I had condoms."

"No, I wasn't." *I was surprised they were red.*

"You don't realize that women want sex the same as men."

"Yes, I do," Larry shot back, but he didn't want sex the same as Lacy. He wanted intimacy, and she wanted to catch a train.

"Whatever, Larry, it was great. Wanna do it again?"

"Now?" Larry saw his life pass before his eyes. He needed a gym membership and a box of Viagra, stat.

"No, whenever. 'Would you buy from this vendor again?'"

No. "I'll call you."

"Fine." Lacy slipped into her skirt, then put on her high heels. "Do you like these?"

"Yes," Larry said, because that was always the right answer with women. He waited for the follow-up questions, like with Allie: *Are they too slutty? Are they not slutty enough? Are you sure? Are you sure? Are you sure?*

"Gotta go." Lacy flashed a smile and left, closing the door behind her.

CHAPTER 65

Allie Garvey

Allie entered the woods. Moving a branch aside, she made her way between the trees, which had grown closer together, the limbs heavier. The temperature dropped in the shade, and she crushed dried leaves and twigs underfoot. Though that night had haunted her ever since, she'd never come back here. The trees were so overgrown, providing a leafy bower that blocked the sun, leaving her feeling like she was back twenty years ago, on the night of her first kiss, and first murder.

Allie felt tears come to her eyes again, but she blinked them away, moving forward, almost tripping on a log underfoot, feeling something scratch her shin. The trail that used to be here had grown over, and she guessed that the track team no longer ran here, after Kyle. She kept going, making her way to the bottom of the hill, finally spotting the bent tree. She felt her heart stop with recognition. The four of them. Kyle. The gunshot.

She breathed, then kept walking down the hill, descending into a nightmare. She reached the tree, which had aged like a person. It seemed stooped, and its branches held fewer leaves. Twenty years was a long time in the life of a tree, as it was in a woman's. She touched the trunk with her fingertips, then looked down at the roots. She remembered where the bullets had been, since it was all coming back to her now. Since she was embracing the memories instead of pushing them away. Maybe they could help, not harm, as awful as they were.

She walked off a few paces, then squatted and moved dried leaves, grass, and twigs, and started digging. It must've rained recently because the earth was soft, but she took off her pump and used it to go faster, scratching the ground with the heel. After a few minutes, she spotted an edge of the box of bullets.

Her heart beat harder. She dug faster, exposing more and more of the box. She wrenched it from the earth. The cardboard was soft and molded in spots, but intact. It was the same yellow she remembered, and on the top it read REMINGTON. CONTAINS FIFTY BULLETS.

Allie sat down cross-legged, tore open the box, and emptied the bullets onto the hammock made by her dress. The bullets rolled around, clacking dully into each other. Their jackets were a shiny bronze. Their rounded tips were copper. They gleamed lethally in the patch of sun, a sight both horrid and lovely against the black fabric, like a jeweler's velvet.

Allie collected her thoughts, trying to stay calm. Sasha and Julian claimed they hadn't loaded the gun the night Kyle was shot, and they had used fifteen bullets at the construction site. If they were lying, there would be fewer than thirty-five bullets in the box. If they were telling the truth, there should be all thirty-five.

"One, two, three, four," Allie said, counting out slowly so she didn't screw up. Her hands trembled. She reached thirty bullets, surprised to see so many still left. She counted off the last ones. *Thirty-one, thirty-two, thirty-three, thirty-four, thirty-five. Thirty-five bullets.*

Allie recoiled, stunned. She counted the bullets again, but reached the same number. Thirty-five. She counted them one more time, just to make sure, and came to the same total. Thirty-five.

Allie sat back, trying to understand the implications. So the bullet that had killed Kyle had *not* come from this box, which meant that neither Julian nor Sasha had killed him. *None* of them had loaded the gun. *None* of them had done it. They couldn't have gotten the bullet elsewhere. They'd been too young to buy bullets. Julian had stolen them from the job trailer, so they'd have no reason to get them elsewhere.

Allie gasped. She felt shaken to her very bones. It was a revelation that changed everything. She'd believed that she had been protecting a murderer, for twenty years. She'd thought she'd been keeping a secret for a killer who deserved to be brought to justice. But she hadn't. She'd been wrong, *all this time*. She'd tortured herself for twenty years. She'd ruined her life and lost her marriage over an incorrect assumption. She'd been completely mistaken about the defining moment in her *own* life. It struck her as an epiphany of the worst kind. Or was it the best?

Her mind was so blown by the thought that Allie might have burst into laughter, if Kyle hadn't died in this very place. It would forever be where an innocent young man had lost his life. Nothing here would ever be funny. But she realized that more than Kyle's young life was lost that night. Barton had been right. Her life was lost here, so long ago, too. David had killed himself. Sasha had washed out of a stellar future. Julian had become a ruthless businessman. They hadn't been punished, so they had punished themselves.

Allie couldn't tell herself that they'd been innocent, because they'd still played a prank and handed a loaded weapon to Kyle. They weren't innocent, but they weren't completely guilty, either. She realized, for the first time, that not guilty doesn't always mean innocent. Justice isn't always black and white. This was gray, like purgatory. Like the City of Refuge. And Allie felt finally that she could live in that grayness. Now she could *live*.

Her heart lifted, just the slightest bit. She breathed easier than she had before, then she *ever* had since that night. She gathered the bullets, put them back in the box, and rose to take them with her, the same as her memories of what happened here. They would always be part of her, and she wouldn't try to suppress them, or pretend they didn't exist anymore. They *belonged* with her, forever. The past and present. The living and the dead.

Allie was going home.

■

CHAPTER 66

Larry Rucci

Larry lay still, trying to recover from sex with Lacy. The luxury hotel room was dead quiet, and the walls must have been thick. He doubted anybody had heard their lovemaking, which was a relief. Lacy had yakked up a storm, telling him to do this, do that, then when to turn her over and back again, like she was a girl steak, done on both sides.

Larry thought of Allie. She didn't give orders or make noise, but he knew when he had pleased her in bed. And with Allie, Larry had been the one who made noise, the guy trifecta of *ahh*, *oooh*, and *yes*. He liked it, all of it. Ovulation sex had made it less spontaneous, but spontaneity was overrated. He liked good, steady consistent lovemaking, like a foundation to their marriage. Their marriage bed had been a *bedrock*. They'd had that, until the end.

Larry swallowed hard, trying not to remember. He

hadn't made any noise with Lacy, and he realized it was because he didn't want to hear himself. He was hiding from himself. He had cheated on his wife, that's what it felt like. He felt regret so deep it could have drowned him, like he could've gone scuba diving. He'd need oxygen tanks to get to the bottom of this guilt ocean.

He got up suddenly, trying to shake it off. He had to snap out of it. He had to move on. He walked to the window, which overlooked Rittenhouse Square. Larry found himself looking away from the park, toward the western part of the city, to Fitler Square. It was outside his window frame, but that was where he belonged, where his home was, where his wife lived. He was homesick, lovesick, wifesick.

He would *have* to get over it. Allie had lied to him about the birth control pills. She had lied every month, when he got his hopes up about whether they'd gotten pregnant. He'd imagine the little baseball mitt he'd buy if the baby was a boy, or the tricycle if it was a girl. He wasn't sexist, no matter what Lacy said. She didn't even know him at all. *Comment section, my ass.*

Larry shook his head. He missed his wife, and he hated himself for that. He loved his wife, and he hated himself for that, too. She didn't want a baby with him, and their marriage was over. He'd already moved on, having broken the seal on meaningless sex that would end in cardiac arrest.

He went to take a shower.

CHAPTER 67

∎

Allie Garvey

Dad!" Allie said, entering the house, and her father
met her at the door, throwing open his arms.

"Honey, come here," he said, his lined face soft with
sympathy, and Allie felt her defenses give way, surrender-
ing to the comfort of a father's embrace. She was surprised that his body seemed so frail, his shoulders knobby
and spine bony through his oxford shirt. He felt like an
older man, which only made her cry harder. She couldn't
lose him, too. She couldn't lose everything. She'd been
such a terrible daughter.

"Dad, I'm sorry."

"It's okay, honey," her father said softly, his voice
vaguely raspy, and Allie breathed in the familiar smells of
faded aftershave and antimicrobial soap from the office.

"I'm so sorry, I should come out more."

"No, stop, honey, don't cry." Her father rocked her

slightly back and forth, and a memory came out of nowhere, but it wasn't of him rocking her, it was of him rocking Jill, when Jill was so sick and hurting so much, which guaranteed the tears would keep flowing.

"Everything is going to be okay. You and Larry, you can patch it up."

"No, Dad, we can't." Allie released him, wiping her eyes. "He wants out."

"Larry loves you, and you've been so happy."

"Dad, you don't understand. Hold on, let me get a Kleenex." Allie set down her purse and headed into the kitchen, where the two hotdogs were frying in butter, cut in half, lengthwise. Their aroma filled the air, and the kitchen looked neat and clean, if unused. The old pictures of her and Jill were still on the corkboard, but Allie tried not to look. She tugged a Kleenex from a box next to the undercounter TV, playing on low volume. She wiped her eyes and blew her nose.

"Honey, have some water." Her father filled a glass under the faucet, then handed it to her.

"Thanks." Allie accepted the glass and took a sip of lukewarm water. It didn't dissolve the lump in her throat, which would undoubtedly remain there until the day she died.

"Take another sip, honey."

Allie put the glass down. "Dad, so much is going on, I don't know where to start."

"Sit down, we'll talk."

"I want to stand, if that's okay. There's so much I need to tell you—"

"First, listen to me. Your mother and I didn't have the easiest time, but our marriage was a good one, before."

Allie felt a twinge. She didn't have to ask what he meant by *before*. She knew. Before Jill died.

"Marriage is about give-and-take, and I know things can go wrong when there's a medical crisis. You know your mother and I had one in a big way, with Jill. But we weathered that, and you will, too."

Allie didn't understand. "We're not having a medical crisis."

"I happen to know you are, honey."

"What?"

Her father hesitated. "Larry told me you couldn't have a baby."

Allie felt her mouth drop open. "What? When did he tell you that?"

"Christmas. He told me not to say anything. He said you wanted to keep it secret, but you know Larry."

"Oh, great." Allie laughed at the irony. A man who couldn't keep a secret married to a woman with nothing but secrets.

"He said you blame yourself because of stress. You have too much stress from your job. It aggravates your colitis. You do too much for those kids, but you have to learn to do for yourself and for a child of your own."

Allie couldn't believe her ears. "He told you all that? He never told me that."

"He was trying to help." Her father smiled shakily. "Honey, it's okay that I know. Stephanie at the office is doing IVF. She gives herself shots for two weeks."

400 ■ LISA SCOTTOLINE

"Dad, no—"

"If you don't want to do IVF, you can adopt—"

"Dad, I'm not having a baby because I don't deserve a baby."

"No, don't say that. You deserve a baby. Remember, we had you tested. You're not a carrier for CF. You can have a healthy baby."

"Dad, I don't—" Allie fell abruptly silent, glancing at the TV. A news bulletin was on, showing a photo of Sasha from their high school yearbook. Underneath, the chyron read WOMAN FOUND DEAD OF SUSPECTED OVERDOSE IN DEVELOPER'S HOME.

Allie gasped. "Dad, sorry, I have to go," she said, heading for the door.

■

CHAPTER 68

Julian Browne

Julian called Allie's cell on his burner phone. "Allie, I have terrible news about Sasha. I wanted to reach you before you saw it on TV."

"I just did!" Allie sounded shocked. "I was just about to call you! I looked up your address, and I'm on my way over. They said on TV she *overdosed*!"

"Allie, you can't come over." Julian shuddered. The last thing he needed was that blabbermouth around the crime techs. "There's police here. It's no time for visitors—"

"But what happened? She overdosed?"

"I don't know what happened. I wasn't home. I can't really talk, I have to speak with the police and I . . . I feel . . . so upset." Julian softened his voice with ersatz grief. "I've known Sasha my whole life, you know? It's so sad this happened in my house, my *home*, and it was just so awful finding her."

"You *found* her?" Allie's voice broke. "Oh my God, you must be beside yourself!"

"I am," Julian said hoarsely. "Coming after David's funeral, I just—"

"I don't know if you saw, earlier, when her purse fell over? The pill bottle fell out, and I wish I had asked her about them, said something, stopped her."

"I know, I saw them, too. I feel the same way."

"Don't you think it was accidental? It had to be, right? She was fine—"

"Excuse me, I have to answer a question for one of the crime techs." Julian covered the receiver, though no one else was in the kitchen, then came back on the phone. "Allie, sorry, I have to go. The police need me."

"But when can we talk? I want to know what happened."

"Sorry, I have to go. I can't stay here tonight. I gave my statement to the police, and I'm going to my place in Jersey."

"Where in Jersey? When are you leaving?"

"As soon as I can, after a meeting with my dad." Julian changed his plan on the fly. He could *hear* Allie wanting to ask to come to his house. She was so transparent.

"Where's your house in New Jersey? Is it far?"

"No, it's in the Pine Barrens, less than two hours away."

"Can I come and see you there? I need to talk to you. I mean . . . there are things you need to know. I've been to Connemara Road. I went to see a lawyer."

"A lawyer?" Julian asked as lightly as he could.

"I didn't tell him about you or Sasha, but you should hear what he told me."

"Okay, let's meet at my house in Jersey." Julian realized Allie was even stupider and more dangerous than he thought, but this was working out beautifully. She was walking into a trap. He would meet with his father and Mac, setting everything in motion.

"What's the address? And is this your cell?"

"Yes. My house is on a country road. Look for the painted rock with the flags on 539. It's a landmark on the left."

"Got it."

"Come around nine o'clock, after my meeting with my dad. You can stay over, if you like. Spend the weekend. It'll give us a chance to talk. You're the only person left who understands."

"I know." Allie sniffled, sounding touched. "I'll see you then."

CHAPTER 69

CHAPTER 69

∎

Larry Rucci

Larry came out of the shower to a ringing cell phone. It lay faceup on the nightstand, and the screen showed it was Allie calling. He was getting a divorce and had already had sex with an acrobat, but even so answered after one ring.

"Hello? Larry, it's me."

"I know," Larry said, his heart beginning to pound. Allie sounded upset, but he knew what she would do next because she had done it many times before. Every time they fought, she would apologize, but nothing would ever change. This time would be no different.

"Larry, listen, I know what you said this morning, but I'm really sorry."

"I don't want to hear it," Larry heard himself say, his heart speaking. "You say that every time."

"No, but this time I mean it, this is going to be different, it really is, I'm really going to change things, and it will heal us—"

"No. Just no." Larry heard the pain in his tone, and the finality.

"Larry, we don't need to get a divorce, and if you just hear me out, we can talk about it—"

"I don't want to talk about anything anymore."

Allie sighed deeply. "I'll call you later, I just want you to know that I'm really feeling good, and it's not your fault, none of it was your fault. It's always been my fault, I know that."

"That's what you always say, but nothing changes, and I finally figured it out."

"Larry, really, I love you, I have to go."

"What do you have to do? Where do you have to go?"

"I can't explain it to you—"

"Oh, no, more mysteries, more lies." Larry's bitterness welled up, and he decided to unload on her. "Do you ever stop lying? Hiding things? You've been taking birth control pills, for a *year*. I found them."

"Larry, I can explain that—"

"You told me we were trying! The ovulation, the mucus—it was all lies. No wonder you put off the testing. You lied to me, Allie."

"No, but I can't say more, I have to go. I'll call you later tonight. I love you." Allie hung up.

Larry looked out the window. She'd sounded different, or was he telling himself that? She sounded clear, like something was new in her voice, but he couldn't put his finger on it. Her tone sounded stronger, charged up. Determined. Driven.

Larry looked down at his phone. He realized he had a way to know where Allie was, without asking her.

CHAPTER 70

Allie Garvey

Allie hung up with Larry, speeding along the turn-pike. The traffic was congested, but she kept switching lanes, her nerves pushing her to keep going.

Julian had sounded so sad on the phone. He'd adored Sasha, and it had to have been awful for him to come home and find her dead. Allie thought of how broken-hearted Ryan had been at David's graveside. She couldn't imagine anything worse than coming home to find someone you loved dead. She had been there when Jill died, but the Garveys had lived in fear of that moment for years.

Allie's thoughts raced. Her stomach knotted. She tried to stay in the moment. She'd heard the wounded, angry note in Larry's voice, and she could imagine how heart-broken he'd felt finding the pills. There was so much she'd kept from him. She should've come clean with him. She should've said what she felt in her heart, that she didn't deserve a baby, that she wasn't worthy of being a mother, that she had killed another mother's child and so she had forfeited her own right to become one.

Barton had been right, she had been in exile from herself. She needed to find a new way to live, in which she could acknowledge that she was responsible for Kyle's death, but at the same time not let it destroy her life. She would explain it to Larry, and all she could do was pray that he'd give her another chance.

Allie accelerated behind a tractor-trailer, watching the terrain change but remain the same, a Jersey strip mall instead of a Pennsylvania one, a New Jersey development instead of a Pennsylvania one. Brandywine Hunt would always be with her, and that was part of her responsibility, too, but she had to move past it. She was truly her father's daughter, because he had stayed in the same house since her mother had passed. He lived within his grief, never moving past it, taking on the responsibility himself, and she couldn't do that to herself anymore.

Allie flashed on Sasha, picking up her pill bottles from the ground. Sasha had lived in her pain, too. Sasha's choice had been to self-medicate, to numb the pain. Drugs couldn't make a City of Refuge, and Sasha had succumbed just as David had, in a different way but for the same reason.

Allie's eyes filled with tears, wishing it had all been different. Wishing she could go back twenty years ago and make it better.

Allie thought unaccountably of Jill, feeling her sister's spirit with her, for the first time in a long time. Jill would've wanted to know the truth, too. Jill would've gotten in the car and driven to meet Julian. Jill would have taken her life into her own hands, if only she'd had the time. Allie couldn't let her sister down.

And suddenly Allie didn't feel trapped in her grief any longer, but felt her sister inspiring her, filling her with breath and purpose. Allie could feel the full measure of the love within her suffuse her, fill her from the center of her being to her very skin. She could love her husband the way he deserved to be loved. She had so much love to give, and now it could be free.

■

CHAPTER 71

Larry Rucci

Larry scrolled to his Find My Friends app, opened it, and watched the map come to life on his phone. He and Allie had gotten the app two years ago, when he got sick of calling around for her.

LOCATING ALLIE'S PHONE read the screen, on top of a map, and then it showed a blue line heading north.

Larry didn't get it. Where would Allie be going? Anywhere in Pennsylvania, but why? She could be going beyond, further north. New York? But she hated New York, said it was *too crazy*. New Jersey? But she hated the beach, said it was *too sandy*. Further north?

Larry hurried to get dressed. He wanted to see what his wife was up to, once and for all.

■

CHAPTER 72

Julian Browne

Julian sped along the turnpike in the fast lane. The needle climbed from seventy to eighty, and the car wasn't even breaking a sweat. It was simply the most stable vehicle he had ever owned, at any speed. He reflected that he himself was the same way. No matter how high the stakes, Julian kept his cool. As he'd told Allie, it was why he made the big bucks.

Everything was falling into place. He'd go down to the police station whenever and reiterate his statement. When the toxicology screens came in, they would confirm his story. The case would be closed in days. That left only Allie, who was driving into a trap, naïve enough to trust him.

Julian loosened his tie. So she'd consulted a lawyer, but at least she hadn't used his name. When she ended up dead, there would be no connection to him whatsoever. They hadn't even attended the funeral together. They barely knew each other, way back when.

Julian zoomed along, switching lanes to maintain his speed. Two cars up was a yellow Lambo, and he could take it but it wasn't the time to risk getting pulled over. There were cameras everywhere on the highway, and he didn't want to give the police any reason to track him or his travels. He wanted to preserve the randomness of it all—after all, it had begun randomly.

Julian thought back to the day they had buried the gun. It was random that Sasha and Allie had stumbled upon him and David in the woods, which had set in motion this chain of events. As soon as he got rid of Allie, he wouldn't worry anymore. He'd managed to forget about Kyle for twenty years, but it had all come back when David died and Allie resurfaced. He'd expected she might come back for the funeral, but he hadn't been certain, that had been random, too. Now the loose ends were about to be tied up.

Julian checked the clock on the dashboard, making good time. He remembered the way there, having gone with his father so many times when he was younger. He'd never realized that Mac was one of his father's *guys*, even when Julian sneaked the bullets from the job trailer. Mac had told him that he had the gun there to prevent theft, but Julian wondered now if that was a lie, or the truth, or if it was random. Not that it mattered.

Julian accelerated. He thought of Sasha, slipping away on his bed. He wished he could have filmed it, then he could've watched it over and over. But that would've been far too risky. He wasn't crazy.

He inhaled deeply, enjoying the cool and the stillness of the Mercedes sedan, motionless even at speed.

■

CHAPTER 73

Larry Rucci

Larry propped his phone up on the dashboard, keeping an eye on the dot that was his wife's car. She was about half an hour ahead of him, and he couldn't imagine where she was going.

He hit the gas, changing lanes, not wanting to lose ground. He couldn't help feeling like an idiot all over again, like he was in denial about Allie, always chasing her around. Now, literally. Was there any better example of everything wrong with their marriage? What the hell was he doing? What the hell was he *thinking*? Why couldn't she talk to him before?

Larry felt his teeth grinding. He was so tired of being put off by her. It was even ridiculous that he had to have a stupid app to know where his wife was. He picked up his phone, scrolled to the phone function, and pressed in Allie's number. It rang and rang, then she picked up.

"Hello, Larry?"

"Allie, where are you?" Larry asked, wondering if she would tell him the truth.

"I'm driving. I can't tell you anything more than that, I don't want to tell you now. I told you—"

"But you didn't tell me anything. Where, exactly, are you?"

"Please, Larry," Allie said, her tone turning firm. "I don't want to explain on the phone, and I can't tell you a little without telling you the whole thing. I want to tell you everything, but I want to do it face-to-face."

"What do you have to tell me? You mean it's a secret?" Larry only half-believed her, but Allie sounded so strong.

"Yes, it *is* a secret. It's a secret I've had for a long time, and it's the reason everything's wrong with us, because I've kept it in my whole life and I don't wanna keep it in anymore."

"Are you serious?" Larry rolled his eyes.

"I really am, and once I tell you, you'll understand why I kept it to myself, and also why I am telling you, finally now, after all this time."

"How long has this been a secret?"

"It doesn't matter."

"It does to me. Was it during our marriage? Like the birth control pills?" Larry couldn't resist the dig.

"No."

"From before you knew me?"

"Yes."

"Like when? College?"

"No, high school."

"A secret from *high school*?" Larry burst into laughter.

She had to be jerking him around. "Did you cheat in French II? Come on. Don't play games, Allie. Haven't you played enough games?"

"This isn't a game. It's a terrible thing that happened. When I tell it to you, I'm not sure you'll want to be married to me anymore."

"Honey, I *don't* want to be married to you anymore." Larry couldn't resist that dig, either.

"Please, I'll tell you everything as soon as I can, I promise. Now let me go. I love you, goodbye."

"Okay, I'll let you go," Larry said, but Allie had already hung up.

CHAPTER 74

Allie Garvey

Allie picked up speed, feeling more tense after she'd hung up with Larry. She hated the way he'd said, *I don't want to be married to you anymore.* Her stomach had done a backflip at the new notes in his voice, of disgust, anger, and emotional fatigue. She wanted to tell him about Kyle, but she didn't want to do it over the phone. She would do it later, after she had met with Julian.

She passed a sleek charter bus, its smoked plastic windows impossible to see in through the darkness, except for the small TV screens flickering on the backs of the bus seats. Night was coming on, dense and cloudy, blocking the moon, as she'd already crossed the bridge into New Jersey. She had only an hour until she got to Julian's, so she focused on the plan. She hoped Julian would agree with her that they should tell Kyle's mother.

Allie let the idea sit a moment, allowing it to settle into her bones. After wondering about it for so long, it seemed incredible that she was finally at this point, but she was. Even telling Larry that she'd kept a secret for so long, for twenty years, had allowed a sliver of light to illuminate the darkness in her soul. Telling Larry the whole truth would be awful, but it would also set her free.

Allie had remembered Barton's question, *if you were Kyle's mother, would you want to know?* It didn't take her long to answer that, in her own mind. Allie would feel comforted if she knew that her son's death wasn't intentional, but a prank that had gone horribly wrong. Even if Allie could never know *how* it had gone wrong, if she were his mother, she would feel better knowing the truth. At least a tiny part of her burden would be lifted.

Allie drove ahead, picking up speed because the traffic lessened at this hour. The very prospect of sitting down with Kyle's mother made her sick to her stomach, but Allie would make herself do it. It had to be done. Maybe Julian would come with her. She would tell him that even if Kyle's mother went to the police, the police wouldn't charge them, and they couldn't be sued, either. Julian's grief over Sasha's death might have already changed his mind about keeping the secret. He'd sounded so upset on the phone.

Allie clenched the wheel, determined. She didn't need Julian's permission to tell Kyle's mother, and she wasn't asking for it. She was going to tell her whether Julian came with her or not. If need be, Allie would keep his name out of it, like she had with Barton.

There was no going back, there was only going forward, and Allie hit the gas.

CHAPTER 75

Julian Browne

Twilight darkened the sky, and Julian zoomed on back roads through a rural area of New Jersey, which produced tomatoes, peaches, and corn. The homes were middle-class, well-maintained, if far apart. Most of the residents were crop farmers, but others were people who preferred privacy, like Mac.

Julian spotted Mac's house behind a cornfield that was bisected by a narrow, paved road, and he turned left and drove between the tall cornstalks. It grew darker and cooler, and the big Mercedes stirred up grasshoppers, gnats, and moths. The bugs died on the windshield, and Julian flashed on a memory of that happening before. Of him coming here with his father, when he was very young. His parents were still married at the time. It had been fun. Being alone with his father, which was unusual enough, and going somewhere strange. His father had told him they were in *New Jersey*, and Julian had thought, *It's new!*

Suddenly he remembered being inside Mac's house, maybe for his first time ever, and there had been women with his father, Mac, and other men. There had been music, too. His father had parked him in front of the TV while they all went in Mac's bedroom. But Julian didn't watch TV. He'd gone to the bedroom, opened the door, and watched them. They hadn't noticed him. They'd been busy. Everybody had been naked, hugging. It had been strange but it had excited him, and he'd never had that feeling before. He remembered the sensation. It had been *thrilling*. He realized that was when it started. The watching.

Julian left the cornfield, which ended in a manicured acre with mulched beds of azalea and rhododendron, with Mac's house in the center. It was a large ranch home of white clapboard with black shutters, cedar shakes, and a generous porch. Mac's black Audi A6 was parked in the circular driveway, in front of Julian's father's Maserati.

Julian pulled up next to the Maserati, cut the engine, and got out. The air was warm and still because the cornfield blocked the breeze, and an American flag hung on a flagpole near the front door. Julian walked up the porch and could hear Mac and his father laughing loudly inside. His father always was a Man of the People when he was with the people, a more raucous version of himself, like a politician going for the salt-of-the-earth vote.

Julian knocked, then Mac hollered to him to come in,

and he entered the house, which was the way he remembered. The entrance hall had colonial molding, the family room was to the right, and Mac and his father were sitting across from each other on couches in front of the fireplace, smoking cigars and having a beer. Mac had aged well, perennially sunburned from golf and fishing, his shoulders still powerful, and his chest a barrel in a collared shirt. He had on golf shorts and Top-Siders.

Both men got up, still laughing. "Julian, you made it!" his father said, grinning.

"Hey, Dad." Julian smiled, crossing the room.

"Julian, get over here!" Mac grinned, the cigar between his thick fingers. "Let me see you."

"Hi!" Julian gave Mac a hug, then let him go. "Good to see you again, Mac."

"You, too, kiddo. When did you get so tall? Nice suit!"

"Thanks." Julian turned to hug his father, placing one hand on his arm, but with the other, he slipped a hunting knife from his pocket and plunged it into his father's chest, burying the weapon to the hilt.

His father's face contorted in agony, only inches from Julian. His hands flew to the knife. He staggered backward when Julian released him.

"Oh my God!" Julian stepped aside, so Mac could see. "Mac, get the knife out! Get the knife out!"

"Scott?" Mac yanked the knife from Julian's father's chest. Blood geysered from the open wound. Mac looked at Julian with wild-eyed disbelief. "Julian! What did you do?"

"Relax, Mac." Julian whipped a pistol from his other pocket, aimed at Mac's chest, and pulled the trigger.

Boom! The gunshot was deafening. Flame spit from the muzzle.

Mac flew backward against the couch, his eyes bulging. His shirt erupted in a burst of crimson blood. He collapsed in a heap. His head dropped to the side.

Julian stood still, assessing the situation. Mac was dead, still bleeding from his chest. His gaze was unfocused, sightless. His jaw unhinged, his muscles slack. His body folded, unnaturally. The knife lay on the rug near his hand. So did the smoldering cigar. All the better if the house caught fire.

Julian turned to his father. He was still alive. Blood gushed from his chest. He would bleed out soon. The skin on his face was already growing pale. He was making gurgling noises. His chest heaved rapidly. He was panting. Pinkish spittle dripped from his mouth. His eyes rolled backward. He tried to keep his head up. His horrified gaze found Julian.

"Wha?" his father mumbled, barely understandably, but Julian couldn't hear anyway, the gunshot ringing in his ears.

"Dad, did you really think I believed you when you said that *we'd talk about it later*?" Julian went to his father's side, speaking into his ear. "Don't kid a kidder, right? As soon as you said you wanted to be my partner, I knew you were going to take my company. So I'm taking yours."

His father shook his head weakly. Blood spurted from his chest, lower than before. There was increasingly less volume for his heart to pump.

"I knew you'd never let me run Browne, even though I'm fully capable of it. I've been working for you since I was little. After we talked, I knew this was my chance. And it wouldn't come again."

Julian's father kept shaking his head, wobblier now. His eyelids fluttered. Pinkish bubbles slaked his chin. Blood drenched his white shirt.

"Almost finished, Dad. It will look like Mac stabbed you, but it won't look like you shot him. Your fingerprints won't be on the gun. There won't be any residue on your hand. We have to fix that."

His father's eyes went glassy. He slumped lower in the couch. He was going into shock. He paled. Blood leaked from his mouth.

Julian placed the gun in his father's hand, wrapped his father's fingers around the handle, and put his father's index finger on the trigger. Julian aimed at Mac and used his father's finger to fire. It wasn't easy, but it was doable.

Boom! Julian winced from the loud blast. Another crimson burst exploded on Mac's corpse, around the shoulder.

Julian let the gun fall from his father's hand. He stepped away, to watch. His father's breathing began to slow. Bloody foam bubbled from his lips. His head dropped to the side. His legs twitched. His breathing stilled and finally ceased.

Julian double-checked the scene. It was perfect. When the police finally came, it would look as if the two men had killed each other. The police would investigate, find that Mac worked for his father, and assume that they'd gotten into a fight while drinking. The gun couldn't be traced to Julian. He'd bought it on the street with the serial number scratched off. The hunting knife could be bought anywhere, and he'd paid cash.

Julian was getting the hang of this. You had to be good in an emergency—that was the key to everything.

He didn't need anyone's help to kill Allie. He would do it himself.

■

CHAPTER 76

Larry Rucci

Larry kept an eye on the dot on the screen that said ALLIE'S PHONE. He was still on the Pennsylvania Turnpike, but Allie had gone over the bridge into New Jersey and had gotten off at an exit. He couldn't understand where she was going.

Larry frowned, trying to figure it out. He had grown up in Clifton, in northern New Jersey, and lived his whole life in the state. He knew it well. He'd never heard Allie mention the name of anybody she knew there. Larry was dying to know what her secret was. It was almost impossible for him to believe that something that happened in high school could be that terrible, other than the fact that her sister had died, but he knew all about that.

Larry switched into the slow lane, hoping to pass the pickup in front of him in the fast lane, who'd been ignoring him flashing his high beams. Allie was about half an hour ahead of him, and he needed to catch up. There was less traffic now that rush hour was over, and he could see the orangey lights of the bridge to New Jersey up ahead, a tall arch that made a bright arc against the night.

Larry bit his lip, beginning to worry. He didn't believe Allie was jerking him around. She'd sounded so certain. Determined. He'd feel better if he knew where she was going. He decided to call her and tell her he was following her. She could get mad at him, but she was the one with the big bad secret.

Larry picked his phone off the dashboard, alarmed to see that the battery icon was on red, at eight percent. He had no idea when that happened. He looked for his car charger in the slot under the radio, but it wasn't there. He went inside the console and felt around, then remembered that he had taken the car charger out the other day and forgotten to put it back in. And he didn't have his extra charger because he'd packed it in his messenger bag, which was back in his hotel room.

Shit. Larry thumbed to the phone function and pressed Allie's picture to call her, but the call wouldn't go through. A warning came up, telling him he didn't have enough power to make a phone call. He thumbed to the text function, found her name, and hit the microphone icon to dictate.

Text me where you are going, it typed, then he hit SEND.

CHAPTER 77

■

Allie Garvey

Allie got a text alert on her phone and glanced over to see the banner on the top of the screen. It was from Larry.

> Text me where you are going

Allie felt touched. He cared enough to ask, but she still didn't want to tell him over the phone. She picked up the phone, scrolled to the text function, and hit the microphone icon to dictate.

> Tell you later, hope you understand, love you

She pressed SEND and set the phone back down, traveling south in the darkness. It seemed like a pretty area, but she couldn't see at night. Allie didn't know much about New Jersey except her in-laws' house in Clifton. She had no idea where she was going.

She double-checked her GPS, but she was going the same way as the blue line. She hadn't known that Julian had two homes. The TV news had shown a video of his beautiful stone home with outbuildings and horses in Pennsylvania. If his New Jersey home was even half as nice, it would be a palace.

She'd know soon enough.

CHAPTER 78

Julian Browne

Julian raced along the back roads. He was on a schedule, and so far, so good. He hadn't taken long at Mac's, and he'd arrive ahead of Allie, as he planned. He doubted she'd get there earlier than he told her to. She was a rule-follower. Fat kid Allie Gravy.

Julian zoomed ahead, swerving this way and that, as the two-lane road went past cornfields and dog kennels. Allie wasn't stupid, just naïve. She trusted him because she'd grown up in the same development as he did, as if geography were any guarantee of character. Sasha had thought the same thing, evidently.

People like us don't kill people, she had said.

Julian shook his head, musing as he drove. Both Allie and Sasha were completely wrong. People like us *do* kill people, and it doesn't matter at all if you grew up across the street from someone. It was random that Julian had grown up across from Sasha, and that the two of them had met at all. Or because he had loved her so much, maybe it was luck. Or fate. Or an Act of God.

Julian veered left, then right, enjoying the sensation of the car hugging the turns. He didn't believe in God, but he was starting to wonder about randomness, fate, and luck. Something was coming together in his life, especially because, since Hurricane Sandy, he was in the Act-of-God business. Every insurance policy had an Act-of-God clause, and that's why nobody was paying off and flood insurance was so insanely expensive. Because nobody could ensure against such a thing.

Julian whizzed by small clapboard houses, their cheap lights on within, their televisions flickering. He felt himself buzzing, thinking more clearly than ever before, all of his senses on high alert, every piston firing like a superb and powerful engine. Killing was an Act of God, after all. God was the only one entitled to give and take life, and whether the killing occurred in a hurricane or as a result of a bullet, Julian didn't see the difference. And if you performed Acts of God, you became God. Or a god. Or at least godlike. Because he had to admit to himself, that's how he was feeling.

Julian breathed deeply as he drove, letting the air fill his lungs, inspired, literally. He was in the zone. He could do no wrong. Everything was falling into place. He was going to run Browne after having been trained to do it, all his life. He had everything ahead of him, and the future was limitless. All he had to do was get rid of Allie, who was driving like a lamb to the slaughter.

Well, the butcher was ready.

CHAPTER 79

■

Larry Rucci

Larry watched the Allie-dot turn onto Route 206 South. He was getting more worried. She would have left behind the suburban sprawl, and it would be getting more and more rural. Route 206 traveled south through the Pine Barrens, a pine and cedar wilderness in South Jersey. It was protected by the Pinelands Protection Act, so there were few buildings there except for the old farms, houses, and ranches that were grandfathered in.

Larry accelerated, trying to make up the distance between him and Allie. He was only twenty minutes behind her, and he knew the Pine Barrens. Growing up, he used to go there with his family, walking the nature trails in the Brendan Byrne and Wharton State Forests and other areas. He'd hated those outings, being too chubby to hike comfortably. He'd suspected that's why his parents had taken him. It was supposed to be exercise but he'd never lost any weight and would come home with ticks in his underwear.

Larry watched Allie moving southward, through the middle of the wilderness. He wracked his brain to think of what she could be going there for. There was nothing there except for pine and cedar trees, for miles and miles. The kids in school used to joke that the Mafia buried bodies there. It was funny then, but it wasn't funny now.

Larry checked his phone screen. The battery icon was down to three percent. He was going to lose her any minute. He watched the Allie-dot go south, driving through Lacey Township.

Funny, Larry and Lacy!

Larry felt a deep stab of remorse. He knew one thing for sure. He loved his wife.

And he wanted her back.

CHAPTER 80

∎

Allie Garvey

Allie drove in the darkness, starting to worry she was going the wrong way. She'd just come off the traffic circle from 70 East to 72 East. After a few ranches and small businesses, the area was getting denser and more forested. She was driving along a two-lane road with almost no other traffic. It was pitch dark because there were no streetlights and no ambient light.

She put on the high beams, and they shone down the road ahead like two cones of light, but she couldn't see beyond them. Moths and other bugs flew into her path, and one time she thought she saw a bat.

She traveled along 72 East. The cell reception flickered off and on. She scrolled to the phone function, called Julian's number, and figured she'd ask. There was no harm in double-checking. He'd been so upset after Sasha's death.

Allie held the phone to her ear, listening to it ring, but

it went to voicemail and she left a message. "Hello, it's Allie. I'm on 72 East heading for the intersection of 539 North. Sound right? Can you call me? Thanks."

She pressed END, replacing the phone on the holder. She checked the reception, but it had only one bar. She hoped the call would get through. She was getting the heebie-jeebies.

She was pretty sure it had been a bat.

CHAPTER 81

Julian Browne

Julian remained on the back roads, his phone to his ear. He was listening to Allie's message, since he'd screened her call. He'd call back after he'd heard the message and figured out how to handle her. He could let nothing go wrong at this stage. He called Allie back, and she picked up immediately.

"Julian, is that you?"

"Yes, I got your message." Julian moderated his tone for maximum soothing. "Don't worry, you're going the right way."

"But it's so dark and there's nothing here. Just woods. And in some places, no cell reception."

"Exactly, it's nature." Julian laughed. "Where are you now?"

"I just got off of 72 East and I'm going up 539 North."

"Did you see the painted rock on your left yet?"

"Not yet."

"You will. Then take the second right. You'll be there in no time. I'll be there ahead of you."

"But it's in the middle of nowhere."

"I know, I bought a parcel from one of the old-timers. I paid a fortune because there are so few, and they're grandfathered in under the law." Julian was telling the truth, technically. "I'll meet you out front because the driveway is long and I don't want you to miss it. I'll wave a flashlight."

"Good, thanks." Allie was grateful, he could tell.

"I picked up a salmon filet and a bottle of wine. We'll have a good talk. It's been an awful day for us both."

"It really has," Allie said, sounding reassured. "See you soon."

"Drive safe."

"I will."

"Bye." Julian pressed END.

It was fun, playing God.

CHAPTER 82

•

Larry Rucci

Larry glued his eyes to his cell phone, watching Allie travel up Route 539. His battery was down to two percent power. The cell reception was spotty. And there was nobody around. No passersby, no police, no lights, no houses. Fantastic.

His mind raced. Allie wouldn't have realized how remote it was until she'd gotten here. The Pine Barrens were a million acres of pine and cedar forest, covering about twenty percent of New Jersey, most of it federally or state protected. Building wasn't permitted, but the houses, ranches, and cabins built by generations past were permitted to stay. The woods included bodies of water, open-pit gravel quarries, and the old Oyster Creek Nuclear Generating Station. Few people outside the area realized how vast it was, or that patches were completely desolate.

Larry shuddered. He knew Allie must have had no

idea because he'd made it sound like an enchanted forest, telling his stories about being the fat kid on the hike. About finding a tick on his *balls*, which his mother had *tweezed* out. Allie had laughed. He'd loved to make her laugh.

"Whoa!" Larry startled as a deer appeared at the side of the road. He swerved, then skidded on the sandy grit of the shoulder, just missing the animal. He braked reflexively. He breathed hard, his heart hammering.

He steered back onto the road, accelerating. He had to catch up. His battery level dropped to one percent, the icon glowing a warning red in the dark interior of the Acura.

Allie was still traveling up 539 North. There was nothing there but trees and dirt roads, most of those unmarked and unnamed. There were some houses, but they were buried in the woods. Larry knew because he had ridden ATVs there with his friends in high school.

Larry accelerated, watching Allie. In the next moment, she took a right onto one of the unmarked roads, into the woods.

"Allie?" Larry heard himself say, his heart in his throat. She was heading deeper into the Pine Barrens.

Suddenly his phone screen went black. His battery had run out.

Larry floored the gas pedal.

■

CHAPTER 83

Allie Garvey

Allie took a right onto an uneven dirt road with thick pine trees on either side. There were no houses in sight. She slowed, and her tires rumbled over bumpy patches in sand. Puddles were here and there. The road was narrow enough for only one car. It didn't have a street sign.

She drove ahead, looking left and right, but still couldn't see any lights among the trees because they were so thick. There didn't appear to be a single house on the street. Julian's had to be set far off the road, and she remembered he said he had a long driveway. She checked her phone. No service.

She lowered her window. The woods were full of sounds, only a few of which she could identify. Crickets, cicadas, and a high-pitched wail that was broken up—an owl, she guessed, but it didn't sound like a hoot. It sounded like *ooh-oooh-oooh*, like a ghost. Allie wasn't a nature girl, and she didn't like the dark. It was pitch black except for her high beams.

She felt a tingle of fear but told herself to relax. Julian had said what to expect, and there was no reason to be nervous. Larry had been to the Pine Barrens plenty of times when he was little and he'd told her the stories. She felt a twinge, thinking about him. She hoped she got the chance to tell him the funny story about how scared she'd been in the Pine Barrens. She figured he would laugh. She remembered him telling her that his childhood trips were hiking, hiking, and more hiking. He'd hated the exercise, but he'd said it was beautiful, and she supposed it would be, in the daytime.

The road wound to the right, then to the left, still bordered on both sides by pine trees. Allie kept feeding the car gas. She heard the noise of running water and looked to the left, surprised to see a stream moving along beside the road. Moonlight glinted off the water's surface, making it look like a giant python. Otherwise she couldn't see anything. Up ahead she saw the white light of a flashlight, waving up and down.

"Thank God," Allie said aloud. It had to be Julian, and she looked to the left to see the lights of his house, but she couldn't see any. Maybe the woods were too dense or his house was very far back. Or maybe he'd just gotten home and hadn't turned the lights on yet. Then again, he said he had salmon. You wouldn't want to leave fish in a car in summer.

She kept going toward the flashlight, which was a big one, and Julian shone it on his face from underneath, to show that it was him. He was smiling, and Allie laughed, relieved. She could see the glint of his gray Mercedes, parked behind him. Okay, he'd just gotten home.

She flashed her high beams, saying hello.

CHAPTER 84

Julian Browne

Julian felt preternaturally calm as Allie drove closer. The only hard part of his plan was getting her here, and he'd managed that. His hammer rested on the ground, hidden in underbrush. It wasn't the subtlest weapon, but it was untraceable and all he had left at the farm.

Julian went over his plan, mentally rehearsing. As soon as Allie pulled up, he'd pick up the hammer and bury it in her skull. It would kill her instantly. Then he'd carry her away from the road, since she wasn't fat anymore. If he couldn't, he'd drag her. No one ever came here, and there were no houses around for miles. It would be a long time before anybody would find her corpse, if ever. Rain would hide their footprints and tire marks. She'd have decomposed, her flesh eaten away by foxes, vultures, and bugs. As for her car, he knew a guy who'd break it down for parts, no questions asked. The plan would work. Evidently, practice really did make perfect.

Allie closed in, twenty-five feet away, then twenty, then ten. She stopped the car. "I made it!" she called out her car window happily.

"Well done!" Julian called back. He dropped the flashlight near where the hammer was hidden, as if by accident. He picked up the flashlight in his left hand and the hammer in his right.

Tucking it behind his back.

CHAPTER 85

■

Larry Rucci

Larry squeezed the steering wheel. Every fiber of his being told him something was wrong. He had to get to Allie. There were almost no houses out here. Allie didn't know anybody who lived here. There was no logical reason for her to be here.

He raced up the road, accelerating to seventy-five miles an hour, then eighty, then eighty-five. He couldn't go any faster without risking hitting a deer or crashing, which wouldn't help Allie.

Larry's high beams pierced the darkness, but they didn't go far enough. He felt like he was outrunning them. Bugs and moths flew crazily, scattering around his car. Air blew through his open window. He was almost at the road where she'd turned right. It must have been an unmarked road, like many of them this deep. They weren't even named on maps.

"Allie!" he yelled out the window.

The woods and wind swallowed his cry.

CHAPTER 86

∎

Allie Garvey

Allie cut the ignition, which turned off her interior lights and high beams, plunging her into darkness. She got the keys out of the ignition and dropped them in her purse.

"I'm proud of you, Allie!" Julian walked toward the car with the flashlight, aiming it on the ground. "You're a country girl now."

"This *is* the middle of nowhere," Allie said as she got out of the car, looking around. There was no light except for his flashlight, and clouds passed in front of the moon. The woods were too dense to see his house. She heard the stream rushing along the road. The air felt cool and damp. The forest was filled with sound. The road was deep sand.

"Welcome!" Julian kept walking toward her, aiming the flashlight on the ground.

"Where *is* your house?" Allie asked. She slowed her

walk to meet him, feeling a nervous tingle. She looked to the left, squinting. There was nothing but trees. And Julian's car wasn't parked in any driveway. Her stomach tightened.

Allie stopped. Julian hadn't answered her question. He kept coming, swinging the flashlight, most of him in shadow. Her eyes adjusted to the darkness. There was no house here, and they both knew it now.

Her mouth went dry. She turned and ran back to the car.

"No!" she screamed, reaching the door and tearing it open.

CHAPTER 87

Julian Browne

Julian swung the hammer down on Allie as she opened her car door. She jumped aside at the last instant. The hammer connected with her right wrist, missing her head. He heard her bone break.

Allie cried in pain. She reached for her wrist, stunned. Her purse fell to the ground.

Julian raised the hammer again, but slipped on the downswing. In that split second, Allie took off running down the road. She screamed for help. No one would hear.

He raced after her, slipping again. His Gucci loafers provided no traction. He had to get her. He was pissed at himself. Now he had to chase her down.

Allie kicked off her heels, ran off the road and into the forest. The woods down here were dense, which was why he'd given her this location. His farm was to the south, still in the Pine Barrens but closer to civilization. The last thing he needed was a dead body near his house, after all of these recent deaths.

Allie screamed for help. Julian entered the woods on the diagonal, following the sound. He aimed the flashlight in her direction. The jittery cone of light located her after a moment. Her dress was black but he could see her. She wasn't that far ahead of him.

He would catch her and bash her head in.

CHAPTER 88

∎

Larry Rucci

Larry reached the street where Allie had turned right. He veered around the corner. The back of his car skidded on the sand, fishtailing.

He hit the gas and steered straight. He squinted to see down the road. The only lights were his headlights. He couldn't see anything.

He accelerated to eighty-five, gripping the steering wheel as the road curved to the right, then the left. Finally, it was a straightaway.

Larry saw something up ahead, on the left. Parked cars. It had to be Allie, and someone else. That couldn't be good.

His high beams shone on the cars as he got closer. The nearer car was Allie's. His heart leapt into his throat. The other car was a Mercedes sedan.

Larry slowed down, parking behind Allie. Her car was empty. The passenger side door hung open. The sight terrified him.

"Allie!" he yelled, honking his horn. "Allie!"

CHAPTER 89

Allie Garvey

Allie ran through the woods, in pain from her wrist. It hung useless, and the jostling made it throb. But she couldn't panic. She ran for her life.

Her heart thudded. Her breath became ragged. She panted from exertion and terror. She used her good hand to clear the branches as she ran. The trees grew so close together it was hard to get through. The branches were thick. The pine needles tore her arm and scratched her cheeks. Her hair got caught.

Julian was going to kill her. She screamed for help. No one was around. She realized that Julian must have killed Sasha. He'd made it look like an overdose. He must have wanted to silence her.

Julian shone his flashlight around. The circle of light found her. He knew where she was. Horror powered her forward. She had to go faster.

Suddenly Allie heard honking and shouting. Someone was calling her. It was Larry. The sound was somewhere behind her. Her heart leapt with hope. She had no idea how he had gotten here, but it didn't matter.

"Larry, help!" Allie screamed at the top of her lungs.

CHAPTER 90

■

Julian Browne

Julian raced through the woods after Allie. He used the flashlight and the hammer to break the branches in his path. It gave him an advantage. He could move faster than she could. He was closing the distance between them.

Pine needles scratched his face and snagged threads on his sport coat. He kept tripping on the underbrush in his loafers, which only made him angrier. Allie was ruining everything. When he caught her, he'd make her pay.

Julian heard honking, then shouting coming from the road behind him. Someone was calling her name. A man's voice.

Julian had no idea how the man knew Allie was here, but it infuriated him.

He ran faster. He swung the hammer, breaking the branches with renewed determination. He recalibrated his plan on the fly. He was still in control.

In the end, he'd kill them both.

CHAPTER 91

■

Larry Rucci

Larry sprinted into the woods. He could hear Allie screaming his name. He followed the sound.

"Allie!" he shouted back to her. The woods were dense, but he'd been in the Pine Barrens many times. He knew what to do. He crouched as low as he could, forming a triangle of his arms in front of his face and torso, like his father had taught him. His father used to say, *Make yourself small*. Larry used to think it was a fat joke, but it wasn't, he saw that now.

He powered forward. He heard Allie call his name. He called back to her. He spotted a flashlight to his right, moving erratically. Someone was using it to clear a path to Allie. The owner of the Mercedes. He couldn't see the man because the woods were so dark.

Someone was trying to kill his wife. Larry didn't know who or why. It wasn't going to happen as long as he drew breath.

"Allie!" Larry angled sharply to the right. Instead of going after Allie, he was going after the man chasing her. Larry always knew he would die for her. Even if she wouldn't for him.

He was funny that way.

■

CHAPTER 92

Allie Garvey

Allie kept running, trying to keep ahead of Julian. She was about to shout back to Larry again, but she realized something. She knew where Larry was because he was shouting for her. Julian must've known where she was because she'd been shouting for help. That was how he'd been able to find her with the flashlight.

She clammed up as she ran, so Julian wouldn't know where she was. Larry wouldn't, either, but he'd sounded farther back in the woods. God forbid anything happened to him. She wished he knew how much she loved him. She'd done Larry so wrong. Now she'd put him in danger.

She struggled to keep running. Her breath came ragged. The flashlight cast around, randomly shining on trees and branches. She heard Julian behind her, breaking branches.

"Give it up, Allie!" Julian called out, taunting her.

Allie felt a bolt of fright. He was getting closer. Gaining on her.

"Allie, don't fight me. I took care of Sasha. I took care of David. That leaves you."

Allie gasped as she ran. Julian had *killed* David. David hadn't committed suicide. Allie had been right about him. But David was dead, and so was Sasha.

Somehow she ran harder. The trees had grown together. She struggled to pass through. The underbrush was a thicket. Her thighs burned.

Her heart was pounding. Her right wrist was killing her. Sweat slaked her face and body. The air felt more humid. Her eyes stung. She couldn't quit now.

The flashlight swept the woods. Julian was looking for her. He would expect her to keep going straight. She had to confuse him.

Allie angled to the left, off the straight line she was on, or thought she was on. She was losing her sense of direction. She looked up but clouds covered the moon. She didn't know where she was anymore.

She kept running.

CHAPTER 93

■

Julian Browne

Julian remained in control, but he could feel rage boiling inside his chest. He wanted to howl with fury.

He'd lost sight of Allie. He'd been using the flashlight to break branches, and she'd finally figured out to shut up. Luckily, whoever was trying to be a hero hadn't. *Larry.*

Julian banged away at a branch, and it broke. He swung the flashlight back and forth, trying to find Allie. Damn her black dress. She blended in. He couldn't hear her anymore. Larry never shut up, like a kid playing Marco Polo.

Julian kept going, following a straight line after Allie. A pond and an abandoned hunting cabin were nearby. The air felt damper. He could smell the water. He hadn't intended to go this far, but that bitch had led him here.

He realized something. Marco Polo would be headed toward him, trying to save her.

Julian looked around, but he couldn't see even a

shadow, much less a man. He swung the flashlight but didn't see anyone.

Julian shut off the flashlight so Marco Polo couldn't find him.

"Allie!" Marco Polo shouted, echoing in the woods.

That was all Julian needed.

He headed toward the sound, hammer in hand.

CHAPTER 94

Larry Rucci

Allie!" Larry shouted, but Allie had gone silent. He realized she didn't want to give away her position, which was smart.

Larry looked to the right for the flashlight, but in the next moment, it blinked off.

Larry realized what the killer was doing. He'd turned off the flashlight because he didn't want to give away his position, either. Larry figured the guy had changed his plan. He'd stalk them and kill them both.

Larry was heading for the killer, and now the killer was heading for him. They should be closing in on each other.

Larry kept moving, pushing pine needles out of his way. The killer would come after him first. He posed a greater threat than Allie.

Larry squinted but couldn't see anyone or anything.

He whirled around. He couldn't see anyone behind him. Trees were everywhere. He couldn't even see the sky. He heard nothing but the sounds of the woods.

He crouched down, felt around on the ground, and picked up a rock.

CHAPTER 95

Allie Garvey

Allie kept going, hearing Larry calling her. She couldn't call back or she'd give herself away. It struck her with horror that if she could hear Larry, so could Julian. Julian would kill Larry. Allie couldn't let that happen. If anybody was getting out of the woods alive, it would be her husband.

She knew Julian had to be closer to her than Larry. There was only one way to save Larry's life, and it was to risk her own. She had to draw Julian to her, not send him away. If she survived, it was all good. If she didn't, Larry would be free to escape. Everything had started in a woods, and it was going to end in one, too.

Allie broke off a branch, and the end splintered like a stake.

Her heart pounded. Blood pulsed in her ears. She gripped the stake in her left hand. She took a deep breath, gathering her courage.

"Larry, run!" she screamed. "Run! Run! Go back!"

CHAPTER 96

■

Julian Browne

Julian turned his head toward the sound. Allie was calling for Larry. She was telling Larry to run. He realized what she was doing. She was offering herself instead of Marco Polo. Fine with him.

Julian switched directions, heading for her. She sounded closer than Marco Polo. She would be easier to pick off.

Julian swung the hammer down on a branch, cracking it off. He got a bead on Allie's shouting. It was getting louder. He didn't need the flashlight to find her anymore. He tucked it into his waistband behind his back.

Julian kept going, pushing through the forest. Allie sounded closer and closer, and in the next minute, he saw her shadow outlined in front of a pine tree.

Allie was standing there, screaming her fool head off. Julian couldn't wait to shut her up for good.

CHAPTER 97

∎

Larry Rucci

Larry stalked the killer, heading for him with the rock. He heard Allie start shouting again.

He turned his head toward the sound. She was telling him to run. He realized what she was doing. She was revealing her position. She was letting the killer know where she was. She was sacrificing herself for him.

Larry's throat swelled with emotion. She was willing to give up her life for him. She was answering the question he'd asked himself since they got married. She loved him as much as he loved her.

Larry moved faster. He had to get to her before the killer did. Allie was his wife until death did them part.

Larry was hell-bent on making sure that didn't happen.

CHAPTER 98

Allie Garvey

Allie spotted movement to her left. She turned. She saw the flash of a white shirt between the pine needles. Julian.

Her mouth went dry as dust. Her heart thundered. Adrenaline surged in her system. All of her senses focused like never before. The pain in her wrist receded.

Larry had gone silent. She couldn't think about him now. Julian was breaking the last few branches between them. She trembled. She told herself not to panic. She stood her ground.

She tightened her fingers around the stake and let her good arm fall. She didn't want Julian to know she had a weapon. She had to draw him in and make her move. He wouldn't expect her to attack. Her best shot would be her first one. She braced herself.

She could hear Julian grunting with exertion. He moved a branch. She glimpsed a flash of his face. He was almost upon her. His white shirt stood out like a target. She waited for him to get as close as possible.

"You bitch," Julian spat out, breaking the last branch between them with a hammer.

Allie lunged forward with the spike and aimed for his chest. Julian jumped aside but was hemmed in by a tree. The spike went into his lower right side.

Julian yelled. Allie drove the stake into him with all her might. Julian dropped the hammer. He grabbed the stake and wrenched it out of his body.

Allie felt for the hammer on the forest floor and grabbed it. Julian kicked her, connecting with her broken wrist. She screamed.

Julian reached down, but she swung the hammer up at his face. It hit him in the cheekbone. He staggered sideways, howling.

Allie scrambled to her feet, holding on to the hammer.

Julian leapt onto her in a rage. He shoved her backward to the ground. His hands went around her throat. He squeezed her neck, strangling her.

She hit him with the hammer but he didn't stop. She hit him again and again. It still wasn't enough. She was too close and couldn't get a powerful enough swing. She kneed him in the groin, but he didn't stop. She couldn't breathe.

She heard gagging sounds and realized it was her. She began to panic. She was losing consciousness. She kneed him and kicked him, but he kept squeezing.

She dropped the hammer, her good hand going reflexively to her neck. She tried to peel his fingers off but couldn't. She was getting weaker. She couldn't breathe. She couldn't keep kicking him.

Julian squeezed harder, relentless.

She tried to hit him, but it didn't help. She poked her fingers in his eyes, but he shook her off. Her hand fell uselessly back.

Allie choked. Julian grimaced with lethal effort, his face inches from hers.

She was out of air.

CHAPTER 99

Allie Garvey

G et off my wife!" Larry shouted, striking Julian on the head with a rock, from behind. Stunned, Julian released Allie's neck.

Allie gasped and coughed for air, her chest heaving. Larry grabbed Julian from behind and yanked him off her. Julian spun around to Larry, punching him in the face.

Larry staggered but punched back, hitting Julian in the jaw. Allie coughed and wheezed for air. She spotted something in the back of Julian's shirt. His flashlight. Julian pulled it from his waistband and raised it to hit Larry.

"No!" Allie screamed, recovering. She lunged forward, grabbed Julian's arm, and hung on it, while Larry started punching Julian. Julian doubled over, dropping the flashlight.

Larry swooped down, grabbed the flashlight, and

swung it at Julian's knee like a baseball bat. Bones broke loudly, and Julian howled in agony. Larry hit him under the chin with a powerful uppercut. Julian collapsed to the ground. His chest was moving, so he was breathing.

"Honey, are you okay?" Larry rushed to Allie, taking her in his arms, and she burst into tears, enveloped in the safety of his embrace.

"Is it over?" Allie heard herself ask through her tears, needing reassurance.

"Yes, unless you want me to kill him." Larry held her closer, and Allie looked up, trying to tell if he was kidding. Her husband's grim smile curved in the moonlight, and she felt a rush of love for him.

"You saved me."

"And you saved me."

"Does this mean you're taking me back?"

"Was there any doubt?" Larry held her gently. "Okay, maybe there was. But I love you, and you really *do* love me."

"I really do." Allie nestled against him.

"Also did you see me in action? Wow."

Allie knew he was trying to make her laugh. She'd missed him, so much. She'd missed his great heart. Maybe she had some of the Rucci luck, too. "So what do we do now? My phone's in the car."

"We go back and call the police. We're in Lacey Township. Ocean County has jurisdiction."

"What about Julian?"

"Is that his name? Who is he? And why the hell was he trying to *kill* you?"

"I'll tell you later, okay?" Allie shuddered, wiping away tears.

"Is he your secret boyfriend from high school? Did you beat him for class president?"

"No." Allie smiled through her tears.

"We leave him here. His knee's broken. He's not going anywhere fast, even if he comes to. We're not far from the road. Let's go, sweetheart." Larry put his arm around Allie, supporting her, and they hobbled out of the woods together, holding fast to each other.

CHAPTER 100

Allie Garvey

The next few hours were a blur of activity that transformed the still, dark woods into a beehive of uniformed authorities and official vehicles with idling engines and flashing light bars. Allie and Larry had called 911, which reached the Ocean County Sheriff's Department and referred them to the Lacey Township Police Department, who'd located them on GPS. Black-and-white Lacey Township cruisers had rushed over, followed by boxy gray ambulances. Uniformed police and EMTs escorted Allie and Larry to separate ambulances, where their vital signs were monitored. A cadre of police and paramedics raced into the woods with a litter for Julian.

Police set up klieg lights and sawhorses, cordoning off the area. CSI vans arrived, followed by a young African-American prosecutor from the Ocean County Prosecutor's Office. Her name was Missy Willis, and she met with Allie and Larry, then agreed to take their complete statements at the hospital, prioritizing their medical care. Allie's ambulance was about to leave when police and EMTs emerged from the woods carrying the litter that held Julian, strapped down and in custody. He'd regained consciousness, but he looked away when he passed Allie.

Allie watched with grim satisfaction. He had tried to kill her and Larry. He had killed Sasha and probably loaded the gun. She hoped he spent his life in jail. The paramedic returned to her side, eased her down on the gurney, and closed the ambulance doors. They lurched off, out of the woods.

They were taken to the Emergency Department at Southern Ocean County Hospital in Manahawkin, New Jersey, where they were examined in adjoining rooms. Larry finished quickly, since he had only a bruise and swelling on his cheekbone, superficial scratches on his face and arms, and a butterfly bandage covering a cut on his chin. He called his own parents and Allie's father, told them briefly what happened, and said that he'd update them later, but that they didn't have to come to the hospital.

He kept Allie company while she was examined, waited while she was taken for X-rays and a CAT scan, and returned to the Emergency Department, having determined that her wrist was broken. Reddish bruises covered her throat, and it hurt to swallow, but the doctor told her the pain would go away in a few days. She had minor bruises and superficial cuts, and she was given a cast, a sling, and some Advil.

Allie felt relieved that it was over, but she braced herself to make her statement to the authorities. It would be the first time Larry would hear the secret she'd kept from him for so long. She felt ashamed for what she'd done, especially since it had almost gotten him killed tonight. But she wanted to tell the story and she wanted the truth to come out, no matter what happened to her, them, or anything. She'd heard that cameras and reporters were already outside.

Allie's concern was Larry. She could only hope he would understand once they'd talked it over, at home. She knew it would take work and time to rebuild their marriage, but she'd do whatever it took. They'd start over, and she sensed they could be better than before, since she was finally shedding the burden of the secret.

When the time came, Allie sat on the end of the examining table, and Larry sat next to her in a chair opposite Assistant Prosecutor Missy Willis, Detective Bill Mento, and a uniformed police officer, who had already interviewed Larry separately. Missy wore no makeup, and she had large, thoughtful eyes behind hip, oversized glasses. She looked professional even dressed in a Rutgers sweatshirt, skinny jeans, and red Toms shoes, since she'd been called in from home. She balanced a laptop on her thighs, smiling at Allie expectantly.

"So, Allie, please tell us, in your own words, what happened tonight."

Allie took a deep breath, glancing at Larry, who took her hand with an encouraging smile. There was so much to tell. She didn't know what of it was appropriate for the police, but she wanted to come clean. She decided to begin at the beginning.

"If you really want to understand what happened, I have to start twenty years ago."

CHAPTER 101

■

Larry Rucci

Driving home from Manahawkin, Larry tried to process what he'd heard. Allie had insisted on driving her car, and he was following her in his, staying behind to make sure she was okay. She'd sworn that she was able to drive, rejecting his idea that they stay in a hotel nearby, to decompress. He knew she had to be exhausted, but she'd wanted to go home. So had he.

He followed her car at a safe distance, keeping a careful eye on her. It was dark, and the air was hot and humid, now that they weren't in the Pine Barrens anymore. There wasn't much traffic on the Jersey Turnpike at this hour, and he was relieved, for Allie's sake. Tractor-trailers made her nervous when they sped up behind her, and she generally drove just under the speed limit, which made everybody who followed her nuts, except him. He'd always liked that about her, that she was cautious.

He could only imagine how she was feeling now, having kept such an awful secret for so long.

Larry swallowed hard, keeping his eyes on her silhouette, in the car. He was especially worried she might fall asleep at the wheel, since giving her statement to the police had drained her. She had cried more than a few times, even when they said goodbye to Missy and the others, who had escorted them through the media waiting outside the hospital.

Larry knew it would get worse before the story finally went away. He doubted it would hurt him at work, but there would be questions to answer. There might be repercussions for Allie in her job. They were both ready to take what came, and the story would lose steam over time. What really mattered was Allie, going forward. Marriage counseling aside, she would need therapy. She had things to deal with that she'd been suppressing for too long.

Now that he knew the truth, so much about Allie made sense to him. Her secrecy, her mulling over the past, her ruminations about her sister, Jill, and high school. Her sleepless nights, her stomach problems. Larry realized he'd constructed narratives to explain her behavior, but they'd all been wrong. He'd based them on assumptions because he hadn't known the life event, or its memory that had shaped her personality—or warped it. He sensed the birth control pills were a part of the same puzzle.

Larry exhaled, mulling it over as he drove. They

would sort it out, with insanely expensive counseling. He was so happy to have her alive and for them to be going home together. Now that she was leveling with herself, and him, things could be even better than they had ever been. It could be the marriage he'd always wanted, and the family, too. He believed the truth really did set you free, and he was going to find out. His heart lifted, with hope.

Allie accelerated slightly, and Larry smiled, feeling better. It had been the scariest night of his life, but he was a lawyer, and there was nothing he liked better than the right result. He and Allie had put Julian Browne behind bars. If the asshole didn't plead out, he and Allie would happily testify against him. Julian could get as much as ten years for their attempted murder, and Pennsylvania would have jurisdiction to try him for Sasha's murder and New York for David's. There would be no legal consequences to his loading the gun the night they played Russian Roulette, which Allie already knew, having evidently consulted a lawyer. Larry wished she had consulted him, but he knew why she hadn't. She'd been afraid he wouldn't love her anymore. Nothing could be further from the truth.

Larry kept an eye on his wife, exhaling. He was no psychiatrist, but he knew it had to have been traumatic for Allie to have lived through seeing Kyle kill himself. And he understood why she blamed herself. He would've felt responsible, too. He hadn't really appreciated until tonight the shades of gray on the spectrum between innocence and guilt, but he would never think about it the same way again. So much of the law was parsing degrees of culpability, but all of those academic distinctions were lost on the human heart.

He breathed deeply. It would be morning in no time, and he would wake up in bed, next to Allie. He would get his clothes from the hotel tomorrow. He would tell her about Lacy someday, of course, but not tonight.

The arch of the bridge to Pennsylvania soared ahead in the darkness, next to the YOU'VE GOT A FRIEND IN PENNSYLVANIA billboard, the state's slogan for tourism. Larry smiled to himself.

He watched her car rising into the sky over the beautiful span of the bridge, with him right behind her, the two of them going home.

CHAPTER 102

Allie Garvey

Allie rested her head on Larry's chest, lying on her left side. Her head buzzed. Her right wrist ached, and her throat hurt, too. She couldn't sleep. Larry was still awake, too, but they were all talked out, having gone over what had happened, traded thoughts, and shed more than a few tears.

The bedroom was still and quiet, and the sun was beginning to rise, sending a pale gray shaft through the part in the curtains. She heard the hydraulic screech of the trash truck, a faraway siren, and a dog barking. The morning sounds of the city. Finally, it felt like home.

Allie's mind was in overdrive, but the one thought that kept coming to her consciousness was Kyle's mother. "Honey, I have a question for you," she whispered.

"Not tonight, dear. I have a headache." Larry chuckled at his own joke.

"No, really. It's serious."

"Like tonight hasn't been?" Larry chuckled again. "I look forward to talking about the weather. And how about those Eagles?"

"Honey, this is really serious." Allie swallowed hard, and her throat stung. "I've been thinking about Kyle's mother."

"Okay. I'm all ears." Larry's tone quieted.

"I've been thinking about her for a long time, and now that this is all out in the open, I want to go to her and explain. I want to tell her. What do you think?"

"Whoa, really?"

"Yes." Allie felt it resonate within her chest. She knew it was the right thing to do. "I know her address. She lives near Brandywine Hunt."

"How would you do it? Would you call first, or what?"

"I guess so, but I want to tell her in person. I think it's important she hear it face-to-face."

"Why do you want to tell her?"

"Because it's the truth, and she deserves to know it. I want to set things right, the best I can. Besides, it's going to come out in the newspapers, sooner or later. I don't want her to find out that way. She absolutely deserves better, and I'm the only one to do it."

Larry sighed, and Allie felt his chest go up and down.

"What?"

"I know you mean well, but slow down, babe. You don't know how she'll take that information. If she were my mother, she'd tear you a new one."

Allie swallowed hard again. She knew it was true. "I know. I expect that, completely. I'll listen to her and whatever she has to say to me."

"It will be very hard for her, and you."

"I know that, but if I don't tell her, I'll feel like I'm keeping a secret from her. It's too big to keep to myself anymore."

"Like a material omission?"

"Exactly," Allie answered, nodding. She didn't always understand Larry's legalisms, but this one she understood completely, because she'd lived it. "I'm trying to come clean, and I can't leave her out of this equation. Kyle was her son. She deserves to know the truth about him, more than anyone. She's his mother."

"I hear you."

"The least I can do for Kyle now is to tell her and listen to her. If she's angry, if she yells, if she throws something, whatever. Whatever she wants to do, I'll take my lumps."

"I get that." Larry hesitated. "There's nothing she could do to you legally, even if she told the police."

"Right, I know."

"Did your lawyer tell you that, too?"

"Yes." Allie heard the hurt in his tone and hugged him closer. "I'm sorry I didn't tell you, I really am."

"I understand." Larry hugged her back. "So when do you want to do this?"

"I'd like to go this morning, if she's available. It's Saturday, so I assume she doesn't work."

"How did I know you were gonna say that?" Larry

chuckled. "My parents and your dad want to come over. Your dad says Saturday is fine, and my parents want to come on Sunday with emergency lasagna."

"Okay." Allie didn't look forward to telling the story to her father and her in-laws, but she wanted them to hear it from her, not from TV. "I can stop in and see my dad after Kyle's mother, since they're in the suburbs."

"Do you want me to go with you? I'd be happy to."

"Thank you, but no."

"You sure you can drive, with your wrist?"

"I'm fine." Allie had thought it over. "I think this is something I need to do myself."

"I get it. When you're going through hell, keep going."

"Who said that? Winston Churchill, right?"

"No, my mother, about the Garden State Parkway."

Allie smiled, then it faded, thinking of Kyle's mother. Her gaze went to the window, waiting for the sun to rise.

CHAPTER 103

Barb Gallagher

Barb went to the front door, relieved to see through the screen that Allie Garvey seemed to be a normal woman in her thirties, dressed in a flowered sundress and sensible flats. She had a cast on her arm and there were scratches on her face, as if she'd been in a car accident. The young woman had called on Barb's landline this morning, asking if she could come over to speak about Kyle. Barb had felt intrigued, so she had said yes, even though the young woman was a total stranger. Barb had called Sharon, who'd raced over to join her, and they'd set up the visit for the afternoon.

"Hi, I'm Barb Gallagher," Barb said, opening her front door. "Come in, please."

"I'm Allie Garvey, and thank you for seeing me."

"You're welcome." Barb admitted her to the living room, gesturing at Sharon, who was sitting on the couch.

"This is my friend Sharon Kelly. Sharon, meet Allie Garvey."

"Good to meet you, Allie." Sharon extended a hand with a reserved smile, and Barb knew what she was thinking. Sharon hadn't been sure they should meet with Allie, after she'd looked Allie up on Google and social media. There hadn't been enough information to satisfy Sharon, who was always looking out for Barb.

"Sharon, hi." Allie shook Sharon's hand.

"Allie, please sit down, make yourself comfortable." Barb gestured at the chair next to the couch. "Can I get you anything to drink? Water or soda?"

"No, thank you." Allie sat in the chair, linking her fingers on her lap and crossing her legs at the ankles. She looked at them both with a smile that was obviously nervous.

"Okay, let me know if you change your mind." Barb sat down on the couch, catty-corner to Allie. She felt nervous, too. "I was surprised to hear that you knew my son. I didn't recognize your name. He never mentioned you."

"I didn't really know him, that's why." Allie swallowed so hard that Barb noticed her Adam's apple going up and down, which was when she spotted reddish bruises covering Allie's neck, only partly hidden by her dress. Barb felt a tingle of concern. "Were you in an accident of some kind? I see your bruises on your neck."

"No, not exactly." Allie's hand flew to her neck, and she tugged up the collar of her dress. "First, let me tell you about me. I grew up in Brandywine Hunt and I work as a child advocate. I'm married to a lawyer named Larry Rucci, a partner at Dichter & O'Reilly in Philly, and we live in Center City. This is my card, and I wrote my home address on the back, so you have my contact information." Allie took a business card from her purse and set it on the coffee table, but neither Barb nor Sharon moved to pick it up. "I can explain, um—I guess, I'll just get right to it. I was attacked last night, with my husband, by someone I grew up with. Someone I knew from my childhood, Julian Browne."

"Attacked?" Barb asked, aghast. She recoiled. "Have you gone to the police?"

Sharon interjected, "You mean Julian Browne, the developer's son? I saw on the news that he was arrested in New Jersey. A woman overdosed at his house yesterday, too."

"Right, yes." Allie nodded. "Julian Browne was arrested for the attempted murder of my husband and me last night, in the Pine Barrens in New Jersey."

"That's terrible." Barb grimaced. "But what does that have to do with my Kyle?"

Allie pursed her lips. "First, let me warn you that this is really upsetting news, and it does involve Kyle. I know this is going to be hard for you to hear, and I didn't want to hurt you further, reopen an old wound, or make Kyle's death harder for you. I wanted to tell you the truth because I think you deserve to hear it. And not from the news or the police, because sooner or later, this is going to come to light."

Sharon interjected again, "*What* is? What are you talking about?"

Barb fell silent a moment, flashing on the night Kyle's body had been found, when she sat next to Sharon in the police station. Barb had gone numb with shock. Sharon had had to do all the talking for her. Barb's heart felt suddenly heavy, just like it had back then.

Allie nodded, glancing from Sharon to Barb. "The police said that Kyle committed suicide alone in the woods off Connemara Road. But that's not the truth. He didn't commit suicide. I was there, and so were three other people who lived in Brandywine Hunt. We were teenagers at the time, fifteen years old. Their names were David Hybrinski, Sasha Barrow, and Julian Browne."

Barb gasped, struck dumb. She felt utterly and completely shocked. She felt her own mouth drop open. She tried to collect her thoughts, but she couldn't. Her chest went tight with pain, with fresh grief.

"Wait, you were *there*?" Sharon asked in disbelief. "You all were? *Four* people? What are you talking about? Why didn't you stop him? What happened? What were you doing there? What were *they* doing there? *Julian Browne* was there, too?"

Allie nodded, stricken. "Let me start from the beginning," she said, and she explained that she and the other three had found the gun in the woods, gotten some bullets, and decided to play a prank on Kyle, telling him they'd played Russian Roulette but they hadn't. Allie had thought the gun was unloaded, and she thought the others had

486 ■ LISA SCOTTOLINE

believed the same thing, and she hadn't known otherwise until Kyle had shot himself.

Barb felt tears come to her eyes, and her chest got tighter and tighter. She felt her heart flutter at the revelation, but she didn't interrupt Allie's story, which sounded true. Sharon took her hand, and the best friends held hands on the couch while Allie continued, explaining how she had hid the secret about Kyle's death until she had gone to David's funeral, and how she'd thought David had shot himself on the twenty-year anniversary of Kyle's death.

Barb had begun to cry, realizing that it must have been the same funeral she'd seen yesterday morning at Gardens of Peace. Sharon got her a box of Kleenex, and Barb held a tissue to her nose while Allie told them that David's apparent suicide and Sasha's apparent overdose were both murders, then how she'd given a statement to the authorities in New Jersey, which would result in them referring Sasha's murder to the police in Pennsylvania, who would probably be calling Barb. Allie finished with how Julian had tried to kill her and her husband so that she would never reveal the truth about Kyle's death. Allie ended saying that she believed Julian had loaded the gun that killed Kyle because he was jealous over Sasha. When Allie finally fell silent, tears glistened in her eyes, but she blinked them away.

"That's the story," Allie said, exhaling. "I am so very sorry that I didn't speak up that night. That I didn't stop them, that I took part in it at all. It was an awful, horrible prank, and it went tragically wrong, and it took Kyle's life. I'm deeply sorry, and that is what I came here to say." She paused. "Now please, ask me anything you like, and I'll answer. Any reaction you have, I'll understand. The least I can do for you now, and for Kyle, is to be here for you. And listen."

Barb sat motionless, still stunned. She didn't know what to say, how to react, or even what to think. The pink Kleenexes sat in her lap like so many crushed flowers. Her mouth felt like cotton and her heart like lead. She could barely breathe. She knew she was being told the truth, and the first coherent thought that came to her mind left her lips before she could stop herself.

"I *knew* he didn't do it," Barb said quietly. "I *knew* he didn't commit suicide."

Allie nodded, teary. "He didn't. He had no idea it was loaded. He thought it was a joke. He even said so."

Barb's hand went to her chest, as if to calm her heart. She had been right, all this time. Kyle *hadn't* meant to kill himself. He had been low, but he hadn't been *that* low. She *hadn't* missed the signs in him, after all. She *hadn't* let him down, in the end. She felt horrified, but she also felt deeply validated, after twenty years. The police had been wrong.

Tears sprang to her eyes. She felt her heart ease, and her breath came a little more quickly. Suddenly, she found herself shaking her head, no. She wished she could go back in time and change it all. She wished she could tell Kyle to stay away from girls like Sasha, who would repay his kindness so cruelly, after he rescued her cat. She wished she could warn him about entitled boys like David, or deadly ones like Julian, or even well-meaning girls like Allie, who didn't stand up for him, or themselves. But what mattered most to Barb—and it was the only glimmer of light in this awful truth—was that at least, at the very least, *Kyle hadn't killed himself.*

Sharon touched Barb's hand. "Honey, is there anything you want to say? That you want to ask her?"

"No," Barb said after a moment. She didn't know if she had any other words. She was just so dumbfounded. She turned to Allie. "This is so . . . shocking, and I need to think about it. I need to think about this. It changes everything."

Allie nodded, her expression sympathetic. "I understand completely. You have my contact information, and if you ever want to talk to me, I'm there."

Sharon sniffled. "Barb, do you mind if I say something to Allie?"

"No, of course not," Barb answered, shaking her head. She felt numb. It was the only word.

Sharon's attention returned to Allie, and her dark eyes flashed. "Allie, I *know* you're not trying to alleviate your own guilt by coming here. Good luck with that. You and your little friends did a horrible, *horrible* thing to a wonderful young man. You handed him a gun, and you pressured him to *shoot himself.*"

"I know, and I'm very sorry." Allie nodded.

Barb tensed at Sharon's anger, but didn't blame her. Sharon had loved Kyle, too, and she was entitled to her feelings.

Sharon scowled, leaning closer to Allie. "And don't

think this is the end of it. I'm going to check out the story, and I'm going to make some calls. The police, a lawyer, everybody. This is *not* the end of it."

"I understand." Allie nodded again, solemnly.

"I'm going to see what we can do about this. David and Sasha will face God's judgment, but there should be charges filed against Julian. He may be going to jail for a long time for what he did to you and your husband, but he should be punished for what he did to Kyle."

Allie nodded. "I understand," she repeated.

"Don't *begin* to think you're off the hook. You're an accomplice. You aided and abetted. You should be *ashamed* of yourself for playing a prank like that, and it's no excuse you were drinking. You were fifteen, but that's old enough to know better, and you *should* have known better."

"I agree; I'm very sorry." Allie refolded her hands in her lap. "I'm sorry for your loss—"

"Stop saying that!" Sharon interrupted, her voice breaking. A tear rolled down her cheek, a single wet line. "How *dare* you kill somebody and then say, 'I'm sorry for your loss'! That won't make it better. Kyle was like *a son* to me. I watched that boy grow up. His mother loved him to the *marrow*. I know how much he had to offer this world. God is the only one who has the right to take a life. Not Julian Browne. I hope he rots in prison for the rest of his life."

"Sharon, have a tissue." Barb handed her the box of Kleenex, stricken.

"Thanks, honey." Sharon's watery gaze met hers. She

yanked a tissue from the box. "I'm sorry, I was trying to keep it in control."

"It's okay," Barb said, patting her on the arm. "But unless you have more you want to say, I think Allie can go now. I want to think this over. Don't you?"

"Barb, I've been wanting to throw this girl out for the past ten minutes!" Sharon jumped up from the couch, stuffing the Kleenex in her jeans pocket. "Allie, let me show you the door. I don't think we'll be calling you. We don't want to hear your voice ever again."

"Thank you for your time." Allie rose shakily and headed for the screen door. Sharon reached it first and flung it wide open. Allie started to leave, then looked at Barb, her mouth downturned and her expression full of sympathy.

Barb looked back at Allie directly, feeling connected to her. Allie had heard Kyle's last words, seen him take his last breath on this earth, and watched him die. Barb couldn't find the words to say so now, but she respected that Allie had told her the truth. It would take years to parse her feelings about today, but Barb collected her thoughts. She acknowledged to herself that the truth helped her. It lifted the burden she had carried for twenty years. She *knew* her own son. She *hadn't* let him down. The thought brought her peace. She couldn't have Kyle back, but she felt . . . consolation.

Barb couldn't smile, but she nodded back at Allie.

CHAPTER 104

Allie Garvey

Allie found her father in the backyard, on his knees in front of her mother's perennial garden. She reached the gate but didn't open it or call to him for a moment, composing herself. She felt upset after meeting with Kyle's mother and her friend Sharon, but she would sort out her feelings later, with Larry, at home. She tried to switch mental gears, to focus on her own father. She dreaded telling him about Kyle, but he deserved to know the truth, too.

She opened the gate, and he was on the far side of their large backyard, weeding. Her mother's garden was still full of purple coneflowers, black-eyed Susans, and pink hydrangeas. It touched her that her father had tended it all these years, though her mother had been the family gardener, not him. He was weeding next to the gardening carryall she'd gotten him for Christmas, his knees resting on his foamy blue knee pad. He had on a short-sleeved madras shirt and khaki shorts, tucked in with a belt, and she always used to joke that he was the best-dressed gardener in Brandywine Hunt. Today, she didn't feel like joking.

"Dad, hi." Allie crossed the backyard to the flower bed.

"Honey!" Her father turned, and his lined face formed an instant mask of concern. "How are you feeling? Oh my God, look at you, in a sling!"

"I'm fine," Allie said, managing a smile, but her father was already on his feet, stripping off his gardening gloves, discarding them on the ground, and coming to her with open arms.

"You didn't have to come out here. I would've come to you."

"I was out already." Allie hadn't told him about Kyle's mother yet. She would've called on the way over, but she'd been too upset and hadn't wanted him to hear her that way without explanation. After all, she was about to give him the shock of his life.

"My God, you were almost killed! And Larry, too! What's going on?" Her father hugged her as soon as they met, and Allie hugged him back, trying not to cry. She wanted to keep her wits about her. She allowed herself to feel the comfort of his embrace. The sun felt warm on her back, seeping into her bones. Birds chirped in the trees, and the scene was so peaceful she hated to disrupt it, but there was no putting it off.

"Dad, I have a lot to tell you," Allie said, releasing him.

"Yes, yes, of course. Let's go inside. I have iced tea, homemade."

"No, let's stay. We can sit here." Allie swallowed hard. Somehow it felt right, to be among nature, near her mother's garden and her father's handiwork. When Jill was alive, they used to eat dinner outside in the garden, on the pretty wrought-iron table with a glass top. It was still there, in front of the hydrangeas, though after that summer, they'd never eaten outside again.

"The glass is dirty. I could Windex it."

"It's fine. Let's just sit." Allie pulled out the chair, which caught on the manicured grass, but sat down, and her father sat next to her, resting his skinny forearm on the glass, its surface dulled from years of rain.

"Are you in pain? Do you need an Advil? You know that helps with the swelling, too."

"I'm fine. Really, Dad." Allie braced herself.

"Honey, do you know what they said on the news? Did you hear?" Her father's lined face collapsed in a frown. Close up, she could see that he was sweating slightly in the heat. "They said that Julian Browne's father was found *dead* in New Jersey, with another man. Scott Browne was murdered. Stabbed to death."

"Oh, no," Allie said, horrified. She hadn't heard. She hadn't had the car radio on and hadn't checked her phone.

"Doesn't that seem strange?" Her father's eyes narrowed. "That Julian's father was murdered? And a young woman overdosed at Julian's house? I forget her name, but you saw on TV. And now he tried to kill *you*. And Larry."

"Okay, well, Dad, that's connected to what I have to

tell you. It's very upsetting, but it's about me, and, well, the summer after Jill died."

"Okay." Her father frowned with sympathy. "I know, you got so sad that summer. I could see it. You used to be happier, lighter, but after your mom went to the hospital, you changed."

"No, Dad, it wasn't Mom's illness that changed me. It was something I did that summer. Julian was involved in it, too, but it's about me."

"I didn't know you knew Julian Browne. How did you know him?"

"I didn't, but I met him because of this thing that happened." Her father blinked behind his glasses. "It's a secret, and I kept it from you, Larry, and everybody. But it's about to come out, and I want you to know about it from me. It happened in the woods by Connemara Road."

"I don't know what you're talking about."

"Dad—" Allie began, then hesitated. There was no going back if she told him, but she had to. "I did a terrible thing, and it changed the way I am. It changed *who* I am."

"You would never do anything terrible. I never worried about you, not for a minute. You were a good girl."

"I was until then." Allie cringed. "See, there was a boy our age named Kyle Gallagher, and he was new. The police thought he committed suicide in the woods, alone. But I was there, and so were my friends, and we told him it was a game. Russian Roulette. We gave him a gun we found, and we didn't think it was loaded—"

"*Russian Roulette?*" Her father's hooded eyes flared with alarm. "*You* played Russian Roulette? *You, Allie?*"

"No, I didn't, but he did, Kyle did. We told him we'd played it but we hadn't, and I didn't know the gun was loaded." Allie collected herself. "Dad, just let me tell the story, and listen, okay?"

"Okay." Her father nodded gravely, linking his fingers on the table, and Allie began at the beginning, like she had the other two times, but it felt harder now because she was telling it to her father, whose opinion mattered so much. She told him everything, how they'd been drinking, how they'd lied to Kyle about playing Russian Roulette, then how the gun had gone off and Kyle was dead.

Allie watched his face contort with anguish, and tears filled his eyes behind his bifocals. She couldn't stop telling the story because she knew he had to hear it, once and for all. She poured her heart out about her nightmares and flashbacks, about how she couldn't stop the instant replays, visualizing the gun being loaded and fired. She told him how she had kept it secret until David's suicide, when she finally couldn't take it anymore, then about meeting with Julian and Sasha after the funeral, the Pine Barrens and Larry, and she ended with her visit to Kyle's mother.

When Allie finished, she was shaking. "Dad, I'm so, so sorry, about all of this. I wanted to tell you, but I couldn't."

"I know, I understand." Her father's expression was etched with agonized lines. His knobby shoulders sagged in his plaid shirt. "But you could have told me, you should have told me."

"I was worried you wouldn't love me anymore," Allie blurted out, her voice sounding childish even to herself, and her father reached over with a deep moan, hugged her close, and didn't let go. She could feel him frail in her embrace, and they clung to each other.

"Oh, honey, I'll always love you," her father whispered in her ear. "But there's something I have to tell you, too."

CHAPTER 105

Dr. Mark Garvey

Mark inhaled, his chest tight. It hurt him to see the bruises on Allie's face. Her broken wrist. The bruising at her throat. He should have spoken up. He should have told her. She could have been *killed* last night. His beloved daughter could have been *murdered* because of him. Allie had risked her life to find out something he had already known.

Mark met the glistening eyes of his daughter, and Allie looked like she had back then, that awful summer, the worst one of their lives. He didn't know how to tell her what he had to tell her. He never imagined he would have to, but he hadn't known she'd been there with Kyle Gallagher. Mark had made so many mistakes that summer.

"Dad, what is it?" Allie asked, teary and mystified.

"Honey, that was such a bad summer, you remember."

"Right, I know."

"I was really hoping the 5K would work out, but it was a disaster. Remember? No one came."

"I remember." Allie nodded.

"We had that big fight at the house later, remember? Fran called me out, and she was right about that, she really was. I failed your mother. I tried to turn it around, but it was too late."

"You tried your best, Dad." Allie patted his hand, and it struck Mark as such a sweet gesture, so like her.

"But my best wasn't good enough. It really wasn't. That weekend, it all came to a head." Mark bit his lip, which trembled. He didn't want to cry in front of his daughter, even now. A feeling of deepest despair washed over him, taking him right back to that day. "Remember, I had spent months on the 5K, and I think it was my way of coping with Jill's death. Setting up the meetings, the waivers, the organizing. It was a way of avoiding my grief."

"I knew that, Dad." Allie's tone was gentle.

"I coped badly, and what I did only made it worse for your mother and you. It isolated her, and you got lost in the shuffle. I told her I was looking out for you, but I wasn't. I was trying to, but I didn't do a good enough job. I let you down, too, and I realized it that weekend."

"You didn't let me down—"

"No, I did, you have to let me say this to you." Mark twisted his wedding ring, which he still wore. "You were so upset that morning, Sunday morning, that your mom had to stay in the hospital, you were scared of losing her like you lost Jill. I knew you would be, I could see it. I knew it was my fault, I'd let her go downhill, like Fran said. I failed you, and I didn't save your mom, and I hurt you so badly, which cut me to the *quick*—"

"Dad, really—"

"No, listen to me." Mark remembered that day like it was happening right in front of him, and he entered his own personal nightmare. His past. "So remember, your mother didn't come home from the hospital, and you got so upset that she would have electroshock, that you were losing her, that she would die, and you ran up to your room and closed the door. As a father, a man, I felt so ashamed, *so* ashamed. Me, the one everybody relies on and looks up to. The breadwinner. The *dad*. I was in pain, Allie. So much pain. I had been, for so long."

Allie squeezed his hand, but didn't interrupt.

"So I went out, I left the house, I went to the woods. I hurt so much, and I wanted to make it stop. I knew the gun was there, in the woods off Connemara Road. It wasn't my gun, it was your mother's. She bought it, and I buried it there."

"*What?*" Allie's mouth dropped open, in utter shock.

"Your mother bought it one day, after Jill died. She bought it in a gun store, with bullets, too, and I found the bag and realized she was really thinking about killing herself. She would say so from time to time, but I thought she was being dramatic. But when she bought the gun, it scared me, *really* scared me, and I thought, I have to get rid of this gun. But I didn't know what to do with it. I couldn't throw it away, but I didn't want it in the house anymore, or the car, or anywhere Mom could get it."

Allie gasped, her eyes widening. "You mean the gun that Julian found *was yours*? *Mom's*?"

"Yes. So I wrapped it in an old newspaper and buried it in the woods by the bent tree. I scratched off the registration number so nobody could trace it back to her. I buried it without the bullets so nobody would hurt themselves if they dug it up. I even checked on it sometimes, at night, to make sure no one took it. I thought I was being so responsible, but I was wrong about that, too. Mom got mad that I took it, but I thought I was saving her life."

Mark felt a wave of shame. He'd kept the secret for twenty years, just like Allie had. She was her father's daughter, in the end. Her hands flew to her face, and she began to cry, but Mark couldn't stop now.

"So I went out there on Sunday, and I dug up the gun, unwrapped it, and I loaded it with a bullet. I put it to my head." Mark's throat thickened with emotion, but he stayed in control. Back then, that day, he'd been crying on his knees, holding the gun to his temple. "But the thought of *you* stopped me, Allie. You saved my life. I told you I was your life preserver, but you were mine."

Tears ran freely down Allie's cheeks, and Mark touched Allie's good arm to comfort her.

"I couldn't leave you alone, all by yourself. Not with your mother so sick in the hospital. Not with Jill gone. I couldn't imagine what would happen to you. I couldn't imagine that you would survive that. I knew I had to stay alive, for you."

Mark squeezed Allie's arm, to steady her. He had to

finish the story. Then he realized his daughter already knew the ending. *She* had lived the ending, not him.

"The next night I heard that a young boy, Kyle Gallagher, had committed suicide. It was in the same spot where I buried the gun. I realized what must have happened. He must have used our gun to kill himself, and I must've left the bullet inside it." Mark wiped tears from his eyes, still guilt-ridden over the boy's death. "Allie, I felt terrible, but I didn't tell anyone. I didn't go to the police or even to his mother, like you did today. I told myself I didn't tell because I didn't want to go to prison, and you would be alone. But the truth was, I felt so terribly ashamed. I didn't have the guts you had today. I'm not as brave as you, honey."

Allie doubled over, dissolving into tears. Sobs wracked her body, and Mark felt his heart break. He put his arms around her and held her close.

"Allie, I'm so sorry, I'm so very sorry. I wish I had said something, and if I had, you wouldn't have had to go through what you have, for the past twenty years. You could have been *murdered* because I kept a secret I never should've kept, and it caused you to keep a secret you never should've kept. I'm so very sorry, honey, and I love you from the bottom of my heart, as I hope you still love me."

Allie shifted in his arms, sobbing. "I love you, Dad, I do, but I think I'm going to throw up. I have to go—"

"I'm so sorry." Mark let her go, and Allie jumped up from the table, covered her mouth, and ran crying into the house.

CHAPTER 106

Allie Garvey

Allie raced into their powder room, closed the door behind her, and leaned over the sink, gasping. She couldn't catch her breath. Her chest heaved, and she leaned forward, choking. Her throat hurt as it had last night. She gulped air, dry-heaving. She put her good hand on the sink for support.

Her body sagged between her shoulders, and without the sink, she would have fallen to her knees. She would have collapsed with what she knew. Not that her father had buried the gun, not just that. Not just that he'd loaded it. Not even that he'd wanted to commit suicide. Or that her mother had, too, that awful summer.

Allie had remembered something else while her father was talking, as he told the story. It had triggered something that she'd thought was déjà vu, but when he'd told her how he'd gone to Connemara Road, dug up the gun, loaded it, and held it to his temple, it had begun to dawn on her with horror that she'd already *known* that her father had done all that. Allie had begun to remember that she had *seen* that, herself. Because *she had been there*.

Allie's chest heaved, and she wheezed in and out, struggling to breathe as the memory surfaced from the depths of her subconscious, recovered from whatever subterranean recess it had been buried in, all this time. She'd thought she'd been visualizing a thumb loading a bullet in the gun, but it hadn't been her imagination, it had been a memory. It had been a trauma, and her brain had hid it deep. What happened that weekend came to life in front of her eyes, right now, as if she were experiencing it in real time and it was happening to her, right this very instant.

The whole weekend was so horrible, after her mother had been so out of it at the 5K, then the fight between her father and Fran, and Sasha hearing it all from upstairs. Then Sunday was worse, with Allie so upset that her mother had been admitted to the hospital, and she fought with her father, blaming him, yelling at him, calling him out for not taking care of her mother, for making her worse. Allie ran upstairs to her bedroom and never felt so awful, so lost, so terrified for her mother. Her mother was in a *mental hospital*, and Allie was worried she might never come home.

She realized that she'd been terrible to her father, and that was the moment she understood he wasn't all-powerful but a human being with faults like everyone else. She felt guilty for the way she'd treated him, and she wanted to apologize. She went downstairs, but the front door had just closed behind her father. He'd left the house. He was going somewhere on foot, and Allie didn't understand. She felt afraid, worried for him.

She left the house and followed him at a safe distance, so he couldn't see her. He went down the street and around the corner, then she followed him as he entered the woods off Connemara Road. She stayed behind him, hiding in the trees so he couldn't see or hear her. He hadn't seen her, he'd been too distraught to focus on anything but his own anguish, but she'd seen him, she knew that now.

She watched him from behind the thick trees, and he began to dig under the bent tree, to her astonishment. She didn't know how he knew Julian's gun was there, and if he knew, why he hadn't yelled at her, but she watched him as he unearthed the gun, unwrapped it from the newspaper, and loaded the gun with a bullet. His thumb had pressed it into the cylinder. Allie remembered it now. She hadn't remembered it before. The memory had been buried until today, when he told her what he'd done.

Now, Allie knew who loaded the gun because she had *watched* him load the gun. It *wasn't* Julian, it was *her father*. She had *seen* her father load the gun. She had buried the memory, only to have it recovered now. She'd watched horrified as he closed the cylinder and raised the gun to his temple, just like Kyle would do only hours later, in the exact same spot.

Her mouth had dropped open in shock at what she was seeing, at what he was doing, but she froze, paralyzed. She wanted to shout to her father to stop but no sound came from her mouth. She couldn't utter a single word. Her father was going to kill himself. He was raising a gun to his head. He was going to fire a bullet into his brain. He was all she had left. Her mother was gone, Jill was gone, and her father was going to leave her, too. Allie would be alone. She would have nobody. No family, no nothing.

Suddenly her father lowered the gun, wrapped it back up, and put it back into the hole, and began to cover it with dirt. Allie turned and ran all the way home, not wanting to be discovered. She got home in no time, panting and crying, running upstairs to her parents' bedroom, to cry there, to keep what she could of them. And then she'd seen her mother's tranquilizers on the night table.

Allie was hysterical, desperate, terrified. She tore off the cap and gulped some pills down with water. She had to get numb. She had to forget what she knew. She couldn't bear the thought that her father wanted to kill himself. She had to escape her own mind. She stayed high all day and took more pills. That night, she felt so calm from the pills, floating on a cloud when she met David at the trail. She felt relieved that Kyle wasn't with Sasha and Julian, so Allie drank vodka, fast. She got more and more out of it. She remembered David's kisses and Kyle being so late. Allie was totally wasted by the time Kyle came. She tried to tell him not to play the game, but it all happened so fast, Kyle played, and the gun had gone off.

Her father hadn't unloaded the gun, and Allie knew

that now. She knew that then, too, but after Kyle had shot himself, that knowledge had been swallowed up in her memory of Kyle putting the gun to his head the same way that her father had, in exactly the same spot, only this time the gun had gone off, killing Kyle.

Allie realized with dread that she had known all along that the gun was loaded. All this time, in the back of her mind, her memory of what her father had done with the gun lay beneath what Kyle had done, and all of her sleepless nights, grisly instant replays, nightmares, health issues hadn't been only about Kyle. They'd been about her father, too. Allie *had* been obsessed with Kyle's death, and her *father* was why.

Tears flowed down her face. Her knees buckled. Her father was at the door, calling her, knocking. He'd loaded the gun that killed Kyle. Someone knew all this time.

And that someone was her.

Allie Garvey

The winter sun filtered through the window, washing the kitchen in a pale light, and Allie sipped her tea, sitting in her cozy bathrobe and flannel nightgown, while Larry sat across the table from her in his sweats. His head was buried behind the sports page but his bare feet rested on hers under the table, a habit of theirs.

We're holding feet, she'd told him once, and they both had laughed.

The Sunday newspapers lay scattered on the tabletop, but she'd read her favorite sections. She could've cleared their plates, but she didn't feel like rushing to do that, either. The TV played on low volume on the counter, showing political talking heads until noon, when the NFL programming machine came on, with its trumpets and transformers, gearing them up for the Eagles game, as if anybody in Philadelphia needed help getting excited over any team. Her father, her in-laws, one of Larry's brothers, his wife, and their two boys were coming over, so there would be a lot to do, but Allie had already gone food shopping, and right now, she found a moment of stillness with her thoughts. She inhaled slowly, then exhaled.

Her tea had gone lukewarm, but she sipped it anyway, feeling like she was catching her breath, maybe for the first time since everything had happened. There had been tears, reporters, and the Bakerton police, who had been called by Kyle's mother and had interviewed Allie and her father about Kyle's death. Larry had held her hand throughout, and Barton had represented her, having advised her to tell them the whole truth and nothing but, which she had done. No charges were filed against her or her father, as Barton had predicted, and she had finally stopped worrying that they were going to change their minds or listening for the phone to ring. Julian had pleaded guilty to their attempted murders, as well as to Sasha's murder, in exchange for a sentence of life in prison without possibility of parole. Larry had been satisfied that justice had been achieved, though Allie was less sure. The district attorney in New York had yet to charge Julian for David's murder, and it wasn't moot to Allie, though it may have been legally.

She was still trying to figure out what justice was in this situation. She had her own responsibility for Kyle's death to deal with, especially after her father's revelation, which had started her back at an emotional square one, throwing her in tumult for a long time thereafter. She'd cut back on her hours at work, increased her therapy to twice a week, and was trying to find a way to live with what she'd done. She was hoping to find the City of Refuge, but there was no map or GPS. Some days it felt like it was around the corner, and other days it was somewhere over the rainbow.

Allie knew it was about forgiveness, but she couldn't forgive herself yet, if indeed she ever could. She was aiming for acceptance, and this morning, just now, she actually felt a moment of peace, just one moment, and that was one more moment than she'd had yesterday or any day before that. She tried to be optimistic, and in fact, she had to be, because the baby was on its way.

They'd found out they were pregnant only two weeks ago, sooner than Allie was probably emotionally ready for, but she was learning that life was anything but orderly. Allie sensed it was for the best, in that the baby was pulling her into the future in a way that she needed in order to go forward, to live her life. She'd always wanted to be a mother, and if she waited until she felt as if she deserved a baby, she might never have one.

Allie's hand went reflexively to her belly, and she was determined to do everything she could to earn the privilege. Having a child changed things, everybody said so, and she found herself thinking of David, about how his having a baby had made him want to come clean about Kyle, and then about her own mother, whose life had changed completely when Jill was born. So had her father's.

Allie kept her hand on her tummy, amazed to think that there was a new life growing inside her. She felt

510 ■ LISA SCOTTOLINE

somehow that the life was connected not only to her, Larry, and their families, but even to David, Jill, and her mother, to the living and the dead, all of the people Allie loved linked together in some eternal skein of life, like a human chain of hearts and souls, forever. Tears came to her eyes, and she didn't know if she was being profound or hormonal, but she allowed the feeling to be, and for a moment, just one moment, it was a beautiful thing.

"Honey, you okay?" Larry asked with concern. He must have been watching her over the newspaper.

Allie looked at him with a slowly spreading smile. "I'm getting there, thanks," she answered simply.

And she realized with gratitude that it was the truth.

Acknowledgments

I'm a big fan of "thank you," and my first thanks go to my readers. I have written thirty-some novels and nine nonfiction books, and over the years, my readers have become even more important to me. Many of you have followed me from book to book and supported me as I expand the type of book I write, going from legal thrillers in Rosato & DiNunzio to deep domestics like this one, and even to the funny books I write with my daughter. I feel so grateful to each and every one of you for being so loyal, in every way. I feel grateful every morning for this wonderful job of mine, not only because I love writing books, but because I love reading them. And I love most of all the reading community, and all of you. So you get my first thanks, today and always.

Someone Knows was especially challenging for me because it required research outside my expertise, and this is where I get to thank those experts who helped me. Usually I specify exactly how my sources help me, but I won't here, because this book has a twist or two and I'm a no-spoilers kind of girl. I owe all of the following people a huge debt of thanks, and if there are any mistakes in this novel, I'm responsible.

Thank you to dear friend and legal genius Nicholas Casenta, Esq., Chief Deputy District Attorney of the

Chester County District Attorney's Office. Thank you, Officer J. Slota and Fran Holmes, Lacey Township Police Department; Lieutenant Robert P. Klinger, Willistown Police Department; Susan Carnes, Clinical Director, Penn State Behrend Health and Wellness Center; David Singer of Singer Specs/Sterling Optical; and Joseph Hurley of Targetmaster. Thanks to Karen Thomas and the Breathe Foundation, and Paul Geller and Laura Wingate of the Crohn's & Colitis Foundation. Thanks also to Francie Fitzgerald.

Thank you to Ivan Held, president of G. P. Putnam's Sons, who inspired me to go deeper than ever before into the domestic story, and I hope I have done so with this novel. Ivan leads by energetic example, and his enthusiasm for this book encouraged me to take it to the next level. I've never before attempted a domestic thriller with so many main characters and such sophisticated themes, as well as a twisty-turny plot. I've been looking at the intersection between justice and family for a long time, but this novel combines them in a way I never have before. Thanks to Ivan!

Thank you so very much to Christine Ball, my new publisher, who welcomed me with open arms, and to my editor, Mark Tavani, who is a delight in every way. Mark's enthusiasm and support powered me through this book, his comments to the manuscript were spot-on, and I look forward to years of a productive and really fun relationship with him. It's all about the sentence, and Mark gets that and then some! Thank you, Mark! And thank you to Danielle Springer Dieterich, for all of her editorial comments, cheerful encouragement, and shared love of the best dogs in the world. They know who they are.

Thanks to Lauren Monaco, a gorgeous ball of sales savvy, and Sally Kim, whom I admire so much. Thanks to Alexis Welby, who made such a splash for me before I had even arrived at Putnam, and to Ashley McClay, who comes up with new ideas for marketing every day. Thanks to Katie Grinch (and her adorable mother). Thanks to Anthony Ramondo and Christopher Lin, for their sensational work on this cover! And thanks to the rest of the great gang who worked so hard on this book: Jordan Aaronson, Philip Budnick, John Cassidy, Liza Cassity, Heather Dalton, Paul Deykerhoff, Andrew Dudley, Daniel Kosack, Benjamin Lee, Erica Melnichok, Kristyn Mendez, Rachel Oben-schain, Emily Ollis, David Phethean, Andrew Rein, Drew Schnoebelen, Kimberly Shannon, Trish Weyenberg, and my old friend, the great Laura Wilson.

Thanks and love to my terrific agent, Robert Gottlieb of Trident Media Group. His tireless advocacy and faith gave me the confidence to strike out in new directions, and he is absolutely dedicated to my career and me, in addition to just being a wonderful human being and a hoot to work with. Special thanks to his amazing assistant, Sulamita Garbuz. Thank you to Erica Silverman, also of Trident Media Group, who has worked with Robert to make such great progress for me in Hollywood. Thanks to Dorothy Vincent for all of her work selling my books internationally. Finally, thanks so much to Nicole Robson and Trident's digital media team, who have been absolutely essential on social media.

Finally, thank you so much to the team of people who support me so that I can write full-time. Writing is not only my life, it's my dream, and I write better books if I don't have to worry about interruptions. My brilliant assistant and bestie Laura Leonard does every single thing she can to free my time, which means she works all the time. Nothing good happens without her, and I can't thank her enough for her loyalty, hard work, and love. Thanks to my amazing assistants at home, Nan Daley and Katie Rinda. They work impossibly hard so that I can deliver the best book possible, every time. Each of them cares as much about my readers as I do, and I know how lucky I am in them. I love you, ladies. Thank you so much for your constant support, friendship, and a hell of a good time, every day.

Finally, thank you so much my bestie Franca Palumbo and to my amazing daughter (and even coauthor), Francesca Serritella. I've been writing about family all my life, because that's what matters most to me. Everything changed the day Francesca was born, in too many wonderful ways to recount here. She's truly a gift, graced with intelligence, a kind heart, and a generous soul. Francesca even talked plot points with me for this novel, which helped so much. She just finished her first novel, and I couldn't be prouder.

Love you, honey, and deepest thanks from mom.com.